ECHOES OF THE CITY

Also by Lars Saabye Christensen in English translation

The Half Brother (2004)
Herman (2006)
The Model (2007)
Beatles (2010)

LARS SAABYE CHRISTENSEN

ECHOES OF THE CITY
Maj and Ewald

Translated from the Norwegian by
Don Bartlett

MACLEHOSE PRESS
QUERCUS · LONDON

First published in the Norwegian language as *Byens Spor*
by Cappelen Damm As, Oslo, in 2017

First published in Great Britain in 2019 by MacLehose Press
This paperback published in 2022 by

MacLehose Press
An imprint of Quercus Publishing Ltd
Carmelite House
50 Victoria Embankment
London EC4Y 0DZ

An Hachette UK company

This translation has been published with the financial support of NORLA

A CIP catalogue record for this book is available from the British Library.

ISBN (MMP) 978 0 85705 916 1
ISBN (Ebook) 978 0 85705 917 8

10 9 8 7 6 5 4 3 2 1

Designed and typeset in Scala by Libanus Press, Marlborough
Printed and bound in Great Britain by Clays Ltd, Elcograf S.p.A.

ECHOES OF THE CITY

PROLOGUE

Kirkeveien begins in Frogner square, where the tram turns east towards the districts of Elisenberg and Solli, if you're going in that direction, of course, and away from Fagerborg, away from Majorstua, away from this city that I love, despite everything, for good or ill; for good – its size and the number of trees suit my temperament; or ill – its desire to grow bigger eats away at that same temperament. A city has to be its age. Otherwise it will be like a child in a dinner jacket or an old man dressed in a sailor outfit. It will just evoke ridicule and not a longing for home. The boy, or rather the young man, because he is in the process of becoming a man, sitting on the tram, the one you can see passing by early this morning while everyone wakes to the saddest news a grateful nation can receive, wants to leave, leave Fagerborg, leave Oslo, everything, just leave. His name is Jesper Kristoffersen and he has a bulging seaman's kitbag beside him on the seat. Take note of his eyes if you can: vacant yet alert, he sees and is seen. Incidentally, below his left eye there is a blue shadow, a relic of the past. Once he was diagnosed as *sensitive*. We are walking in the opposite direction, on the left-hand side of Kirkeveien, alongside Frogner Park with the magnificent, some might contend overblown, Gustav Vigeland sculptures, which in autumn, now, can call to mind the great gardens in Russia at around the turn of the nineteenth century: abandoned, melancholy and, by no means least, artificial collections of sculptures that carry the bank of clouds on their backs. In spring and summer, however, the park dances to a different tune. Mothers sun themselves on the benches, but don't allow their children playing on the grass out of their sight. Teenagers feed the swans, but that is only to disguise their true intention, which is to flirt. The crumbs of bread they throw into the pond are the pure grist of love. And in the two restaurants, Broen and Herregårdskroen, fathers sit in their white shirts drinking beer from chilled, foaming glasses. Everything is blithe and languorous. Everything is carefree and of the moment. Everything is eternal, a blue sky reflected in the clear light of the pond. At times like these it is not art that we rate highest but life. In the winter it is different. Then life is in the background and the sculptures come to the fore, columns of frosty granite, a frozen army, and you could almost believe the park is a Gothic battlefield or an extension of Vestre Cemetery, which is not far away, with its gloomy crematoria and black, jagged cypresses. Winter in general turns this city into a wretched, oppressive place, even though it is winter we are most used to. Winter hems us in between drifting snow, banked-up piles of ice and barren dreams. Winter is the time for serialised fiction, penitence and the radio. Now, as I have indicated, it is September and not just any September. It is the saddest September day so far this year. The leaves are falling like yellow tears. I can truly say this: the leaves are falling like yellow tears. A newspaper boy comes running by with the special edition of *Aftenposten* in his cart. Is it because Jesper Kristoffersen is signing on to join M.S. *Bergensfjord*? Hardly likely. Young boys and men, indeed some girls too, go to sea every single day without anyone getting particularly upset, apart from maybe a mother, a sister or a sweetheart. That is how it should be. You tear yourself away, however much it hurts. On the tennis courts the nets have been taken down. A white ball lies in the shale, like a full stop after the final serve of the summer. But at Frogner Stadium opposite the Sørensen & Balchen car workshops in Middelthuns gate it is always high season: speed skating, figure skating, bandy, athletics and football, a full calendar of sport all year round. Women in the city will probably have a special memory of Sonja Henie's floodlit grand entrance: gliding onto the ice like an angel, to wild applause, skating backwards, her arms outstretched like wings, it was as if she were about to take off. Men will probably remember Oscar Mathisen beating the cocky, over-rated Bobby McLean here, and Frogner Stadium being called the American Waterloo for that very reason. As for the Norwegian world champion, he lost on the last bend when the ice beneath him had melted. He shot his wife first and then took his own life. I often think about that: weren't all the medals he received enough to console him? Or was it a case of the higher you rise, the harder you fall? As a matter of fact, there is someone else running around the stadium now, lap after lap in the heavy shale, wearing a knitted jumper and blue shorts over tights. It is, as everyone knows, Dr Lund, a specialist in the everyday, as he likes to say. He is still oblivious of the night's sad events. And had he known, he would doubtless have run twice as far, fifty laps, that is, twenty kilometres. In fact it was Dr Lund who had called Jesper Kristoffersen sensitive, but later gave him a clean bill of health: *The boy is in good health and fit for any kind of work.* Let us continue, not that there is any rush; on the contrary we have plenty of time. But to those who wish to accompany us, please adjust to our pace. That is the custom here. At Maries gate we stop anyway and have a look at Majorstua School, where the caretaker, ex form master Løkke, also called Uløkke, an allusion to *ulykke*, misfortune, has put on a black suit and is carrying the Norwegian flag across the empty schoolyard. We notice he is holding the flag in the same way you would carry a dead or an injured child. Then we reach the Salvation Army premises. The front door is adorned with this motto: *Through Blood and Fire*. It is odd to think that these timid, polite, unarmed soldiers who never die but who are transported to eternity in *Aftenposten* obituaries, should have such a violent slogan. And the magazine they sell, especially in the Valkyrien area of Oslo, is called the *War Cry*. Form and content do not always coincide. Then we are finally in Majorstua, the junction that might be called Kirkeveien's St Peter's Square. This is where the buses and trams turn. Here you can take the Holmenkollen underground to the National Theatre, down to the very centre of the city. And from here you can travel up to the forested region in the north, Nordmarka, which for many is the ultimate proof of God's existence: eternal life is found between Lake Tryvann and Mt Kikut, where you can meet lean, hardy men with dripping noses and auras of sweat, ski wax and spruce. It may also be mentioned that this same Nordmarka is used in a threat by desperate parents when idle youth prefers to lie in on a Sunday: If you're not in Nordmarka by ten o'clock you're in deep trouble. And then you might end up on Bastøy, the prison island in the Oslo Fjord where under-age murderers and other uncivilised boys are taught discipline and a fear of God with the aid of the iron maiden, a sarcophagus in which you go to sleep a child and wake up a broken old man. Incidentally, we retract the comparison with St Peter's Square and prefer to say that the Majorstua junction is Kirkeveien's Times Square. Here there are banks, opticians, chemists, delicatessens, kiosks, hairdressers, perfumeries, telephone booths, ladies' hosiery shops, travel agents and waiting rooms with weighing machines that tell you your fortune on small cards. The advertising signs on the roofs should be mentioned at this point: in the dark season you can read the Bible in the light from them: *Blue Master* and *Frisco*. Not forgetting the two cinemas of course: the Colosseum with its enormous dome and Kinopaleet, which because of its pillars looks more like a Greek temple. Now I have it: Majorstua is Kirkeveien's Acropolis. The watering holes, as they say in local parlance, are also easy to find: Gamla, Valka, Larsen, Vinkelkafé and Tråkka. There are never any problems quenching your thirst in Majorstua. And we still haven't touched on all the bakeries. Nowhere are there more bakeries than in Majorstua – Samson, Møllhausen, Hansen, and a bit further away, in Industrigata there is little Manfred's bakery. In the morning an aroma of freshly baked bread wafts over this part of town. The birds sate their hunger merely by flying overhead with their beaks open. Not today though, not today. Today there is no fresh bread. Today the adverts don't light up. Today the darkness persists. As we start on the long, gentle climb that culminates at Vestre Aker Church, which as far back as 1856 gave its name to this street where Fridtjof Nansen's mother once planted an avenue of trees, we see what we initially believe to be leaves on the steps of Majorstuhuset, but they turn out to be Red Cross raffle tickets. They must have come from the autumn charity bazaar. No doubt people with losing tickets just threw them down. This is depressing: a city full of losing tickets. We cross the road and finally start on the ascent that many, especially delivery boys on bikes and strangers, under-estimate. Not only is this part of Kirkeveien long, you also have to factor in the wind, which originates from beyond the glaciers in Svalbard, bringing with it the salty sea-air from the Finnmark coast, it rushes down through northern Norway and Trøndelag, picks up speed over Dovre and catches the end of Lake Tryvann before crossing Suhms gate with teeth of steel. By now we have passed the Clothing & Shoe Repairs Expert and the Priests' Church, a solid, unassuming place of worship which was built with money collected by priests and their families in the capital. Some wags claim that more people have seen the light at the Clothing & Shoe Repairs Expert than during church services and even more have seen it at the Valka pub. But we don't want to talk about that here. Lights come on and lights go out. Hopefully it all comes to the same. For what has caught our attention now is the shop window at Melsom's. The butcher, Melsom, is leaning over the counter, taking down a picture of his son Jostein, who is advertising Valcrema skin cream in a ladies' magazine, and in its place he puts a portrait of King Haakon bordered by black ribbon. Outside, his wife, eyes red-rimmed, gives her husband instructions, watch out, the black silk mustn't touch the ham, the portrait has to be closer to the door, stop, not *so* close, and it's probably best to replace the ham with some parsley and entrecôte. We leave them to it and continue past Marienlyst, which is on Fagerborg's western fringe. There, set back like a palace, is the Norwegian Broadcasting House, which for the rest of the day will commemorate the King and play funeral music. Some say that is why Jesper Kristoffersen decides to go to sea on this morning of all mornings; he cannot stand all these slow, sombre melodies. That is probably incorrect. As already mentioned, he is no longer sensitive. Then we are in Jessenløkken, which might be considered Fagerborg's Versailles: the large, rectangular blocks of flats with sunny yards in the middle and facades facing Kirkeveien, Jonas Reins gate, Jacob Aalls gate and Gørbitz gate. They were designed by Harald Hals, built between 1916 and 1920 and are the first example of modern town-planning in Norway, inspired by the Viennese architect Camillo Sitte. An idea that transcended the norm in this quarter where tradition almost always rules: social modernism started in Fagerborg. We were the first! The apartments were also ahead of their time with all modern conveniences in situ, double glazing, cellar laundries, balconies, sculleries, and there was also a secret room everyone knows about: the vestibule. The vestibule is the room without windows. The vestibule is useless and dark. The vestibule is at best an ante-room. The architects thought the vestibule would lend the apartment a stamp of distinction, bourgeois finesse, so to speak, which would also endow the apartment with its desired gravitas. This vestibule, on the first floor of Kirkeveien 127, has been Jesper Kristoffersen's room until now, his ante-room, this Jesper Kristoffersen who not so long ago caught the tram from Majorstua down to the City Hall square and from there walked to the Vippetang headland to sign on with M.S. *Bergensfjord*, which was operated by the Norwegian-America Line. Still standing on the little balcony are Maj Kristoffersen, his mother, and Stine, his younger sister, who are watching him leave. It is not difficult to work out who they are shedding most tears for, King Haakon or Jesper. Let me phrase it like this: you don't always put yourself first. You put *family* first. We, for our part, have a way to go before we reach the end of Kirkeveien. The graveyard below Vestre Aker Church is steeper than the landing slope of Holmenkollen ski jump. Do not suffer from vertigo if you die in Fagerborg. Most people, however, would prefer to be buried in Vestre Cemetery, even though it is a bit further away. After all, it is flat and clearly set out and you seldom receive unexpected visitors. We inhale the anaesthetic-like smell of oil and petrol from the Esso garage on the corner and cross the tramlines leading to Bislett which in some way mark Fagerborg's eastern boundary. Inside Ullevål Hospital, which in its day was the biggest in Europe, the flag is also flying at half-mast. The number of those who die will probably rise today. It increases if you lose a king. When you lose a king you lose part of your life. And even though we are now outside Fagerborg's absolute limits we keep walking, past another graveyard, Nordre Cemetery, and come to Geitmyrsveien, and there, on the other side of the road, is the school garden. That was what I wanted to show you. The apple trees stand in line, the soft fruit bushes, too. The little field has been ploughed into beautiful, even furrows, dark, fertile waves. In the shed hang the tools: spades, forks, rakes. By the way, someone has left behind a pair of gloves. They almost look as if they are still working the soft, friable soil. I wanted to show you this tidy school garden to remind you where we have come from, regardless of how modern most things have become, what with blenders, colour films, biros, sputniks, electronic music and T.V. test patterns: everyone in Fagerborg comes from the land.

A SHORT RESUMÉ OF OUR
FIRST YEAR, 1947

The Norwegian Red Cross, in order to rationalise and ease the workload, mapped out the city of Oslo and divided it into departments, each with its own board. In June 1947 a department was established in Fagerborg. In the church office we identified those members who belonged to our newly established district. Our first task was to enrol new members in September. We signed up around five hundred, some of whom have become life members.

At the bazaar from 12th–19th September we took 1,264.80 kroner. The income from membership fees was 595 kroner, so our total reserves, after necessary expenses, were 1623.87. We were promised 650 kroner in start-up capital by the main office.

At the end of November and the beginning of December Fagerborg put forward several members to help sort and pack clothes for Europe Aid. Our cash contribution was 200 kroner.

We were also assigned a quantity of wool, which we shared round, and started on various knitting projects: socks, mittens, scarves, hats, trousers etc. These are intended to be distributed to people in our district or wherever in the country acute help is required. For example, a substantial package was sent to Tromsø, where a family was left destitute by a fire.

In May our department received a request from Fru Fougner (the chairwoman of the Sewing Association founded in 1907) for help with sewing seams on linen and labelling emergency blankets, to be precise at a communal field hospital. In addition, Fagerborg department were asked by the working committee to take care of and feed 47 Jewish children who were going to stay in Norway for two months. On their return it was also our department that took care of the children, a pleasant and interesting task.

In August our members held their first meeting at the chairman's home. The turnout was very disappointing. Of the fifteen members who had promised to come only three actually turned up. We had decided beforehand to make a doll with accessories to be given away and we shared this work between the three loyal members and the board.

In Red Cross Week, which lasted from 18th to 26th September, we started off on the 18th with a floral float and children dressed in a Red Cross uniform in a motorised procession. The takings were poor and according to the working committee this activity will be dropped in future.

Unfortunately, enrolment was sluggish. As we all know, the fee was raised this year from two to four kroner for annual members and from twenty to fifty kroner for life members. This is probably too much.

The bazaar brought in: 1,874.05 kroner
The sale of charity stamps: 206.10 kroner.

During this month a budget proposal will be drawn up to decide what to do with these proceeds.

INDIAN SUMMER

Maj Kristoffersen is at Kirkeveien 127, standing in the shade
on the little balcony and watching all the children playing in
the yard below. There are lots of them. These are the war generation. These are the peace children. Many were born before
the war was over, but they are still the peace children. Her boy,
Jesper, was one year old when an ammunition dump exploded
in the Filipstad area of Frogner and many thought then the
whole city had been blown up; even in Fagerborg windows
shook, and these tremors became a part of the heritage of the
war, cracks in the ceiling, fissures in the walls, burst eardrums,
crooked chandeliers; everything that would be repaired when
peace came, but for which ultimately there was no time and
which was put off until the following day, because peace-time
is busy, unlike the slow, pointless war, apart from when there
were explosions in Filipstad. Jesper is sitting in the corner, he
lifts his hand and waves to his mother or perhaps he is just
restless and ill at ease again. His sweater might be too thick, or
it is prickly, and he scratches his neck. It is the first Saturday in
October 1948. But the air is still mild. The sun still has warmth.
It hangs over the rooftops and catches the fiery Virginia creeper between the windows. Meteorologists call this an Indian

summer. Maj Kristoffersen is enjoying it. She moves into the light. She takes off her jacket and would light a cigarette if she had one. If only it would last. But in a month's time conditions will probably already be right for skiing. Then she loses sight of Jesper. He is nowhere to be seen, not by the rubbish bins, not by the swing, not by the bench. She is seized by panic. She knows he isn't far away. The door to Jonas Reins gate is always locked. Nonetheless she is panic-stricken. He can't have gone down into the cellar, to the laundry. He may have wandered up to the drying loft. There are dangers everywhere. She is on the point of shouting. She is on the point of dragging herself away from the Indian summer. Then Margrethe Vik opens the window above her and leans out.

"Telephone call for you."

"Is it Ewald?"

"I didn't ask. It's a woman though."

Maj Kristoffersen casts a final glance over the yard, but still can't see Jesper. Then she goes to the back stairs and runs up to Fru Vik, who accompanies her to the hallway where the black receiver lies on the bureau waiting. Maj Kristoffersen turns to Fru Vik.

"Could you have a look for Jesper while I'm on the telephone?"

Fru Vik gives a slight toss of the head and wipes her hands on her apron.

"Right. I don't want to be in your way."

"Oh, that's not what I meant. It's Jesper. I couldn't see—"

"I was busy making lunch."

"Yes, it smells delicious."

"Answer the telephone quickly before they ring off."

Fru Vik goes out and closes the kitchen door firmly behind her.

Maj Kristoffersen lifts the receiver and says her name. A Fru Lund from Ullevålsveien is at the other end. She is ringing on behalf of the Red Cross, and for a moment Maj Kristoffersen thinks it is Jesper she wants to talk about, he has been up to mischief and the Red Cross itself has been brought in. She is both terrified and furious. They shouldn't meddle. No-one should meddle! She can manage on her own! She doesn't say this. She just thinks it. Or has there been an accident? Has something happened to Ewald? Has Jesper managed to hurt himself in the short time he was out of her sight? But Fru Lund has quite a different matter on her mind. She asks whether Maj Kristoffersen would be willing to attend a board meeting of the Norwegian Red Cross, Oslo Division, Fagerborg department, possibly as a co-opted member. They need new women. In fact, she has been told Maj is very good at keeping accounts. Maj Kristoffersen breathes out with relief and feels like shouting "yes", but composes herself.

"I'll have to confer with my husband first," she says.

Fru Lund has complete understanding. A post at the Red Cross is not something you take on lightly. It involves the whole family. She gives Maj Kristoffersen her telephone number and asks her to call when she has made up her mind, preferably over the weekend, because the next meeting is on the Wednesday coming. They ring off. Maj Kristoffersen can hear that Fru Vik is back. Water is running from the tap. Jesper is screaming. Then everything is still. She joins them in the kitchen.

"He was behind the birch tree," Fru Vik says.

Jesper looks at his mother and, as always, it is impossible to know whether he is going to laugh or cry.

"So that's where he was."

"He was having a pee."

"Having a pee? Goodness me . . ."

"But now at least he's washed his hands."

Jesper starts crying. That was good at least. Laughing on this occasion, in Fru Vik's company, would have been much worse. Maj pulls her son close to her. As usual he is reluctant and amenable at one and the same time. She doesn't understand how this can be, but he is exactly like an impossible string on an instrument, both slack and tense.

"Sorry for the intrusion," she says.

Fru Vik opens the kitchen door for them and gives Jesper a Marie biscuit, which he goes to put into his mouth, without a second thought, but changes his mind at the last moment, stops crying and quickly slips it into his pocket. Maj squeezes his neck a little harder.

"Thank you," Jesper mumbles.

Fru Vik pats him on the head as she turns to Maj.

"Perhaps the Red Cross can help you to get a telephone?"

"And perhaps it was you who told them I was *very good* at doing accounts?"

Fru Vik smiles.

"That's what your husband says anyway."

NORWEGIAN RED CROSS, FAGERBORG DEPARTMENT. REGULATIONS

The Norwegian Red Cross, Oslo Division, Fagerborg department is affiliated to the working committee of the Norwegian Red Cross, Oslo Division, as an independent group.

The department is led by a board consisting of up to five persons including co-opted members. The board is elected by the general assembly for two years at a time.

The general assembly is held every year before March. The chairman gives notice at least a week in advance either by contacting members entitled to vote or placing an announcement in an Oslo newspaper.

The department has one representative on the working committee.

The aim of Fagerborg department is to promote Red Cross objectives within the local parish.

INTER ARMA CARITAS

The four gentlemen standing at the bar in Hotel Bristol are loud, boastful and assertive. Their names are Ravn, Johnsen, Strøm and Kristoffersen. They mean well. When Ulfsen, the bartender, tells them to quieten down a bit, he doesn't actually say so, he only raises an eyebrow and they are silent for a second and can hear the lounge pianist playing *Rondo Amoroso*, probably for the old dears eating open sandwiches at the other end of the bar, by the stairs. Then the men order a round of gin and tonics, apart from Ewald Kristoffersen, who prefers to drink beer, although today he has a small aquavit now and again, not to miss out on the fun. They all work for Dek-Rek; two are graphic designers, two are interior designers and they have every reason to celebrate. Oslo Council has commissioned their agency to organise the displays for the city's 900-year jubilee. It will be in 1950. Two years away. There is no time to lose. They already have some ideas. They can see it in their mind's eye. They can see the future. It is drawing closer. But for now they have to drink and afterwards get the music to swing. Ewald Kristoffersen is sent over to the grand piano. He waits for the pianist to finish the piece. It seems this cannot be done in the flick of a lamb's tail. It takes time.

The pianist is doodling. This is the nature of lounge music. This is how *background music* is. Finally Ewald Kristoffersen places a hand on the pianist's shoulder.

"My friends would like to hear something more upbeat," he says.

Enzo Zanetti, the resident pianist at the Bris, looks up as he continues to play, smiling, but his eyes are weary, and the flaps of his collar, which look impeccable from a distance, are curled at the edges. He speaks in a soft voice with an accent:

"Upbeat? Any suggestions?"

"If I have any suggestions? No, I leave that completely to you. Maybe something by Louis Strongarm though?"

"Strongarm?"

"Or Elling Duketon? As long as it swings."

Ewald Kristoffersen is afraid he might not have expressed himself clearly enough, but on his way back to the bar he hears the pianist change his repertoire and start to play *The Hall of the Mountain King*. That will have to do. His colleagues applaud. They raise their glasses. Down the hatch, they say. Soon afterwards they go their various ways. Someone is waiting. See you on Monday if you're over your hangover. Ewald is the only one left. It is his turn to pay. It is always his turn to pay, it strikes him. He takes out the rectangular brown envelope, the reward for all his hard work, and places a fifty-krone note on the bar. Now he understands why barmen are called conjurors. The note has gone before he can heave a sigh. And fifty isn't enough, either. It has disappeared into thin air. Ewald Kristoffersen has to add a tenner, but with the change at least he has enough for a "green sweater with a high neck", a glass of port and a beer. Suddenly he feels guilty and drains both glasses. Then he has to go downstairs and relieve himself. It takes time. Ewald Kristoffersen thinks: Pissing is freedom. That could be a slogan. But for what? Life? He can still hear *The Hall of the Mountain King*. As he is washing his hands he catches sight of his face in the mirror. Deep down, he is astonished that any woman could love him. He puts a krone on the table by the lavatory attendant, who in return gives him a small, wrapped bar of soap, Sterilan. When he goes back up he slips a five-krone coin to Enzo Zanetti, who nods imperceptibly, says something in Italian and plays *Mood Indigo*, mostly for the women who have come for a coffee and something a little stronger. Then Ewald Kristoffersen fetches his coat and hat from the cloakroom, gives fifty øre to the pocket Venus there, goes out and feels an unexpectedly gentle wind blowing down Rosenkrantz' gate. He is almost in the mood to take a stroll down Karl Johans gate. No, he has to go home. He decides not to take a taxi anyway. Money saved is money earned after all. He walks down Kristian Augusts gate, past the National Gallery and Tullinløkka Square, which is the lowest point in the city. Everything runs down to here from the mountains in the north, east and west. Instead of rounding Grotten, Henrik Wergeland's Swiss-style house, he takes a detour through the Palace Gardens. The trees seem confused in this fifth season, the Indian summer. It is the light that makes them seem young again, for as long as it lasts. For as long as it lasts is sometimes long enough. He continues towards Bislett, where straight, grey Thereses gate opens onto the curves of the sports stadium. In Norabakken, which is a steeper street than he can remember, he has to have a rest and he takes it at the urinal below Fagerborg Church. There is a strong stench, it is not like at the Bristol, but despite that it feels good to have a pee. There is no attendant here. People manage on their own. After he has finished he sits down on a bench in Stens Park, wipes the sweat from his brow and watches the clouds that are already casting a shadow over Mt Ekeberg. It is exactly as if the city is shrinking. How can you best show that this city is 900 years old? It is 900 years old and still it hasn't grown up. You have to start somewhere. Ewald Kristoffersen doesn't yet know where. He only knows why he has a bad conscience. It is because of Jesper. Jesper is hard work. Time away from him is a relief. Jesper is not a peace child. He is a war child. Ewald Kristoffersen gets to his feet and walks the last bit. He is a bad father. He is terrible. A shiver runs through him. He should have bought something for Jesper. He should have had a flower with him for Maj. They are sitting in the kitchen waiting. Maj hears that he has finally arrived. He bangs around in the hallway. He changes his clothes in the bedroom. He is in the bathroom for an age. He is not in a hurry. This time she won't spare him. He is two hours late. Jesper looks down and clenches both fists. But when Ewald Kristoffersen shows his round face in the doorway and twangs his braces, his stomach spilling over his belt, she relents after all. Even Jesper relaxes for a moment and sticks one hand in his pocket. The father of the house takes his place at the table.

"The porridge is cold," Maj says.

"Oslo Council gave us the commission."

"So you've been celebrating, have you?"

"Just a little snifter at the Bris."

Ewald puts the envelope in front of Maj. She opens it,

counts the notes with nimble fingers and looks at him again.

"*One* snifter?"

"It was my turn to buy a round."

"Wasn't it last Saturday as well?"

"I don't want to be seen as a tightwad."

"A tightwad? Talk properly, Ewald!"

"A miser."

"No, you can leave being a miser to me. So that you can be extravagant."

Ewald Kristoffersen secures the serviette firmly between the top buttons of his shirt.

"Anyway, cold porridge is my favourite," he says.

He eats the rest, scrapes the deep bowl at the end and licks the spoon. Then Jesper takes something from his pocket and places it on the table. It is a Marie biscuit. Ewald looks at his son.

"For me?"

Jesper nods.

Ewald Kristoffersen's eyes well up. He has always been easily moved. The boy has a good heart. He dashes into the hallway and comes back with something after all. He gives the little bar of soap to Jesper, who unwraps it and is about to put it into his mouth. At the last moment Maj manages to stop him and glares at Ewald.

"Have you been shopping as well?"

"Just a trip to Cirkus Schumann."

Jesper starts crying. His whole body shakes. His face distorts. His hands beat the air. When his mouth snaps shut, his crying becomes a low howl. Maj has to hold him. She has to hold him tight. Ewald looks away. Jesper calms down. This never lasts long. But it is long enough. Ewald turns slowly to his son, who is sitting on his mother's lap, pale and limp.

"It isn't really the famous circus, you know. I only went to the toilet."

Ewald laughs and Jesper lifts his head, a little smile on his face.

"Cirkus Schumann is the place where men like you and me stand and have a pee. So why's it called Cirkus Schumann? Well, it's simply because it's round and there's room for exactly seven men. *Syv mann*, Schumann. One day you'll have to come with me, Jesper."

Afterwards they wash up together, all three of them. Jesper has to dry the spoons. He can do that without dropping them on the floor. Ewald eats the Marie biscuit when he is in the sitting room drinking coffee. Jesper goes to bed early and falls asleep, fortunately. He has a bed in the little vestibule between the bathroom and the hallway, in the room with no windows. Maj joins Ewald and sits on the sofa. The news that reaches them, either on the radio, which Ewald is listening to, or in *Aftenposten*, which Maj is flicking through, may be this: the last execution has been carried out and the judicial settlement of war-time treason is considered to be over. Ex-minister Ragnar Skancke has been shot. Biros are already popular in Norway despite costing 25 kroner. It has also been announced that the Nobel Committee will not be awarding a Peace Prize this year. There is peace, but no-one can be given a prize for that. In addition, football pools have been an unqualified success, except that at many workplaces efficiency drops by twenty-five per cent every Wednesday when the coupons have to be handed in.

"Was it you who said I was good at doing accounts?" Maj asks.

Ewald turns off the radio.

"Might've been. Why?"

"The Red Cross rang. Fru Lund wants me on the board."

"And what did you say?"

"That I would confer with my husband."

Ewald chuckles.

"Oh, I think you've already decided."

"Maybe I need something different to occupy my mind."

They are silent for a while, listening. Not a sound is coming from the vestibule. All they can hear is the rain falling.

"But have you got the time?" Ewald asks in a whisper.

Maj's turn to chuckle:

"Time? I've definitely got lots of that."

"What about Jesper?"

"Fru Vik can look after him at a pinch. And there's another advantage."

"Yes?"

"Maybe the Red Cross could help us to get a telephone. Then we won't have to . . ."

Ewald Kristoffersen, who doesn't usually lose his temper – he is more inclined to melancholy and frivolity – thumps the table.

"We don't need charity!"

"And now you've woken Jesper."

Maj goes to see him. Ewald can hear her singing. It makes him sleepy as well. Jesper continues to cry for a while. Then it is as if all the sounds of the apartment block have been switched off.

When Maj and Ewald go to bed they can't sleep. They lie listening to each other's restiveness.

"I'm a bad mother," Maj whispers.

Ewald sits up in bed.

"How can you say things like that? You're . . ."

"I was on the balcony and couldn't see Jesper. But instead of going to look for him I went up to fru Vik's and answered the telephone."

"Maybe he could do with a brother. Or a sister."

Ewald leans gently over to Maj, but she pushes him back.

"Don't wake Jesper again."

"We can have a bit of jig jig, can't we?"

"You jig jig yourself. Let's get some sleep now, before he wakes us up."

They lie, each on their own side of the bed, oblivious to who falls asleep first. An ambulance comes down Kirkeveien casting a blue, flickering light through the curtains as it passes. The sound of tyres on the wet tarmac causes time to stand still in the flat.

BUDGET PROPOSALS 1948/1949

Each department is to send its budget proposals to the working committee during November and state how the board plans to spend its income.

It was suggested that a loan stock of medical items be built up in those departments that do not already have one. It was likewise suggested that infants' requisites should be acquired. Preferably bandages, for loan stock, and one item of aid equipment held in reserve in case of emergencies. Most departments have their medical items stored with the parish nurse or privately, if that is more convenient, and then usually with a hospital employee. Lending out of equipment is either free or at a fixed rate per week. It was reported that Plesner was the most used company for obtaining goods. When equipment is on site, there is an announcement in the parish magazine or the daily newspaper.

A model of a cradle, in iron and painted white, with removable leather lining, was borrowed from the Danish Red Cross. The working committee will invite tenders for the production of these. A loan period of six months at a time for the cradle was suggested. After applications to the department for support and requests for loans of equipment have been granted, information re. the applicant should be obtained from the Oslo Charity Register.

Personally, I suggest setting up a crèche in Fagerborg.

Current activities in Oslo:

1. Aid Course starts on 9th Nov at the Rikshospital.
2. Medical training with the Home Guard at Riis School for 150 attendees.
3. Patient Friends: hospital visits, reading to patients, library work etc.
4. Private arrangements: walking, bridge tournaments, local raffles.

A nurses' training course at Wergelandsveien Clinic was proposed for the Fagerborg department. Seven people on every course, one for every day of the week. Personally, I would suggest two, minimum one, extra auxiliary nurses as back-up in case of illness, travelling etc. The training period should be three mths in Med, then three mths in Ops, or whatever might suit the hospital.

Oslo 9.11.48
Fru Lund

FRESH SNOW

It is snowing in Vestre cemetery. The footprints behind Fru Vik soon begin to merge into one. Every single step she takes becomes the first. It is so quiet. That makes the loss all the greater. It opens up spaces inside her she would prefer to keep closed. She stops by the last grave under the silver firs, which also merge into one, crouches down and sweeps snow off the stone with a brush she keeps in her bag. The inscription is still white and she has to scrape out hardened snow from the engraved name: Veterinary Surgeon Halfdan Vik 18.3.1890 – 2.6.1945. Beneath it there is plenty of room for Fru Vik. She won't take up much room, either. What will her final date be? She turned fifty-two this summer. She could live for another thirty years. Then it will be 1978. Or forty years: 1988. It hardly bears thinking about. What is more, she had an aunt who lived until she was one hundred and two. If Fru Vik gets that far she will be able to see into the next millennium. She would prefer not to. There won't be anyone's name beneath hers. She removes one glove and touches the man's name. *You idiot*, she whispers and straightens up. At that moment the chapel bells ring. Snow hangs in the air. A cortège comes out onto the steps. At the front stands a stooped man who is all too thinly dressed. A young boy throws a coat over his shoulders. Behind them waits a long line of people. The snow continues to fall. Fru Vik walks past them and reaches Borgen Station on the metro line. As the doors close the grieving man enters and keeps them open to allow the rest of the procession to come in and sit down. At length the train sets off for Volvat. Fru Vik shows her ticket to the conductor. She can use it both ways. The conductor shakes his head and says she has to buy another. Her ticket is more than an hour old. Fru Vik is astonished. That can't be right. Did she lose track of time? Had she been standing by her husband's grave for so long? She looks at the stamp: 12.58. She checks her watch. It says two o'clock. How embarrassing. She lowers her eyes, ashamed, humiliated, mumbling as she rummages for some money in her bag, *I didn't mean to, I didn't mean to*. Her purse is under the brush. She can't get at it. The train stops at Volvat Station in the tunnel. Passengers start to get on. A queue forms. She almost drops her bag, but eventually finds some coins, which she gives to the conductor, who is at last able to give her a valid ticket. Fru Vik sits down on the first free seat and averts her eyes to avoid meeting anyone's gaze. Perhaps they are thinking she is a fare dodger. How embarrassing. She repeats the words to herself, *how embarrassing*, all the way down to Majorstua, where she quickly alights. The thinly dressed man in mourning watches her. Then he walks down to Sørkedalsveien, turns right and opens the door to Restaurant Larsen for the rest of the mourners. Together, they walk up to the function rooms on the first floor, where there is a table set with open sandwiches, shrimps, roast beef, salmon and Camembert. Two waitresses are serving white wine. At first conversation is muted and sporadic. Soon there is laughter. With the coffee comes apple tart and cream. The man, Olaf Hall, stands up and looks at the guests. They are friends and colleagues, not his but Ragnhild's. They drink more white wine, even though many of them have to be on stage in only a few hours. They turn to him. He doesn't know them. He fixes his gaze on Bjørn, Ragnhild's son, his stepson. Where is his grief? He is mature enough now to show grief. Olaf Hall can see no sign of it. He takes a mouthful of water and starts to speak:

"I noticed a lady on the way here. Her ticket had expired. She thought she could return on the same ticket. But it was invalid. And then I thought: life's like that, too. There's no such thing as a transfer ticket. And we should bear that in mind while we're alive."

Olaf Hall raises his glass. A hush descends over the assembly. It is the kind of hush they call in the theatre *restless*. Then an elderly actor also raises his glass and shouts: *Bravo! Life is like the Holmenkollen Line. First class, second class and standing room only!* Some cannot stifle a laugh. It doesn't matter. Afterwards Olaf Hall goes over to Bjørn and suggests walking home together. The stepson doesn't look at him. He has made other arrangements. Olaf Hall wants to say something. Other arrangements on the day his mother is buried? He refrains. When he steps outside it has stopped snowing. Footprints are visible in the snow that has fallen.

A board meeting was held on 10/11/48. Unfortunately the secretary was unable to attend. But a new woman attended on a trial basis, Maj Kristoffersen, who, we all felt, made a good impression.

On the agenda were the matters that were raised at the working committee's meeting on 20th Oct. It was decided that Fagerborg department would welcome an auxiliary nurses' training course at Wergelandsveien Clinic. With regard to the collection of membership dues it was agreed to employ someone on a commission basis (10% of the amount). The chairman announced that the department had contributed 20 kroner for flowers at the funeral of the actress Ragnhild Hall. She performed for us on a few occasions. Otherwise we discussed budget proposals, and this topic will again be on the agenda at the next meeting.

We received a letter from Herr Henry Karlsen, Grønnegt 19, asking for a woollen blanket. The Red Cross has a number of blankets for sale at a price of 25 kroner, and we will try to supply Herr Karlsen with such a blanket, provided that enquiries made to Oslo Charity Office show he is entitled to help.

THE CHILDMINDER

Maj Kristoffersen rings Fru Vik's doorbell. It takes her a long time to open the door and Maj doesn't have a lot to spare. Jesper is standing beside her, erect and quiet. Suddenly he sticks his hand through the letter box. Maj grabs his arm and pulls. His hand is stuck. It won't budge. Or is it because he has clenched his fist? She is on the verge of tears. She stamps her foot. It is five minutes past seven. It started at seven. She is about to box the boy's ears. At last she hears Fru Vik in the hallway. There is silence for some moments. Then Jesper pulls his hand out of the letter box and slips a syrup biscuit in his pocket. Fru Vik opens the door and looks down at Jesper, who is standing as erect and quiet as before, his hands behind his back.

"Is it the postman?" she asks.

Jesper doesn't answer.

Maj almost pushes her son in front of her.

"Could he stay with you for a couple of hours?"

"Has something come up?"

"Red Cross meeting. And Ewald had to go to the office again."

"So late?"

"He's busy with the jubilee."

"Well, Jesper can stay here. If he wants."

"Have you already started your Christmas baking?"

"I like to be well prepared."

"Me, too. Thank you very much."

Maj Kristoffersen runs down the stairs.

Fru Vik goes inside with Jesper and closes the door. They sit down in the kitchen. This is where she is happiest. The rest of the flat is too big. She pours some juice for them. He says nothing and doesn't touch the glass. She studies him. You might imagine the boy was shy or very defiant. However, Jesper is on edge. His eyes flit. They are never still. Fru Vik thinks he is looking for a way out. Doesn't he like it here? Is he afraid?

"Are you looking forward to Christmas?" she asks.

Jesper doesn't answer.

"What are you hoping to get?"

Again he doesn't answer.

"Are you hungry?"

This time she doesn't wait for an answer. She just warms up some leftovers in the pan and puts them on a plate, which she places in front of Jesper. The boy doesn't eat.

"What's the matter with you?"

Did he smile? No, it was more like a grimace, a gust of ill wind across his face. Fru Vik rests her elbows on the table, to get closer.

"I don't suppose you remember Herr Vik, my husband, do you? No, you don't. He was stupid enough to die when peace came. Can you imagine? He fell headlong in Kirkeveien and that was that. He was a vet, by the way. That's a doctor for animals. But during the war he had to operate on humans as well. In secret. What could I say? Do you know where the Veterinary College is? It's not far away. Herr Vik worked there. And do you know what they have in the cold storage room? Dead animals. Sometimes he brought some home. And still they send me fresh supplies. What's on your plate is the remains of a calf."

Jesper pushes the food around with his forefinger.

"I fall, too," he says.

"Do you?"

"At night."

"Do you get up?"

"No."

"How do you fall then? Out of bed?"

"In my sleep."

Jesper starts eating. He eats until the plate is empty and finishes the juice as well.

Afterwards they wrap up warm and go down into the yard. Three boys from 123b are making a snowman by the clothes drier. The string on it hangs in heavy, white loops. Fru Vik wants to take Jesper over to them, but he resists. He is stronger than her. His whole body is tense. They go back upstairs. Then they take a seat in the sitting room. It is dark. The furniture is brown and green. The pictures on the wall also lack light. The big cushion on the sofa is yellow, however, and has four tassels, one at each corner. Jesper sits next to it. His feet stick out. One of his stockings, the left one, has a hole in the heel. Fru Vik reflects on how her life might have been. She casts these thoughts from her mind, fetches a pair of her husband's socks and puts them on Jesper's feet, over his stockings.

"Shall we play a game? Dice?"

Jesper shakes his head.

"We could play patience?"

Jesper clenches his fists and looks away.

Fru Vik sits down in the wing chair, which still smells of tobacco, an odour that will probably always be there, even if she throws out the chair and buys a new one, a modern chair which is easier to keep clean, but perhaps no better to sit in. Anyway, she will keep the wing chair. She misses the flame that could suddenly appear at the end of a pipe. The vet is still there as a smell, as a smokiness, as stains. Then she has to leave the room on some urgent business. She also uses the opportunity to relax. Jesper can be strenuous company, even if he only sits there gawping. There is something about him that drains you. When she goes back to the sitting room Jesper has found a book he is slowly leafing through. Fru Vik moves closer. It is Francis Harbitz's *Manual of Forensic Medicine*, with eighty illustrations and four plates. Jesper is studying the picture of a boy with his eyes closed, an open mouth and car tyre tracks over his face. He doesn't bat an eyelid. He is as reticent as ever. Fru Vik seizes the book from his hands and puts it back on the shelf. Then she switches on the radio. At first it crackles. Afterwards there is a hiss between stations, names of towns, but soon the sound is crystal clear in the sitting room, a piano, a simple melody, melancholic and light-hearted at the same time. It was like a clown pouring out his grief. She turns to Jesper. He has put the yellow cushion on his lap and is resting his elbows on it. His mind eases. He closes his eyes and is calm.

———

The board meeting was held on 15/11 at the chairman's home. As Frøken Dagny Schelde, the vice-chairman, asked to be released from her post, Fru Berit Nordklev took her place. The co-opted member of the board, Fru Ingrid Arnesen, was made permanent, and Frøken Løvseth is the new co-opted member. It was agreed that Maj Kristoffersen should take on the post of treasurer, which she accepted. The chairman stressed the importance of punctuality at meetings.

Our meeting was called principally to discuss some of the items that had come up at the working committee session, especially the budget proposals for the following year.

The following was decided:

20 Christmas boxes at 20 kroner each	400
Earmarked for loans stock	500
Earmarked for baby materials	500
Earmarked for crèche	500
Earmarked for reserve fund	1000
Earmarked for running expenses	350

The board discussed what tasks should be undertaken in our department, but for the time being we are going to continue putting money aside and eventually try to establish a crèche for the district. It was also agreed to purchase some medical equipment for renting out.

The department received a request to put forward the names of seven ladies to be trained as auxiliary nurses at Wergelandsveien Clinic, and we have already reached this target.

The chairman informed us that some knitwear and
other clothes have been sent to a fisherman in Nordland. His
family lost everything they owned in a fire.

GRATUITIES

Dr Per-Fredrik Lund has already examined the head waiter, the other waiters, the cooks, the chambermaids and the barman. All of them, except the barman, who is troubled by constricted nerves in his left forearm, appeared to be in good shape, at least there were no signs of anything alarming on the horizon, that is, they wouldn't be dying tomorrow. However, Dr Lund would have liked them to take better care of themselves. The war had to shoulder part of the blame. It still haunts the body; it is the last, defiant occupying force. But poor nutrition, bad habits and tobacco can not be ignored. Peace makes people more casual and they deserve this after five lean years. He doesn't want to judge. A happy person is casual. A happy person puts on weight. But it can't go on for ever. Peace also requires discipline. He himself ran the 400 metres in seven international competitions for Norway before the war and he wears the Norwegian Sports Federation's badge of achievement. Dr Per-Fredrik Lund is the medical officer at Hotel Bristol and once a year, in December, he casts an eye over the employees. Now there is only the lounge pianist left. He is new at the hotel. His name is Enzo Zanetti and he is from Italy. A dark, slightly stooped man comes in and takes a seat. He places his coat and hat on his lap and is about to light a cigarette. Dr Lund raises a hand and the pianist puts the packet back in his pocket.

"Sorry."

"You can smoke outside."

"I should give up."

"Yes, I agree."

"I shouldn't have started."

"Then we agree on that, too. But take it step by step. And then, when you've given them up, don't start again."

Dr Lund takes his blood pressure and his pulse, and listens to his breathing. It is really not looking good. The only point in the musician's favour is that he isn't overweight. However, he is too thin. You can count the ribs on both sides. That isn't a good sign, either. They are the legacy of war. Peace is moderation. Peace is the golden middle way.

"Do you eat properly, Herr Zanetti?"

"I live alone."

"I see. But you should eat healthily and regularly in any case."

"I eat mostly at night."

Dr Lund sits down and makes a note in his papers.

"Incidentally, how did you end up in Norway?"

Enzo Zanetti shrugs and looks outside:

"I was touring with a jazz band. We were actually supposed to be going to America. I stopped here when war broke out and the band split up."

He has an elegant, rounded accent with a lilting cadence.

"You speak good Norwegian," Dr Lund says.

"It's like rehearsing a new repertoire. I don't know all the notes yet."

44

"You should do more exercise."

"Do you mean walking?"

"That would be good. Or running. You don't have to run fast. Just enough to get your breathing going."

"I tried skiing, but I kept falling over. Unlike you Norwegians, I wasn't born with skis on my feet."

"Just keep moving. Anything else bothering you?"

"Customers."

Dr Lund gets up and laughs.

"Yes, I can imagine."

They wish each other a happy Christmas. Enzo Zanetti puts on his coat and scarf and goes out into the snow-covered street. Dr Lund watches him from the window. Zanetti stops by a lorry loaded with firewood and lights a cigarette. He has to strike several matches. Brun, the hotel director, comes in and stands beside Dr Lund.

"Are my staff up to a full workload?"

"I would say so. But if you want me to give them a full examination, they will have to come to my surgery."

"Then they'll have to make an appointment in their own time."

"As you wish."

"And my pianist?"

"He's in a poor way."

"He's very highly regarded. He brings people in."

"He's lonely."

"Even I could've come up with that diagnosis. All lounge musicians are lonely."

Brun takes off his jacket and shirt. He smells faintly of sweat. His aftershave can't hide this. His stomach hangs over his belt. Dr Lund carries out his examination.

"You should spend the Christmas holiday with your family," he says.

"What did you call it? A holiday?"

"We aren't as young as we used to be."

A sudden gravity hits Brun.

"Is there something wrong?"

"Everything's a bit too high, old chap. Blood pressure, pulse, weight. Just like last year."

"Good! I can demand as much of my employees as I do of myself, can I then?"

"I beg to differ."

"In what way?"

"I ran 400 metres in 49.9. I don't expect my patients to do the same."

"That's several years ago now, old chap."

Brun puts his shirt back on. Dr Lund packs up his equipment. When they look out of the window again, Enzo Zanetti is still smoking on the corner. The low sun around him is pale. Shadows sharpen and lengthen. People hurry past, carrying full net bags in their hands and presents under their arms. Soon everything is as it was before. Some youths pass by carrying skis over their shoulders. Their laughter erupts from their happy faces.

"He often daydreams," Brun says.

"Perhaps he's teaching himself better Norwegian."

"His accent has such charm. Besides, he has an artistic soul. Unlike us."

"What's that supposed to mean?"

"He's a man with deep feelings, Per-Fredrik."

The hotel director gives the doctor an envelope emblazoned with the hotel logo, the Christmas gratuity. Enzo Zanetti looks up as the two men move away from the second-floor window. He closes his eyes. He thinks about women. They are the subject of his dreams. He has to have a woman soon. Most of the women in Norway are interested briefly, then suddenly they don't want to know. They give him their little finger, but not the rest. They play hard to get. He could go down to Tollbugaten or ring one of the numbers the barman has, but he won't sink so low. There is no joy in paying for the pleasure. But if he doesn't get some soon, there will be no other option. Home is too far away. He doesn't forget to send money, but he won't be going home this Christmas, either. Enzo Zanetti crosses his arms and flicks the cigarette away, it lands in the snow and the glow disappears in a black hole. Then he walks down to Karl Johans gate, past the Christmas displays, which don't raise his spirits, even though shops are now full of commodities that had been in short supply. He carries on through Borggården and stops in the nigh-on deserted City Hall square. He likes standing here. He likes watching men working at Aker Mekaniske Verksted shipyard. He likes watching the gantry cranes with the blue cabins. They resemble prehistoric animals, skeletons, especially in the winter when they are covered with snow and rime frost. He likes to see the smoke, the welding flames and the unfinished ships in the docks. He likes to hear the noise of the power hammers. It evokes in him a bitter-sweet nostalgia. It is the sad resonance of exile. When he turns to face the Filipstad quays below the Fortress he can see the yellow derricks and men unloading Marshall Aid from a Cormack liner. He lingers for a while and scans the fjord, which at this time of day, when there is a clear sky, takes on a red hue all the way past Dyna Lighthouse and out to the Nesodden peninsula. Then Enzo Zanetti shivers and hurries into Automaten, a bar where you can fill your beer glass yourself from a tap in the wall, the only luxury that comes to mind in this melancholy city, with which he is now fully in harmony. However, he drinks only one glass and smokes another cigarette. He usually says: I drink only when I work. When the other tables become too noisy he goes back to Hotel Bristol. Down in the staff quarters he changes into a dinner jacket. He can already hear the loud voices from the bar and laughter from around the tables. December is a dreadful month. Drunken customers and children are the worst. He stands in front of the mirror, straightens his bow tie and combs his hair. The lines on his face are unmistakeable. He will soon be forty years old. How much deprivation can a face take? How much capacity is there in a normal heart for great distances? This is a life of broken Norwegian. These are days with a foreign accent. He decides to start with "White Christmas". On his way out he meets Aina Strand, the chambermaid from Tvedestrand with a voice like sandpaper and hair in the shape of a walnut. She has finished her shift and blocks his way.

"Did you have a medical as well?" she asks.

"Yes."

"Did he find anything?"

"Not as far as I know. How about you?"

"The doctor said I had a stiff neck, but I already knew that."

"You've got a stiff neck?"

"It's because I have to lift mattresses. Feel."

Aina, the chambermaid, bows her head and lifts her

flaming hair. Her neck is a smooth curve. What a beautiful sight it is. But Enzo Zanetti hesitates. She becomes impatient, takes his hand and puts it on her neck. He feels her warm, slightly moist skin. He feels a beating pulse, a soft metronome inside her.

"You've got delicate fingers," she says.

Enzo Zanetti pushes Aina away, afraid he will he want more and be rejected once again. Too violently. She almost falls. She clings to the wall and looks at him with frightened eyes. Then her gaze changes to contempt and she turns her back on him. Enzo Zanetti goes up the staircase. It is steeper than usual. No, he won't open with "White Christmas". Some clod will ask him to play it during the evening anyway and he can't face doing it twice. He'd rather open with "Undecided", which he learned when he was on the way to America and got stranded in Norway. Perhaps he could sing as well:

First you say you'll play
And then it's no.
Then you say you'll stay.
That's when you go.
You're undecided now.
So what are you going to do?

On the last step Enzo Zanetti stops and puts on his lounge-pianist smile. It comes naturally to him. Then he takes a seat at the grand piano. The laughter and the voices carry on unabated. That is how it should be. He is the background. His closest family is the Christmas tree. They could change places. He changes his mind again and instead plays Erik Satie's

Gymnopédie No. 1, which he heard on the radio the other evening. He doesn't notice that the customers in the Bristol go quiet and sit up straight as they listen to these notes that belong in both the circus and the cemetery.

MINUTES FROM WORKING COMMITTEE MEETING, December 12th, 1948.

Frogner department, represented by chairman Fru Heide, put forward a proposal that, because they had the Red Cross clinic and the nurses' home in their district, their department should see their first priority as improvements to and modernisation of the Red Cross nurses' home, which was badly run down. The accounts show a deficit, such that it was out of the question to burden them with further expenses.

The first item on the agenda was the suggested purchase of a potato-peeling machine that was now available. The price is 1,700 kroner. Frogner would pay 500. The proposal, which was approved and strongly backed by Fru Galtung, was based on the other twelve departments in Oslo contributing 100 kroner each. The money would be sent to Fru Scheel with a note explaining what it was for. It was further suggested that every department should renovate and maintain one room each at the home, which, for example, might be named after the department responsible. It was decided that an interior design consultant (preferably a woman) should calculate the costs and suggest the décor, which of course should be uniform.

Christmas boxes this year would be sent to old people's homes and orphanages in Oslo.

A baby's bed modelled on the Danish "cradle" was

demonstrated. Delivery time: about three weeks. Child Aid is ordering some beds. Child Aid had also designed an application form, in conjunction with a list of available equipment. In the New Year infants' clothing should be distributed in exchange for textile coupons.

After the meeting there was an informal gathering at the nurses' home, in the cosy dining room, which had been beautifully decorated with candles and flowers for the occasion. Fru Galtung was given a splendid silver bowl with an inscription; she had been chairman since 1944. Fru Berg presented her with the gift and gave a warm speech of gratitude. In addition, the senior nurse at the home held a fine speech. Fru Scheel passed on her thanks on behalf of the other board members. Fru Diesen, who had been present at the previous change of chair, gave a summary of Fru Galtung's period of office. Finally she welcomed the newly elected chairman. Fru Molstad, on behalf of Child Aid, expressed her gratitude and handed over a bouquet of flowers. Fru Galtung thanked everyone for all their kindness.

Fru Lund attended on behalf of Fagerborg department.

THE CHRISTMAS WISH LIST

Maj Kristoffersen takes Jesper by the hand as they go through the swing doors of Steen & Strøm, the large department store on the corner of Prinsens gate and Kongens gate, 12,000 square metres spread over seven floors, which after the war's great shortages, when the Nazis had closed it down, was just beginning to get going again. Department stores are the yardstick of a free society. Buying involves making democratic choices every single day and not just every four years. The more goods there are, the freer we become. People buy. People sell. It is the true referendum of the people. But still there is little on offer. However, it is more than enough for Maj Kristoffersen. She is inclined to think there is too much. Do we really need all of this when it comes down to it? Maj Kristoffersen, at least, can manage easily without most of it. Nevertheless, she has stopped underneath the lights, amid the sweet fragrances from the perfume counter on the ground floor, they pervade the whole building, perhaps the rest of the town as well, making everything redolent of parties, insouciance and dreams: Soir de Fête, My Sin, Fille d'Eve, J'aime and Heure Bleue. Then she feels Jesper pulling at her hand. He drags her back into the world. He has seen an escalator. He wants to go on it. She holds him back. Escalators are dangerous. Children should be accompanied by an adult. Escalators are dangerous for adults, too. She had read in the paper about a woman whose dress had got caught and she had been dragged in between the steps, which didn't stop moving until only her head was left visible. It had happened outside Norway, at Harrods in London, but nevertheless. They walk over to the little queue that has formed where the staircase rolls out of the floor. Some people are nonchalant, step on and are carried up. Many are hesitant and let the more confident pass. Others give up and stay on the ground floor or find a staircase that doesn't move. It is Maj and Jesper's turn. Jesper doesn't hesitate. He pulls his mother along with him. It is a bit like boarding an aeroplane. They take off. They rise at an angle through the light of the department-store universe. Even the hand rails move with them. Jesper laughs. It is not every day that Jesper laughs. Then they have to get off. This is even more important than getting on. They stand on the same step holding each other's hands. They are enjoying themselves. They would like it to last longer. They count down. They land on the sports equipment planet. Maj buys Ewald's Christmas present here, a pair of blue gaiters. Then he can't complain about snow in his pitch-seamed boots and stay at home every Sunday. But Jesper wants to go higher. And Maj is in a good mood. Which is because Jesper is easy to handle. They are both in a good mood. That is so rare. They take the escalator to the next planet: Ladies' clothing. In the nearest corner is *The New Look*, a row of long creations. It is new, although it looks like the old look, just in a different way. The old has become the new. It is Dior. Maj Kristoffersen cannot contain herself. She walks over to

53

the stand and slowly passes her hand along the dresses. She pushes the branches aside and enters deeper and deeper into the forest of beauty. Jesper is wide-eyed. He wants to join in. An assistant on high heels comes over to them and watches Maj as she moves along the line of clothes hangers.

"Do you need any help, Madam?"

Maj can't help but notice the friendly forbearance in the assistant's eyes. Does she perhaps think that Maj doesn't have the money?

"I'd like to try on the blue one," she says.

The assistant looks at her again, but this time it is more to determine the right size. Then she shows them the way to the fitting room and carefully lays the dress over the back of a chair.

"I'm nearby if you need any help."

The assistant draws the curtain, but they can see her shadow outside. It doesn't move. Is she keeping guard? Maj sits down. Her face is hot. It is glowing. That is how it feels. Jesper is keeping a close eye on her. He senses something in the air. He doesn't want to miss it. It is a long time since he has been so present, so *there*. Maj sees the price tag attached to the neckband: 1,865 kroner. It is beyond belief. It is more money than the Red Cross take at the tombola. Her heart skips a beat. Her fingertips itch.

"What do we do now?" she whispers.

Jesper touches the dress and Maj is on the point of screaming. What if he spoils it? What if there is so much as a tear in it, a loose thread? Then she will have to pay. But Jesper doesn't spoil the dress. He gently passes it to Maj, who starts getting undressed, until she is standing in only her underwear and can slip into the soft, tight material. She is thirty-two years old and still has a pretty figure. She looks in the mirror. The dress fits her like a glove. She whirls around. She dances. With her dark hair she could have been French and sinful today. Jesper laughs.

"How are you doing?" the assistant asks.

"I'm afraid it doesn't quite fit," Maj Kristoffersen says.

"It doesn't fit? Shall I get you another size?"

"No, this isn't right for me. It . . ."

"Are you decent?"

"Yes, of course. I'm . . ."

The assistant pulls the curtain to the side and looks in.

"You have to see it in the light!"

She pushes Maj Kristoffersen towards the other ladies, who are only looking without daring to touch, turn to her, smiling and envious, probably suspicious, too. Can *she* afford such a showpiece? She cannot. Maj is on the verge of tears. Will she never be able to get out of this king's ransom in blue, *The New Look*? She just wants her old self back. That is all. She is Maj Kristoffersen from Fagerborg. They come to a halt in front of a large slanting mirror by the wall under a yellow lamp. She sees an unfamiliar woman. The assistant pulls the zip up to her neck, looks over Maj's shoulder and sees the same, but through different eyes.

"And you're telling me it doesn't fit?"

Maj Kristoffersen looks around. Jesper is still standing by the fitting room watching. For a moment he seems unhappy and angry. She will have to hurry before this goes all wrong. She will have to get it over with. She will have to tell the truth.

"It's much too expensive for me."

"No, it isn't. It's Dior. Perhaps you didn't realise?"

Maj scurries back to the fitting room, ashamed and determined; she changes clothes at speed and takes the dress to the assistant, who appraises her again.

"You should know, Madam . . ."

Jesper takes his mother's hand and squeezes it. She bends down.

The assistant comes closer.

". . . that no-one has looked better in that dress than you."

Maj Kristoffersen looks up and blushes. She feels a sudden, strange pleasure. It is a long time since she has experienced anything similar, she feels proud and light-headed. She wants to say something, thank you, but before she can, Jesper pulls her towards the escalator, which takes them back down to earth. And there, amid the fragrances in the perfumery department, she remembers what she really came here for, not just to buy gaiters for Ewald, she has to have a Christmas present herself as well. She takes out her purse, kneels down and gives Jesper exactly 42 kroner. He holds the money in both hands.

"Now you go over to the counter and buy a bottle of eau de cologne. 4711. Then you ask the lady to gift-wrap it. Can you do that?"

"Yes."

"4711. Say it after me."

"4711."

"It's a perfume. Can you remember that?"

"4711. Perfume."

"And now I'll turn away so that I can't see what you're giving me for Christmas."

Maj Kristoffersen straightens up and looks in a different

direction. She hears Jesper go over to the counter. It takes time. She is on the point of looking over her shoulder. Perhaps it is too much for him. She resists. She said she wouldn't look. She will keep her promise. Instead she eyes the Christmas tree in the middle of the shop. Suddenly she dreads the New Year, when she will have to sweep up all the pine needles in the sitting room, and not just there but everywhere in the flat. Sometimes she even finds needles when she does her spring clean. You simply can't get rid of them. They are like a curse. Nevertheless she hopes Ewald will be out and about early and get the biggest tree. Then at long last Jesper is back. He doesn't stop. He just walks past her towards the swing doors, which are just as dangerous as the escalator. Maj had read about a woman who kept going round and round for hours and finally got stuck. That was in Harrods too, or perhaps it was Magasin du Nord in Copenhagen. Anyway, she hurries after Jesper and they emerge together in Prinsens gate. It is two o'clock. It isn't snowing. The clouds are drifting away. The clear sky is sinking over Oslo. Jesper's breath around his face is white. He gives the little bottle to his mother.

"Didn't they gift-wrap it?"

Jesper shakes his head and quickly shoves his hands back in his pockets.

"But you did ask, didn't you?"

Jesper nods. Now it is Maj's turn to shake her head.

"That wasn't very nice of them. We'll have to do it ourselves."

She puts the eau de cologne in her bag. Then they walk to the National Theatre and catch the train to Valkyrie Plass. Jesper likes to be at the front when they go through the tunnel.

At Melsom the butcher's, by the end of Kirkeveien, they buy five pork patties, one for Jesper, one for Maj and three for Ewald if, for once, he can make it home for dinner.

The board meeting was held at Fru Lutken's on December 9th. All five members were present. Fru Nordklev read the minutes from the previous meeting of the working committee (see above). It was decided to give 100 kroner towards the purchase of the potato-peeling machine for the nurses' home and to participate with the other departments in the renovation and modernisation of the nurses' quarters.

Fru Lutken had, since the last board meeting, talked to the parish nurse, Inger Bø, to find out if there might be room available in the parish hall for the planned medical equipment stock. As this was proving difficult to resolve the chairman promised she would examine other options. Fru Lutken was asked to see what it would cost to acquire those medical items we have been advised are necessary.

As far as a stock of infant supplies is concerned, the parish nurse thought there was no great need for any and we therefore agreed that the 500 kroner set aside for this purpose could be used on medical equipment instead.

With reference to the crèche, Fru Lutken had been informed that the parish was looking to set up a nursery. Fru Nordklev promised to write to the Chief Housing Officer to find out if room could be found for a crèche in a new building.

As there is still a considerable lack of clarity with regard to the demarcation of our department's responsibilities, Fru

Aasland promised to consult the Red Cross office in Fredrik Stangs gate to establish complete clarity.

This year twenty-two Christmas boxes will be handed out at a cost of 20 kroner each, according to the parish nurse. Melsom the butcher, Smør-Petersen the delicatessen and Samson the bakery have all made a contribution this year.

CHRISTMAS SPIRIT

"What do you think of the pianist?"

"He looks lonely."

Dr Lund leans closer to his wife.

"I mean the music."

They are sitting at a corner table in Hotel Bristol, each with a cocktail, before they go into the Mauriske Hall restaurant and dine on a superior dinner. It is this year's Christmas gratuity for the in-house medical officer. He is dressed in a dinner jacket and drinking a manhattan. Tove Lund is wearing a long, grey skirt, white blouse and a shawl, and she is sipping with relish at a dry Martini.

"I suppose the music is how it should be," she says.

"You mean drowned out?"

They can barely hear each other speak. Over at the bar there is optimism. It is the start of the loud season. Dr Lund regards the enthusiastic men smoking with one hand, drinking with the other, while wildly gesticulating and shouting over each other. They deserve it. Just so long as it doesn't become a habit. Just so long as they don't come here every night with their big-shot ways. He has a motto: It is the rule, not the exception, which makes you happy. But when he gives this some more thought, unfortunately he realises it isn't true. Had he not been at his happiest when he set the Norwegian 400-metre record? The record isn't the rule. But happiness is not the same as pleasure. Dr Lund would put it this way: the rule is pleasure and the exception is all the rest. His wife takes his arm and nods towards the doors.

"Can you see who that is?"

Dr Lund looks in the direction she indicates, but doesn't recognise anyone. He laughs:

"No. These gentlemen all look exactly the same."

"The slightly plump one. No, very plump. He appears to come here quite often. It's Ewald Kristoffersen."

"Maj Kristoffersen's husband?"

"Yes. By the way, she's our new treasurer. Apparently they have a difficult son."

"Difficult in what way?"

"Stubborn. Angry. Pees in the yard."

"Doesn't he go to school?"

"No. He's a bit . . . behind."

They sit in silence watching Ewald Kristoffersen. He is together with some younger men, probably colleagues. They give their coats to the wardrobe attendant and make their way towards the bar where their glasses stand filled and ready. It doesn't take them long to down them and immediately they want more. It is easy to understand why the barman has constricted nerves in his left forearm. Dr Lund is happy he is responsible only for the employees and not the customers.

"High blood pressure," he says.

"Who?"

"This Ewald."

"You're not at work now, Per-Fredrik."

Then the head waiter comes to summon them. Dinner is served. They follow him to the Mauriske Hall, a large room in ornate Moorish style. It will be good to have the noise behind them. When you eat you don't have to talk all the time, fortunately. One can at a pinch make *polite conversation* and you do that in a low voice. It is war that has made people so talkative and loud. For five years they had to keep their voices down. Now at last they can raise them. Dr Lund walks behind his wife and can still enjoy the sight of her. Enzo Zanetti lifts his hands and glances as she passes, catches sight of the doctor, they nod to each other, then he goes on to play "Silent Night", even if no-one is listening. Maybe the doctor can give him some painkillers. Or something to help him sleep. He should have asked. Then he hears the life and soul of the party again, the one who always asks for Louis Strongarm. Has he got a request tonight as well? Enzo Zanetti makes sure he doesn't meet his eyes. Instead he smiles at the two middle-aged ladies who are drinking tea by the stairs and have kept their hats on, looking timeless and lost. He plays "We'll Meet Again" for them. They can't hear anything anyway. No, the life and soul of the party is only going to the toilet and holding on to the shiny banister as he totters downstairs to Cirkus Schumann, as the wits call it. When he comes back up he has combed his hair and straightened his tie, but he hasn't noticed that one collar flap is sticking up. And so the evening goes on. At nine Enzo Zanetti has a break, goes outside and lights a cigarette. It is cold. He shivers. He should have put on his coat. But it is still better to be here. The street lamps' miserly light makes it even darker. Suddenly someone grabs him and drags him round the corner. He can't fight his way free. There must be at least two of them. If they are going to rob him, they won't find much, not even a Christmas gratuity. One of them snatches the cigarette from him and stubs it out on the back of his left hand. Enzo Zanetti screams, but the other man covers his mouth and not a sound escapes. He tries to wriggle loose. He receives a punch to the stomach, and another, this time in his kidneys, he doubles up and another punch lifts him from the ground. The assailant leans closer, braces himself and head-butts him. Enzo Zanetti, the lounge pianist, hits his head against the brick wall as the blood seeps from his broken nose.

"Keep away from our girls, Wop," the man says.

"Which girls?"

"*My* girl, Greaseball!"

The man takes his right hand, forces his forefinger back until there is the sound of a dry crack. He lets go and is about to start on his left hand as well. The man holding Enzo Zanetti whispers:

"Hey, not both of them."

"Why not? Doesn't he play with both hands?"

A tram rattles down from Pilestredet or perhaps it is something else that startles them. At any rate they let Enzo go and run up towards Teatergaten. He slumps down to the snow and stays there. The tram passes by. The faces in the carriages, why can't they see him? He tries to stand, but can't. Soon he is no longer cold. It is warm. It is darker. It is almost pleasant. He just floats off. He doesn't know where. It doesn't matter. Perhaps he is on his way home. Then he can manage after all, to stand up, that is. He staggers around the corner, spits blood, holds his mutilated hand in the air, his nose stuck to his cheek, that is how it feels, he can only breathe through his mouth. In this state he enters the bar in Hotel Bristol. The closest customers scream. He staggers past them, to the piano. He is going to play. That is his job. It is such a long way. Why does no-one help him? The barman runs into the Mauriske Hall. Finally someone takes his arm, gently. But Enzo Zanetti pulls away. He doesn't want another beating. He doesn't want any help. He is going to play. He falls over the stool and almost drags Ewald Kristoffersen down with him. He lies on his back. Looking up at the Christmas tree, the star, is it only a street lamp going out? Faces soon cover the light. Now Enzo knows what he is going to play. He is going to play *Sonatine Bureaucratique*. Then he recognises the medical officer, who pushes Ewald Kristoffersen away and kneels down.

"Oh, my goodness," says Dr Lund.

Ewald Kristoffersen fetches his coat from the cloakroom and goes out as the ambulance arrives. The sirens remind him of war. It is a long time since he thought about war, even though it is not a long time ago. He turns up his collar, walks to the National Theatre and catches the metro. There are only empty seats, but he prefers to stand at the front and watch the darkness appearing and disappearing. This feeling of speed appeals to Ewald Kristoffersen. When the train vibrates beneath his feet it is even better. He usually gets off at Valkyrie Plass – the station there was the result of an accident, a street collapsed at this very spot – but he stays on until Majorstua. So that he can have a beer at Tråkka before he makes a start on the long climb up Kirkeveien. It strikes him that no matter which direction he comes from, the last bit is steep. He thinks about Oslo. Where to begin? He doesn't know yet. He needs some ideas. That is his job. If he doesn't have any ideas, he won't have a job. What about just forgetting the 900 years and celebrating the future? Why should we always carry history with us? Ewald Kristoffersen reckons that is a brilliant idea. It will never be accepted. He unlocks the door to the hallway as quietly as he can, hangs up his coat and scarf on the hooks and puts his snow boots on the old newspapers on the shoe rack. Jesper is asleep in the vestibule. Ewald Kristoffersen tiptoes past the bed just as quietly. Then he stops. Maj is sitting at the dining table doing the accounts. She has her own book to write in. She doesn't notice her husband. And he knows at once where to begin: women. That is quite an idea, thinks Ewald. He will start with Oslo's women.

On 16/12/48 Fagerborg department received 48 Canadian tins of food from the Oslo Red Cross for distribution. We added some other food and gave twelve parcels to the elderly. They had applied to the Red Cross earlier for parcels from America. The chairman responsible for the handover said there was great joy when they received them.

DECEMBER 23rd

Fru Vik removes the snow with a little spade. Once that has been done, she places a wreath and a short, thick candle by the gravestone. Then she takes out some long matchsticks and tries to light the candle. The wick burns at the third attempt. Then she quickly puts a glass tumbler over the flame, which flickers for a moment, then settles into a nice upright position. Fru Vik straightens up, wraps the spade in newspaper and puts it and the matches in her bag. Some distance away a man stands watching her. She is not mistaken. It is her he is watching. He has been doing so all the time. She turns to walk to Borgen Station, but changes her mind and makes for Frogner Park instead. There is no reason to hurry. She is a widow. Besides, the sun is shining. The shadows from the graves stretch out. She has to look down for a moment not to be dazzled. The man is following her. She starts to walk faster. He does, too. She hears his footsteps coming closer. He soon catches her up. Fru Vik stops and turns.

"What do you want?"

The man looks down, dazzled as well, or maybe only embarrassed.

"I didn't mean to frighten you."

"You didn't."

Then Fru Vik recognises him. He was standing on the steps of the chapel early this winter, not wearing a coat. He is as thinly clad as before.

"I've been watching you," he says.

"I beg your pardon."

The man proffers a hand.

"Olaf Hall. I saw you by your husband's grave when Ragnhild, when my wife was buried. And I couldn't forget you. I had to see you again. And I was sure you would return today."

"Were you now?"

"And if you hadn't come today, you would've done tomorrow."

"How so?"

"Because you're a loyal woman."

Fru Vik can hardly believe her ears. It is her turn to be embarrassed. What is he up to? Is he making an advance? But that is not on. It is highly inappropriate. The ground frost has barely thawed and there he is, in the cemetery, in his shiny suit, making a pass. Nevertheless, she shakes his hand, although she lets go quickly.

"Margrethe Vik."

"I knew I'd get to see you again."

"And now you've seen me."

"I'm grateful. Perhaps—"

She interrupts him.

"And now we're no longer going the same way, Olaf Hall. On the contrary, we're each going our own way."

Fru Vik goes out through the gate, tramps across the dog-walking area of Frogner Park without daring to look back.

This is terrible. She is confused. She is annoyed. The moment has been ruined. She becomes angrier and angrier. Only when she is sure he can't see her does she look back. She can only see the Monolith. There is something about this massive stone pillar in the winter. It is covered with rime frost. It vanishes in the cold. It is loneliness. It is the wind and the sun. Fru Vik bends her neck, holds her hat and peers down Middelthuns gate to Kirkeveien. From there it is a short walk home. In Majorstua men rush into the vinmonopol while women queue at Melsom the butcher's a bit further up. Fru Vik has everything she needs. She needs so little. Definitely not much. Outside the entrance to her apartment block in Gørbitz gate she meets Maj Kristoffersen and Jesper, unfortunately. She isn't in the mood to talk to anyone. She wants to go in. She wants to go to her flat, collect herself and stay there.

"Aren't you well?" Maj asks.

Fru Vik has to stop after all.

"Yes, I am. Of course. What makes you think I'm not?"

"I just thought . . ."

Fru Vik points to the net shopping bag.

"Are you delivering Red Cross parcels today as well?"

"We had one left. Fru Lund asked me to deliver it."

"That will make someone happy."

"Yes, they're very grateful when we turn up. Why don't you join our local department by the way? That would be so nice."

Fru Vik takes out her keys.

"That's for you young ones. I'm too old for that sort of thing."

Maj Kristoffersen laughs.

"Too old? You? Not at all. Do you think Fru Vik is too old, Jesper?"

Jesper looks up and gives the question some thought.

"Don't know."

Fru Vik pats him on the head.

"You can visit me tomorrow if you're bored."

Jesper nods and follows his mother down to Majorstua, where they take the Disen tram for four stops and get off at Uranienborg. Maj Kristoffersen checks the address on the piece of paper in her hand again: Jørgen Moes gate 12. It is not far away. But the snow piled at the side of the pavements is high and they have to make large detours to cross the road. The church clock says ten past two. They are beginning to hurry. Eventually they arrive at the right corner. Inside the entrance to the flats there is a smell of gravy and burnt Christmas biscuits. On the second floor they see the name on the door of the lucky recipient: Enzo Zanetti. It is a strange name. Fru Lund has explained that he is Italian and lonely. And Maj explains that to Jesper. Italy is a faraway country where oranges grow and it is hot all year round. Enzo Zanetti is an Italian name. So he is Italian, too. He even makes his living by playing the piano. She hopes he can speak some Norwegian. She forgot to ask Fru Lund about that. All they have to do is hand over the parcel, though, not make conversation, and everyone knows what the Red Cross is wherever they are from. Didn't it all start in Italy anyway? Jesper is allowed to ring the bell. Then they wait. Time passes. Jesper rings again. The same: nothing. Perhaps he isn't at home? But Fru Lund said Enzo Zanetti was unable to go out. That is why he is getting the parcel. Maj rings the doorbell. She does it twice to be sure. Soon they hear footsteps approaching, slowly.

"He'll be pleased now," Maj whispers.

She takes Jesper's hand and they step back a pace so that they aren't standing on the mat. Then the door opens, not wide, but enough. A dark-skinned, quite short man peers out at them. He is wearing only a dressing gown and supporting himself on a stick with his left hand. His right hand is in plaster. His face is in no better condition. It is already lined and weather-beaten. And in addition to a black eye, almost closed, he has a bandage across his nose, and his forehead is dark green and swollen beneath the thick, black hair that in places, especially by the temples, is grey and wilting. Maj Kristoffersen asks:

"Enzo Zanetti?"

The man nods very cautiously.

"Yes?"

"Do you understand Norwegian?"

The man nods again and appears suspicious.

"Yes."

"We have a Christmas box for you from the Red Cross."

"From what?"

"The Red Cross. Fagerborg department."

"Why?"

"Because . . . because you need it, I suppose."

Maj Kristoffersen lets go of Jesper's hand, takes the parcel from the net bag and hands it over. Enzo Zanetti opens the door wide, leans on his stick and stares at the parcel.

"What's in it?"

"Tins of food from Canada, salami, sugar and a pair of socks. Which we knitted."

70

Enzo Zanetti starts laughing, the laughter subsides into coughing, he has to bend over and stands in the doorway doubled up as his whole body shakes. Maj is at a loss as to what to do. Then at last the dark-skinned man in the dressing gown is still, he straightens up slowly, his face shiny, and stares at her.

"You can take your damned parcel and keep it! *Adesso!*"

Enzo Zanetti slams the door and hobbles back to the sitting room, where the grand piano occupies most of the space. He sits down on the stool, drains the glass on the piano, pours himself another and plays Satie with one hand, the melancholy left hand. Then he feels guilty. Some people are so kind they give others a bad conscience. He stops playing and goes over to the window. On the window sill is a pile of old sheet music. He looks out. To the right is Briskeby Fire Station. To the left the towering Uranienborg Church. Enzo Zanetti lives in Jørgen Moes gate, a street named after the author of folk tales, which lies between the church and the fire station. Then he spots them between the banks of snow, opens the window and shouts:

"I'd like your parcel after all!"

He smacks the window shut and goes to the hallway, unlocks the door and waits. He is cold. He could get seriously ill standing here in the draught. He is ill enough as it is. The Red Cross is making him ill. Damn the Red Cross. It is the boy who finally brings up the parcel and hands it over.

"Thank you," Enzo Zanetti says.

He is about to close the door with his foot. But the boy is still there. His eyes are determined, yet restless. He seems troubled. He is burning to say something.

"I've heard you play," the boy says.

"Have you now? Where?"

"At Fru Vik's."

"Fru Vik? Do I know a Fru Vik?"

"She's our neighbour."

"I see. And I played there?"

"On her radio."

Enzo Zanetti laughs.

"That probably wasn't me. I only play at Hotel Bristol."

The boy looks to the side or past him, pensive.

"It was the same tune," he says. "But . . ."

"But?"

The boy pulls away, both shy and curious.

"Your playing was softer."

Enzo Zanetti is taken aback, then he understands the context. He raises his plaster and knocks it gently against the door frame.

"That's because I play with only one hand. But when I'm well, I'll play with two. Thank your mother."

Jesper nods and runs down the stairs. Maj is waiting for him impatiently on the next landing. She takes his hand and they dash out and back the same way to the tram stop.

"What took you such a time?"

"Nothing."

"Was he being stubborn again?"

"No. He was nice."

They just reach the tram in time and find seats on the bench. Maj shows her tickets. Everything is fine. They have transfer tickets. Transfers are the best. She turns to Jesper.

"Nice? What do you mean by nice?"

Jesper shrugs. He would rather be standing outside. Then

he could imagine it was him driving the tram, even if he is at the back, driving along Riddervolds gate, around the corner by the Trade & Commerce building, down Drammensveien and Glitnebakken, from stop to stop through a network in which sooner or later everyone in this city is caught. Standing at the back is best. From there you can see everything you leave behind. However it is not Jesper steering the tram. Not even the conductor is steering. It is the rails. It is the people who laid the rails, who perhaps died years ago, who are still steering the tram.

They get off at the National Theatre and can see the towers rising inside the scaffolding around the new City Hall, which is due to be finished for the 900-year jubilee. Then they follow Karl Johans gate, past the Christmas tree in Universitetsplassen, where the famous Salvation Army Slum Sisters stand collecting money and old clothes. Maj Kristoffersen nods to them. They work in the same area as her. They are helping. They are helping those worse off. But the Slum Sisters are not collecting much. Nowadays everyone is worse off. It is cold helping on December 23rd, but it warms your heart anyway. Jesper stops and looks up.

"Are we going to have a tree as big as that?"

"Doubt it," Maj Kristoffersen says.

It is starting to snow. Soon the shops will be closed. Whatever you have forgotten to buy now you may as well give up on. But Maj has everything she needs at home, except Ewald and the Christmas tree. Suddenly Jesper goes over to the big piggy bank, rummages through his pockets and puts in a coin, a krone. For a moment he stands with his back turned to Maj, confused it seems, pulls his hat down further over his ears while the Slum Sisters pat him on the shoulder and smile at Maj. Then she and Jesper continue to the Grand Hotel and walk up Rosenkrantz' gate. At number 12, between Det Nye Teater and the B.U.L. building, they go in and take the lift to the fifth floor. Jesper likes taking the lift. It is slower than the tram, but it shakes more. Maj, for her part, is anxious. She stands in the corner with her eyes closed.

"Was that why you said he was nice?"

Jesper doesn't answer.

"Because he gave you a krone?"

"Yes," Jesper says.

"You're nice, too. But we should never take money. The Red Cross doesn't allow it. That's why it was good you passed the money on. And take off your hat."

The lift comes to a stop, Jesper pushes the gate to the side and Maj squeezes out. Here, Dek-Rek has offices on the whole floor. First they meet the secretary, Frøken Bryn, sitting at an oval table on which there are two telephones. Behind her is a world map painted straight onto the wall. Norway is almost unrecognisable. She shows them through to the design office, where there are eight desks with slanted drawing boards and lamps that can be twisted in any direction. The lamps are switched off. It is the end of the working day. The designers hang up their white coats, loosen their ties and are quiet. Ewald Kristoffersen is one of them. He hasn't had time to change yet. In his breast pocket he has a line of pencils and pens. They look like a military distinction. He is the one who talks most. Someone fills small glasses and they toast. He is the one who toasts loudest. Jesper sees his father and hardly recognises him. This is a different father. This is a father in disguise. He doesn't know which one he likes more. His mother lets go of his hand and at that moment Ewald turns and catches sight of her. There is a silence. The men say hi, a little perplexed, almost embarrassed, no longer unrestrained, just even more subdued. The moment has lost its magic. They have been seen. Ewald comes over to them.

"Is anything the matter?"

"We're going to buy the Christmas tree you should've bought three weeks ago," Maj says.

Ewald is cross, but tries to hide his emotions.

"I thought you didn't want a Christmas tree. So that you wouldn't have to sweep until June."

"You'd better ask Jesper if he wants a Christmas tree, Ewald."

Ewald looks down at his son.

"Shall we have a Christmas tree this year, Jesper?"

The boy shrugs again.

"I don't mind either way."

Maj sighs and is about to say something, *see, see what you've done*, but before she has a chance Frøken Bryn is there. She gives Jesper a ginger biscuit and looks at Ewald.

"Rudjord wants to talk to you."

"Now?"

"This minute, Kristoffersen."

Ewald bows and Jesper sees another father, a cowed one. That at least is sure. He doesn't like the cowed father. Ewald signals to Maj and follows Frøken Bryn, past the reception desk, into the inner sanctum. His colleagues are shrugging on their coats and already leaving. If only he could join them. Then he could have a beer as well. What can this be? What would Rudjord want from him on December 23rd? Are there too many of them? Will Ewald Kristoffersen have to go? But aren't times good for the company? Hasn't Dek-Rek been given the assignment for the council's exhibitions in connection with Oslo's 900-year jubilee? He can feel some pressure around his heart, his breathing stops for a second. He is forty-one years old and can't die now. He is forty-one years old and can't get the boot now, not now when Maj and Jesper are waiting for him. He would rather die while they are here. He adjusts his white coat and Frøken Bryn opens the door to Rudjord's office. Ewald Kristoffersen takes a deep breath and goes in. The door closes behind him. Rudjord is standing with his back to Ewald at the window, smoking a French cigarette, which has a sweet smell. His left arm hangs down limp, a war injury. He was in the office when Filipstad exploded. He always wears a waistcoat with a suit and a pocket watch. He would like to appear like the firm he founded in 1930: modern and traditional at the same time. Rudjord turns at length and taps the cigarette into a small silver ashtray.

"Haven't you taken off your work-clothes yet?"

Ewald Kristoffersen looks past him. From here he has a view of Hotel Bristol on the next corner. If only he could be sitting there. All he wants is to be free of worry. Being free of worry is synonymous with being happy. Is that too much to ask?

"I keep going to the end," Ewald Kristoffersen says.

"You can have a break now."

What is that supposed to mean? A break? What does Rudjord mean? Is it a warning? Is the idea that Ewald is to take a break and never return? He laughs.

"I have no choice, I suppose."

Rudjord puts his cigarette in the silver ashtray.

"Your wife's waiting for you outside, isn't she? Maj?"

"Yes. Maj."

"And Jonas?"

"Jesper."

"Jesper. Sorry. There are so many children now that I can't remember all the names."

"Yes, the place is crawling with them."

"How old is Jesper now?"

"He turned seven in October."

"Then he'll be going to – let me see – Majorstua School?"

"He won't be starting until next year."

Ewald looks down and rearranges the pencils in his breast pocket. Rudjord comes around the desk.

"What I wanted to say is that I like your idea."

Ewald looks up.

"Sorry?"

Rudjord laughs, flips another cigarette out of the blue packet and lights it. All with one hand.

"Don't you remember your own ideas, Kristoffersen? The women! I like it."

"You like it, sir?"

"My God, Ewald. Drop the formality. Yes, I like it. Start with women. It's different. It's special. And Dek-Rek has to be *special*. But never *controversial*."

Rudjord passes Ewald the packet. However, Kristoffersen is too bewildered to smoke.

"I got the idea when I was watching my wife," he says.

Rudjord puts the cigarettes in his pocket and laughs again.

"Yes, I can imagine."

"When I came home one night and saw my wife in the sitting room doing the accounts for the Red Cross. She's the treasurer for the Fagerborg department. And . . ."

"It's an excellent place to start, Kristoffersen. With women volunteers."

"Yes, that's what I was thinking. Excellent."

"That was all I wanted to say. And to wish you and your beautiful wife a wonderful Christmas. Not forgetting Jesper, of course."

Rudjord pats Ewald Kristoffersen on the shoulder. It is a blessing. He goes out, taking the blessing with him. He is going to bless everyone. He kisses a surprised Frøken Bryn on the cheek and tears off his white coat as he almost runs to the design office where Maj and Jesper are still waiting. And now Jesper sees another father, this must be the third one, or perhaps the fourth in the course of a very short time. This is the father he likes best and he notices that his mother does, too: this is the proud father returning to his family.

"Now let's go straight to Universitetsplassen and buy this Christmas tree," Ewald Kristoffersen says.

However, they go to Ullevålsveien instead, and it strikes him that it is all uphill there, too. But today no inclines are steep. He is light on his feet. He is light in his heart.

"What's got into you?" Maj asks.

"Rudjord liked my idea. And do you know what?"

"No. What?"

Ewald Kristoffersen stops, holds Maj with both hands and kisses her. And he does this in the middle of the street, on December 23rd, not far from Our Saviour's Cemetery, where, amongst others, Wergeland, Welhaven, Ibsen, Bjørnson, Collett and Nordraak are buried in Æreslunden, the famous burial ground, all these people who are commemorated in street names throughout the city. Jesper is wide-eyed with happiness.

"It was you who gave me the idea."

"Which idea?"

"Women! Behind every town there is a woman!"

"Oh, give over, Ewald."

But there are only two trees left when they see Jubalon, as he is called, the old man who fells part of his forest every Christmas and transports the trees to the tram loop in Adam-stuen and sells them there. One is more spindly than the other. Ewald Kristoffersen takes out his wallet and points to the first one. Maj thinks they should take the other one.

"At least it's dropped its needles once and for all," she says.

Then Ewald and Jesper carry the tree to Fagerborg whistling "Silent Night". Maj walks behind them. It is a miserable specimen of a spruce. It is the one no-one wanted. It doesn't matter. Today it doesn't matter. Ewald and Jesper whistle, not exactly in unison, it sounds like two tunes, but anyway. They carry the tree together, even though Ewald carries most of the weight. When they get to their house entrance, Maj spots Fru Vik standing in her window keeping a lookout or lost in dreams. Has she really still got her outdoor coat on? Maj waves to her. Fru Vik raises her hand too and shakes her head thinking: what a Christmas tree. Actually it doesn't matter. If you decorate it well enough no-one will notice. Ever since her husband died, she has stopped buying a Christmas tree. She just puts a wreath on the door, for appearance's sake. She will have to decorate her own grave. She chuckles. It isn't a happy chuckle. Then she hears the Kristoffersen family on the stairs, it would have been better if they had used the rear entrance, then there wouldn't be any pine needles on the stairs. Actually that doesn't matter, either. The tree was so bare you could see right through it. Ewald stops whistling, and she hears his heavy breathing instead, while Jesper whistles something like the melody he heard on the radio, *Gymnopédie No. 1*. It is an odd, almost unsettling combination, a child whistling Satie. She sits down in the wing chair, with her coat on. She is cold. It is quiet. She doesn't feel like eating. Though she isn't angry anymore. She is just sad and frightened. Everything sinks slowly inside her and what is left is a sense of loss. She goes to bed early and can't sleep. She isn't frightened any longer, but the sadness turns into something it is hard to identify. It is so long ago. She has forgotten what it was like. She is out of herself. This is how it was for Fru Vik on the night before Christmas Eve, 1948. She gets up, wraps a shawl around her shoulders, fetches the telephone directory and finds Ragnhild Hall, *actress*, Nordraaks gate 11. It strikes her: the dead are still listed in the book. Is Halfdan as well? She has to look. He is. Of course he is. It is an old directory. It is from before the war. It is out of date. But *she* isn't in it. Fru Vik shudders. In the end she finds Olaf Hall under *Hall's Antiquarian Bookshop*, also Nordraaks gate 11.

But when she goes back to bed and can't sleep this time either, she gives up and shuffles into the kitchen. She heats some milk, which she pours into a cup. It is still dark. It isn't morning yet. This is going to be the longest Christmas Eve for many years. The curtains are drawn in the other windows.

Only the snow gives light. Then she takes a stack of *Aftenposten* newspapers from the pantry, peruses the obituaries and starts reading:

> Ragnhild Hall, formerly Stranger, made her debut as Solveig in Peer Gynt at the National Theatre in the autumn of 1923 and already then her performance drew standing ovations. She had a versatile career on a variety of stages, both at home and abroad. She was widowed early when her first husband director Oskar Stranger died in a drowning accident and she was left with her son Bjørn. She married Olaf Hall in 1936. In her last years she was mostly to be found in the Chat Noir and Edderkoppen theatres. She spread happiness wherever she went and was held in high regard by both her audiences and colleagues. She will be missed. J.H. Wiers Jenssen and Leif Juster.

There is a ring at the doorbell. It isn't seven o'clock yet. Something must be wrong. Fru Vik opens the door. There is nothing wrong. It is only Jesper standing on the cold, narrow staircase, still in his pyjamas.

"I'm bored," he says.

———

1949

The first board meeting of the New Year was held on January 10th at Fru Ingrid Arnesen's. Those present were: the chairman, Fru Lutken, Fru Nordklev, Fru Lund and Fru Kristoffersen.

Christian Plesner estimated the price of the items needed for the medical resources stock at 430 kroner. The equipment will be acquired at once and the chairman will store it. We are short of bed protectors, but now we have been promised enough material by the Red Cross to make eight.

A members' meeting was proposed for February 21st in the parish hall.

An application for a room for a crèche/day care centre will be sent to the Chief Housing Officer in Oslo.

THE EXCHANGE

At Steen & Strøm the Christmas decorations have been taken down and the shelves that had been almost empty are now completely empty. There are no rare scents coming from the perfume counter, only draughts, and even the assistants have stopped putting on make-up. They scowl at the tight-fisted, dissatisfied customers bringing back their presents. Even the escalator has lost its lustre. It is no longer a plane, just a steep, restless pavement. Besides, Maj Kristoffersen thinks this is embarrassing. Jesper stands in front of her. They get off at the sports department. The same assistant as last time sticks his sports magazine in his pocket. Maj Kristoffersen stops, places the gaiters on the counter and looks down.

"I'd like to exchange these," she says.

The assistant picks up one gaiter with two fingers.

"You haven't worn them, have you?"

"No, no. Not at all. I mean, my husband hasn't worn them."

"Your husband. Didn't they fit him?"

"Yes, they did, but apparently he wants something else."

"Such as what?"

"If I could have my money back, then we could give that some thought."

Maj Kristoffersen looks up warily. The assistant doesn't seem very amenable at first.

"The best I can do is to give you a voucher."

"Not money?"

"This is not a second-hand shop, Madam. This is Steen & Strøm."

"I was just asking."

"How about some ski wax? We have a set of three brands for all kinds of snow."

"I don't think so."

"Or what about some ski straps?"

"Actually, my husband's not very keen on skiing."

"We can all make mistakes, Madam."

"I think I'll take the voucher then."

"As you wish."

The assistant sighs and takes a form he starts to fill in.

"Can I use it in other departments as well?" Maj asks.

"Let me explain the conditions to you. You can use the voucher anywhere in the store, but not with sale items."

"But there's almost no choice."

"Correct. And the voucher has to be used within a week of today's date. What's your name?"

"Maj Kristoffersen. That's unfair."

"Unfair? Surely you can't expect to buy something at full price and then exchange it for something else on offer, thereby getting double the benefit?"

"Why not?"

"I've wondered the same."

The assistant throws the form over his shoulder and looks at Maj Kristoffersen while lowering his voice.

"I'm going to damn well give you the money because we don't stock-take until tomorrow!"

Jesper suddenly seems nervous. Maj turns and at once sees three people getting off the escalator. The assistant looks at them too and smells trouble. He quickly lays the item-exchange form back on the counter and busies himself filling it in. There are two men, one younger, one a little older, both wearing dark suits, and the assistant from the perfume counter. She stops and points at them. The men come closer, serious, determined. One stands behind Jesper. The other takes Maj's arm.

"Would you mind coming with us?"

"What?"

"Please don't make a scene. Just come with us."

All four of them go to an office beside the fitting rooms. Maj and Jesper are shown to a chair. Both men stand in front of them. The older of the two looks down at Maj.

"Is this your son?"

"Yes. Of course he's my son."

"What's his name?"

"Jesper. What do you want?"

"We have reason to believe Jesper stole a bottle of perfume from the ground floor just before Christmas."

Maj Kristoffersen jumps up from the chair.

"That can't possibly be true. I gave him 42 kroner exactly! Which is the price of 4711! And your assistant didn't even gift-wrap it!"

She raises her hand to her mouth, slowly sinks to her chair and turns to Jesper, who is sitting with his hands in his pocket, motionless.

"Did you pay for the perfume you bought me, Jesper?"

He doesn't answer. Maj leans closer.

"Jesper, did you pay?"

Jesper doesn't answer now, either. Soon Maj can't take it anymore. She loses her temper. She shakes him. His head lolls from side to side. She doesn't give up. In the end the younger man has to stop her. The second man asks:

"Are you sure you didn't tell your son to do it?"

Maj takes a deep breath.

"To do what?"

"Steal the bottle, Madam."

"How . . . how could you ever think such a thing?"

"You spent a very long time in here."

Maj releases her breath in a sob and hides her face in her hands. Jesper rocks backwards and forwards in the chair. The older man passes Maj a tissue. She blows her nose in it. Suddenly Jesper falls forward and lands on the floor. He lies there, on his stomach. Maj lets go of the tissue, crouches down and tries to turn Jesper over.

"Did you hurt yourself? Did you hurt yourself, Jesper?"

He doesn't want to turn. He makes himself heavy and impossible to move. Maj lays her cheek against his. He is smiling. Is he smiling? Jesper is smiling. Maj eventually coaxes him to his feet. He manages to stand. The two men are apparently sick of the whole performance. The younger one opens the door. The older one leaves the white tissue where it is and leans closer.

"Never show your face in Steen & Strøm again, Madam."

Maj Kristoffersen takes Jesper by the hand and drags him along. Over by the counter the male and female shop assistants watch them. They can just keep the gaiters. They can keep the voucher, too. Maj heads for the escalator. It goes so slowly. Someone has slowed it down to torment her. She can't get out fast enough. It is snowing. The snow is grey. The streets are narrow. Everything is a detour. She is silent until they are finally in the hallway at home. Then she grabs Jesper as hard as she can and asks:

"Did you do that on purpose?"

He looks past her.

She has to grip him even tighter.

"Answer me. Did you fall on purpose?"

Jesper shakes his head and Maj lets him go. She doesn't know what to believe anymore.

"Where's the money?"

"In my pocket."

"In which pocket?"

Jesper lowers his gaze. Maj sticks her hand in the pockets of his windcheater and rummages through them. In the first she finds a stone, a clothes peg and an elastic band. In the other she finds the money: three notes and some coins. She counts them. It is exactly 41 kroner. One krone is missing. She knows her sums. She can add two plus two. It is the krone Jesper gave to the Slum Sisters, which he said the Italian pianist had given him. Maj is on the verge of tears again. She has a chancer for a son. He has had the money in his pocket the whole time. How does he dare? She puts the money in her bag and goes to the bedroom. Jesper follows her, curious. She takes the bottle of perfume, goes into the bathroom and empties it down the toilet. She turns to Jesper thinking: Now I've got him.

"We won't tell Pappa about this," Maj says.

———

On January 11th a meeting was held at the Oslo District office to discuss the need for more nurses. Those present were: Fru Esther Andresen (new chairman of the working committee), Fru Alfa Heide, Fru Schlytter, Herr Holm and Fru Berit Nordklev. Fru Schlytter reported back on her work at Bærum Nursing Home, which has now lasted three mths. After an interview with Fru Schlytter in the daily paper approx. 40 volunteers have applied to the Red Cross office. The applicants will be registered and initially do a short course (6 hours) before they are assigned to a hospital.

It was decided that the Fagerborg department would still try to start without "qualifying". The previous day we had been requested by Wergelandsveien Clinic to make available some volunteers. It was pointed out quite firmly that they would have to sign a legally binding professional pledge and also do the same course when it materialises.

In the evening we had a meeting at Fru Berit Nordklev's. At such short notice it wasn't possible to assemble many volunteers. The senior nurse at the clinic, Sofie, was present and led the class. A schedule was set up and personal details and any other requisite information were taken from those present. At the same time the pledge was signed. It turned out that the ten volunteers we had mustered wasn't enough. There should have been double that number as the clinic was in sore need of help. The two first volunteers started the very next day on the evening shift. Shifts are organised as follows: one set on the first floor and one on the second. Times are arranged to suit individuals, mostly women, also some professional women. The first ones start at eight o'clock or a bit before, the others at nine. They work till noon, some right through till four. The afternoon shift also has a variable start-time, from four to five or six o'clock through to the end of the day, that is, to ten or eleven. Many women do two shifts a week, the chairman herself has three and occasionally four. We call the Sunday shift "optional", but so far we have provided auxiliaries for the Sundays we have had.

Schedules are displayed on both floors, women take note of their shifts and go to the same ward so that the hospital can organise nurses' work and free time accordingly. In the case of illness they report in so that replacements can be found and arrangements are disturbed as little as possible. We hope this will be a help for the hospital, and a good one. At any rate the volunteers are full of energy and like the work a lot.

SALE

Fru Vik is walking down to Majorstua. At first she thought of taking the tram, but she continues walking along Kirkeveien. So she has more time to change her mind. She is carrying a net bag. In the net is Francis Harbitz's *Manual of Forensic Medicine*. She doesn't want Jesper flicking through it anymore. It might be the grim pictures in it that make him so uneasy. At Frogner square she turns left. It isn't quite as cold down here as up in Fagerborg, where the winds from the Nordmarka region can make life tough for everyone. Fru Vik stops. She can still turn around and go back home. She doesn't. She walks on. She looks at the street names. There it is: Nordraaks gate. In the middle of the gradual incline she finds no. 11. It is an old brick house. Outside there is a sign: HALL'S ANTIQUARIAN BOOKSHOP. She has to go through a gate to reach the entrance, which is beside the main door. She knocks. No-one answers. Fru Vik goes in. After all it is only a shop. The smell of books, of leather and paper, hits her. It reminds her of nature, a forest. There are books from floor to ceiling, novels, dictionaries, collected works, bibles, atlases, poems, plays, encyclopaedias and telephone directories. This is what she sees as she looks around. Then Olaf Hall appears between the shelves. He is wearing glasses today and is reading Izaak Walton's *The Compleat Angler or the Contemplative Man's Recreation*. He puts it down on a desk, looks up and it is his turn to catch sight of her.

"I'd like to dispose of this," Fru Vik says.

She passes him the manual. He takes it, leafs through slowly and looks up again.

"A classic."

"I'm clearing my husband's things."

"I thought your husband was a vet?"

Olaf Hall suddenly seems shy and runs the back of his hand across his mouth. Fru Vik smiles.

"He was quite interested in everything that was dead."

"I can give you fifty kroner."

"Fifty? That's a lot."

"I'm thinking of the sentimental value."

"It hasn't got any now."

"I'd like to give you a good price anyway."

"I think you should give me an honest price."

Olaf Hall takes a step closer.

"Then I can't offer you anything."

"Oh dear, now you've been horribly honest."

"This is the sixth edition and medical students use only the latest. Besides, there's some writing in the margins."

Olaf Hall goes to give the book back to Fru Vik.

"I can't get rid of it, it seems," she says.

"You can leave it here."

"That's nice of you."

"And if you have any more books, I'd be interested of course."

They stand around for a few moments, silent and uncertain what to do. Perhaps eventually you get used to a smell like this and barely notice it. Dust floats in the sparse light. Fru Vik looks at her watch.

"Well, I'd better—"

Olaf Hall interrupts her.

"You can come upstairs and have a cup of tea. Or something else. If you feel like it."

"I don't think so."

"I live there. It's very practical."

"With your son?"

Fru Vik is embarrassed this time. Olaf Hall smiles.

"I'm sure you've made your arrangements as well," he says.

"I saw the obituary."

"It's my stepson. From Ragnhild's first marriage."

"We didn't have any children."

"Neither did we."

Both of them look down, equally embarrassed now. They search for words. One of them has to say something. Fru Vik does:

"Perhaps another time."

Olaf Hall looks at her.

"Another time?"

"Yes, for a cup of tea."

Fru Vik rolls up the net bag and moves towards the door. Olaf Hall dashes past her and opens it. Snow blows in over the threshold.

"Perhaps you think it's better to meet somewhere in the middle?" he asks.

"That will have to be up to you."

"I'd prefer not to go to the Theatercafé. But what about the Bristol? It's supposed to be nice there."

"That's not exactly in the middle."

"I'll take that as a yes."

Olaf Hall locks the door after Fru Vik, scuttles up the rear staircase to the house's first floor and stops by the kitchen window. He watches her walking between the banks of snow, slightly bent, perhaps she is frightened of falling. Will she turn? Why would she turn? She doesn't know that he is there watching her. He is interrupted by Bjørn, who comes in with snow melting under his shoes.

"Who was that?"

"Who was what?"

"The woman who just left."

"Ah, her. A customer of course."

"Of course. Is the shop going well?"

"Have you been outside watching?"

"I've just got home."

"Are you staying?"

"Maybe. For a while."

Bjørn takes off his coat and goes to his room. Olaf is about to say something, but refrains. Instead he takes a cloth, quickly runs it over the floor and hurries onto the terrace where he wrings out every drop of the dirty water. He just catches a glimpse of Fru Vik at the crossroads by Sigyns gate. She has the feeling the boy, or the young man, she met at the gate is watching her. It was probably the son, the stepson. He didn't seem very friendly. Or perhaps he is just shy. Has Olaf Hall said anything to him? *Said* anything? What would he have said? Nothing has happened. Fru Vik carries on to Munthes gate. She wants to walk through the narrow streets. She doesn't want to be seen. Is it written all over her? She is being unfaithful. She is being unfaithful to her dead husband. It is a disgrace. It hurts. She walks along the smallest streets. And yet she feels a sweetness. It is shameful and sweet. Fru Vik is already thinking about what she is going to wear. Perhaps the sale is still on at Steen & Strøm.

The board meeting was held at Fru Lessund's. Those present were: the chairman, Fru Nordklev, Fru Kristoffersen, Fru Lund and Frøken Løvslett.

Fru Lessund was asked to find out whether either Fagerborg parish hall or the nurses' home in Gabelsgate was free on March 14th. If they were, it was decided to hold the general assembly there with new elections.

Fru Lund undertook to talk to some famous artiste to provide some entertainment at the meeting. The names of Robert Levin and Randi Heide Steen were suggested.

Fru Nordklev had written a letter she thought could be duplicated by stencil and sent to all the life members. She didn't know how many there were of them, but Fru Lessund said she would find out and list their addresses.

Also on the agenda was the question of whether to continue asking for a membership fee. Both the one for 1948 – which hadn't been paid yet – and for 1949. It was proposed to raffle a doll to bring in more money.

Fru Lessund was to ring Plesner and ask how it was going with the medical equipment that had been ordered for their stock and the department had not yet received.

Off the agenda, the treasurer asked whether it would be possible for her husband, Ewald Kristoffersen, employed at

Dek-Rek AS, an advertising and internal design company, to attend a meeting as an observer, in connection with Oslo's 900-year jubilee celebration next year. No-one opposed the request, but the chairman thought it would perhaps be best if he came to a meeting of the working committee, where the turnout would be a little bigger.

THE BOX OF RAISINS

The four women take their leave of each other in Lyder Sagens gate while Fru Lessund waves to them from her sitting-room window in no. 24. Fru Nordklev and Frøken Løvslett tread carefully down towards Suhms gate. Fru Lund and Maj Kristoffersen accompany each other to Kirkeveien. The sky is clear and invisible above the rooftops in Jessenløkken. The moon makes the snow gleam. It is slippery; there is ice in places. Fru Lund, who is ten years older than Maj, puts her arm under Maj's.

"If one of us falls now, both of us will go," she says.

They walk more gingerly. This suits Maj fine. She has something on her mind. She is about to breach the topic, but Fru Lund speaks first.

"I think Fru Lessund's right."

"About what?"

"Your husband should come to a working committee meeting."

"Yes, maybe."

"We have to have something that's ours, you know. Just like the men. It's not always a good idea to mix things."

"I'll tell him that."

"But it's a brilliant idea, isn't it? The women behind the city. You must be proud."

"Yes, Ewald's received a lot of praise."

"And you? Aren't you happy in our department?"

"I'm very happy," Maj says.

Fru Lund laughs and holds her arm a little firmer.

"You don't need to be so *polite*. If you have a complaint, say so."

"I think it's wrong that members don't pay the sub on time."

"Yes, it's shameful."

"We're going to be in arrears. And that affects our work."

"We have to be patient. We're still short of money."

"People have got the money when they go skating or to the restaurant."

Fru Lund laughs at the young treasurer.

"You shouldn't be so strict, Maj. People have to enjoy themselves as well."

They walk in silence over the last part and stop below Fagerborg School. There is still a star hanging in one of the dark classrooms. Now Maj Kristoffersen has to speak or it will be too late.

"Fru Lund, would it be . . .?"

"No need to be so formal, Maj. My goodness, I feel so old when you're so polite."

She tries again:

"Could your husband have a look at Jesper one day? Our son."

"Yes, I'm sure he can. Is there something wrong?"

"I don't know. He's just so . . . difficult."

"Difficult? Well, that's not exactly Per-Fredrik's speciality, but I'll talk to him. Then I'll let you know."

"Thank you."

"I'm sure it's nothing to worry about. Everyone's a bit difficult at times."

Fru Lund walks on to Ullevålsveien, while Maj crosses Jacob Aalls gate and lets herself into the yard. Someone has left a toy in the snow, a little ski jumper in mid-leap, but who has unfortunately fallen. She puts the ski jumper on the railing by the kitchen steps and runs up the five floors to the drying loft. She feels the clothes, mostly belonging to Ewald – socks, shirts and trousers. They aren't dry yet. They never get completely dry. The air here is too damp and cold. She puts them in the basket anyway. They will have to stay in the dining room tonight. Then she can iron them early tomorrow. She notices two dresses hanging on the far clothes line, one blue, the other green, both are full-length and brush the floor. Maj hasn't seen these dresses before. It is like a party, a party in the drying loft. She feels an urge to try one of them on. She doesn't of course. Instead she puts her bag on top of the clothes and carries the basket downstairs, carefully, so that she doesn't trip on the steep steps. On the second floor Fru Vik's door opens a fraction.

"Come in," she says.

Maj sighs.

"I have to go down to Ewald and—"

Fru Vik interrupts her.

"You have to help me. You owe me that much."

Maj puts down the basket. Fru Vik lets her into the kitchen and quickly closes the door. Now Maj can see she is wearing only underwear.

"There's nothing wrong, is there?"

"Yes, there is! I need a dress! And not one of them fits!"

She kicks at a black outfit lying on the floor.

"Are they yours in the loft?"

"Yes. And they don't fit, either. You can have them."

"What do you want a new dress for?"

Fru Vik glares at Maj.

"What do I want one for? I just feel like dressing up! Anything wrong with that?"

"No, no. I didn't mean anything like that."

Fru Vik sits down and composes herself.

"It'll soon be four years since Halfdan died. And . . ."

She doesn't say any more. Maj picks up the black dress and hangs it over a chair.

"Of course you can dress up," she says.

Fru Vik sighs.

"I wore the green one for our silver wedding anniversary."

"And you still have a good figure."

"I wish. I've sagged since then. Anyway I look pale in green. I look ill."

"The blue one then? That suits you."

"I wore that when the Veterinary College celebrated its fiftieth anniversary. Which I would prefer to forget."

"Why?"

"Amongst other things, because someone had put a snake, an adder, in my bag."

"No! Was it alive?"

"Alive? I didn't have a chance to see because I fainted."

"A snake! Who would do a thing like that?"

"Vets. They call it humour. Are you collecting your washing so late?"

"I use the kitchen door so as not to wake Jesper. And I'd better be . . ."

Maj is about to leave. Fru Vik suddenly gets up.

"You must come with me to Steen & Strøm."

Maj stops in her tracks.

"Why?"

"To buy a dress."

"I don't think they have any."

"At Steen & Strøm? Don't they have the best selection?"

"I was there before Christmas. Just fancy French dresses. Dior."

"They must have others as well."

"Not as far as I could see. I can go with you to Franck. Or Øye."

Fru Vik opens the door shaking her head.

"It's not certain it'll come to anything anyway."

Maj goes out and picks up the basket of washing.

"What'll come to anything?"

Fru Vik is gone for a second and comes back with a box of raisins which she puts on the bag.

"There's something I have to tell you, by the way," she says.

Maj looks at her and is about to put the washing down again. "Yes?"

"Something Jesper told me when he was here. He said he falls at night."

"He falls? How do you mean?"

"Those are the words he used. *He falls.*"

"He says a lot of strange things."

On her way down the last steps Maj starts crying. She can't help herself. Suddenly it is too much. Suddenly the weight of it is too much. She takes a deep breath, rests the basket on her knee, wipes her tears with the back of her hand and unlocks the door. Ewald is sitting at the kitchen table with a bottle of beer and a sketch pad. He looks at his watch.

"Been chin-wagging, I suppose."

"If you can be bothered to look up you'll see I've been getting the clothes."

"And what did the chairman say? Will I graciously be allowed to attend a meeting?"

"She said it'd be best if you came to a working committee meeting instead."

"What's that?"

"It's what we in the Fagerborg department come under. And who we report to."

"*Report?* Report what?"

"What we do, of course."

"Why can't I be with all of you?"

"I'm sure you can. But . . ."

"Do you have secret discussions? Which it's best I shouldn't hear."

"We do not. You can read the minutes."

At last Ewald looks up, surprised for a moment, then he gets to his feet.

"What's up with you?"

"What's up with me?"

"You could've said. I would've gone for . . ."

"If I told you every time, Ewald, I wouldn't have time for anything else."

Ewald takes the basket from her and puts it on a chair.

"Dearie me. I'm not sure the Red Cross is doing you any good."

"Is Jesper asleep?"

They go into the vestibule. Jesper is lying on his back in bed, his eyes closed, his hands folded on the duvet. He seems calm. Is he falling now? Maj wonders. Is he falling in his dreams? She puts the box of raisins on his pillow.

ANNUAL REPORT

In 1948 there were six board meetings and one members' meeting. The Fagerborg department knitted a number of items, which were then given away. In addition, at Christmas 34 parcels of food and other items were given away, as well as 50 kroner to a housewife. The department successfully participated in the bazaar, earning 1,874.05 kroner gross. Christmas charity stamps were also sold. The department now has a stock of medical equipment.

At present the department is providing Wergelandsveien Clinic with twenty voluntary nurses, most of whom are registered as members of this department. We have plans to set up a nursery, perhaps a crèche, in the parish.

The annual report and a copy of the accounts have been sent to the parish council.

1949

Dr Lund is standing by the window in his office in Ullevåls-veien watching Maj Kristoffersen and Jesper rounding the corner at the end of Pilestredet. Sometimes you can see it at once. You can see there is something wrong with a person. There is something about their movements. They are too abrupt or too limp. There is something about their facial features. They are too indifferent or too intense. This Jesper seems limp and indifferent. But all children dread going to the doctor. Perhaps it is just his way of exhibiting dread. Dr Lund opens the waiting-room door.

"Take a blood sample from Jesper Kristoffersen. He's coming with his mother now."

"Right."

The nurse, Frøken Ågot Rud, gets up, goes to the medicine cabinet and takes out the equipment.

"And be a little slapdash."

She turns.

"Slapdash?"

"A couple of attempts at finding a vein. Ruffle him."

Dr Lund closes the door and sits back behind his desk. Soon he hears them arrive. He hears the mother say something to her son. Then all goes quiet. It is completely quiet for a good while. Then the nurse opens the door and lets in Maj Kristoffersen and Jesper. They sit down. Jesper has rolled up his shirt sleeve and is holding his left arm at an angle. Some blood is dripping onto the floor. The nurse puts on another plaster and leaves quickly.

"She was clumsy," Maj says in a low voice.

Dr Lund looks at Jesper.

"Did it hurt?"

Jesper shakes his head.

"Did it hurt?" Dr Lund repeats.

Jesper looks past him.

"No."

Maj Kristoffersen leans forward.

"That wasn't meant as criticism. And thank you for . . ."

Dr Lund smiles at her.

"Of course not. Take his shirt off."

Maj unbuttons his shirt, Jesper raises both arms and she pulls it carefully over his head. The boy is much too thin, but in these times he isn't the only one. Most boys are too skinny. It doesn't mean they are ill. They are hungry and healthy. Dr Lund stands up and walks around Jesper. He listens to his heart and lungs. He looks down into his bristly, brown hair. At least he hasn't got head lice. Dr Lund sits down again and pushes a pencil and a sheet of paper towards Jesper.

"Can you write your name for me?"

Jesper takes the pencil with his right hand and forms six letters. The P is upside down, but otherwise everything looks correct.

"Very good. Are you looking forward to starting school?

You start this autumn, don't you?"

Jesper lets go of the pencil and doesn't answer.

"What's your favourite meal, Jesper?"

Maj nudges him. He still doesn't answer. Dr Lund leans closer and looks him in the eye, but can't catch his attention.

"You must have a favourite."

"Raisins," Jesper says.

Maj blushes.

"Just so that you know, I feed him properly every day."

Dr Lund leans back in his chair and tries once again to catch Jesper's restless eyes.

"Perhaps you'd like to come running with me one day?" he says.

Maj puts a hand on Jesper's knee.

"Did you hear that? Doctor Lund is an old sportsman. He's set lots of records."

Jesper nods briefly.

Maj looks up quickly.

"I didn't mean old. I meant . . ."

"That's fine. Is there anything else you have to tell me?"

Maj places her hand on Jesper's knee again.

"Tell the doctor what you told Fru Vik."

Now Jesper's eyes stop moving. You can touch his gaze. The indifferent features tense up. He looks like an old child. He says nothing. Maj pats him on the cheek.

"Just tell Dr Lund as well. Nothing'll happen to you."

Jesper clenches his teeth. A sharp grinding noise comes from his mouth. Then he starts to talk. It strikes Dr Lund that his voice seems to come from a different place, from another, less tormented body. It is even and gentle.

"I fall. I fall backwards. Sometimes forwards, too. Mostly forwards."

Dr Lund leans closer again.

"You *dream* you're falling, don't you?"

"I just fall."

"Do you hurt yourself?"

Jesper laughs suddenly and doesn't say another word.

Dr Lund stands up. Maj does the same. Jesper goes to the nurse to get dressed. Dr Lund holds Maj back and closes the door. She becomes uneasy.

"Is there something . . .?"

"No, no. I just want a word with you privately."

This doesn't make Maj any less uneasy and she glances at the door.

"He's not so comfortable with strangers," she says.

"Does he wet himself?"

Maj spins round to Dr Lund and blushes again.

"No. That's behind him, long ago."

"And he doesn't wet his bed at night?"

"Not as far as I've seen. And I would've seen, I think."

"What's your opinion about what he says? His falling?"

"It must be something he dreams."

"Obviously, Fru Kristoffersen. He's a robust lad."

"Is he?"

"And that's good. It'll stand him in good stead. I asked the nurse to be a bit rough with him."

Maj laughs and holds her hand over her mouth.

"Oh, right. Jesper took it well."

"Exactly. We'll have to see if the blood samples show anything, but I'm fairly sure they'll be absolutely normal.

So you don't need to worry at all."

"Don't I?"

"No, Fru Kristoffersen. Jesper's a fine boy. But may I ask about his father? What's the relationship between father and son like?"

Maj looks down and feels a desire to wash the floor.

"My husband works a lot."

"Yes, we all have to do our bit."

"Have you anything special in mind?"

"It's important for a son to have a good relationship with his father."

"He does have."

"Good! And, as I said, don't worry. If you do, you'll make Jesper worried too."

"But what's causing them, these falls he talks about?"

"He's a sensitive lad, Fru Kristoffersen."

Maj Kristoffersen looks up warily and doesn't quite understand:

"Is Jesper sensitive too? You said he was robust."

"One quality doesn't exclude the other."

Dr Lund opens the door for her. Jesper is dressed and ready to go, sucking a caramel the nurse gave him. Maj takes his hand and on the way home she buys cod, parsley and a packet of mayonnaise from the fish man at the top of Kirkeveien. Jesper is restless again. He can't stand still on the chequered floor. They rush on. They have the wind at their backs. Then all of a sudden it is in their faces. February is a mischievous month. The weather can change in a second. She hopes Jesper won't get ill, now that he is healthy. He walks ahead, still with his left arm at an angle. Maj can barely keep up. Nevertheless she feels light, almost carefree. She laughs into the wind. At last they arrive at the entrance to their block. Jesper takes two steps at a time. He still hasn't finished the caramel. Maj pats him on the cheek.

"Now let's go and see Fru Vik first, to tell her everything went well," she says.

Jesper turns his back on her.

"Don't you want to?"

Jesper doesn't answer.

"Do you need the toilet?"

Jesper changes his mind and goes upstairs with her to the second floor after all. Maj rings the bell. It takes a while. Then Fru Vik opens the door, but only a crack. She has curlers in her hair.

"What is it?"

"Are we disturbing you? Are you going to a party?"

"What is it?" she repeats.

Maj pushes Jesper ahead of her.

"Tell her, Jesper."

Jesper says nothing. Then he leans forward, takes a deep breath and spits out the caramel. It pings down in front of Fru Vik's lacquered toenails and she gives a cry of surprise. Maj does, too. Jesper squirms loose and runs off. The two women look at each other.

"What was he supposed to say?" Fru Vik asks.

Maj picks up the caramel with two fingers.

"He's sensitive," she says.

"Sensitive?"

"Yes. Dr Lund said he was healthy and sensitive."

At that moment the telephone rings. Fru Vik immediately

panics and lets go of the door. It slams shut. Maj is about to go, to go down to Jesper, but before she can get that far Fru Vik opens the door again.

"It's for you. I'll look for Jesper in the meantime."

Maj goes into the hallway, where the smell of perfume is all-pervasive, and picks up the receiver. It is Ewald.

"Maj? I might be late home today."

"Why's that?"

He speaks in a lower voice.

"Because I have to present my plans to management. Rudjord has assembled the whole shooting match."

"Have to hope you get on fine then."

His voice rises again.

"Of course I'll get on fine. So don't wait up for me with dinner."

"Oh, no. And I've bought your favourite meal."

"I can't do anything about it. I—"

"Just a moment, Ewald. Fru Vik probably wants . . ."

Maj holds the receiver to her chest, looks at her and almost has to laugh. Fru Vik is standing in the doorway looking even more flustered. One of the curlers in her hair has come out.

"I can't find Jesper!"

"Isn't he downstairs?"

"He's gone. He spat at me!"

Maj lifts the receiver again and holds it with both hands.

"I have to ring off."

"Aren't you going to wish me good luck?"

"Yes, Ewald. Good luck. You're clever. But don't go by the Bristol today."

"Go *to* the Bristol, you mean. Not by."

109

"Do you promise?"

"Yes, yes."

Ewald stands with the receiver in his hand for a few seconds before he hangs up and lights a cigarette. He doesn't understand why it is necessary to make him feel guilty. *And I've bought your favourite meal.* Maj probably doesn't know what his favourite meal is because he says he likes everything she makes anyway. Then Ewald feels guilty because he is being unfair to her. She means well. He mustn't let his concentration wander now. He drops the cigarette into a half-full cup of coffee and goes to his drawing board in the design office. Should he take his sketches with him? He leaves them on the board. His colleagues are sitting hunched under their angle poises and don't look up. Should he take off his white coat and meet them in a suit? No, he should know his place. He tidies the pens in his breast pocket. At one o'clock Ewald goes to the office. Frøken Bryn opens the door. Rudjord gets up from behind his desk and beckons him in. They sit down. There is no-one else present.

"Let's hope the City Hall is ready for the jubilee," Ewald says.

Rudjord laughs and places the packet of French cigarettes on the desk.

"We'll do our bit anyway. By the way have you been to any of these Red Cross meetings?"

Ewald looks around.

"Isn't anybody else coming?"

"It'll be just us."

"No, I haven't. Not yet. But there's a general assembly soon and then . . ."

Rudjord proffers the packet. Ewald coaxes out a cigarette.

Tobacco spills out from both ends. He fires it up with his own lighter and starts coughing. Rudjord goes over to the desk, pours two whiskies and gives one to Ewald, who knocks back a mouthful and shakes his head.

"Jesus."

"You're not the first to react like that."

"I'm not used to these French fags."

"You said it. They smell of perfume and taste of dynamite." Ewald laughs.

"We should have Gitanes as clients."

"It won't be necessary for you anyway."

"Mm? Excuse me, what won't be?"

Rudjord sits back down.

"To go to this Red Cross meeting."

Ewald straightens up and can't see anywhere to put the damned cigarette.

"Strictly speaking, it's not necessary. I've already got a good enough picture, so . . ."

"We rate your idea very highly, Ewald, but we've come to the conclusion that we need something more *official*."

"What's that supposed to mean?"

"History. Art. Literature. We're going to keep your idea in mind. I'm sure it can be used on another occasion."

"Perhaps for the 1000-year jubilee?"

"Good idea. By then the next generation will have taken over. Johnsen will update you on the latest plans."

Rudjord stands up and looks at his watch. Ewald doesn't move.

"Aren't women official enough?" he asks.

"Maybe. But they're probably best for private indulgence."

Ewald goes to the toilet first. He throws the glowing French dog-end into the toilet bowl and washes his face with cold water. `Then he looks at himself in the mirror. The collar of his shirt is cutting into his neck. There is a fold of fat over the edge. Soon he will be choked. He loosens his tie and opens the top button. The blood drains from his head, down into his heart, which pumps it further with dramatic, heavy beats. His heart is out of proportion. He leans against the wall and exhales three times. Then Ewald goes back to the office. Johnsen has put some sheets of paper on his desk in the meantime. He must have known the whole time. Everyone knew the whole time. Ewald is the last to know. They have been fooling with him. He glances at the sheets. He sees Vikings, Ibsen, Munch, Vigeland, skiing tracks and transatlantic liners. They are official. They are also utterly boring. Didn't they have it banged into their skulls from day one? Be specific, not general! A city isn't general. A city isn't representative. It is made up of individuals. It is specific. Someone calls out from behind him:

"Was Rudjord in a good mood, Kristoffersen?"

That must be Johnsen too, calling over in a chummy voice.

"I was allowed to try one of his French cigarettes," Ewald says.

"Yes, Rudjord has stopped smoking, hasn't he. His lungs."

Ewald Kristoffersen thinks: Now I'll get my favourite meal after all. He sits at his desk doing nothing. He is empty. He will have to start again or continue where Johnsen left off. He can't do either. At four o' clock he takes off his white coat, hangs it on the hook, fetches his outdoor coat, goes over to the Bristol and hands it over to the pocket Venus in the cloak-room. Then he sits at the bar. There is a beer already waiting for him. Two hours later he orders a gin and tonic from Ulfsen, who raises an eyelid, very slightly. There is no rush, Ewald thinks. Even if he is late for dinner, it is still early. A man sits down beside him. Ewald recognises him. It is the pianist. He still has a blue shadow over his forehead and seems otherwise groggy. Ulfsen proffers his left hand.

"Welcome back."

Enzo Zanetti nods.

"Thank you. A glass of red wine, please."

Ulfsen raises both eyebrows and his brow puckers.

"Here?"

"Yes. A glass of red wine please."

Ulfsen is still not quite in tune. He leans across the bar and lowers his voice.

"You can have it in a coffee cup."

"In a proper glass please."

"As you wish. But don't blame me."

"I don't start work for an hour."

"And there was me thinking you only drank during working hours."

Ulfsen shakes his head and reluctantly does what Zanetti asks. Ewald raises his glass.

"Pour me a few drops as well, Ulfsen. And no ballerina piss this time."

That is Ewald's sense of humour. It is always there. He tries to suppress it, but he can't. As soon as he begins to sink, he rises again. He was born wearing a rubber ring. He looks around. Customers glide in through the doors. The women go to the toilet while the men hand their coats to the pocket Venus, who at this time has to have help from a slip of a girl called Jenny. *Hurry up there, Jenny.* The cloakroom is the men's last stop before the parties and the conquests. Soon there is a smell of cigars and laughter and perfume. Ulfsen puts the drinks on the bar. Ewald turns to Enzo Zanetti and bends his elbow.

"Majoring or Minoring?"

"I beg your pardon."

Ewald laughs.

"Which key are you in today, major or minor, my friend?"

"Mostly minor, I suppose."

"Yes, you got a bit of a pasting last time."

Enzo Zanetti looks up:

"Were you here?"

"If I was here? I would make so bold as to say I almost saved your life."

"Yes, you're here almost every evening. But thank you, anyway."

Ewald laughs again. Is this how he is to be remembered? As someone who is always here and still forgotten?

"Someone thought you were hitting a few bum notes, did they?" he asks.

Enzo Zanetti finishes his drink, lights a cigarette and eyes Ewald.

"Have you any requests? Apart from Louis Strongarm and Elling Duketon?"

Ewald Kristoffersen isn't listening any longer. He has caught sight of Fru Vik. He shudders. What the hell. Can't he be left in peace here, either? She stops by the entrance, out of breath and lost. An elderly gentleman with grey, nearly white, hair makes his way through the scrimmage and helps her off with her fur coat and hands it in to the cloakroom girl. Then they go back to a corner table. Fru Vik is wearing a long, blue dress. She is overdressed. She is a Christmas tree in February. She casts a quick glance over her shoulder. Ewald Kristoffersen ducks. He isn't doing anything wrong, but he still doesn't want to be seen.

"Maybe the *Flight of the Bumblebee*," he says.

But Enzo Zanetti is already sitting at the grand piano. He is playing to deaf ears. It doesn't matter. He is part of the noise. All the sounds flow down a drain and disappear somewhere in the fjord, apart from a bird pecking at the inside of his head. Then someone goes over to him and asks quietly:

"Can you play Chopin?"

Enzo Zanetti nods, and even though people generally have to be considered idiots, at least at Hotel Bristol, life is worth living for a moment. Can he play Chopin? Finally a civilised request. He plays a prelude while Olaf Hall goes back to Fru Vik. The waiter brings her a glass of sherry. He drinks a whisky. They clink glasses and listen for a while to the Polish sorrow, mixed with a little Italian humour. It puts an elegant damper on the noise around them. Then they both talk at once. They laugh and go quiet.

"You first, Fru Vik," Olaf Hall says.

"No, Herr Hall, *you* first."

"Shall we be more informal with each other?"

"It was a good choice."

"What was? The Bristol or being informal?"

"Chopin."

"It was for us."

115

Fru Vik holds the little glass with both hands.

"A boy went missing in our apartment block today. That's why I was a little late."

"That doesn't matter. You found him, I trust?"

"Yes, eventually. He'd hidden in the drying loft. What about you, Herr Hall? I mean, Olaf."

"I set off in good time."

"I mean, what was it you wanted to say?"

"Do you like Chopin?"

"He's wonderful."

"The pianist's right hand is wobbly. Don't you think?"

"I don't know much about music. But I think he's a good pianist."

"Everyone knows something about music. They just don't know they do."

Fru Vik sips her sherry and tries to concentrate on Chopin. It isn't easy. She can't hear any difference. The right hand is no worse than the left. Furthermore she is put off by the looks she is getting. Or is it just her imagination? Who's that Ragnhild Hall's widower is out with this evening? So soon.

"Do you know a lot about fish as well?" she asks.

Olaf Hall is taken aback at first, then he laughs.

"Ah, you're thinking about *The Compleat Angler*. You're observant."

"You were skimming through it."

"I like observant women."

"How could I not see . . .?"

They are interrupted by the waiter from the Mauriske Hall giving them the menus. Olaf Hall leaves his untouched. He watches Fru Vik running her finger slowly down from meal to meal. He can't help but notice her ring. Of course she wears it. He has removed his.

"I thought we might eat in a private room," Olaf Hall says.

Fru Vik looks up.

"Sorry?"

"I've ordered a room for us."

Fru Vik looks at the menu again. There are no prices on it. The prices are on his menu. She gets up; he does the same.

"I just have to spruce myself up," she says.

"There's an en suite."

"It'll only take a moment. Sorry."

Fru Vik goes down to the toilet, locks herself in a cubicle and starts to cry. This is worse than a snake in your bag. She cries some more and can't breathe. Someone knocks on the door and asks if there is anything the matter. There isn't. Nothing. At length she calms down, takes out her handkerchief, blows her nose and opens the door. Her face is drying. She washes her hands, drinks a mouthful of water and straightens up. A young woman in a tight skirt is leaning against a wall. She passes Fru Vik a small, shiny hip flask. Fru Vik shakes her head, clings to her handbag and stumbles past a group of loud women coming in. Again she can't breathe. She stops at the bottom of the stairs, on the soft, dark-red carpet. She hears voices from the floor above, a rush of angry sounds. That is all she can hear, squalls of noise. Someone is coming round the landing. She moves to seek refuge in the toilet again. It is only the pianist. Fru Vik waits for him to pass.

"Is there another exit?" she asks.

Enzo Zanetti stops.

"*Another* exit?"

117

"Apart from the one upstairs."

He eyes the woman, who seems like a lost fugitive standing there in a dress that is far too long, her handbag in front of her like a soft shield. She was the woman sitting in the corner. Was it her he played Chopin for? It didn't help much, if so. He nods. He has a certain sympathy for anyone who wants to sneak away.

"There's an exit behind the kitchen."

"Would you mind showing . . .?"

"But haven't you got a coat in the cloakroom?"

"It doesn't matter. Just—"

"I can get it for you."

"No, just show me . . ."

Fru Vik follows the pianist, along a corridor, around a corner, through the kitchen, where the chefs are running between pots and pans and everyone is shouting, and at last, past the freezer room, they come to a door, which Enzo Zanetti opens.

"Can you find your way now?" he asks.

Fru Vik staggers out into Rosenkrantz' gate and for a moment she seems too small for this city. She is surrounded by mist, distant lights and shadows. Enzo Zanetti lights a cigarette and watches her walk up Pilestredet, unsteady on her slender high heels, her bare shoulders white and angular, she is shivering. A taxi stops at the rank nearby and she gets into the back. Zanetti sees his mission as accomplished, flicks the cigarette end and walks back the same way. He has forgotten what he was going to do. Oh, yes, he wanted a piss. And a cigarette. And to sneak away. The white-haired gentleman in the tweed suit is waiting by the ladies' toilet. He is looking at his watch. He is uneasy. He can still have such a good time, Enzo Zanetti thinks, walking slowly up the last steps and massaging the fingers of his right hand. The head waiter is waiting for him at the first table.

"The hotel director would like a word with you," he says.

Enzo Zanetti looks at the shelf above the reception.

"In his private room," the head waiter adds.

"Am I getting a reprimand? I haven't had such a long break, have I?"

"I know nothing about that."

Enzo Zanetti chuckles.

"I'm sure you do."

The head waiter places a hand on his shoulder, an unusual, almost frighteningly tactile gesture for him.

"I've always thought you added a certain style to this little place of ours. So long as you know your limits."

"Didn't you like the Chopin? Have customers complained?"

"Director Brun is waiting," the head waiter says.

Enzo continues up to the second floor. Is it because he was drinking in the bar? He is already out of breath by the first floor. The lift is not for staff. The lift is only for guests. He stops outside a door marked Private, knocks and walks in. Brun is sitting in the leather chair by the window thumbing through a pile of papers. He glances over his shoulder and thumbs a bit more before standing up.

"We didn't think you would come back," he says.

Enzo Zanetti looks at his shoes; they are polished and impeccable.

"I did."

"There have been a few changes in the meantime."

"Am I not welcome?"

"We're going to start playing jazz here."

Enzo Zanetti looks up.

"I play jazz, sir."

"A jazz band. Which means—"

"I know what it means. Dancing."

Brun fetches two envelopes. In one is his wage for two months. Enzo Zanetti puts that in his inside pocket. The other is from the chambermaids.

"Aina started a little collection while you were away," Brun says.

"Aina?"

"Yes, she's the one from Kristiansand. With the hair and rolled 'r's."

"I know who Aina is."

Enzo Zanetti doesn't want any collection. Brun insists.

"The maids have really pulled out all the stops. Don't disappoint them now."

Enzo Zanetti puts this envelope into his inside pocket as well and walks into the corridor. He passes an open door, stops and looks inside. It is one of the suites that has to be ready for the following day. Aina has her back to him and is making the beds. The light from the ceiling lamp makes her hair gleam. The used sheets are on the floor. He can see how heavy the work is from her body.

"You didn't have to do that," Enzo Zanetti says.

She turns to him and drops a pillow cover.

"I just wanted to make amends."

"I don't need charity."

"Everyone needs something."

Aina looks down. Enzo Zanetti doesn't budge. The man who always knows what he is going to play is suddenly blank and unprepared. The two of them are at the bottom of the hotel hierarchy, the chambermaid working overtime and the dismissed lounge pianist. At the top are the customers. They don't decide anything, but they still have the power.

"So you wanted to make amends?"

"Thank you for not reporting him."

"I don't know who it was."

"We don't go out together anymore."

Aina gently raises her eyes. They gaze at each other for a while.

"Perhaps we'll see each other."

Then he takes the lift down. As he moves between the tables, past the piano, it strikes him that no-one has noticed he is leaving them. He doesn't have even the tiniest impact on the evening. The customers keep coming as before. The drinks taste the same as before. The conversations continue in the same vein. The laughter lasts just as long. He stops outside the steps, buttons up his coat and lights a cigarette. A man stands next to him. It is the humourist from the bar. He takes out a cigarette and Enzo lights it. Ewald Kristoffersen turns quickly and fortunately he can't see Fru Vik anywhere, but he does notice the peacock fetching her fur coat from the cloakroom.

"Early night tonight," Ewald says.

Enzo Zanetti walks down Kristian Augusts gate and disappears between the street lights as he used to disappear between the tables at Hotel Bristol.

When Ewald arrives home Jesper is asleep. He is sleeping

heavily. On the other hand, Maj is very awake. Ewald is basically happy she doesn't ask how the meeting went, but is
disappointed that she has forgotten it. She has other things on
her mind.

"I'm worried, Ewald."

Ewald pulls Maj close, not knowing what to think. There
is so much to be worried about that you can't be worried for
any length of time.

"What about?"

"I was standing by the window waiting for you. And a taxi
stopped outside. And I thought it was you."

Ewald holds her a bit longer before letting go.

"I'm at home now. I couldn't get away from Rudjord so
easily."

"But it was Margrethe. She arrived in a taxi wearing only
a dress and she looked quite dishevelled, poor thing."

"Did she come home wearing only the floor-sweeping
gown?"

"Yes, Ewald. I went up and rang her bell, but she didn't
open the door."

"Oh, dear."

"If she doesn't open up early tomorrow morning, I'll have
to ask the caretaker . . ."

Jesper sighs in his sleep and the husband and wife are
silent for a few seconds.

"Has he been good today?" Ewald asks.

"Yes."

"Yes? Quite sure?"

Maj switches off the ceiling light.

"Just a bit restless."

Ewald has to hold her again.

"And he's got that from his father."

The next morning Maj rings Fru Vik's doorbell and she doesn't open the door this time either, but she does at least respond.

"I've got a cold," she says and seems very distant.

"Do you need any help?"

"No."

"Don't you want me to do some shopping for you, either?"

"I'm not hungry."

"What about the *Aftenposten*?"

"There's nothing in the paper anyway. Just go."

Fru Vik didn't take in the newspapers until a week later. She is doing it as Maj opens her door and picks up the evening paper from the mat. She can see her working on the floor above. If she has some secrets, she should be allowed to have them in peace, at least for a while.

"Are you feeling any better?" Maj calls.

Maj hears only the door closing upstairs. Then she goes back in to Ewald, who is in the sitting room with Jesper. He has come home for dinner every day recently, sometimes even earlier. Jesper is kneeling on the sofa. Maj suddenly remembers what she forgot to ask Ewald about and is ashamed.

"How did it actually go at the meeting with Rudjord?"

Ewald shrugs and throws a sock at Jesper, who laughs.

"Fine."

"How fine?"

"Fine fine. How else would it have gone?"

Maj laughs and shows him the advertisement on page 12: *General assembly for Fagerborg department of the Norwegian*

Red Cross 3/3/49, 7.00 p.m. in the Priests' Church. Simple fare.

"You can go there for some more inspiration," Maj says.

Jesper throws a sock at Ewald, who is sitting and thinking of an excuse for not going, but nothing springs to mind. Nothing comes to mind, damn it. He is about to explode. He has no ideas. He has no excuses. Even lies are in short supply. Soon his shirt won't be able to hold his heart in place.

"Aren't you going?" he asks.

"Someone has to look after Jesper."

"Can't Fru Vik?"

Jesper jumps down from the sofa, knocks over an ashtray, goes into the vestibule and kicks the door shut after him.

Ewald looks up at Maj.

"Perhaps I can take him with me. And then you can go, too?"

"I think you should go on your own," Maj says.

There is another advertisement in the evening edition of the *Aftenposten*, immediately beneath the previous one: *Enzo Zanetti, private piano lessons, classical, jazz and hits. All day. Not on Mondays. Tel: 558456.*

GENERAL ASSEMBLY, PRIESTS' CHURCH, 3/3/49

The turnout was decidedly poor. The annual report and accounts audited by the department's accountant were read out. No-one had any remarks to make, except for Ewald Kristoffersen, who was present as an observer in connection with Oslo's 900-year jubilee. He thought the poor turnout was due to a lack of advertising. No-one, according to Ewald Kristoffersen, has a better commodity to sell than the Red Cross. He said he would be happy to give advice on this if it was desired. This was well received and fell on fertile ground. Incidentally, Ewald Kristoffersen is married to Maj Kristoffersen, the treasurer for the Fagerborg department. Some thought, however, that it was inappropriate to use the word "commodity". Ewald Kristoffersen said he could equally well have said "attitude".

Paragraph 2 of the regulations stipulates, among other things: "Every year half of the board are to step down". It was decided that two members of the board should step down every year. The deputy chairman, Frøken Dagny Schelde, retired at her own request in August 1948 and Vanda Aasland, the secretary and ex-treasurer, has to temporarily withdraw for health reasons. She agreed to remain on the board as a co-opted member.

The following five board members were appointed: Fru Maja Lessund, Fru Else Larsen, Fru Maj Kristoffersen, Fru Ingrid Arnesen and Fru Berit Nordklev. Fru Vanda Aasland and Fru Ingrid Foss agreed to remain as co-opted members.

Neither Randi Heide Steen nor Robert Levin was able to come and entertain us, but at the last moment and by roundabout means we were able to contact an Italian pianist, Enzo Zanetti, who is resident in Oslo. At first he seemed so uncomfortable and uninspired that Chairman Fru Nordklev was on the point of speaking to him. But he warmed up and played really well, also some Christian Sinding songs, and told us that he came from Solferino, which in 1859 was the scene of a bloody battle and claimed the lives of 40,000 soldiers. And three years later our founder, Henri Dunant, wrote *A Memory of Solferino*, urging the world to help the war-wounded. It was very moving. How small the world is! Enzo Zanetti was also able, amid great excitement, to teach us ladies some Italian, and rounded off his performance with the slogan Tutti Fratelli and made everyone say it in unison.

THE EVENTS OF THE DAY

Bjørn Stranger looks at the dead woman and faints. He comes to in the Dean's office. Now it is Bjørn Stranger who is stretched out. He is lying on the green sofa wishing he were also dead.

"You're not the first," the Dean says.

Bjørn Stranger gets up.

"I'm sorry."

The Dean gives him a glass of water.

"It'll be fine. As I said, you're not the first."

"Thank you."

"Nor the last, I don't doubt."

Bjørn Stranger holds the glass with both hands, takes a swig and looks down.

"I'm not suited to this."

"Don't be so sure. But you should give it some consideration."

"Give what some consideration?"

"As you yourself said, to whether you're suited or not."

Bjørn Stranger had perhaps hoped for a different answer, but is still happy with it. He collects his things from the lecture hall and goes out into Universitetsplassen, where the students stand in groups chatting, laughing and smoking. Some glance at Bjørn Stranger. Most don't notice him. He crosses Karl Johans gate, without a backward glance, and follows Drammensveien up to Bygdøy allé. Roof gutters are dripping. Pavements will soon be free of snow. Bjørn Stranger has a sudden feeling of immense freedom, options are queueing up, time itself is waiting for him, but the next second this same freedom seems oppressive. What is he going to do with it? He throws his lecture notes in the litter bin by the taxi rank in Fredrik Stangs gate. At that moment the telephone rings on the post. There are no taxis around. Bjørn Stranger laughs. There are no taxis. He feels a need to talk to someone. He looks around. The telephone keeps ringing. He takes it. A woman asks for a taxi to Gabelsgate 19, it is urgent.

"Be right there," says Bjørn Stranger.

He hesitates for a moment as he hangs up: it is so easy to do something bad.

When Bjørn Stranger arrives home he fetches an empty box from the pantry and goes into his mother's bedroom. No-one has been there since. The air is heavy, the bed unmade. He opens the window first. Then he opens the wardrobe. Her clothes hang there as before, a line of costumes from the Theatercafé down to Larsen Restaurant. This is not what he is going to tidy up. He crouches down and starts picking out the empty bottles, mostly gin, Gordon's, they are easy to stack. Afterwards he carries the box into the kitchen and puts it down on the worktop. Then he goes down to the antiquarian bookshop. His stepfather is standing with his back to him. He usually does. He barely notices that Bjørn is there or perhaps that is precisely why he doesn't turn round. Bjørn sees the fur coat hanging on a hook by the door. Has his stepfather also started tidying up?

"That's not Mamma's," Bjørn says.

Olaf Hall gives a start, but doesn't turn round.

"What?"

"The fur coat."

"No, it's not Mamma's."

"Don't say Mamma's."

"It's not Ragnhild's."

"Whose is it then?"

Olaf Hall turns. Bjørn is sitting on the stool Olaf uses to reach the top shelves.

"A customer left it."

Bjørn laughs.

"You destroyed Mamma, you did."

Olaf Hall takes a step closer:

"Did I destroy Ragnhild or did I destroy things for her?"

"Comes to the same thing."

"No, it doesn't."

"I'm glad I was allowed to keep our name."

"Of course you were allowed to."

"Ragnhild *Hall*. From the day she took that name things went downhill."

"You don't have to say that, Bjørn."

"She started with Ibsen and ended up at Chat Noir. You just have to read her obituary. Juster wrote it."

Olaf Hall looks at this boy, this young, immature man, who closes his eyes and rests his head on his hands. Nothing moves on. It all stays inside him. There is already a bitterness etched in his face, a crucifix in both corners of his mouth.

"Do you think it's only others who are to blame when things go wrong?" Olaf Hall asks.

Bjørn Stranger looks up.

"By the way, I've put a box of empty bottles in the kitchen. In case you want the deposit."

Then he gets to his feet, goes to the door and opens it. The wind blows up the papers by the cash till. Olaf Hall reaches out a hand and tries to hold him back.

"I sold a book the other day. *The Compleat Angler*. To the secretary at the English Embassy. Guess how much for."

"Five kroner."

"Times a thousand. Five thousand."

"I won't be home for dinner."

"Lecture?"

"What does it matter?"

"Shouldn't you be wearing more clothes?"

"That's the only thing you've taught me. How to freeze."

Bjørn Stranger kicks the door shut.

Olaf Hall thinks the same as Bjørn: it is so easy to do something bad. But he adds another thought: it is so difficult to make amends. Fru Vik doesn't answer when he rings. He hardly knows how many times he has tried. But she doesn't pick up. He has to make amends. That is all he knows. He writes a greeting on an old postcard, puts it in the pocket of the fur coat and opens the door. Bjørn is still standing there hesitating by the gate.

"Could you do me a favour?" Olaf Hall calls.

Bjørn reluctantly returns.

"Yes?"

"Could you deliver this coat to Fru Vik in Kirkeveien 127?"

"What do I get for it?"

"A reward in heaven maybe."

Bjørn shrugs.

"Do I have to say anything?"

Olaf Hall puts the coat in a bag.

"Only that I'd very much like to see more books."

"You're glad Mamma is dead."

Olaf Hall looks at his rigid features. It occurs to him that this is not bitterness. Bitterness demands a certain gravity, which his stepson does not possess yet. He turned twenty-three this winter. It is more a grievance, bitterness in its puberty. Bjørn is still in emotional puberty.

"You shouldn't say that," Olaf Hall says.

Bjørn takes the bag and walks towards Majorstua. Number 127 must be almost at the top, closer to Ullevål Hospital. At first he follows Jacob Aalls gate, crosses Bogstadveien by Valkyrie Plass, and on the other side Jacob Aalls gate changes character. It becomes wider and more elegant. In front of the apartment buildings, which are adorned with Berlin-style stucco plaster, there is room for small lawns, which are brown and soaked now, in March. Children are playing everywhere. They are making a racket and are filthy. There are more prams than cars. A horse is in one gateway. Bjørn walks in the middle of the street. What should he do with the fur coat? He could chuck it, give it away or destroy it. But he is curious. He wants to see how Fru Vik reacts when he gives it back to her. Who would leave a fur coat behind? At Suhms gate he turns left and heads for Kirkeveien. Behind the lawns and the sports ground in Marienlyst he sees the Norwegian Broadcasting Corporation, a white building that looks like a palace from a distance. It is twenty to two. As he rounds the corner in the district known as Jesseløkken he hears brakes being jammed on, a scream and a dull thud, an almost inexplicably dry sound. Bjørn Stranger hears all this at once and is unable to decide in which order the noises come. He turns and sees a trolley bus askew between stops. The overhead wires are down and hanging in clusters on the roof. In the middle of the crossing lies a figure, a boy, on his stomach, face down on the tarmac. People have stopped on the pavements and are staring at the boy, who seems unapproachable and lonely. Bjørn Stranger is the first to run over and kneel beside him. Blood is running from his scalp. His hair is a black, sticky tangle. His right leg is twisted. His eyes have rolled backwards, his face is a different colour, shiny and blue. Bjørn Stranger holds a hand behind his neck, opens his mouth, sticks two fingers inside and pulls out his tongue. Then he breathes life into the boy, who jerks and groans. Now people are running over to him. The ambulance is already on the way. Bjørn Stranger lets go of the boy, stands up, walks past people who hardly pay any attention to him, picks up his bag and covers the final distance to number 127, whose entrance is from Gørbitz gate. The ambulance passes him. The sirens are like a kind of silence. Bjørn Stranger feels empty, alien, he thinks: it is so easy to do something good. Fru Vik lives on the second floor. He rings the bell. She doesn't answer. He rings again. When Fru Vik doesn't answer the door this time either, he assumes she isn't at home. Bjørn Stranger can't make up his mind whether to leave the bag on the mat or come back later. Then he hears a voice from inside:

"Who is it?"

"A messenger, Fru Vik."

Fru Vik opens the door, at first no more than a fraction, then the whole door. She immediately recognises Bjørn Stranger, even though she barely cast a glance at him as they passed each other in Nordraaks gate.

"What do you want?"

"I was asked to deliver this," Bjørn Stranger says.

He regards Fru Vik for a moment, more he cannot bear. Everything about this ordinary woman, grey from top to toe, from her flat hair to her equally flat slippers, repels him. Then he casually takes the fur coat from the bag and gives it to her. Even her embarrassment is ordinary. She stands there with it in her hands and at first doesn't know what to say. She could say that she will never wear it again. He can just take it with him, take it back. She doesn't want it. Give him my regards and tell him that from me. Bjørn makes a move to go.

"Would you like to come in?" Fru Vik asks.

He stops and breathes in.

"I'm going to a lecture."

"You study medicine, don't you?"

"What else has Olaf told you about me?"

Fru Vik looks at Bjørn Stranger, who studies the floor. He is a good-looking boy, a little weak, almost transparent, just like his thin, fair hair, which he has combed forward, probably to hide the already deeply receding hairline. There is a tear in the knee of his grey trousers. Has he had a tumble?

"I'm very sorry about your mother," she says.

"Do you usually leave your fur coat lying around?"

"I saw her once at the National Theatre. As Fru Alving. She was brilliant."

Bjørn Stranger looks up, his brow damp with sweat.

"Could I have a glass of water?"

Fru Vik lets him in. He takes a seat in the sitting room, on the edge of a chair. She fetches a glass of water from the kitchen and takes it to him.

"You can have something else. Coffee?"

He drinks the water in one long swig and sits with the empty glass in his hands, exhausted, at a loss to know what to do, seemingly.

"Thank you."

"Are you unwell? You—"

"I just came up the stairs too quickly."

"You must know best yourself. Studying medicine."

Fru Vik laughs. Not for long. Bjørn Stranger gets up and stands with his back to her.

"I was also asked to say Olaf would be happy to see more books."

Now it is Fru Vik's turn to study the floor.

"You can say that unfortunately I don't have any more."

"*Very* happy, he said by the way."

Bjørn Stranger turns, gives the empty glass to her and is suddenly pressed for time. Fru Vik accompanies him to the door. Afterwards she goes to the window and watches him hurry towards Jacob Aalls gate. At that moment Maj and Jesper round the corner by Kirkeveien. Each carrying a net bag. Fru Vik steps to the side. Soon she hears them on the stairs. Then the bell rings. Can't she be left in peace? Fru Vik bundles the coat in the cupboard below the clock.

"Now you open the door for me this time!" Maj shouts.

Fru Vik goes into the hallway and opens the door.

"Why wouldn't I?"

"Because your door's been locked for days. We were starting to worry."

"You don't need to. But thank you anyway. Was there anything in particular?"

Jesper hides behind Maj, who puts down her bag.

"Perhaps you heard it?"

"Heard what? I can't hear anything."

"The accident."

"What accident? Tell me now. I haven't got all day."

"Jostein. The butcher's boy. He was hit by a bus near Suhms gate."

"My goodness. I've always said that crossing was dangerous. Is he alive?"

"Yes, thanks to a young man who was there."

"Which young man?"

"Well, I don't know. He just left when the ambulance arrived. But he knew his first aid and saved Jostein's life. There you can see how important our Red Cross courses are."

Fru Vik is lost in thought, she smiles, it is extremely inappropriate, and she says:

"Isn't that what we all want?"

"What?"

"To save a life."

Fru Vik moves to close the door. She wants to be alone. Maj is quicker. She pushes an unwilling Jesper in front of her.

"And now you say sorry to Fru Vik!"

"There's no need."

Fru Vik places her hand on his head. He shakes it off. Maj holds him even tighter.

"Yes, there is. He spat out a sweet. Say sorry, Jesper!"

Jesper looks up at Fru Vik and there is something in his eyes that frightens her, something that blasts everything in its path.

"You're the one who should say sorry," he says.

Jesper squirms free and slides down the banister to the first floor. Maj sighs:

"I'm still finding pine needles when I do the dusting."

Then she runs after Jesper, she has learned from experience, he won't get away this time. Fru Vik closes the door and is suddenly tired. Fatigue comes over her. She feels like going to bed. It is too early. This is how you start dying. You go to bed too early. She heats yesterday's leftovers, which she doesn't finish. Tomorrow will be too late to reheat them. Twice is fine, but not three times. That is the limit for remains. She scrapes them into the bin, but can't be bothered to take it downstairs and hopes it won't begin to smell overnight. Before she turns out the lights in the flat she collects her fur coat. She has made up her mind. She will never wear it again. Besides, the season is over. The coat has to go into cold storage. It can hang in the refrigerated room at the Clothing & Shoe Repairs Expert. Then she can give it to the Red Cross bazaar in September. When you get older, most things come in the wrong order, she thinks. She gets rid of the fur coat and hibernates herself. The events of the day sink in as the remainder of the day sinks towards the onset of night. Then she finds a postcard in one pocket. There is an old picture of Boulevard St Michel with Café Fleur and Café Odeon, each on a corner. She sits in the wing chair, beneath the dark yellow light, and reads: *Dear Margrethe. Forgive me. I don't know what is too early because I am afraid that it will all be too late. I only know that when I saw you, first at Vestre Cemetery and then on the tram to Majorstua, I knew you were my ticket, my transfer ticket to the life I want to lead. Your Olaf.* Fru Vik reads it all again. Transfer ticket? Your Olaf? What a fool. She tears the card into as many pieces as she can and throws them away with the remains.

THE WORKING COMMITTEE MET ON MARCH 6TH

A variety of letters from pensioners and others thanking the Red Cross for the Christmas boxes, as well as New Year greetings and best wishes to the working committee from Fru Bergljot Galtung, were read out. The annual report was read by Fru Petra Scheel, our secretary, plus the audited accounts for 1948. A copy of which has been put in the department file.

Regarding the bazaar, it was announced it would be held from 10th–21st Sept. As usual, 35% goes to the church, which is a regional decision. Max number of prizes: five. A course for Patient Friends has been held and a new one starts soon. Twenty volunteer nurses have started at Wergelandsveien Clinic. The Fagerborg department report was read by their chairman, Fru Esther Andersen. The volunteer service will now be extended to the Rikshospital, Adamstuen Nursing Home and Vanføre Clinic.

Special mention was made of the courses held in home nursing, first aid and baby care for girls in the seventh grade. Apparently it is accepted that these courses will be funded by the council and form a part of training. Home Guard courses in first aid were held at Huseby School, plus a four-hour course for volunteer nurses.

Intense efforts are being made to find a larger home with

fifty rooms for retired nurses. Negotiations are in progress with Obos Housing Co-op. According to the chairman, this was urgent.

On 7/3/49 the board meeting was held at Fru Berit Nordklev's. She read out the minutes of the last general assembly/ working committee meeting.

COMMUNICATION

Jesper hears voices. He doesn't tell anyone. He still hears them.
When he puts his ear to the sitting-room wall, the one facing
Kirkeveien, he hears voices, although no-one is talking. His
father is full-length on the sofa reading the paper. He hasn't
said a word for a long time. And his mother isn't at home. The
voices must be in the wall or outside somewhere. They are
clearest in the evening, like now. Jesper can hear them. Is it
only him who hears them? At any rate his father can't. Otherwise he would have put down the paper. Jesper is afraid and
relieved. They are speaking for him. He can hear the butcher's
boy whisper: *I don't want to die.* He can hear the bus driver
shout: *He ran straight in front of me.* He can hear Dr Lund's
comforting words: *You're not going to die. Everyone has to die.*
They don't know that Jesper can hear them. He hears Fru Vik
pray: *Our Father who art in heaven.* He hears the butcher's boy
again: *Why is everything so quiet?* He hears his mother:

"Did you absolutely have to say something?"

Jesper turns and sees her in the doorway, in her outdoor
clothes, and angry. Pappa lazily peers over the newspaper.

"Did I say something?"

"At the general assembly!"

"I thought it was only right and proper to make my presence known."

"You were supposed to be there as an observer. That was the agreement."

Ewald places the newspaper on the table.

"Are you ashamed of your husband?"

It is only now that Maj catches sight of Jesper sitting in the corner with his arms around his knees.

"Hasn't he gone to bed?"

"Obviously not. Are you ashamed of me?"

Maj takes a step closer to Jesper.

"Go to the bathroom and get ready for bed. I'll be along in a minute."

Jesper gets up slowly and skulks out.

Maj turns to Ewald again.

"Would you like it if I burst into Dek-Rek and told you how things should be done?"

Ewald laughs out loud.

"I didn't burst in."

"Why haven't you put Jesper to bed?"

"Anyway, the two things can't be compared. Dek-Rek's my job."

"Oh, is that so? Sorry for existing."

Ewald isn't laughing anymore.

"What do you mean?"

"Everything you do is so much more important."

Ewald gets to his feet.

"I earn the money. Do *you*? No, you don't."

Maj lets Ewald chunter away and goes to the bathroom, where Jesper is standing next to the sink cleaning his teeth. He has buttoned his pyjamas up wrongly. She goes to button them up correctly, but changes her mind. Then she goes with him to the vestibule. He lies down and turns his back on her.

"You mustn't be angry at Fru Vik," Maj says.

Jesper doesn't answer.

"If you have to be angry at someone, it should be me."

Jesper still has his back to her. Maj leans across him.

"Fru Vik told me what you'd told her because she loves you. Jesper?"

The sound of his breathing was like a whistle.

"Are you falling now?"

Maj holds him tight. When she is sure he is asleep, she lets go and goes back to Ewald, who hasn't finished talking.

"Has the Red Cross managed to get us a telephone yet? Eh? No, the Fagerborg department of the Norwegian Red Cross in Oslo has not."

Maj closes the door gently behind her and Jesper hears her say:

"You'd like that, wouldn't you? Then you wouldn't have to ring Fru Vik to get hold of me every time you were ensconced in the Bristol."

"It may have escaped your attention, but I come home for dinner. Or have I become invisible recently?"

Jesper listens, but these voices are different from the ones he heard before. These are alien, even though he knows them, even though these voices are closer to him. They don't talk for him. They don't talk to him. They just talk past each other until one of them gives up and both are silent for a while. Then Mamma says quietly:

"Let's not argue."

Pappa lowers his voice as well.

"We can have a bit of rumpy-pumpy instead."

"Ewald! You're waking Jesper!"

But they can't wake Jesper because he isn't asleep. He is lying in the narrow bed in the cramped windowless vestibule and his head is electric. His head is a pin cushion. Soon he hears his parents getting ready for bed. He sees their shadows creep past leaving a veil of tobacco and perfume in the darkness. Soon he hears the silence that isn't silent anyway. The sounds race in all directions. There are sounds between the voices. There is a crackle. There could be an explosion at any time. There isn't. The sounds continue. Jesper gets out of bed, opens the hall door and closes it behind him. He slips his feet into his father's snow boots and puts his coat on over his pyjamas. He goes out. The city is quieter than the flat. The world is quieter than the vestibule. He looks up at the brick wall beside their sitting-room window. A bundle of wires is attached there. They hang in a gentle curve towards the thin cables the trolley busses pass beneath and that often crackle, blue, almost four-sided flashes of lightning. There are no flashes now. Jesper follows the cables down Kirkeveien. They remind him of the escalator in Steen & Strøm. He stops by the butcher's. There is a sign on the door: CLOSED DUE TO ACCIDENT. Isn't everything closed at night? Jesper wishes it had been him. He walks on to Majorstua where the cables continue in all directions. It is impossible to see where one stops and the next starts. He remembers he caught the tram with his mother before Christmas. He walks that way. There isn't a soul out. Jesper is the only person. The boots are so big he can barely lift a foot. The coat drags along the pavement. He comes to a church at the top of a hill. The clock in the steeple resembles a full moon with hands: a quarter past four. Then Jesper hears music. A window is open in a narrow side-street. Someone is playing a piano. He has heard the same tune before. This is the third time. The notes are far apart, they hesitate, they are drawn out, but they never fail. They fall into place, exactly where they are supposed to fall, and Jesper falls into place too. He recognises where he is. This is where he wants to be. Music is better than the voices. He cries. He doesn't know why. It is that longing of which we know nothing. It is what we only sense, vague and intangible, it is what will reveal itself one day, clear and grounded in real experience. Then the music is drowned out by sirens, which also rent the darkness. Briskeby Fire Station is responding to a call. Jesper puts his hands over his ears. The fire engines slew around the corner by Eilert Sundts gate. There is a fire somewhere. The sky is burning. The night is ruined. Jesper walks home. He hasn't got a key. He sits on the steps and waits. Soon the paper boy comes. He runs past and the *Aftenposten* has barely landed on the door-mat before he is on the next floor. On his way back down he is stopped by Fru Vik, who asks him to calm down and stop stamping, he is waking up the whole house. The paper boy doesn't have time to worry about this, he just laughs, then sets off again and says, what on earth do you want the *Aftenposten* for, if you're not awake, lady. Fru Vik leans over the banister and is about to give him a piece of her mind, but she spots Jesper sitting under his coat. She goes down and sits beside him.

"What are you doing, Jesper?"

"Not saying."

"Do you want me to apologise first?"

Fru Vik gently puts her hand on his shoulder.

"Can't you sleep, either?"

Jesper doesn't look at her.

"What's the name of the song I heard in your flat?"

"Which song?"

"On the radio."

"Well, I don't remember."

Jesper starts to hum it. He closes his eyes and hums Erik Satie's *Gymnopédie No. 1*. Fru Vik looks at him. His tight mouth is all of a sudden soft and supple. When Jesper opens his eyes he is quiet again, but the elasticity of the melody stays with him for a while, a gentleness on his face, a child's melancholy.

"Shall I sit here until Ewald comes to get the paper?" Fru Vik asks.

"You can do."

"What shall we tell him?"

Jesper shrugs.

"That I've been out looking for a telephone for them."

On 4/4/49 the members' meeting was held in Fagerborg parish hall. 1500 circulars were distributed in the district beforehand, as advised by Ewald Kristoffersen.

The programme included a talk about the work being done in Fagerborg department by the Red Cross, by Fru Berit Nordklev, the chairman, a lecture about Red Cross work in Norway and other countries by deputy secretary general Jens Meinich, as well as musical entertainment by Bjørn Wall. Afterwards Herr Bendiksen, Deputy Head of Majorstua

144

School, gave a moving talk about Grini concentration camp and his later transfer to Bergen-Belsen. Hearing how the Red Cross saved lives and gave comfort both here and in Germany affected us all and strengthened our resolve and optimism.

A basket of groceries was raffled and brought in 180 kroner.

Also, the chairman has received twenty pairs of shoes from the Oslo District Red Cross, a present from American Relief for Norway. The shoes have already been handed over to the parish nurse, who has undertaken responsibility for their distribution, so that the shoes will reach the needy in our parish.

The total costs of the meeting, such as the renting of a room, flowers and not least copies of the circulars etcetera amounted to 214 kroner.

160 people attended.

HUSBANDRY

Fru Vik is sitting by one of the round tables on the terrace waiting. She has never seen the city from here. It seems so small. Karl Johans gate is no more than a thin line of twine hanging from Oslo East Station. The light erases the buildings. Ris Church, on the other side, is like a white stain on a green curtain. And if you didn't know any better you might think that the commercial building known as Havnelageret was the Royal Palace. The Danish ferry is docked at Vippetangen, the tip of the Akersnes peninsula, and in Bjørvika Bay the cargo boats are queueing up. An open double-ender boat crosses the fjord between Hovedøya Island and Dyna Lighthouse. The sun shines uninterruptedly. Nevertheless a chill in the air can make the shadows darken beneath the trees on the steep slope down to the train lines. The waiter comes over to her. She says she is still waiting. He smiles knowingly and slowly retreats, so that she has time to change her mind. At Ekeberg Restaurant you are allowed to change your mind. Fru Vik looks in a different direction. At the other tables are couples who don't belong together. She has heard the rumours. Now she can see it with her own eyes: office workers and women who are not exactly their spouses. For that they have dressed up too much. No woman goes to so much trouble for her own husband. And everyone is speaking in such low voices they may as well have been silent. What they are trying to hide is obvious. Hands on table cloths are too restless. They fidget. It is repugnant. The weather is close, despite it being spring, May. Fru Vik regrets having come. She has already made one blunder, agreeing to go to Hotel Bristol. Now she is about to do it again. Why did he want to meet here of all places? And in addition arrive late. Why not at Herregårdskroen Restaurant, which is closer? Or they could have just gone for a walk. Yes, that would have been the best, a walk, perhaps in Frogner Park, and then each go their own way. That is normal. There are no demands made. That is what you usually do. It is simple. Fru Vik puts on her gloves and pushes her chair back. Then she catches sight of Olaf Hall on the hill. He seems hot and out of breath. He looks up, waves and almost runs the last stretch. Then he sits down, places his hands on the cloth, but removes them immediately and doesn't quite know what to do with them.

"Are you cold?" he asks.

"No, why?"

"You're wearing gloves."

"I was just about to leave."

"Sorry. Today's been so busy. I'm really sorry."

"It doesn't matter."

"Well, as I said, today's—"

He is interrupted by the same waiter, who places a menu between them. They order coffee and apple cake. While they wait, their conversation stalls. They say nothing before the waiter is back with their order. The cake is hot with a little portion of whipped cream on top. They taste the coffee first. Olaf Hall puts cream in, Fru Vik doesn't.

"Has the shop been busy?" she asks.

"No, I'm closed on Tuesdays. But a letter came. An intolerable letter. I had to make a few telephone calls."

Olaf Hall takes out an envelope and places it between them. There is the Red Cross logo in one corner. The addressee is Ragnhild Hall. Fru Vik doesn't touch it. She doesn't want to read other people's mail. Olaf Hall leans across the table and appears vexed. He presses a finger on the letter.

"This is an invitation from the board of the Fagerborg department of the Red Cross. To Ragnhild. Asking her to perform at their general assembly. Have you heard?"

"No. But that's not good."

"Not only has it passed them by that she's dead, but they think she's common enough to do charity and monkey tricks."

Fru Vik says nothing, although she wanted to say something, for example she could have said that charity work is not common and is not comparable with monkey tricks, either. But she can understand Olaf Hall, she found overdue letters in her letter box too, addressed to Halfdan Vik, and it hurt. Olaf Hall is breathing heavily and puts the letter back in his blazer.

"I seldom get angry. But I have been today."

"And you have every reason to be."

They eat for a while. The cream is thin and runs off the fork. A gust of wind lifts Fru Vik's serviette. Olaf Hall grabs it and passes it to her.

"Perhaps it's the truth I can't tolerate," he says.

"Which truth?"

148

"In the end that was what she became. Entertainment in the interval."

"It wasn't that bad."

"Yes, it was that bad. She couldn't even get any work at the Edderkoppen Theatre. No-one wanted her. Or only when everyone else had been asked and she did it for free."

"She had some big roles too, didn't she?"

"At the beginning, yes. Then she fell apart. She destroyed herself. There are people who choose to destroy themselves. To destroy all the brilliance they have."

"I'm not certain it's a choice, is it?"

"I don't know anymore. I only know there was nothing left of the person I once fell for."

Olaf Hall goes quiet and gazes across the fjord that is now bathed in a blue haze. The mountain ridges behind are colourless and merge with the sky. The air quivers. Fru Vik dislikes this conversation. It is not right to sit here at Ekeberg Restaurant talking about the dead, especially not about Ragnhild Hall. She realises that this is a mistake, but is unable to rectify it.

"Do you come here often?" she asks.

He looks at her.

"Thank you for wanting to meet me at all."

"It's not every day I receive a postcard in my coat."

Olaf Hall chuckles and puts down his cutlery.

"But I like the view. And if we couldn't go to Café Fleur or Café Odeon in Paris, I thought this was the best."

"I have a book with me by the way," Fru Vik says.

She takes an old hardback from her bag and puts it on the table. It is *Husbandry* by Bernt Holstmark, published by

Grøndahl & Sons in 1913. Olaf Hall leafs through absent-mindedly, stops at some of the colour plates, various breeds of horse. There are some notes written in the margins.

"Tell me about your husband," he says.

Fru Vik looks down. Can you be unfaithful to the dead? She hears laughter somewhere behind her. She has to choose her words with care.

"Halfdan was responsible for the king's dogs."

"He seems like a good person."

"Yes, he was a good person. Except that he took his leave much too early."

"May I ask how?"

Fru Vik raises her eyes. Olaf Hall has hung his blazer over the back of the chair. His white shirt is freshly ironed, but has a yellowish tinge; it has been in the wardrobe for too long. She suddenly feels a kind of tenderness for him.

"You're never cold, Olaf, are you."

She hears the familiarity in her own words and he notices it, too. It is a concession. She is conceding that she is attentive. He approaches her with a hand.

"It's May. The sun is warm. Are you sure *you're* not cold?"

Fru Vik pulls her arm away.

"He died while lecturing to students at the Veterinary College. About the insemination of pigs."

"Yes, the war took its toll."

"It wasn't the war. It was his heart."

"It's always the heart."

She wants to talk about something else:

"You're not interested in husbandry?"

"The colour plates are interesting."

Olaf Hall opens the book again and puts on a pair of thin, round glasses. He is silent for a while, then he peers at Fru Vik over the top.

"May I read to you?"

"So long as it isn't from the chapter about pregnant sows."

Olaf Hall pushes the glasses up his nose and starts to read aloud. His voice is pleasant and slow. It reminds her of the radio.

"This manual makes no claim whatsoever to be original; to do that I lack the necessary practical experience in husbandry and the extensive theoretical knowledge that would enable me to deal with such comprehensive material independently. For this reason I wished only that a man with the requisite qualifications would perform this task. As, however, no-one showed willing, the lack of a suitable manual drove me to make an attempt myself, the book you are holding. Bearing this in mind, I hope you will judge the book with charity and leniency."

Olaf Hall closes the book, takes off his glasses and looks at Fru Vik.

"Shall we have a glass of white wine, Margrethe?"

Fru Vik is so surprised that she can only nod, she regrets her action at once, but by then it is too late. Olaf Hall has already caught the waiter's attention and soon two chilled glasses are on the table. They raise their glasses and toast each other. Afterwards he leans forward.

"I'd like to tell you something in confidence."

"You really don't need to."

"Yes, I do. I insist. You're the first person I'm going to tell."

"You'd better tell me then."

"Are you ready?"

"I think so."

"I'm writing a collection of poetry."

Fru Vik doesn't quite know where to look. She decides on the entrance to the restaurant. She can rest her eyes there.

"I just have to powder my nose," she says.

Olaf Hall quickly takes her hand and lets it go at once.

"Don't run away from me this time."

Fru Vik finds the toilet by the cloakroom. Fortunately it is empty. She leans against the washstand. What is this make-believe? She is well over fifty. She is a widow. Life has already brought her to a halt. She looks up. The face in the mirror is red. That must be the sun, the wind. It must be all the light. She dabs on some powder, takes a deep breath and walks back to their table.

"What are your poems about?" she asks.

"Life and people. Human life."

"That's a big area."

"I felt exactly the same as this Holtsmark. I had to write my own book because it didn't exist yet."

"Is it finished?"

"You can't rush it. You have to give it the time it needs. I work at night."

"Perhaps you could read me a verse one day?"

Olaf Hall puts his hand on hers and doesn't take it away immediately.

"Nothing would please me more, Margrethe."

They can choose between taking the tram and walking. They decide on the latter. The afternoon is pleasantly cool, with occasional gusts of wind that make the fjord foam. Olaf Hall leaves a five-krone note as a tip under the ashtray, so that it doesn't blow away. It strikes Fru Vik that he appears to be at ease with tipping. For her part, she thinks it is lavish. At least half would have been more than enough. She says nothing. It isn't anything to do with her. They walk through the woods, across the tramlines and past the Seamen's School. Keeping a little distance between them. If you saw them and didn't know any better you would imagine they were walking separately. On the steep bend, just afterwards, where you can see north to where the city ends, they do however come closer again.

"You must be proud of your son," Fru Vik says.

"Stepson."

"Bjørn. Really proud."

Olaf Hall stops and holds her arm. There is some unease in his eyes, some torment, it almost hurts.

"Have you anything particular in mind?"

"Hasn't he told you?"

"He tells me very little."

"He saved a life the day he brought me the fur coat," Fru Vik says.

Her arm twitches.

"Yours?"

Fru Vik laughs.

"No, it wasn't that bad. He saved the life of the butcher's son."

Olaf Hall is motionless for some seconds, then lets go of her arm and runs a hand through his white mane. Fru Vik straightens her coat sleeve. The air is clear and still. Then they continue walking past the ruins of Hallvard Church and disappear down into Oslo.

———

On May 14th the board meeting was held at Fru Ingrid Arnesen's. Those present were the chairman Fru Berit Nordklev, Fru Ingrid Arnesen, Frøken Vanda Aasland and Fru Maj Kristoffersen. On the agenda: the written answer to their enquiry which they had received from the Chief Housing Officer in Oslo, who informed them that at present there was no suitable accommodation for a crèche in the Fagerborg District. The chairman said she would keep an eye on the matter and come back to it later.

A request had been sent to the Textile Office for linen for our medical stock.

The Red Cross Head Office had passed on a letter from Torstein Malm, Fagerborg District, requesting help for him and his family. The chairman would examine the case more closely with the parish nurse.

A doll had been bought for the raffle at the Red Cross bazaar in September and work on sewing clothes and accessories for it had begun.

It was noted that we had received two thank-you letters from recipients of a pair of shoes.

Our department accidentally sent an enquiry to the actress Ragnhild Hall asking if she would perform at our general assembly. We regret this, as Ragnhild Hall passed away last year. Flowers and a letter have been sent to the widower, Olaf Hall, who has also been offered a free two-year membership of the Red Cross.

CONSTITUTIONS

Fru Vik wakes with a start, not because of the hollering of the elated school-leaver running up Gørbitz gate to Fagerborg School, but from a dream. She had been dreaming about a horse rolling in mud. And this dream reminded her of something while she was still asleep. She is sitting in bed and has to hold tight: *Husbandry*! Holstmark's *Husbandry*! Did she leave it at Ekeberg Restaurant? Or did Olaf Hall take it with him? Should she ring him and ask? She has already told him twice she didn't want to spend today with him, and if she rings to ask after the book, he might think that she has something else on her mind, that she regrets saying no and wants to meet him after all. But she doesn't. They can meet on normal days. They don't bind. But not on May 17th, Constitution Day. Festivals are binding. Festivals promise too much. Anyway, it doesn't matter if Olaf took the book with him. *She* forgot about it. She noticed the tip, him putting the banknote under the ashtray, but not whether the book was there. Fru Vik sinks back down on the pillow, turns to the wall and cries. It is Halfdan himself lying up there in Ekeberg Restaurant, traded in, abandoned. That is how it feels. She goes into the bathroom. There isn't enough water in the cistern for a shower. She has to make do with cold water over her face and a cloth under her arms. It doesn't matter. She will keep her distance from people today. She looks at her hands. They are getting old, too. They are changing colour. They are getting liver spots. They are disgusting. She tries to pull off her wedding ring, which Halfdan bought at David Andersen's in 1917 and he slipped on her finger in April of the same year, when her hands were young, before they had their hands full. It won't budge. She rubs Vaseline around it. That doesn't help, either. The ring is stuck. She gives up. It is the ring which is wearing her, not vice versa. Fru Vik takes it as a sign, gets dressed, pins on her May 17th rosette, drinks a cup of coffee and makes it on time to the service in Fagerborg Church. She sits on the last pew. There aren't as many people as there were the previous year. The congregation is dwindling year on year. Pastor Bergesen gives a masterful sermon promulgating responsibility and joy based on the Gospel of John chapter 12 verse 35: *A little while longer the light is with you. Walk while you have the light, lest darkness overtake you.* They sing psalm 432. They say the Lord's Prayer. They receive the blessing. Afterwards the sun shines on the church steps. People greet one another, shading their eyes. The young ones are impatient and are held back by mothers who aren't free today, either, but feel free. Fru Vik would prefer not to shake the pastor's hand. However, there is no escape.

"The sermon was food for thought," she says.

Pastor Bergesen smiles and pats her hand.

"Don't be too serious today."

Fru Vik thinks about what he said as she makes her way home through the crowds. She is not quite sure if she understands his words, but they do her good anyway. Don't be too serious. A weight falls from her shoulders. She straightens her back. That is how easy it is. There is room for her. Stens Park is green. At the top, by the little pool, birds are weaving blades of grass on high. Some people are in the way. It is the Red Cross ladies: Fru Nordklev, Fru Arnesen, Frøken Aasland and Fru Lund. But Maj Kristoffersen isn't there. They aren't in the way though. Fru Vik is happy to stop. The men for their part have gathered in Pilestredet. They are laughing at something and smoking cigarettes, all of them apart from Dr Lund. Perhaps it is his endless warnings that have provoked the laughter.

"That was generous of you to donate the fur coat to our bazaar," Fru Nordklev says.

Fru Vik smiles:

"Now that you mention it, I'm afraid I have changed my mind."

"Changed your mind?"

"Yes. I've simply had second thoughts. It would be terrible to meet someone walking around in the very coat that Halfdan gave me."

The ladies are silent for a moment and exchange glances. Fru Lund collects herself finally and also smiles:

"We can understand that. But please don't let us down like this another time. We need all the help we can get."

"I didn't mean to. I'd happily donate something else. Halfdan's skis are still in good condition. And his pitch-seam boots . . ."

"You can go to the flea-market with them. We're holding a *bazaar*."

The men have become impatient and are coming closer. They are still in high spirits and shaking their heads. Herr

Nordklev, who likes to start festive days with a snifter, kisses Fru Nordklev on the cheek and reveals what was so funny and at worst scandalous:

"And here's your doctor who doesn't like children's processions. Have you heard?"

Fru Lund nudges him good-humouredly.

"That's just what he says."

"Not to us. Tell the ladies, Per-Fredrik."

Dr Lund doesn't need to be asked twice.

"I only mean that I'd rather see weapons and soldiers on Karl Johans gate than noisy, stiffly dressed children."

There is a silence. The board of Fagerborg department, Oslo District, Norwegian Red Cross, except the treasurer, look at each other, uncertain how to react to such a statement. Is Dr Lund serious? At length the chairman, Fru Nordklev, bursts into laughter, just to be on the safe side:

"That was mean of you!"

"To whom?"

"To the children, dear Doctor."

"I won't hear a bad word about them. I'm just being realistic. We've seen how it went in 1940. Does anyone believe that a children's procession armed with flags, ice cream and silly trumpets represents a deterrent?"

"But a children's procession isn't supposed to be a deterrent. It's supposed to be a festive celebration!"

"Yes, we've already become lazy and smug."

Herr Nordklev sighs:

"Isn't it wonderful to be lazy and smug?"

Fru Lund tries to subdue her husband, in vain, however; he has got the bit between his teeth now:

"I would say the Eidsvoll men who drew up our constitution in 1814 – May God be with them – were more preoccupied with the gravity of the situation and the nation's interests than bands and tomfoolery. It was that drunk, Henrik Wergeland, who wanted festivities."

Fru Vik senses that the laughter and merriment will soon be unable to hide the bad atmosphere that is developing. So she taps the doctor on the arm and says:

"We have to remember the pastor's words. Don't be too serious today."

Herr Nordklev raises his hat.

"I'll second that."

Then the group disperses. Some of them go to the square in front of the Royal Palace, some go to Sim. Solberg bakery in Hegdehaugsveien to eat layer cake, some go to Stortorget where the children's procession starts in an hour, while others walk arm in arm through the streets and enjoy what the day has to offer. Fru Vik goes home. On the staircase she meets Maj and Ewald coming down with Jesper between them. Maj is wearing a green, flowery dress and high heels, which she is bound to regret in a couple of hours, probably before they have reached Karl Johans gate. Ewald is wearing a grey suit and a light coat. In addition, on his lapel he is wearing the biggest rosette in Fagerborg; it is big enough for the whole family. Maj has only the Red Cross badge on her chest and Jesper refuses to make a hole in anything. He is also in his best clothes, a blazer which at present is much too big for him, a white shirt buttoned to the throat, grey pressed trousers and polished shoes. But his face isn't dressed for the occasion. It is tired and defiant. He is the antithesis of other children at this time.

He is unwilling, tormented. In his eyes Fru Vik can see what seems to be anger, but it isn't, it is pain. At once she thinks: the boy isn't sensitive; he is aware.

"And you've already had a word with Our Lord?" Ewald says.

"Only the pastor. And Dr Lund."

"Well, that's almost the same thing."

They laugh. Jesper doesn't. He wants to go back. Maj holds him and moves so that Fru Vik can get past.

"Would you like to join us?"

"Thank you, but no. I need to have a little lie-down."

She continues up the stairs while Ewald almost has to push Jesper out into Gørbitz gate and around the corner. Maj rushes after them and they hold his hand to be sure they have him. Then they are on their way to the city. They *are* in the city and are on their way to the city at the same time, which in this regard means the area between the National Theatre and Stortinget, the Norwegian Parliament, in other words Karl Johans gate and its cobbled side-streets.

"She's been so odd recently," Maj says.

"Who has?"

"Fru Vik."

"If only you knew."

"Knew what?"

"I really don't know."

"Come on, tell me."

"I think she's found herself a . . . how shall I put it . . . a chum."

"A chum?"

"On the grapevine I heard she was with a tweedy gentle-man at Hotel Bristol not so long ago."

160

Maj stops and holds her hands over Jesper's ears.

"What? At the Bristol?"

"And someone saw her with the same gentleman at Ekeberg Restaurant recently."

"Ekeberg?"

"Isn't that nice?"

"Nice?"

"That she's found herself . . ."

Jesper tries to wriggle free, but Maj grips him even harder.

"It's not that long ago her husband died," she whispers.

"The sourpuss. Fru Vik really deserves a—"

"Sshh!"

Ewald stops talking and smiles and Maj can safely let Jesper go. Then they walk past the butcher's shop, where Norwegian flags and a polished photograph of King Haakon stand between legs of mutton in the window. It is the same picture that will be there eight years later, but then it is an hour of grief, not of joy. In Bogstadveien there is a mass migration towards Karl Johans gate, towards the *city* in the city. In the Sim. Solberg café, where Bogstadveien has already imperceptibly joined Hegdehaugsveien, sit the Nordklev and Lund couples with coffee and the speciality of the house, square meringues. Fru Nordklev catches sight of Maj, waves and goes out.

"Goodness, I needed a breath of fresh air," she says.

"Is there something wrong?"

"Only the doctor. He'd rather have a military parade than a children's procession."

"Ugh."

"He won't talk about anything else. Is this Jesper?"

"Yes. He's looking forward to hearing the bands. Aren't you?"

Fru Nordklev bends down to talk to Jesper, who seeks refuge behind Ewald. She has to straighten up again.

"By the way, it's nice to see you wearing our badge today," she says.

Ewald takes a step forward.

"I hope no-one thinks it's the Danish flag."

Fru Nordklev doesn't think that was funny. She pulls Maj aside.

"I can't make it to the working committee meeting next month. Family visiting, you know. And neither the co-opted members nor Lund's free. Are you?"

"Do I have to write the minutes?"

"You'll manage that fine."

"But Vanda and Ingrid are so good. Can't—?"

"I'm sure Ewald can help you. Thank you, Maj. That's nice of you."

Ewald takes another step forward.

"By the way, how's it going with the telephone?" he asks.

Maj flinches and Fru Nordklev doesn't quite understand.

"Excuse me, which telephone?"

"If Maj has more to do, we must soon be getting a telephone. Isn't that only right and fair?"

"Yes, I think it is. You'll have to get in the Televerket queue and cross your fingers."

Fru Nordklev hurries back to the others. Maj tousles Jesper's hair. Ewald turns to her.

"Cross our fingers? Can't we rely on the Red Cross either now?"

Maj says nothing and they carry on to Wergelandsveien, follow it past the Kunsternes Hus Art Gallery and the honorary artist's residence known as Grotten, turn right by Fredriks gate and find some space in the crowd where the gentle incline up to the Royal Palace starts. People are vying for a good view. Some have even brought a step-ladder so they can climb up to see better. But then they block other people's views and the atmosphere turns nasty. A policeman decides that anyone with a step-ladder should stand at the back, as they can see over everyone else anyway. Tempers calm. Ewald wants to lift Jesper, but Jesper doesn't want to be lifted. He wants to be at the bottom. The king and the crown prince appear on the balcony between the pillars at the top of the light. Birds take off from Abelhaugen Hill casting fleeting little shadows behind them. The first school bands set off: Bolteløkka, Ullevål, Tøyen, Uranienborg, Sinsen, Majorstua. Jesper is breathing heavily at the bottom of May 17th. It is almost unbearable. Bursts of noise break out here and there, drum rolls, tubas, school-leavers shouting, trumpets, dogs barking, flutes, male choirs and three cheers. Sometimes the sounds stretch into distinct threads drawn from ear to ear. The next moment the sounds tighten into knots that will never loosen. Then Jesper sees a dark, sad figure he recognises at once. It is the Italian, the man with the piano. There is a worn flag sticking out of his pocket. He is standing behind the step-ladders, stooped and holding his ears. Jesper does the same. He holds his ears. It helps a little, but not much. What can stop the noise? What can get rid of it? Silence? Not when the racket is already in your head. Enzo Zanetti catches sight of Jesper and recognises the troubled, inquisitive boy. He remembers the mother as well, the Red Cross woman, who is dressed to the nines. She has done her best. That should be enough. But she doesn't seem to feel at ease. She is probably finding it difficult to enjoy or endure her outfit. Her high heels are already at an angle, her dress is creased above her hips, her back and calves obviously hurt, and her complexion is pale. But it is impossible to miss her brave smile. She is leaning against a man who is quite plump, almost square, with a kind, blank face, which often characterises carefree people who think they are happy. Enzo Zanetti turns his gaze to Jesper again and smiles at him. Jesper smiles back. They smile at each other. It is a sign. No-one else in the world is holding their ears in Karl Johans gate today except for Jesper Kristoffersen and Enzo Zanetti.

Maj nudges Ewald and motions towards Jesper, who has his eyes closed as well.

"How stupid we are," she says.

"What was that?"

Maj leans towards Ewald:

"Of course Jesper's fed up."

"Why?"

"He should've been in the procession. If everything—"

Ewald interrupts her and he it is, in the end, who lives up to the pastor's humanistic counsel, not to be too serious, as he says lightly:

"He's a lucky man who can look forward to the following year instead."

Jesper sticks his hands in his pockets and May 17th breaks over him again. He opens his eyes. He just glimpses Enzo Zanetti, bowed, walking down Fredriks gate. It is the wrong direction, but crossing Karl Johan today is impossible anyway. It will take him at least an hour to reach Automaten; he will probably have to go round Oslo East Station or Solli Plass. He takes the flag from his pocket and flutters it. Two police horses pass by and the constables salute. Enzo Zanetti bows and has the smell of the animals in his nostrils for a long time, it reminds him of a childhood in an ochre countryside, which he will soon have forgotten. Then he continues alongside the Palace Gardens, stops outside Kunsternes Hus, but can't see a single free table in the café. At Krølle Kro in Uranienborgveien there is a queue, mostly young students, and the bar in West Hotel between Riddervoldsplass and Vestheim Private School is too expensive. He passes on Sim. Solberg as well. The white serviettes and the sound of cutlery, especially the small cake forks, make him nervous and depressed. And he definitely can't be bothered to walk all the way down to the Bristol. Besides, he never goes there anymore. Enzo Zanetti goes home. The entrance to his apartment block is cold and quiet. He takes out his bunch of keys and opens the post box. It is empty. Isn't there anyone in this wretched, megalomaniac city who wants to learn to play the piano? Then Enzo Zanetti remembers there is no post on Constitution Day in Norway.

The first thing he sees when he opens the door to his flat is the suitcase. It is in the hall. From the bathroom she has removed her toothbrush, perfume and combs. There is no red hair in the sink. He glances into the bedroom. The bed is made. Her shoes have gone. He isn't surprised. He knew it would happen. He has noticed it in her eyes. She doesn't see him anymore. She sees only a boring, older man. She has drawn her own conclusions. She is sitting in the kitchen, which is so cramped they cannot avoid touching, whatever they do.

"I'm never going into town again," Enzo says.

"Isn't today a nice day for it?"

"A nice day?"

"You could've woken me up. I would've gone with you."

"Why do you Norwegians have to make such a din when you're happy?"

"Because we're so quiet normally."

"You've been quiet recently."

Aina stands up and runs her hand over his fingers.

"Are you managing?"

"The Red Cross might use me again."

"You deserve better than that."

"And you? Are you managing?"

"I've got into the Railway Academy. In Kristiansand."

"Congratulations."

"Railway jobs in Norway are secure. There's nothing more secure."

"But that's not why you're leaving."

Aina doesn't answer and goes into the hall. Enzo Zanetti follows her.

"We might see each other on a train one day," she says.

"Do you think so?"

"Absolutely. When you're touring the country."

She kisses him on the cheek and disappears down the stairs. Enzo Zanetti goes over to the sitting-room window. Soon he sees her cross Jørgen Moes gate. She leaves her youth behind her and is on the way to the tram stop on the bend. He hopes she doesn't turn around.

————

The working committee meeting for the Oslo District of the Red Cross was held at the nurses' home on June 10th, 1949. Those present were: the chairman, Fru Andersen, the deputy, Fru Dybvig, office manager, Holm, as well as the chairmen from most of the departments, apart from Fagerborg, who were represented by Maj Kristoffersen.

After a welcome speech by the chairman, the Oslo District secretary, Fru Petra Scheel, read the minutes from the previous working committee meeting. Then Fru Dybvig talked about the division of labour in departments and gave some guidance regarding the planning of their work. Fru Dybvig read out the relevant section of the Norwegian Red Cross regulations. Office Manager Holm then reported on the planned Red Cross week in September, which will be spread over two weeks. Personally, I believe this to be too long. One week would be enough. As before, the bazaar will be held in Håndverkeren Restaurant while the market will be moved from Studenterlunden Park to Skansen. Holm touched on the following two issues: the help needed to organise the "week" and admitting new members via former members. (He added there would be a "no-charge raffle" for two electric Elna sewing machines and every member who signs up one or more members would receive a corresponding number of free raffle tickets.) The procedures regarding the acquisition of new members and the payment of membership fees were discussed. Along with the sale of Red Cross stamps (1 krone) and possibly balloons, and how boys and girls would be organised to sell these items. I commented that we had enough volunteers in Fagerborg.

The chairman informed us that Lillebrog department

had donated 100 kroner towards the redecorating of the nurses' home and thanked them.

In addition, the committee addressed a number of other matters, such as the setting up of four field hospitals, each with 24 beds, which were now erected. Fru Diesen and Fru Falling were asked to inspect the hospitals once or twice a year. The chairman mentioned the possible purchase of plots in Ullernåsen to build homes for retired nurses or the aged. There was also discussion of whether departments should set up a list of what yarn and material they might need to knit/sew clothes to be distributed in their areas and send a joint request before the summer holidays to the rationing authorities to buy in whatever was necessary, without using coupons. Another issue was whether departments should work together when there is a particular need for help.

The question of the potential loaning (lending) of departments' medical resources will be on the agenda for the working committee.

Fru Nordklev suggested that Fagerborg department should at some point try to arrange a tour into the countryside for the old, and has looked into the costs of bus fares and catering. Nothing was decided for the moment. There was a call for volunteers on the board to help. Personally, I would like to do something for our old people. In my opinion the trip should not be so long that there is only time to go there and back. I suggest Tyrihøgda, where they also have simple fare. Drøbak is another possibility.

15/6/49 Maj Kristoffersen

RHUBARB

Summer plunges this city even deeper between the mountain ridges while raising those people who remain after the others have gone, raising them into majestic loneliness. Summer here isn't a season. Summer is a moment in time. This is also true of Fagerborg. Let us see: Kirkeveien seems broader than normal. You could call it a boulevard, though a deserted boulevard. Dr Lund has closed his surgery and gone to Hvaler with his family. Melsom the butcher's is unlit and the counter is empty. Melsom has a brother-in-law who knows someone who has a cabin in Øyeren, not so far from Sunnaas, where Jostein will stay until the start of school. They can visit him at the weekend. It is a national holiday. Savour the words. They feel good. Most things are national in this post-war period, before affluence grows too much and everyone has to look after themselves and not others. Most things that happen are the same and people talk about the same. That doesn't mean you say the same. But we remain in the city, apart from on one day, Wednesday, July 6th. Then Maj Kristoffersen has to go on a trip with the old folk, organised by the Fagerborg District of the Red Cross. Ewald and Jesper accompany her to Fagerborg Church, where the bus is due to leave at eleven. Fru Else Larsen and Fru Ingrid Foss are already there. Jesper stays in the background, as does Ewald. One shouldn't interfere too much. But he thinks it is unreasonable of the Red Cross to lay claim to Maj's time right now. Then the old folk begin to arrive: widows and widowers, couples and eternal bachelors, they come from all sides, from Sankthanshaugen, Jessenløkken, Valkyrien and Ulleval, dressed in their best summer clothes, which are no longer appropriate. They haven't been for a long time. Fru Else Larsen checks names against the register while Fru Ingrid Foss and Maj help the people board the bus taking them to Tyrihøgda. The driver hoots twice, the passengers wave, but don't know who they are waving to, and the bus heads towards Bislett Stadium and soon disappears down Josefines gate. Ewald and Jesper are alone again in the city. They stand silent in the forecourt of the grey church. Fortunately the pastor isn't present. The sun shines in Suhms gate and streams down Pilestredet. They have been lucky with the weather. But Ewald is suddenly uneasy. He feels lost, almost afraid. They are alone. What are he and Jesper going to do all day? He can't remember having been with his son for such a long time. Thinking back, he never has been. What can they do? Should they go home and wait? Ewald goes down to the circular urinal first and Jesper follows. It smells even worse there as it is summer. The floor is sticky. The walls are wet. In the trough there are cigarette ends, corks and something Jesper can't identify. It looks like a dud balloon. Ewald unbuttons his fly. Jesper follows suit. Ewald looks at him and smiles. Feet slightly apart, so you're well balanced, like that, yes. Ewald is in full flow. Jesper strains and strains. Hardly a drop comes out. Barely any flow. He turns away. Ewald sighs, shakes his peg and packs it away. Jesper follows suit. They find a tap behind the church where they can wash their hands. It is very important. You should always wash your hands after you have had a pee. And you have to remember the order of events. You can do it before you pee, but you have to wash your hands afterwards as well. Ewald considers this a promising start to the day. He takes Jesper's hand and they walk down to the city centre. They go slowly, so that they are in step. This is what is called *strolling*. They stroll past Frydenlund Brewery in Pilestredet, turn right by Parkveien, reach the Palace Gardens and stroll through. The king isn't at home, either. The king is away in the national holiday as well. The king doesn't want to be worse off than most people, nor better off. The canopies of trees and the grass meet in the middle, in a quivering green belt. Beneath the hill from the Royal Palace, a gentle ski landing slope down to the city, to the very centre of Oslo, Karl Johans gate floats in the heart of the light. An old lady is sitting on a bench holding an umbrella. The sun turns the umbrella into a parasol. When they can see the fjord they just continue past the cinemas, the Scala, Saga and Klingenberg. Then they stop in the deserted square in front of the new City Hall. Only the bells are missing. They are supposed to ring on the hour and the half-hour, perhaps every quarter of an hour as well. Ewald isn't sure if he will like being reminded of how much time there is to go and how much has gone. The two towers, however, are impressive. Jesper agrees. He shades his eyes from the sun and almost gets a crick in the neck. This City Hall puts Ewald in a bad mood. It reminds him of the jubilee. They walk down to the quays, but have to stop for the goods train coming from Oslo East Station and going to Oslo West. The steam locomotive is pulling at least fifty-two wagons and moves so slowly it is almost standing still. This depressing lentitude puts Ewald into a profound mood. What he sees is time pulling away from him, loaded with everything that is no longer necessary. Over at Akers Mekaniske Verksted the shipyard is silent. Work has come to a standstill. The cranes are hanging their heads. The ships have no name. The world is waiting to be launched. Ewald glances at Jesper. Is he alright? Or is being with his father boring? It is hard to know. His face doesn't give anything away. It strikes Ewald that Jesper seems older than he is, not with regard to his size or height, but in his facial expression. It is his eyes that do it. They are unrecognisable. They look in a different way. Ewald is almost frightened. Is it a torment being with his father? Or is there something else? Is his life a torment? But he definitely doesn't complain. So it can't be that bad. The quayside train has finally passed and they can cross the railway lines. The Nesdodden ferry is ready to leave. Most of the passengers are on the deck. They are wearing broad sun hats and carrying big baskets. It has become so hot that the islands at the end of the fjord have vanished in a blue haze, which the occasional yacht cuts through. Ewald removes his jacket, loosens his tie and opens his shirt at the neck. Jesper does the same, except that he is not wearing a tie. Ewald feels a tenderness welling up. This is how it should be. The son trying to be like the father. They walk back to Karl Johans gate. Pensioners are sitting on the benches in Studenterlunden Park, hidden in the flickering shade beneath the trees. The pavements are wide. A lone professor is standing in the university square. The students don't come until September. Everything is on hold. This is the national holiday period. Ewald is thirsty. They can drop into the Bristol and have an open sandwich, but Maj might not like them going there. He has a better idea. He will show Jesper the future. Ewald takes him to Dek-Rek. In the lift Jesper finally smiles. There is no-one at work now. But Ewald has keys. He unlocks the door. This is Ewald's second world. His first world is Jesper and Maj. At times, however, the second world has to come first. The empty offices seem alien. The doors are ajar. A piece of carbon paper is on the floor behind the secretary's desk. It looks like carelessness. As no-one sees it, it has no significance. Ewald shivers, but pulls himself together before Jesper notices. They go into the design office. Blank sheets lie on the drawing boards. They are the future. Ewald tells Jesper to notice the size of the sheets especially. Jesper is tired. He is given permission to sit on the secretary's chair for a while to rest. It can swivel. In the meantime Ewald goes into Rudjord's office. He cannot comprehend what he is doing. It is like a dream. If an air-raid warning had gone off now he wouldn't have been alarmed. He pours himself a whisky and drinks it. He allows himself another tiny drop, replaces the carafe on the shelf, exactly where it was before, and dries the glass. The lowest drawer in the desk is full of pencils, all kinds – soft, hard, medium. He takes one of each. There is no point having a future if you don't have the tools. Ewald hurries back to Jesper, who is swivelling round in slow circles with his eyes closed. Ewald waits for the chair to stop. Jesper is sitting with his back to him. Ewald gives the chair a little push and passes the pencils to Jesper, who opens his eyes. Then they go home and wait. Maj doesn't come until eight o'clock. Her footsteps are so heavy on the stairs that you can hear every one. In the hall she has to sit down and breathe out. Ewald and Jesper look at her. She appears to be suffering. She loosens the cord around her dress and that helps a little.

"My God," she says.

Ewald bends down.

"What's the matter? Has—?"

"We ate the whole time. From when we arrived to when we left."

"Were the old folk hungry?"

"And how! They never stopped eating! They were never full! And we had to keep them company. I'm not going to eat again until Christmas."

Ewald helps her up, laughing.

"Yes, I can see you've really put on weight since I last saw you. Especially . . ."

Maj swats him away, but she has to laugh, even if it hurts.

"What sort of time did you have?"

She looks at Jesper, who nods.

"Fine, I think."

"You think? Did you get something to eat?"

"We completely forgot," Ewald says.

Maj sighs.

"I can't leave you for a second without something going wrong."

Actually, Ewald considers this comment undeserved.

"Couldn't you have brought back something instead of eating it? If you were so full?"

"Steal, you mean? Steal from the Red Cross?"

"That's no worse than you stuffing yourselves, is it?"

Maj sighs again and goes into the kitchen. She fries a

couple of eggs and heats a tin of stew. Just the smell makes her feel sick and she has to hold the stove to remain on her feet and not to throw up. She summons her remaining strength.

"Don't forget to buy rhubarb tomorrow," she shouts.

But this excursion to Tyri Fjord with Fagerborg's famished old people is the exception to summer's golden rule. As I said, we stayed in Oslo. No-one talks more about the weather than those left in the city. We sometimes complain and blame the Meteorological Institute, which isn't far away, in Blindern. But when it starts to rain, which often happens in this area, no-one breaks into a run. They just continue walking at the same quiet pace, going nowhere in particular. When it stops, you notice that the buildings are a different colour and gleam in a different way. No renovation work has been done and it is not the rain's fault, either. It is the light breathing on the facades, especially in the evening, slowly drawing out the day. Inside the abandoned flats the furniture is covered with sheets, which soon fade and resemble yellow bandages when the residents return in August. The flats sicken at being vacated, but on days with cloudless skies, which generally come one at a time, the people left in Oslo know where they are going. To Ingierstrand Beach, Lake Sognsvann or Fornebu Airport to watch planes taking off. Fru Vik is going to Vestre Cemetery. It is a long time since her last visit. She walks through Frogner Park. She has bought a begonia. A man in shorts and a hat is standing in the sun taking photographs. A mother is pushing a pram towards him. Fru Vik hears the baby cry. She could have gone with Olaf Hall to his country retreat in Nesodden. He invited her. She said no. It isn't right. It isn't done. Holiday is also a festival. But she was on the point of saying yes. No, it isn't right. It simply isn't done. It would be saying yes to more than that. She dare not think about it. She has to stop for a moment and rest. Then she crosses the dog-walking area of Frogner Park, which even the smallest poodles have abandoned, and opens the gates to the cemetery. In the shadow of the poplars it is cool, almost chilly. She stops by the untended grave. She is a bad widow. She places an old newspaper on the ground, crouches down and starts to tidy it. She weeds, clears the ground, plants the begonia, washes the gravestone and cleans his name: Halfdan Vik. It occurs to her that she has the capacity to forget. She stands up, fetches a watering can and soaks the dry earth. What could grow apart from the begonia? On her way back she meets other widows coming with the same purpose. They exchange a few words, predominantly about how quiet it is in Oslo now that everyone has left. Everyone has gone. That is the widows' refrain. Fru Vik tries to discern whether their grief is like hers, whether they are equally bad widows, but she can't see, though there is enough sorrow. Sorrow is dignified. Sorrow requires discipline. Sorrow is the slowest of all emotions. She walks home through the Frøen District and in Kirkeveien she bumps into Ewald coming from Smør-Petersen in Majorstua with a bunch of rhubarb. His white shirt is grey with sweat and hangs outside his trousers. Do you have to be sloppy even if it is a holiday? Sometimes it is difficult to like Ewald Kristoffersen. Anyway, they walk the last bit together. Ewald at once notices that Fru Vik is not very talkative today. He doesn't feel like saying much, either. But he can't stand such long silences, especially if no-one else is speaking and it is as quiet as now. It makes him nervous, impatient.

"I actually like the city in the summer," he says.

"I'm not so sure about that."

"No? Don't you enjoy the silence?"

"Is that why you don't go anywhere?"

Ewald dislikes this question.

"Jesper needs some calm," he says.

"Is he worried?"

"No. Why?"

"I thought everyone dreaded starting school."

Ewald holds the door open for Fru Vik and they go in through the front door.

"Besides, we are going somewhere," he says.

"Where?"

"The back yard."

He takes the short cut through the cellar and comes out by the rubbish bins. At this time, at ten minutes past two, there is sunshine from the flag post to the bike stands. The Virginia creeper, which almost covers the windows as well, makes the yard look like a room with green wallpaper. Jesper is sitting on a stool beneath the birch tree flicking through a book. Maj is stretched out on a deckchair by the roses and couldn't even eat breakfast this morning. The sight pleases Ewald Kristoffersen immensely. He puts the rhubarb down beside her and sits on the steps.

"She's lost weight," he says.

"Who has?"

"Fru Vik. Really. The only dimples you can see are on her knees."

"Ewald! Shhh."

"And why should she have a telephone when we don't?"

"Because Halfdan Vik was a doctor."

Ewald lights a cigarette.

"Doctor, Maj? He was a vet. And a sourpuss. Did he call the animals? Or did they call him?"

Maj doesn't have the energy to laugh.

"She can hear you, Ewald."

"No, she can't. She lives behind closed windows. And by the way, the vet's dead."

"And you're nasty."

"What does she need a telephone for when she has a refrigerator?"

"Now you're talking rubbish."

"I suppose she has to call that posh friend of hers."

Maj sits up and lowers her voice.

"How did you know they were at Ekeberg Restaurant by the way?"

"How?"

"Were you there as well perhaps?"

"No, do you know what? If I had been, I would've invited you as well."

"And I would've said no, thank you. Can't you put another shirt on?"

Ewald stubs out his cigarette, flicks it down the drain and brushes ash off his shoes.

"Rumours, Maj. Rumours roll down the Ekeberg mountain, through the Old Town, across the square outside the station and straight into Dek-Rek."

"You lot are a right old bunch of fishwives."

Maj lies down and Ewald laughs.

"Nothing has faster legs than a secret."

"I'm not interested in secrets."

"I even know what his name is."

"I'm not interested. That's their business."

Ewald takes a stick of rhubarb and puts it in his mouth. Maj straightens up again.

"Go on, tell me then."

"I thought you weren't interested."

"I'll count to three. One . . ."

Ewald leans over to her and whispers the name. Maj raises her hands to her face.

"The actress's widower?"

"The very same. A real charmer."

"My goodness me. We asked Ragnhild Stranger if she would perform for us at a meeting seven months after she died."

"That was a trifle late."

"And we had to send Olaf Hall some flowers and an apology."

"That's what I told you. This city is small."

The shade reaches the deckchair. Maj starts to peel the rhubarb.

"How's it going with the jubilee by the way? And your women?"

"What's Jesper reading?"

"I took out some old school books. Don't disturb him. He's been so calm all day."

"Why would I disturb him?"

Maj looks up for a moment and smiles.

"I think he enjoyed it yesterday."

"Why wouldn't he?"

Ewald bites off a piece of rhubarb and strolls down to Jesper anyway. There isn't room for two on his stool. Ewald stands.

His shirt is wet against his back. He loosens his braces. On the ground is *My First Reader* by Gundersen and Munch. Jesper is reading another book, Margrethe Munthe's *Let's Sing*. Ewald thinks Jesper should be reading the other book, but refrains from saying so. Jesper also seems most interested in the musical notes printed at the top of every page. He runs his index finger slowly along the small, black symbols that look like crumbs hung out to dry, but he knows, despite not understanding them, that this strange pattern has meaning.

"Let me have a look," Ewald says.

At length Jesper looks up and passes him the book open at the page. The song on the page is "In the Window", and Ewald is humble and proud. He sings it so loudly that the whole block of flats can hear it, but there is no-one at home anyway:

When pappady goes
I press my nose
To the window and peer.
He looks around
And smiles abound,
We are always so near.
Then he raises his hat
I grin and clap at that.

Ewald gives Jesper the book back and breathes out.

"That's a really good choice."

Jesper closes *Let's Sing*.

"I can't read," he says.

"I know, Jesper. It doesn't matter. That's why—"

Jesper jumps up and interrupts him.

"I need a piss."

Ewald glances at Maj, did she hear? She is still peeling the rhubarb. So he takes care of Jesper, who is hopping up and down.

"For now, we say *pee*, Jesper. When you're thirteen we can say *piss*, but never at home. Outside, we usually say *have a leak*. *Slash* is also—"

"And Cirkus Schumann."

Ewald laughs.

"But that's just in a restaurant. And at school we say *lavatory* or *loo*. Frøken, may I go to the . . .?"

Jesper runs to the rear entrance and Ewald follows him. He waves to Maj, who straightens up for a moment and runs the back of her hand across her brow. Then she is alone in the green yard. An obvious and terrible thought strikes her all of a sudden: *I never have a holiday.* For a moment she hates the rhubarb, she hates her fingers, she can't stand the thought of all the meals in front of her like a never-ending menu. Then it is over. She looks around, ashamed, afraid that these thoughts are so intense that someone might see them. Then Fru Nordklev comes up from the laundry cellar carrying a basket. Maj goes over to the clothes lines and helps her with the bed linen.

"I thought you'd left ages ago," she says.

"I've just popped back. And I brought the washing while I was at it. It's so difficult in a mountain cabin."

"You've got a nice tan."

"You too, Maj. The sunshine's here, too."

They finish hanging up the washing and Maj is about to speak, but Fru Nordklev says:

"To tell the truth, I would've rather stayed here. My goodness, how wonderful it is to be on your own."

She puts the remaining pegs in the basket. A wind gusts around the yard and lifts the clothes on the lines: a sheet, two pillow cases, two jumpers, a pair of trousers and a white shirt.

"It'll be dry by the evening," Maj says.

Fru Nordklev lifts the basket and shakes her head.

"I probably won't have the time. To be on my own. There's a lot to do before the Jewish children get here. Poor things. Anyway, we don't have much to complain about here in Norway, do we."

Maj looks down at her sandals and for a moment she is convinced Fru Nordklev has read her thoughts. She is ashamed.

"Is there anything I can do? I'd like—"

"Actually Frogner District is responsible. Besides, you've had enough on your plate already. I heard rumours that the trip yesterday was – how shall I put it? – a challenge?"

Maj laughs.

"Yes, you could say that. I think it's almost wrong to eat so much."

"Yes. The Jewish children would've liked some of it. We have to fatten them up and send them back to Germany happy."

"The bill for the trip doesn't make for happy reading."

"We'll have to recoup it at the bazaar."

"Tell me if you need me."

"That's kind of you. Have you got enough sugar for the rhubarb?"

The sunlight is moving closer to Jacob Aalls gate. The sun shines into Maj's eyes and she looks away.

"We have more than enough sugar. Thank you anyway."

Fru Nordklev starts walking towards the kitchen steps on Jonas Reins gate. Maj is burning to say what is on her mind. But then Fru Nordklev turns round.

"By the way, you did a good job on the minutes, Maj."

"Thanks. Thank you very much."

"But don't be so personal. We always have to stand back."

"I didn't mean to."

"Although you were absolutely right. A Red Cross week shouldn't be more than a week."

Maj goes upstairs and takes extra special care with the stewed rhubarb while Ewald has a nap before they eat and Jesper sits on the chair in the hall studying Margrethe Munthe's notes. She lets the stalks simmer until she takes them off the heat and makes sure they don't go dark. Then she mixes in sugar and cinnamon. When the rhubarb is soft enough she pours off the water and adds potato starch. Then she brings it to the boil, it has a lovely, yellow-ish colour, and she calls Ewald and Jesper. They come at once and sit at the table.

The Kristoffersen family go to bed early. The sun and, not least, the rhubarb compote, have made them tired, lazy almost. The vestibule door is open so that there is a little current of air from the kitchen window, which Maj has left ajar. Jesper doesn't wear pyjamas and only has white underpants on, which are too big. The bedroom window facing Gørbitz gate isn't closed, either. The night is hot and light and full of tiny noises that reinforce the sense of stillness. Maj is lying on her back and has kicked off the duvet. She hears the telephone in Fru Vik's flat. It is so quiet that she can hear the ring tone. She looks at her alarm clock. It is half past ten. It could only be *him* ringing so late. Fru Vik answers the telephone almost at once. Has she been sitting in the hallway waiting for him to ring? Time passes. Then she rings off.

"If I die before you, how will you talk about me?" Maj asks.

Ewald doesn't say anything for a long time, but she can feel his heartbeat and his heavy breathing. Then he turns to her. His voice is low and frail and laden with a seriousness that is unlike him:

"Are you ill, Maj?"

"No. I'm not ill."

"So why do you say such things? You must never speak like that."

"I was only wondering, Ewald. Sourpuss. Is that what you would call me?"

"Now you have to stop. Sourpuss? You aren't a sourpuss. You're a ray of sunshine, Maj. For me anyway."

"That was nicely put."

"Besides, I'll die before you."

"Ewald!"

"I'm overweight, short of breath and I suffer from sleeplessness."

Maj strokes his shoulder.

"It'll be a long time before either of us dies anyway."

Ewald's seriousness passes. Most things pass with Ewald.

"How would you talk about me? Would you call me a cackbag?"

"I don't even know what a cackbag is."

"Or would you find someone else?"

Maj snuggles up to him.

"You're right. We should never talk like this. Sorry."

Eventually they fall asleep, a light summery doze, they

just float on the surface, but sometimes they dive deeper and dredge up unusual dreams from the depths, ones that don't let go until they are sitting in the kitchen the following morning having breakfast. Jesper isn't hungry.

"What does cackbag mean?" he asks.

Maj and Ewald exchange glances and Ewald is about to explain while Maj is wondering what to say about the rest of what Jesper must have heard. Then there is a ring at the door. She gets up quickly, goes into the hall and opens up. It is Fru Vik. She is standing by the banister in a light coat, flat shoes and a broad-brimmed hat. In her hand she has a small suitcase. She appears embarrassed.

"Could you water the plants for me?" she says.

"Of course."

"I wouldn't like them to wither while I'm away."

"Yes, in this heat."

"And look after the one in the sitting room. The snake plant. I've had it ever since . . ."

Fru Vik falls quiet and has to lean against the banister for a moment. She is out of balance. Her life is teetering. Maj takes a step onto the landing and leaves the door ajar. She speaks softly.

"Where are you going?"

"Not far."

"But you have a suitcase with you."

Fru Vik smiles, but it is a sad, hesitant smile.

"Well, in fact, I'm going a long way. I've never been so far before."

"Is it to . . .?"

"Do you know?"

"I know nothing."

"Then it'll stay between us."

Fru Vik gives the spare keys to Maj, who cannot bite her tongue, the words just tumble out:

"You are coming back, aren't you?"

Fru Vik nods, lingers a while, then goes down the stairs with the light suitcase that suddenly feels heavy. Every step is a struggle. She should never have asked Maj to water the flowers. What does it really matter if they wilt? Flowers are supposed to wilt. The taxi is waiting on the corner of Kirkeveien. Some children from Adamstuen who aren't away on holiday either flock around the black Mercedes in which you can almost see your reflection. The driver has a hard time keeping them off. No-one is allowed to touch his car. He opens the door with one hand and raises a clenched fist with the other. Fru Vik gets into the rear and places the suitcase beside her. Eventually the driver sits behind the wheel, rolls down the window and mutters a few curses. Then he turns round.

"And where can I drive you on this beautiful morning?"

Fru Vik is aware she can still change her mind.

"The Nesodden ferry," she says.

———

At the request of the Mission of Israel the Norwegian Red Cross, Oslo District, along with members from the Fagerborg and Frogner departments, arranged board and lodging at Vestheim Private School for approx. 50 Jewish children from Germany who travelled via Oslo on their way to foster parents around the country. The children, who are to stay for three months in Norway, arrived at the school at nine in the morning of August 1st and were immediately given breakfast. Lunch (stew and fruit compote made by the Dampkjøkkenet Company) and an evening meal were served during the day, and at eight in the evening the last children left the school with their group leaders. A number of the children were picked up by their foster parents.

The trip for the elderly took place as planned on July 6th. According to Fru Foss, Fru Larsen and Fru Kristoffersen the excursion, which was blessed with wonderful weather, was a great success. There were 34 passengers on the bus including the three ladies mentioned above. The trip left Fagerborg Church at eleven and went to Tyrihøgda, where coffee, cakes and waffles with sour cream and jam were laid on. Later participants had steak and for dessert pears and plums with cream, and at the end of the day coffee and a Danish pastry. The bus left for Oslo at seven.

TIMETABLE

It is the morning Jesper is to start the first class at Majorstua School, August 22nd, 1949. Everything is packed and ready and it has been all summer: in his satchel he has a pencil case, a timetable, a packed lunch and a notebook. Ewald got hold of the pencils and rubbers, and Maj ironed his shirt and trousers hanging in the bathroom ages ago. But during the night she is taken ill. She goes hot and cold in turns. She can barely get out of bed. This is not like her. Ewald tells her to go and see Dr Lund. He can take Jesper to school. Of course he can. Maj cries and is too weak to argue. However, Ewald thinks of an alternative plan, which in his opinion is far better. First he will have to go with Maj to see Dr Lund. After all, she can barely stand. In addition, there is a morning meeting at Dek-Rek he just remembered, and his presence is simply indispensable. Jesper sees a glimpse of hope. He can go on his own. That is what he would prefer. He wants to go alone. So that he can skip off as well. Skiving from school on the first day must be a record. It doesn't matter. He is a year late anyway. In the end it is arranged that Fru Vik will accompany him to school on his first day. Incidentally, she is back from Nesodden with some colour to her cheeks. Jesper will be hearing this for a long time: Is your mother *that* old? Is that why you're so late, because your mother is actually your grandma? And Maj will keep repeating that she should have accompanied him anyway and she will be plagued by a guilty conscience for many years. Jesper and Fru Vik are both serious and silent as they walk down Kirkeveien. Outside Melsom the butcher's he holds her hand. This moves Fru Vik and she is grateful. But when they are past Majorstua and around the corner of Maries gate, where there is already a whole crowd of expectant, nervous boys and girls and their proud, coiffured mothers, Jesper lets go and stops. He definitely wants to do the last bit on his own. Fru Vik cannot allow that. She is going to accompany him to the school. She promised she would. She is going to watch him go into the playground. She is going to watch him find his class. She wants Jesper to understand this. Jesper understands. But holding her hand again is out of the question. And Fru Vik understands that, too. They walk to the gates. Jesper recognises many faces, but he doesn't know anyone. Then he catches sight of Jostein. In the accident he lost his hearing in his right ear. Jesper joins him. They stand next to each other, in the two rows that form 1G.

"My mother's ill," Jesper says.

But Jostein doesn't hear because he is standing with his deaf ear to him.

The bell rings for the first day. Jesper turns and sees Fru Vik wave at the gates.

With their teacher, Herr Løkke, at the head they march into the classroom. Jesper has to sit at the biggest desk along the wall while Jostein is put at the front of the middle row. The rest of the boys can choose. Løkke, whom they will have for three years and who is wearing a double-breasted suit for the occasion starts calling out names: Petter, Rolf, Øivind, Birger and Ulf. Jesper stands up when it is his turn.

"I hope you will be happy with us," Løkke says.

Jesper sits down. He is uneasy. Why didn't he say that to the others? Shouldn't they also be happy with us? Too much friendliness makes him suspicious. He consoles himself with Løkke having to call Jostein's name three times before he reacts. Then Jesper hears the rest of the names from a great distance: Stein, Halvor, Asle, Tor, Lars. He is somewhere else, in his mind, in his unease. He fidgets with the ink well in the hole in the corner of the desk. He feels an urge to unscrew the lid and dip his fingers. So he does. The ink well is empty.

"The idea is that you should follow what's going on."

Jesper looks up. Løkke is standing over him with an erect back and his hands down by his side.

"So that you can remember the names. Don't you want to do that?"

Jesper screws back the lid, looks around and points:

"Petter, Rolf, Øivind, Birger, Ulf, Stein, Halvor—"

Løkke interrupts him.

"Good."

"Asle, Tor, Lars—"

"That's enough."

Løkke stands looking down at Jesper and for a moment he doesn't know what to do. Then he hangs his jacket on a nail by the door, changes into a brown smock with a belt and positions himself behind the teacher's desk.

"Now we're going to work! And then we're going to work more!"

And twenty-six boys from Fagerborg and district fill in the time-table that will last for the rest of their lives.

When they are let out into the playground again, the inevitable takes place, it happens in all playgrounds when the first day of school is over: a magnetic attraction draws some boys together, and friendships are made that will also last all their lives, while other boys are repelled, or dispelled, to an equally significant loneliness. Jesper stands perfectly still in this throng and sees Fru Vik still waiting at the gates. He is self-conscious, but doesn't want to show it. He doesn't want to show it because of her. Jesper senses something in Fru Vik that pains him, too. Fortunately she doesn't wave this time. Then Jostein passes, with his head at an angle. He is in a hurry. He is surrounded by distance. Jesper sticks his hands in his pockets, walks over to Fru Vik and together they follow Jostein, around the corner, across the Majorstua intersection and up Kirkeveien.

"When I started school I had to walk ten kilometres one way and ten back," Fru Vik says.

"Why?"

"Because we lived in the country."

"Did you live in the country?"

"Everyone in Oslo comes from the country, Jesper."

"I don't."

"But your mother does."

That startles Jesper.

"What do you think is wrong with her?"

"Probably a little stomach upset. Don't you worry about it."

Now they see Jostein taking off his satchel and waiting for them outside the butcher's. They stop. He says nothing.

Perhaps you talk less if you are hard of hearing, because you can't hear what people say.

"Did it hurt?" Jesper asks.

Jostein leans closer, but forgets which ear is deaf.

"What?"

"When you were knocked down."

"I can do."

Jostein hurries into the shop. Through the window they can see his parents behind the counter, both in white coats, but only his mother is wearing a hair net. His father goes over to the meat slicer and cuts up a sausage. Then Jostein comes back with two slices of cervelat wrapped in paper.

"Shall we go to school together tomorrow?" Jostein asks.

"We can do."

Jostein gives the meat to Jesper, who puts the package in his pocket. Then he and Fru Vik walk the last bit. She doesn't want to let him go yet and tells him they will walk back together. She wants to hand him over in the same state she found him. Besides, she wants to hear how Maj is, despite it being only a stomach upset. She is sitting in the kitchen with her hands in her lap, studying them when they arrive. Her hair has more life, but she is still pale. A plate with a half-eaten slice of bread and marmalade is on the worktop. Jesper puts the cervelat there and is uneasy again.

"How was it?" Maj asks.

Jesper nods.

"Good."

Fru Vik lays her hands on his shoulders.

"And Jesper already has a new friend. Jostein, the butcher's boy."

Jesper pushes her away.

"He's deaf."

Maj gets up and stretches out a hand.

"You can still be his friend even if he's a bit hard of hearing."

"And I don't like sausage."

Jesper goes over to the window. He can hear the rustling of the Virginia creeper outside, a dry, withered sound that fills him with a sadness that is also good to feel, if only he can listen hard enough. He stands with his back to them. Maj puts the meat in the refrigerator and slumps down again. Fru Vik pours her a glass of water.

"But how are you? Did the doctor find anything?"

"Yes, in fact he did."

"What?"

Maj sighs and looks at Jesper.

"You're going to have a little brother or sister."

Jesper turns slowly.

"I'd rather have a piano," he says.

On 21/8 the board meeting was held at Fru Else Larsen's. The chairman, Fru Nordklev, informed the board that she had received eleven parcels of baby clothes and three dress fabrics on 13/8 from the Norwegian Women's Association in Washington. Some of the items that weren't finished (shirts) were divided between board members, who will complete the sewing. Fru Nordklev read out the letter of thanks she had sent to the chairman of the Norwegian Women's Association, Fru Ragnild Brekke, the day after receiving the parcels.

A doll purchased for the bazaar has been passed on to Fru Lie, who will see to the clothing. Knitting yarn for gloves has been given to Frøken Else Lange.

Torstein Malm's family, mentioned in the minutes of the board meeting on May 2nd, has received clothes, shoes, etc delivered by Fru Nordklev.

An application to Bergens Privatbank (see tel. conversation on June 1st, 1949, with Herr Torp) for three places at a children's holiday camp has been rejected because of the overwhelming response this year. Herr Torp has, however, promised to try and help next summer. Fru Nordklev suggested that the sum of money allocated to the three children this summer (500 kroner) should be sent to Fagerland holiday camp instead.

The board is pursuing its request for a crèche with the Chief Housing Officer.

The department is looking for helpers on the X-Ray days before and during the Red Cross week. Working hours would be: 9 a.m.–1 p.m. and 3–10 p.m. Contact Fru Lund. Our district will have a bus at Fagerborg Church on September 13th. It will then go to the other departments in turn.

We managed to finish thirteen parcels with more or less the same content, i.e., a cotton blanket, wax cloth, fifteen or sixteen nappies, terry towel or cloth, rubber pants, two or three shirts and a ball of knitting yarn. The parish nurse in Fagerborg will help to distribute them.

X-RAYED

Johnsen places another sheet in front of Ewald and makes some witty comment that isn't witty. Ewald laughs anyway and ripostes, *Got to saw timber with a bloody nail file again, have I,* but by then Johnsen is back on his chair. Ewald has to design Oslo's timeline, 900 flipping years, and symbols, or logos, tied to any events that are worth mentioning, all in harmony with the company's founding principle: tradition and modernity. That means from Harald Hardråde to Haakon VII. That means the city's guardian angel St Hallvard. That means the royal residence and the petit bourgeois province. That means textile factories along the river Akerselva and Edvard Munch's last will and testament. That means shipping and forestry. That means bloody Vigeland. Of the city's 453 square kilometres 320 are forest and yet more forest. Oslo is a forest. Not forgetting Karl Johans gate and Studenterlunden Park. Ewald feels like adding a scurrilous anagram of Studenterlunden in brackets, the one people used after 11.00 p.m. Not even the famous, healthy Oslo breakfast is spared. Ewald is bored. At least his idea was eye-catching. This is no better than three hairs with a centre parting. But he obeys. To design is to obey. Ewald designs what the others have thought up. He is a technical designer. It isn't his job to have ideas. To have ideas is another way of obeying. You obey your own voice. You are your own boss. That doesn't mean Ewald doesn't have ideas. No-one has more ideas than he has, but no-one will get to see them. Now Ravn is looking over his shoulder.

"Jesus. What would we do without you, Ewald, eh?"

"Go to hell in a handcart."

Ravn laughs and puts another pile on his desk.

"Not that I want to stick my nose in, but make loads of space between the type so that the print shop can see the drawings. Understand?"

"Clear as crystal. You speak Norwegian as if you were born speaking it."

Ravn pats him on the back.

"And you're surpassing yourself once again. By the way, Rudjord's called an extraordinary general meeting for two on the dot."

Ravn sits back on his chair, puts his feet on the desk, lights a cigarette and has a coughing fit. Ewald Kristoffersen sharpens his pencil and changes pen. He is in a bad mood. But it soon passes. Actually Ewald is in a good mood. Isn't he perhaps surpassing himself? He thinks about Maj. He is not only in a good mood. He is happy. He should ring her and ask how she is. But then he would have to talk to Fru Vik first and he can't be bothered. It is a shame they don't have a telephone. They are disconnected. He wants to be connected. He wants to be connected to the world. What good is having a piano if you don't have a telephone? Ewald laughs at himself. He has a way with words. He thinks about Jesper. Has he made any friends? Is he keeping up? Does the teacher send him into the corridor?

Jesper would like a piano. Perhaps a piano could make Jesper happy, too. Ewald doesn't understand it, but he has realised that most things are incomprehensible and the rest is downright unbelievable. He fetches the telephone directory and looks up *Musical Instruments*. By then it is already two and Rudjord is gathering his colleagues in reception. He says that they, and he is including himself here, have to make great demands on themselves, greater than ever before. Everyone knows this means overtime. But, as he has said before, Dek-Rek is a modern agency that will also take care of its employees' welfare. Demands and care go hand in hand. In other words, the whole lot of them will have to be X-rayed. According to the Act of December 12th, 1947, everyone is required to present themselves for an X-ray of their lungs. And there is a Department of Health bus at Deichmann Library where Red Cross workers receive the public. So they are performing a good deed at the same time, supporting the Red Cross. This is also part of the jubilee: Oslo taking care of its community. Bear that in mind. So the Dek-Rek crew troop up to Deichmann and queue outside the bus, Rudjord at the head. He wants to set a good example. Two Red Cross nurses ensure the system runs smoothly. Ewald hasn't seen them before, but of course this is a different district. Ravn can't stop coughing and Ewald, who is in front of him, gets a blast straight into his neck. He hears a gob of spit land on the pavement. It is not exactly an embellishment. Ewald turns.

"You've got full-blown TB with bells and whistles, and no mistake."

"Shut up."

"You can frame the pic afterwards and send it to the autumn exhibition."

"Kristoffersen, you're not at all funny. And you never have been."

Ewald can see that Ravn is pale in the gills and his mouth is trembling. His yellow fingers are trembling as well. The whole of him is trembling. Ravn is frightened. He fears the worst. Ewald feels guilty and laughs.

"Everyone coughs in September," he says.

Inside the bus they have to bare their chests. Ewald sees, perhaps for the first time, how fat he is. His stomach, white and repulsive, is hanging over his belt. He is embarrassed, not because of the way he looks, but because the Red Cross nurses might think he over-indulges, that he gorged himself on the fat of the land during the war and still does. Ewald says Ravn can go before him, so that he can get the damn X-ray over and done with, but Ravn doesn't want to, on the contrary he loses his temper. Does Ewald think Ravn is so contaminated he has to be let past, that his case is urgent? Should we be letting people jump the queue? Ewald shrugs and takes his place in the machine, which is like a space capsule, but it is a journey to inner space, to the Milky Way and the black hole of the lungs. He is instructed to press his chest against the screen. It is cold. He does this as best he can. Then he hears two clicks, sees a flash and it is over. He goes out and quickly dresses with his back to the others. It is Ravn's turn. The nurses have to help him in. Afterwards Rudjord lets them off for the rest of the day, so that they are extra ready for the morrow's challenges. Once Rudjord has gone, Ravn suggests going to the Bristol and celebrating the X-ray. The others laugh and walk down Akersgata, where the newshounds wave as they pass, after all they are almost in the same industry. The X-ray photos are not a lot to celebrate, but who would turn down a drink at the Bristol? Ewald Kristoffersen does. His refusal is received badly. Does he want to ruin the atmosphere? Ravn coughs and comes up alongside him.

"I didn't mean what I said."

"Already forgotten. What was it you said?"

"Bloody hell, Ewald, come with us. It's not the same without you."

Ewald feels like saying it isn't true that everyone coughs in September. Ewald doesn't, for example.

"My wife's expecting," he says.

Ravn turns to the others in the expedition.

"Ewald's pregnant!"

So he has to go to the Bristol after all and this time it is Ewald who is treated. But to only one beer. And perhaps a snifter into the bargain. Ulfsen has already filled his glass. They shout *skål*. Ewald looks at the grand piano standing abandoned between the tables and plants. He drinks up and is allowed to leave. First of all he hurries back to Akersgata and in the *Aftenposten* office he finds the newspaper containing Enzo Zanetti's advertisement. Then he catches the tram to Majorstua. It is not quite three o'clock yet. He can wait for Jesper. They can walk home together. He sets off towards Sørkedalsveien, to the gates. But he soon loses heart. Perhaps Jesper won't like it. Perhaps Jesper will be embarrassed and that is the last thing Ewald wants. He thinks: If I were Jesper would I appreciate my father coming to pick me up? He wouldn't. He slows down. Parents, and particularly fathers, should keep their distance from school. In the end Ewald comes to a total halt. When he hears the bell ring, he turns and takes a detour home. He drops by the Post Office and fills in another form, which he sends to Televerket. On a separate sheet he adds that his wife, Maj Kristoffersen, is in the family way and if Televerket accepted their application they would all be in seventh heaven.

The working committee meeting was held on 2nd Sept. Those present were: Fru Esther Andersen, chair, Fru Esther Dybvig, dep. chair, reps. for Child Aid, Sewing Union of 1907, Gifte Red Cross Nurses' Association, reps. for the bazaar committee in Red Cross sub-divisions, except for Sagene and Majorstua.

First point on the agenda was the Red Cross Week, which the Norwegian Broadcasting Corporation is to open on 10th Sept.

On 17th and 24th Sept. there is a draw for the Elna sewing machines mentioned previously.

There will be a balloon sale all over Oslo from 10th to 24th Sept. Departments have the opportunity to sell in their district (purchase 75 øre, sale 1.50 kroner). Fixed stalls: Kontraskjæret, Oslo East and West stations, Majorstua and Studenterlunden.

A concert in Calmeyergaten (no details as yet).

On 24th Sept. a children's show in Bislett with a ballet performance, a police shoot-out with hosepipes, gym pupils from Odd Bye Nielsen School, and much more. At the entrance children are given free chewing gum and a balloon. The same day (24th Sept.), a matinee at the Colosseum Cinema (revue). Flag parade with a band marching from the fire station up Karl Johan to the bandstand every day. Demonstration by emergency services in Frogner Park. Kontraskjæret Market with various stalls, wheel of fortune, hot dogs, ice cream, a spit grill etc. In addition, from 19th Sept. to 30th Sept. an exhibition of American plastic in a tent, with a display for the spectators. Small objects will be shown, such as thimbles, combs, egg cups and so on, which the Red Cross can sell to make some income.

A car has been purchased for a raffle, but at present we don't have permission to sell raffle tickets.

The bazaar: posters for windows are available from Fru Scheel. Fagerborg has table No. 12 at the top on the left.

Sale of stamps: Fagerborg suggested applying to the authorities for permission to sell stamps on Sunday 1st Sept. – children are not at school and there is also an international football match at Ullevål Stadium. The working committee will look into this.

Øksfjord Infirmary, in Finnmark, has been given 5,000 kroner by the working committee for an X-ray machine. This is the first permanent hospital since the scorched earth campaign. Oslo District has also financially supported the hospital.

Last week the Red Cross was visited by ladies from the French Red Cross. They were here to take home 45 French children who have been in Norway this summer. According to Esther Andersen, the children, who mostly came from a strike-affected region, benefited enormously from the stay. Shortly after the French children came to Norway, 150 Norwegian children travelled to France (NB at their own expense).

Enquiries were made with all Oslo churches regarding collections for the Red Cross. It is considered especially important that priests dedicate a few words to the Red Cross in their services. The priests were positively disposed.

THE DAY OF RECKONING

Dr Lund likes talking to Melsom the butcher. He has both feet on the ground. And he knows his business. He slices off neck cutlets with the precision of a surgeon. But what he likes best is that they disagree on most things.

"Have you read *Donald Duck*?" Dr Lund asks.

"Jostein reads *The Phantom*."

"I was asking about what *you* read, Melsom."

"Since Sigrid Unset died I've skimmed through her books."

"She's unique. Even though I think she leans towards sentimentality."

The butcher chops off the fifth cutlet with a well-directed blow, this time it was more soldier than surgeon.

"She writes it as it is."

"You mean as it *was*. She said that the human heart doesn't change. As a doctor I can state with some certainty that she's wrong."

"By the way, I don't believe these comics do any harm. They're fun, Doctor. Isn't that healthy too?"

Dr Lund takes out his wallet.

"Yes, it's healthy. But not all fun is healthy. We shouldn't kill ourselves laughing, either."

Melsom rinses his hands laughing.

"I'll remember that one. We mustn't kill ourselves laughing."

"But do you think the Labour Party will win again?"

"Who else is there?"

"The Right could make inroads."

"Then they'll have to run faster than you, Doctor."

"Oh, I don't run fast any longer, so there the battle is lost."

"But the communists are probably past their best."

"Have they ever had a best?"

Jostein comes from the backroom, with a satchel on his back, and scampers to the door. His father calls:

"Say hello to the doctor, Jostein."

He stops and performs a hasty bow.

"School going well?" Dr Lund asks.

Jostein looks up, his head at an angle, apparently resting on his left shoulder.

"I mustn't be late."

"No, you mustn't. Quick, off you go now."

Jostein runs out and at that moment Jesper appears, too. The two boys shake hands, like two adults, a strange sight, then they walk together down to Majorstua School.

"How's he getting on?" Dr Lund asks.

Melsom puts greaseproof paper between the chops and wraps them.

"He doesn't hear well."

"There are hearing aids."

"It's not just that. He hit his head, as you know."

"If I can be of any assistance, don't hesitate. Do you promise me?"

Melsom hands the packet of meat to Dr Lund with a smile.

"Are you having a party?"

"My wife has invited some ladies round to celebrate the Red Cross week."

"That's some time away yet though, isn't it?"

"Yes, it is. But she likes to celebrate before the event, in case something goes wrong."

"I'll remember that for next time as well."

"And fortunately I only have to fetch the food and keep my distance."

Dr Lund pays, goes out and stands for a moment enjoying the gentle circulation of the air. Kirkeveien on a Saturday morning in September has something special. There is something about the smells, a faint aroma of malt from the brewery in Pilestredet mixed with the freshness of Nordmarka's forest. Everything has a slowness to it, the light, the people. Then he continues to his surgery, gives the packet of chops to his nurse, who puts it in the refrigerator with the medicines. They exchange a few words before he slips on his white coat, the clogs he always wears and sits down. He hears the nurse humming. He likes that. Ågot Rud may have a date this evening. One can only hope so. She is thirty years old, but most people think she is this side of twenty-five. He is extremely content. He is content with life. It is Saturday. The schedule open on his desk is almost empty. No-one asks for an appointment on a Saturday. That is the strange thing. Most people would prefer to be healthy that day. Then his good mood is gone. Ewald Kristoffersen is coming at twelve. Dr Lund takes the X-rays out of the envelope he received from the Rikshospital, looks at them once again before re-reading the case summary. It doesn't offer any hope. The stain on the left lung leaves no doubt. The cancer is spreading. Although it is at an early stage, an operation is not recommended. Dr Lund closes the envelope. It is a death sentence, no less. It isn't the first time he has had to tell a patient it is too late. That doesn't make it any easier though. It is worse. He has to choose his words with care. He has to support both the patient and the diagnosis. He has to find a balance between solace and objectivity. And this objectivity is merciless. So the solace is mostly cold comfort. He refuses to use the word "hope". The nurse knocks on the door and comes in with a cup of coffee.

"You're in a good mood today," Dr Lund says.

Ågot Rud blushes.

"Sorry."

"You don't need to be. Have you got any plans for this evening?"

"I'm going to Skansen Restaurant with some friends."

"Take care then, let me say."

"I can take care of myself."

"Yes, I know. But don't overdo it."

"Was that everything?"

Dr Lund nods and Ågot Rud is on her way to the door, erect and offended, without either of them knowing quite why. There is some work to do anyway:

"Ewald Kristoffersen has an appointment at twelve," Dr Lund says.

Ågot Rud stops.

"That's true. Has the Rikshospital given him the thumbs down?"

"If he hasn't left before half past twelve, knock on the door and say the next patient's on the way."

"He's the only patient today. There's no-one else."

Dr Lund interrupts her.

"You know what I mean."

"Unfortunately I do."

"I'm afraid that I don't think you do. I'm not asking you to do this to let me off the hook. I'm doing it to put pressure on myself."

Ågot Rud closes the door quietly, makes a note on a piece of paper that Dr Lund mustn't forget to take the chops or write out next week's schedule. She is not dreaming about meeting the man of her life at Skansen this evening. She just wants to have a good time. The man of her life doesn't exist. She is sure of that. She doesn't need him, either. Everyone says she needs a man, but they are wrong. They don't know what she needs. Ewald Kristoffersen is punctual, that is, at five minutes to twelve. Ågot Rud helps him off with his coat and hangs it on the coat stand. For a moment she is close to tears when she sees the heavy man trying to be happy. She smiles and searches for words. Ewald Kristoffersen finds them first.

"I suppose you're off out with the doctor for a whirl on the town tonight?"

"I beg your pardon?"

"Well, the doctor's wife has organised a ladies' night and so you and the doctor are free."

Ågot Rud laughs and shakes her head.

"Perhaps the two of us should go out?" she says.

"I'd say three cheers to that three times over."

They stand looking at each other for a moment, silent,

and at once Ewald senses the seriousness of the situation. Through the silly banter he can see he is doomed. He can't put it any other way. He is going to die. Ågot Rud is about to say something, but holds back and instead opens the door for him. Dr Lund is standing by the window, with his back to Ewald. Ewald goes in. Dr Lund remains there for a few further seconds, then turns and proffers his hand. Ewald shakes it. They sit on either side of the desk. Dr Lund shuffles through his papers.

"My wife's going to your dinner party tonight," Ewald says.

"It's really my wife's party. Anyway, I've bought the finest neck chops for it. Don't say anything."

"I promise. Not a word."

"How's it going with Jesper?"

"Fine. But now I think we should talk about me and not waste any time."

Dr Lund looks up and is tempted to smile. He doesn't. He likes the man sitting in front of him. Some say he has no core, but they're wrong. Ewald Kristoffersen's core is his zest for life. Accordingly this becomes even more difficult.

"The X-rays show a stain on your left lung. It's cancer. There's little we can do. But of course we will do our best."

Ewald waits a while before asking:

"And that is . . .?"

"Pain management. Medicines. Care."

"Will it hurt?"

"Not necessarily."

"That answer is meaningless."

"It will hurt."

"How can I be ill when I feel so healthy?"

"That's the nature of the illness. At this stage you don't notice anything."

"But now I do, Doctor. Now that I know."

Ewald leans forward and has to hold the edge of the table so as not to fall. Dr Lund fetches him a glass of water. Ewald drinks, but cannot manage more than a sip. He breathes out and leans back. Dr Lund places a hand on his shoulder.

"It'll be fine, Ewald."

"It bloody won't."

"You're absolutely right."

Dr Lund sits down again and is actually relieved. This is what he was waiting for, a reaction, if not all the unease would collect in another tumour and explode.

"Perhaps it's a good idea if your wife comes with you next time. Next week—"

Ewald interrupts.

"I don't think so."

"It's your decision."

"It is."

"But it usually helps to share—"

Ewald bangs the table.

"You mean less pain for me and more for Maj?"

He withdraws his hand, embarrassed, exposed, yes, he feels exposed. Dr Lund looks at Ewald's large, nervous face, searching for his zest for life.

"She'll have to know sooner or later anyway."

"Yes, sooner or later. But not now."

"As I said, it's your decision."

"I just have to fill the cage with air and sprinkle pepper over the food."

"I don't understand a word you're saying."

"I'll cross the bridge when I come to it. Find the courage."

Ewald Kristoffersen gets up. Dr Lund does the same. The two men stand looking out of the window. The trees in the central reservation of Kirkeveien are beginning to gain height. The leaves are still green. It isn't half past twelve yet.

"We're going to have quite a bit to do with each other soon," Dr Lund says.

"I suppose that's inevitable."

"What are you going to say to Maj when you have an appointment here or at the Rikshospital?"

"That I'm off to the Bristol."

"You'd better stick to water, Kristoffersen."

Both of them laugh. Ewald takes a step closer to the window and lays his palm against the glass and stands like that for a moment.

"Will I be able to see our child?" he asks.

Dr Lund looks at his watch again. It is half past twelve.

"Yes."

Ewald turns to him.

"Took you a long time to find that one little word."

Dr Lund meets his eyes and there is no room for doubt.

"You'll see your child," he says.

There is a knock at the door and Ågot Rud enters. Ewald claps his hands.

"Good you came. I was just about to go."

Ewald follows her. She helps him on with his coat, brushes the shoulders and is considerate to a fault. He catches sight of a mirror and looks at himself. He sees no difference. Yes, he does – he seems younger. He can't understand it. Ågot Rud waits behind him.

"Are you alright, Ewald?"

"I'm afraid I'll have to say no to your invitation. I'm busy this evening all of a sudden."

"That's a shame. Perhaps another time then?"

"We could go to Rondo. I used to go there."

"I'm sure you did."

He laughs:

"I was a real showman, you know. And as thin as a Belsen inmate."

Now it is Ågot Rud's turn to shake her head and laugh:

"The way you talk."

"Don't you believe me?"

She stops laughing and looks down.

"Wasn't everyone before the war?"

When Ewald emerges into Kirkeveien he has no idea which direction to take. He has lost his sense of place. He could be anywhere. Suddenly Fagerborg doesn't exist. He just has a feeling that Dr Lund is keeping an eye on him from the window. Then Ewald Kristoffersen knows where he is after all. He comes to. He walks around Marienlyst, not wanting to bump into anyone – he might bump into Maj of course – and continues across the Tørtberg fields. He stops by the football goal down near the Police College, leans against a post and sinks down onto the damp, worn grass. Ewald Kristoffersen is amazed. He feels no fear. He feels only sorrow and freedom. He can't fathom it. Yes, sorrow he can understand, but not this sense of freedom. It is almost heretical. He is an autocrat. He is invulnerable. He gets to his feet. The damp has gone through his coat. The back of his trousers is wet and he walks towards Majorstua with his legs wide apart. Enthusiastic representatives of the political parties are handing out leaflets. The Høyre Conservatives have positioned themselves on the steps where passengers on the Holmenkollen line come out. The Venstre Liberals and the Workers' Party have taken up a position outside the vinmonopol. The Christian Democrats have, as usual, the corner by the chemist and fortunately the communists are nowhere to be seen. But the agrarian Bondeparti rep is alone by the telephone kiosk, arm outstretched. Ewald walks past without noticing them. He continues down Arbos gate and stops beneath the arched school gates. The bell rings for the last lesson. He catches a glimpse of Jesper walking with another boy, who is leaning close to him. It is Jostein, the son of the butcher, the one who nearly died at the Marienlyst intersection. That is a relief to Ewald. His son might have made a friend. Then Jesper stops, turns and sees his father, who raises his hand and smiles at him. His father seems different. He could easily have been a different father standing there. Jesper doesn't know what makes him think that. There is just something. Jesper shivers and runs after Jostein. The classroom is restless, but it is a happy restlessness that even Løkke can bear. The last lesson on Saturday is the best. On the board the class monitor has written: *Keap the Sabith holey.* Løkke uses the sponge and corrects the mistakes while explaining letter by letter. There is at least one mistake in three of the words. Even Jesper can see that. But he is somewhere else again. He is in his thoughts. He is thinking about his father. There was something. Jesper could see there was. Jesper saw it. He felt it, a twitch, a movement, a resonance. The way he was standing there. Jesper becomes nervous. He has to do something, drop his pencil case on the floor, knock over the ink well, hit something. He could say he needs a pee. He does. He has to pee. But the line is drawn there. Jesper Kristoffersen can pee as much as he likes all the rest of the weekend. The class laughs. The monitor stands by the board and rewrites the sentence: *Keep the Sabath holy*. Løkke heaves a deep sigh. At least it is an improvement. Perhaps the board monitor could write *Sunday* instead? Preferably with one *n*. The boys by the window aren't following. They are almost sitting with their backs to the board. Is there maybe something going on in the playground that is more important than what is happening on the board? This is impossible behaviour. Løkke tells them off, but gently, it is Saturday, and even he can sense a longing to be free. Jesper is itching to go. Jostein is sitting in the middle and can't see anything. So he can't send Jesper a sign. Then Løkke writes this month's verse on the board, two while he is at it, as there is soon a change of month:

August brings the sheaves of corn,
Then the harvest home is borne.

Warm September brings the fruit;
Sportsmen then begin to shoot.

The class has to read these lines in unison, but before they have finished the bell rings. Their satchels are already packed. Who will reach the door first? Løkke lets them run. And despite four breaches of the school rules he can't but like what he sees. He sees happiness and fleetness of foot. This hardened man's heart softens every time. He, too, packs his things with studied slowness and tightens the strap around the worn, brown bag. Jesper is still sitting there. Løkke is astonished. He is about to say something. Then Jesper finally stands up, bows quickly and leaves the room. Løkke stops in the doorway and watches him with concern. The boy isn't badly brought up. It isn't that. He is merely unconcentrated. He might also say: *The boy is one of a kind.* On Monday Løkke will say the boy is lagging behind. He will have to call in the parents for a word before autumn is over. Then the corridor is empty. But the echo of their footsteps is still there. That is the footfall of pupils over many years that only an old teacher can hear. The last he hears is Jesper Kristoffersen disappearing down the stairs and out into the playground, where his father is still waiting. Jostein is standing by the drinking fountain. Jesper sends him a signal that only the two of them understand and goes over to his father. Ewald lays a hand on Jesper's shoulder and they walk up Kirkeveien together.

"Shouldn't we wait for Jostein?" Ewald asks.

They stop and soon Jostein catches up. They say goodbye by the butcher's shop. Jesper and his father walk on. Jesper lets his father hold his hand.

"Have you become friends?"

"I hear for him," Jesper says.

"That's good. And what does he do for you?"

"He's my pal."

When they reach home it strikes Ewald suddenly that he is living dangerously. It is unusual for him and Jesper to come home at the same time. Anything unusual arouses suspicion. He has to be like the person he was and not the one he no longer is. He shouldn't be too like him though, because that arouses suspicion, too. It takes nothing to give yourself away. But Maj is too busy trying on dresses and other adornments that Jesper and Ewald have no understanding of and for the time being are none of their business. They sit in the kitchen buttering bread. Maj has already made lunch, which they can reheat later after she has gone, it is pork rissoles. They can sort out the potatoes themselves and there is red whortle-berry jam in the pantry. Then she calls them. She grants them an audience. They go into the sitting room. Maj is wearing a crimson dress Ewald can't remember ever having seen before. It frightens him. She hasn't so many dresses to choose between. He thinks she looks wonderful. She is the most wonderful woman he has ever seen. She turns round slowly so as not to leave anything unseen in the shade, while holding her hands over her belly, which is beginning to be visible. She looks wonderful all the way round. And Ewald understands that it is even more important to dress up in the company of women. Maj looks wonderful all the way round. Ewald repeats that to himself. Nevertheless he is frightened to say something out of turn.

"It suits you," he says.

"You look much better in blue," Jesper says.

Maj stops and glances at Jesper. Ewald doesn't need to pretend this time. He gently squeezes Jesper's neck.

"You know nothing about dresses."

"Nor do you."

"That's enough, Jesper. Tell your mother she's the most attractive woman in Fagerborg."

"But she would've been more attractive in blue."

Maj smiles at Jesper, a smile Ewald doesn't understand. He lets go and gives Maj a kiss, which she receives with surprise. Now he has to be careful. This could go wrong if he is too nice. Then there would be no option but to lay his cards on the table and say he is going to die. If he doesn't, she might think he has someone on the side. Maj is in the bath so long that Ewald is afraid she forgot to hang her arms over the sides. He tells Jesper. Mamma must have forgotten to hang her arms over the sides. Jesper doesn't laugh. At half past four she goes, Ewald and Jesper stand on the little balcony and wave to her. Then they are alone. Ewald heats the rissoles in the pan and agrees with Jesper that they won't bother with the potatoes. Then they can put on even more whortleberry jam. At six they listen to Children's Hour together. It is a repeat of Schibbye's *Uncle Einar and Oscar in the Studio*. Ewald can remember something this Schibbye had said; in fact it made quite an impression in the advertising industry: *On Saturday afternoons children should be able to sit by the loudspeaker for half an hour as free people.* He looks at Jesper. Is Jesper a free person now? It is hard to say and he is not going to ask. Jesper isn't going to die, not for a long time, and consequently he is attached to people, places, habits, duties, he is attached to everything around him. But Ewald wished Jesper could be free too, as he was, detached from his moorings. After Children's Hour they stand by the window and watch for Maj. She won't be coming home yet. It is a long time before she will come. Ewald says he has heard rumours that they are going to eat neck chops at Fru Lund's, and that sort of thing takes time. Besides, they have to drink coffee and chat and that takes even longer. Jesper stands by the window anyway. Ewald regrets telling him about the chops. Jesper might ask Maj how the chops were and then she will know how he knows that was what they ate. He has to be cautious. Ewald lights a cigarette. It doesn't matter now. He can smoke two at once if he likes. Jesper turns to him every so often, but doesn't look him in the eye. Is he sorry for his father? It seems so. Why would he be? It gives Ewald a shock. Has he let the cat out of the bag anyway? How is that possible? Now he knows. Jesper is sorry for him because Maj went out on her own. Ewald sighs with relief, goes over to Jesper and puts a hand around his shoulders. That is how a father and son should stand. They don't have to say anything. That is what is so good. Then they catch sight of Dr Lund. He is walking briskly down Kirkeveien, in a tracksuit, hat and with a big, light-blue shoulder bag. He glances up at the window where Ewald and Jesper are standing. He is pleased to see them together. Nevertheless it is a sad sight. The certainty makes it sad. He waves, but perhaps they don't see him. He walks on past Majorstua, where some youths are pushing each other by the taxi rank while two thinly clad girls are shouting at them. Dr Lund ignores them. He has his own concerns. He reaches Frogner Stadium and goes onto the track, which is shrouded in darkness now, abandoned and still. He takes a bottle of water from his bag, has a drink and changes into running shoes. Some people think thick soles are best. Dr Lund knows better. They should be as thin as possible. He has seen Africans running barefoot, at an athletics meeting in Edinburgh before the war. They won, but were disqualified. He sprints and then jogs, stretches out again and has a sip of water, until he has done 25 laps, 10,000 metres. It takes him 39 minutes. It is laughable. When you are young and have plenty of time you run short distances. When you are older and you have less time you run long distances, half-marathons, marathons. He listens to the city around the stadium as he rests, music from somewhere, the tram, a dog barking, voices that barely carry. A stadium is the city's exception when the stands are empty, like now. He remembers the full stands in Bislett, the Store Stå section, the cheering that was worth a tenth of a second, maybe two. Dr Lund is getting on for fifty. Then he runs twelve and a half more laps, 5,000 metres, and can do it in 19 minutes. Without pushing it. It is a pleasure, an escape which still requires a strong presence. But one day he will stop timing himself. Then it is over. Afterwards he sits in the stands by the clubhouse, changes his shirt and shoes, puts the sweaty hat in his bag and enjoys the moment. He often says this: Everyone has to have their moment and they have to enjoy it in peace. On the way home Dr Lund bumps into Maj Kristoffersen below Fagerborg Upper Secondary. It is early to leave the party. It isn't nine o'clock yet. Weren't the chops to her liking? Or has Ewald told he is going to die?

"Everything alright with you?" he asks.

"Oh, yes. We had such a nice time. Why?"

"It's early to be going home. I thought perhaps you had . . ."

Maj shakes her head:

"No, everything's fine with me. Ewald and Jesper are on their own."

"I'm sure they can manage."

"I wish Ewald was as fit as you."

Dr Lund searches for words, the right ones, it is not like him, and in the end says:

"You should go walking together."

"In my condition?"

"At least for a couple of months. Before the snow. Then it will be a fit baby. By the way, how were the chops?"

"Very nice. I think there is some food left for you."

Dr Lund laughs.

"That was certainly the idea."

When Maj gets home Jesper is already asleep. She hangs her coat on the hook, pulls off the tight shoes and rubs between her toes. Then she opens the vestibule door and tiptoes over to the bed. Jesper is sleeping on his back, with the duvet up to his chin. He looks peaceful. He isn't falling. But his eyelids are swollen, his cheeks streaked. He wakes up and looks at his mother.

"What is it?" she whispers.

"Nothing."

"Have you been crying?"

"No. We've had a good time."

"Do you want to get up for a bit or sleep?"

"I want to sleep."

Maj kisses him on the cheek and goes into the sitting room where Ewald is on the sofa waiting. She sits down beside him and leans against his shoulder. They don't say anything at first. Ewald realises that he has to speak. She is used to him saying something.

"Was it nice?" he asks.

"I'm so full."

"Didn't you bring anything for us?"

"Give over."

"You could've just wrapped a chop in a serviette and slipped it into your bag."

Maj straightens up.

"How do you know we had chops?"

Ewald gazes at the window and curses under his breath.

"Chops? Did I say that?"

"You did indeed."

"I met Melsom earlier today."

"And?"

"He said he had some chops for sale. Neck chops. And the doctor had bought a whole load."

Maj leans back and yawns.

"We should go walking together more," she says.

"That's fine. What made you say that?"

"The doctor suggested we should."

Ewald can see that he will never have any peace. Perhaps it is best to tell her the truth: that he is dying. But then Maj won't have any peace, nor will the child she is carrying.

"Was he there? I thought it was only a Red Cross hen party."

"I met him on the way home. He had been out running."

"And he said we should go walking?"

Maj rests a hand on his stomach and there is plenty of room for it.

"Don't you think you need some exercise, too?"

"And have you forgotten you've got a bun in the oven?"

Ewald places his hand on hers and the red dress, which is tight and changes colour as the room darkens.

"This is a little person you're talking about, Ewald."

He suddenly leans over against her shoulder in an uncharacteristic movement.

"We can go for a walk before the first snow comes," he says.

———

On 5th Sept the board meeting for the Fagerborg District of the Red Cross was held at Fru Lutken's. In addition to reading the previous minutes Fru Nordklev reported back on the work she had done since the last meeting.

The following letters had been sent:

To Fru Kringlen, Majorstua School, asking her if she could drum up some schoolchildren to sell stamps.

To Ågot Groth and Frøken Astrid Myhre, asking about potential continued help at the hospital or, if not, the return of Red Cross aprons etc, and possible help for the bazaar.

To Tyrigraven Restaurant, thanking them for feeding the elderly and the special food on the summer trip.

To Fru Vestby, regarding her request for help with baby essentials.

Fru Nordklev had received a letter of thanks from the Norwegian Mission of Israel for helping the German children. At the same time she received a bouquet of flowers, for which she thanked them in a letter dated 29/8.

Fagerborg department had been contacted by Fru Gunvor Johansson, surgical ward 3, Ullevål Hospital, though belonging to Kampen District, regarding help of some form, such as yarn for knitting etc. This will be looked into.

Finally, Fru Nordklev wished us luck with the Red Cross Week and urged everyone to get involved.

HOUSE CLEARANCE

Olaf Hall is standing by the bookshelves in the sitting room of the recently departed merchant H.W. Larsen, who was a familiar figure in the city's business community. During the war he earned substantial sums procuring mechanical equipment and genuine coffee for the occupying powers. His enemies called him the Village Shopkeeper. Others considered him a man of honour. If it takes time to amass a fortune, it takes very little to lose it. Anyone can do it. His son did it in two years. Now H.W. Larsen Jnr is leaning against a door frame lighting another cigarette and he is impatient. Olaf Hall feels unease or rather a kind of sadness. He has seen it before: a home no longer a home. But this is also a part of his work, going through a deceased's library. He sees at once what he has to deal with: collected works, Ibsen, Lie, Bjørnson and Elster stand in line, immaculate spines, probably unread. If he can get them cheap, he will take them. Young couples like to furnish their homes with collected works, but not at any price. Then Olaf Hall's gaze is attracted by a book at the very bottom, between the Gyldendal encyclopaedia and the Norwegian Kennel Club journals. The unease and sadness have gone. He feels the joy that is not unknown to fishermen when they have a bite.

He bends down and carefully takes out the book. It is Skeibrok and Kittelsen's *True Tales*, published in Kristiania 1913 and illustrated by Kittelsen himself. He is holding a treasure in his hand. It is gold and it is worth gold. Olaf Hall turns.

"A hundred kroner for Elster's collected works and this."

Larsen Jnr stubs out his cigarette and comes closer.

"Can't you take the whole pile of crap?"

"I'm afraid I don't have the room."

The son walks over to a desk, takes something from a drawer and shows it to Olaf Hall. It is a photo album. Olaf Hall is overcome by unease and sadness again. When those left behind want to sell the family album as well, they have sunk so deep that there is nothing left to lose. However, the worst part is that they think it is valuable because it is, or was, so valuable for them. But memories have no price. It is only the album that costs anything.

"There's a picture here of my father with King Haakon," Larsen Jnr says.

"I don't sell photos."

"It's from the inauguration of the Radium Hospital."

"I think you should keep the photo album."

The son throws it on a chair, both hurt and aloof.

"150," he says.

"It's a deal."

Olaf Hall lays two banknotes on the table. Then he puts the books into a little suitcase he always carries with him on such occasions. The son doesn't shake hands. He just lights another cigarette and casually stuffs the money in his pocket. Olaf Hall walks out, through the garden, and turns right into Josefines gate. Few areas in Oslo are more beautiful in the autumn than

Homansbyen; one would be Jessenløken in Fagerborg parish when the Virginia creeper is at its reddest. He stops for a moment and breathes in. One day this will happen to him, too. He can see it now: his home is no longer his. He can see Bjørn picking it apart and selling every bit to the highest bidder. Olaf Hall strides out and tries to enjoy his coup. If he can find the right collector he can sell *True Tales* for 800 kroner, maybe a thousand. On reaching Hegdehaugsveien he spots a stall at the corner of Oscars gate. It is the Red Cross bazaar. It is the Fagerborg department on top of that. Three women are trying to lure people in and not always succeeding. Olaf Hall strolls over. He still has a bone to pick with them. The raffle tickets cost three kroner each and the prizes are nothing to shout about. But that isn't the point. It is the cause that is the point. He asks for two, gives one of the women ten kroner and she gives him nos. 18 and 19 and four kroner back. He asks for a Red Cross stamp as well. The two other women are blowing up balloons. There is no prize, but if he buys another ticket he will be in the draw next Saturday and could win an Elna sewing machine. They don't recognise him. Olaf Hall suddenly feels sorry for them. He doesn't know why. It has something to do with their enthusiasm. He hasn't the heart to complain even.

"Thank you for the flowers and the membership," he says.

The air goes out of the balloons, the women turn and he carries on:

"But it wasn't necessary. Anyway, my wife would have appreciated the invitation."

It is only now they realise who he is and become animated. This is Ragnhild Hall's widower. That is all he is for them, the widower of a once acclaimed and latterly just a well-known actress. But he is something else for Maj Kristoffersen. For Maj Kristoffersen he is Fru Vik's, well, what is he actually? She can't quite find the word. He is her friend. That will have to do. She puts down the balloons and goes over to him, still breathless.

"Our pleasure," she says.

She proffers her hand.

"Maj Kristoffersen. I'm the treasurer of the Fagerborg department."

Fru Nordklev and Fru Larsen watch in amazement.

Olaf Hall shakes hands.

"Olaf Hall. Nice to meet you. Everything going well here?"

"We haven't really got started. Have we?"

Fru Nordklev and Fru Larsen shake their heads. Olaf Hall lets go of her hand.

"At least you've chosen a nice spot for it."

Maj points to his suitcase.

"Are you travelling?"

Olaf Hall laughs, opens the suitcase and places Kristian Elster's collected works on the counter.

"You can raffle these with pleasure. Then we can say we're absolutely quits."

Fru Nordklev comes over as well, introduces herself as the chairman and thanks him on behalf of the whole district. She can barely find the words. Olaf Hall is beginning to be embarrassed. This is too much friendliness. After all, it is only Kristian Elster. He closes the suitcase.

"Well, I wish you luck."

Olaf Hall is about to leave. Quickly, Maj leans over the

counter while Fru Nordklev and Fru Larsen are busy with a class from Uranienborg School who have come with their teacher to buy raffle tickets they have saved up for since the summer.

"I think we have a mutual acquaintance," she says.

Olaf Hall turns and looks at the quick-witted lady in the Red Cross pinny with a scarf tied under her chin. She reminds him of someone he has seen in a film, but can't remember who.

"Have we?"

Maj suddenly panics. What is she doing? Why can't she keep her mouth shut? This is not like her. She isn't herself. It is true. She isn't only herself. There are two of her. She should have stayed at home. She looks down, ashamed and angry.

"Have we?" Olaf Hall repeats.

"Margrethe Vik is our neighbour," Maj whispers.

When she looks up Olaf Hall is still there and she wishes he had gone. There is something refined about him, something men like to call affected: silk scarf around his neck, hat, pale hands. Ewald would probably go so far as to call him a ponce. Besides, he is much too thinly clad, only a suit and a cloak over his shoulders. The sun is shining, but it is unreliable and half-hearted in September. Maybe it is part of his profession. Working with old books must demand a different kind of care, training in the use of fingertips.

"How is she?" he asks.

Maj Kristoffersen regrets getting herself into this.

"She lives on the floor above us," she answers.

"I hope she's well. I haven't seen her since before the summer."

Maj rests on the counter for a second as a cloud draws shadows along the tram lines in Hegdehaugsveien. She laughs, much too loudly, inappropriately.

"Have you forgotten she visited you this summer?"

"I beg your pardon?"

Olaf Hall puts down the little suitcase. Maj is on the verge of tears. Whatever she says now, she won't get out of this.

"I thought she visited you."

"Did she say that? That she was going to visit me?"

Maj swallows and is calm again. It is too late to lie.

"Yes, that's what she said. She'd even packed a suitcase and ordered a taxi."

Olaf Hall says nothing for a while. Maj has to bring this to an end. The schoolchildren have been given their tickets. The first raindrops fall, heavy and scattered. Then they hammer down on the tarpaulin over the stall and people run helter-skelter. This is a different kind of rain from the summer showers that tend to invite peace or play. Fru Larsen saves Kristian Elster's collected works. Fru Nordklev takes Maj by the arm and her voice is as stern as only a chairman's can be:

"Now you cut along home before you get wet and cold."

Olaf Hall leans closer, he is already dripping.

"You're not ill, are you?"

Fru Nordklev answers for Maj:

"Our energetic treasurer is expecting a child, but trying to get her to rest is difficult of course."

"Then come with me. Don't argue. I insist."

Olaf Hall goes into the street and raises his arm, ignoring the rain. Soon a taxi arrives from the rank in Holtegaten and pulls up in front of the stall. Fru Nordklev and Fru Larsen help

Maj, who doesn't need any help, onto the back seat. Olaf Hall sits on the other side. He is silent, although Maj feels sure he knows the address.

"Kirkeveien 127," she says at length.

The driver crosses Bislett, goes up Norabakken, past Fagerborg Church and Jesseløkken. The autumn is losing its colour. It is falling with the rain. By October Oslo is already bare and waiting for its winter clothing. The taxi stops at Gørbitz gate. The driver switches off the meter. Maj is suddenly unsure. Should Olaf Hall get out with her?

"You mustn't get the wrong idea," he says.

"I haven't."

Olaf Hall stays seated. He glances up at the windows. The Virginia creeper will soon resemble steel wires criss-crossing the facades. He turns back to Maj.

"Do you think you can be happy twice?"

Maj doesn't like this conversation. It is too intimate. Fortunately the driver starts getting impatient.

"I already have a son and now I'm expecting a second child, as I said. So I would think you can."

"Would you at least say hello to Margrethe from me?"

"I will."

"And one more tiny thing."

Olaf Hall hesitates.

Maj wants to get away.

"Yes? What?"

"I'm happy to come along to one of your meetings and entertain."

"You entertain?"

"That may not be quite the right word. I read poems."

"What kind of poems?"

"My own. It's just a suggestion. Or an offer. Now I've said it."

Eventually Olaf Hall gets out, goes around the car and opens the door for Maj. She doesn't want any help. She can manage on her own. He looks up at the windows again. A curtain twitches. Then he gets in and the taxi goes to the top of Kirkeveien to turn there and carry on back down through Majorstua. The rain is soon no more than a shower, but the air is cold. There isn't a hint of summer in it. Maj shivers. It is warmer on the stairs. In summer it is the opposite. Then you can seek refuge in the cool shade here when it is more than 24 degrees outside. She has to hold the banisters. Fru Vik comes down from the second floor and helps her up the last part. Everyone wants to help Maj today. And she would rather manage on her own. But Maj has no choice when Fru Vik moves to support her. She wants to enter the hall as well, to be sure. She is worried about Maj. But after the door is closed she has other concerns on her mind.

"I simply want an explanation."

Maj hangs her coat on the hook and kicks off her shoes.

"An explanation of what?"

"Don't pretend. You know very well what I mean."

Maj has no choice now, either, and it strikes her she never has had.

"He came to our stall. And when it started raining he offered me a lift home. In a taxi."

"What did you say?"

"What did I say? I don't think I said anything. We spoke about Kristian Elster."

"Kristian Elster? What on earth has he got to do with anything?"

"He donated Kristian Elster's collected works to the raffle."

"What did you say about me, Maj?"

"I said we were neighbours."

"Did he bring up my name?"

"No, not as far as I remember."

"But why did you say we were neighbours then?"

Maj Kristoffersen can't stand it any longer.

"I recognised him. And—"

Fru Vik interrupts her.

"I suppose it was Ewald and his blabbermouth friends who couldn't restrain themselves."

"Ewald hasn't got anything to do with this."

"What did you say to Hall?"

"He said it was a long time since he'd seen you and so I asked him if he'd forgotten you went to see him this summer."

Fru Vik hides her face in her hands and leans against the wall.

"Oh, no. Oh, no."

Maj lays her hand gently on her shoulder.

"Didn't you go to see him after all?"

"I went to Hvitsten instead. To the hotel where Halfdan and I used to stay every summer."

"Perhaps that was for the best after all."

Fru Vik drops her hands and her face is calm, almost reconciled.

"How difficult this is," she says.

She walks to the door, stops and turns again.

"What do you think of him?"

Maj had hoped she wouldn't ask.

"He seemed like a gentleman."

"I can assure you that nothing has happened between us."

"And he offered to read his poems to us."

"Humph, I suppose you said no."

"Have you read them?"

"No, but that's hardly necessary . . ."

Fru Vik falls quiet. She is thinking about all the gossip, the voices behind her back, the glances.

"And he said hello. He was insistent I tell you. Say hello to Margrethe, he said."

The two women look at each other, smile for a moment and don't need to say another word for now. Maj closes the door behind her and goes into the sitting room. Ewald is in the armchair, in his outdoor clothes. She gives a start, frightened, not because Ewald might have heard what they were talking about, that doesn't matter, but because he was just sitting there with his coat on and his hat in his lap and it is only two o'clock.

"I'm going to ring the Red Cross personally and ask for you to be taken off duties in your condition, if you don't come to your senses soon," he says.

Maj breathes out, but not completely.

"What are you doing home so early?"

"There's something I have to tell you."

Ewald gets to his feet, takes a brown envelope from his inside pocket and pulls a type-written sheet from it. Maj is frightened again. Has Ewald been dismissed? Do they owe money? Or is it from the school? Has Jesper done something? Can't he keep up? She suddenly thinks: so much can go wrong. Most things can go wrong. Everything can. And Ewald? Hasn't he changed? Hasn't he become different, calmer, more attentive? But that's all for the good. The change ought to be a joy. She clenches her fists behind her back anyway and braces herself.

"Tell me then."

Ewald looks at her.

"We've got a telephone, Maj."

———

The board meeting was held on 3rd Oct at Fru Ingrid Foss's. The treasurer, Maj Kristoffersen, reported that the bazaar had made 1,275.20 kroner and the sale of stamps 4,644 kroner net, which exceeded all our expectations. The chairman informed us that she had a list of the names of the stamp sellers, which might be useful for a later occasion. Re.: the bazaar, we agreed that it was imperative for the closest districts to discuss in advance what prizes they want to purchase. We also agreed to take approx. 10,000 Christmas charity stamps to sell and perhaps some Christmas comics.

Maja Lessund had visited a woman in Ullevål Hospital who had asked the Red Cross for help because she had no possessions. A pawn ticket for shoes to the value of 12.40 kroner was redeemed for her. ML thinks the Red Cross cannot do any more as Poor Relief is the proper authority.

THE WINDOWS

The Kristoffersen family go for a walk. Ewald thinks it is best to go for walks before they have a telephone installed. Otherwise someone might ring while they are out. Maj laughs. Who would it be? Ewald reels off a few names: Rudjord, Ravn, Johnsen. There are also many others, it could be customers who want to get hold of Ewald or other agencies to make him tempting offers he unfortunately has to turn down because he is happy where he is. People have telephones quite simply to answer them when they ring and then you cannot be anywhere else.

"And Dr Lund," Maj says.

Ewald takes her hand and a thought occurs to him: Dr Lund could ring and tell her he is dead. He doesn't say anything for a while. It is Sunday. October has already sharpened the air. They walk past Gaustad Hospital. No-one would believe the insane lived there. Gaustad Hospital is like a castle and the red Virginia creeper that grows wild hides the last signs of the seasons. It is always autumn.

"And Jostein can ring Jesper," Ewald says.

Ewald lets go of Maj's hand and turns. Jesper has stopped halfway up the hill. He doesn't come when Ewald calls. Ewald goes down to him. Jesper is staring at the buildings. Ewald looks in the same direction. Someone is moving in a window, a shadow gliding past. In another window a face comes into view. The long, dark hair emphasises the white skin. It is smooth and transparent. They can see it right from where they are standing.

"Are there women inside, too?" Jesper asks.

"I suppose so. Ugh."

"What have they done?"

"Done? Well, they haven't done anything. They've just got bats in the belfries."

Ewald is about to explain this technical terminology from the Bristol and environs, but stops when he hears the serious tone to Jesper's voice.

"Why are they there though?"

"Someone has to look after them."

"Why?"

"Now that's too many questions, Jesper."

"Why?" he repeats.

"Because they can't look after themselves. Now let's go."

Ewald takes Jesper by the arm, but he won't budge.

"That's not true," he says.

Then the face in the window disappears, not to the side, it just merges into the darkness in the background while the light from the white skin lingers for a few seconds before it too is gone. They walk uphill to Maj and carry on to the fields that stretch all the way to Lake Sognsvann and shine like molten silver. The forest fringe is displayed in all its colours. There are other people out walking too, friends, married couples, lovers. They seem happy. Smiles all round. No-one is in a hurry, but they still keep a good pace. It is the kind of day when life is actually eternal.

"This should be in the jubilee, too," Maj says.

Ewald stops:

"What should?"

"Nature. That's Oslo as well, after all."

"Yes, most of it is nature."

"So it'll be women and nature, will it?"

Ewald shrugs.

"Unfortunately we have to put in some history."

Maj looks at him.

"Is Rudjord still as enthusiastic about your idea?"

"There are always lots of ideas. And the best one wins. Or we take a bit from each and cobble them together."

"I'm sure yours is best."

"Yes, from the first Norwegian feminist Camilla Collett to Maj Kristoffersen."

Ewald kisses her on the cheek.

"Perhaps we should turn around," she says.

They take a different way back, down Damefallet, a line of grass between Nordberg and Sogn, so that they can visit Ewald's father in Tåsen Old People's Home. It is sensible after all to find a purpose for a walk. Alf Kristoffersen is no more than seventy-two years old, but when his wife, Signe, passed away in 1939, all too early, he couldn't manage on his own, he stayed with Ewald and Maj during the war and then moved here. Ewald begged him half-heartedly to stay, but there was no question of it, and everyone was happy about that. Alf Kristoffersen had been a rep for Herkules Confektionsfabrik, a textile factory in Thorvald Meyers gate, and he criss-crossed the country selling suits, coats, shirts, pyjamas and ties. The company's slogan was *The well-dressed man's clothes*. He isn't in the dining room where mostly women are sitting. In general the residents are mainly women. They outlive men, apart from his mother. Men die like flies, Ewald thinks. A menu hangs on the wall by the door: *Wednesday: Curried fish balls. Fruit soup. Thursday: Pork sausage. Salad. Macaroni pudding. Friday: Porridge. Saturday: Peas. Pork. Jelly.* Jesper is holding his nose. Maj quickly grabs his hand. In the end they find Alf Kristoffersen in the smoking saloon. This is where the men have sought refuge. He spots his son, concludes a heated conversation, puts his pipe in the ashtray and accompanies them to his room. Ewald is pleased his father is still well dressed and wears a watch chain in his waistcoat. On the wall above his bed he has a photograph of Ewald's mother. Otherwise he has found room for an armchair from the flat where they lived, the rest of the furniture belongs to the home. On the windowsill there is a busy Lizzie. It is dry. Maj fetches a glass from the corridor and waters it. Alf Kristoffersen sits down in the armchair. Jesper stands by the door.

"What were you talking about?" Ewald asks.

"What we were talking about?"

"It sounded a little spirited in there."

"We were discussing this new city hall. And we decided we would call it the Brown Cheese."

Ewald laughs.

"The Brown Cheese. I'll remember that, Pappa. The Brown Cheese."

"There's not much to laugh about, I'm telling you. That

junk blocks a view of the fjord. Oslo is no longer a city by the fjord, but a city behind the City Hall."

"I'm inclined to agree with you."

"Akselsen in No. 8 thought the opposite of course. He always does. He's dreadfully annoying."

"But at least it makes for a conversation."

"He has to be so *modern*. He wears a wig. What good is being modern when we're going to die?"

"You don't have to say that, Pappa."

"Why have you come here?"

"Why? To tell you you're going to be a grandfather again."

Maj stands in front of Alf Kristoffersen, who holds her hips and smiles. The old charmer appears between a glint of happiness and melancholy.

"Now I can see. Well I never."

Then he turns to Jesper, who hasn't moved from the spot, but Jesper speaks first.

"What do you eat on Sunday?" he asks.

Alf Kristoffersen lets go of Maj and considers the question.

"What the dickens did we eat today? I remember. They fry up all the leftovers from the week and serve them with crisp bread."

Maj laughs:

"Come on now."

They are silent for a moment. You can feel the weight of the place. You can feel it in the slowness of everything, a kind of horizontal gravity. Here, everyone is on a plodding walk. Jesper opens the door and sees two carers pushing a bed past. Someone is in the bed. He closes the door.

"Can you do me a favour?" Alf Kristoffersen asks.

Ewald puts his hand on his shoulder and for a moment is unsure which of them is trembling.

"Of course, Pappa. What's the favour?"

"Go down to the grave and say hello to Signe from me."

"We will."

"And take the flower with you."

"Don't you want to come with us? We can take a taxi."

Alf Kristoffersen shakes his head and interlaces his fingers in his lap.

"I don't want her to see me like this."

"Pappa, you're perfectly presentable. You could even come with us to the Bristol."

"I should've followed her. I should. We should've gone together."

Ewald asks Maj and Jesper to wait in the corridor. When they are alone, he sits on the bed and looks his father in the eye.

"I don't want you to talk like that when Jesper is in hearing distance. And especially not when Maj's in the family way. What's got into you?"

Ewald's father looks down at his hands in his lap.

"I just miss her more and more."

Ewald thinks that it is only right and fair, now it is his father's turn to miss Signe, his mother missed Alf when they were both alive, and he has a lot of catching up to do.

"That was a nice thing to say."

"It's not just something I say. Like you do."

"Let's not start that again, Pappa."

"And it would've been best if I'd died as well."

"There you go again. I don't want to hear it, either. Do you promise me you'll never say it again?"

Alf Kristoffersen looks up.

"I don't think I can."

Ewald takes the plant from the windowsill, goes out to Maj and Jesper and they walk down to Vestre Cemetery. Signe Kristoffersen's burial place isn't far from the chapel, closer to Frogner Park, where you can hear the dogs barking. Actually, that is unseemly. The silence of the graveyard is shattered. Signe Kristoffersen worked part-time at Jacobsen's grocery in Skillebekk. She was mostly responsible for the cash register when Jacobsen was busy elsewhere. She was born in 1881 and died in 1938, from a heart attack, one morning she didn't wake up. Ewald usually says that Maj has inherited her economical ways from his parents while he has inherited his common sense from her parents. And it strikes him that Maj might think the same as his father: that she should follow Ewald when he dies. The thought is unbearable. Maj must carry on living, just like today, live for ever, and it doesn't matter if she finds someone else, so long as he is good to her, Jesper and the new child. Ewald wants to explain this to Maj, at least some of it, he simply wants to unburden his heart, but this is impossible. He has to carry this alone. It is heavy. It is his choice. Instead he gives the dry house plant to Maj and says:

"Mamma might've been a busy Lizzie, but this weed's not going to be on her grave."

"It's what Alf wanted."

"He wasn't himself today. Brown Cheese! Chuck it away. Jesper and I'll fix her grave in the meantime."

Maj finds the refuse bin by the tap and disposes of the busy Lizzie, pot and all. Then she spots a young man crouching by a grave. He isn't doing anything. Just crouching. Maj thinks there is something familiar about him, fair, slightly thinning hair, a face that seems weak and kind at the same time. Then she remembers. It is the young man who saved Jostein's life. She closes the refuse bin quietly and walks the short distance over to him. Now she can see the name on the gravestone too: *Ragnhild Hall.* Bjørn Stranger becomes aware of her presence and straightens up. Maj shouldn't have done it, gone over to him. She regrets going over.

"Is she the actress?" she asks.

"Yes. Why?"

"She was famous."

"I'm her son."

"She died much too young. She could've given us pleasure for many more years."

Maj stretches out her hand. Bjørn is embarrassed, he rarely, or never, hears anyone say anything like this, something nice about his mother, the last person was that lady, Fru Vik, to whom he took the fur coat. But she talked about the old days, about Alving and Ibsen and the big roles. Then people often said nice things about her. Afterwards people stopped talking about Ragnhild Hall. He shakes hands with Maj and lets go just as quickly. He is cold.

"Actually the name on the grave should be 'Ragnhild Stranger'."

"Oh? I only know her as Hall."

Bjørn looks at Maj and feels revulsion.

"I'd like to be here on my own," he says.

Maj can feel herself blushing.

"Sorry. I only wanted to thank you."

"Why? What for?"

"You saved Jostein's life. My son's friend."

"I didn't save anyone's life."

"Yes, you did. In Kirkeveien. The boy who was knocked down. I saw you."

"You're mistaken."

Maj is about to dig her heels in, it *is* him, but she doesn't. She prefers to beat a retreat. Bjørn Stranger crouches down by the grave again and watches the woman walking back to the others, obviously her husband and son, and saying something to them. They turn towards him. The boy raises his hand and waves. Probably he was told to. Bjørn Stranger is furious. They won't leave him in peace. Suddenly he thinks how it must have been for his mother in those days, *in her day*, never being able to walk in peace down the street, all the looks. He stands up, brushes the knees of his trousers and walks over to the stupid family. He walks at a fast, determined pace. The mother pulls the boy close. The father just stands there, heavy, legs apart, stretches out his arms and watches Bjørn carefully. He is protecting his family. Bjørn is laughing inside. This father is like some insignificant person who is never going to find his place in the world because he doesn't know any better. *Doesn't know any better.* That is Bjørn Stranger's favourite expression. *They don't know any better.* That is how it is with most people. They don't know any better. Bjørn Stranger knows better. He stops in front of the woman and is about to open his mouth. He is going to express his opinion. At that moment the boy looks up at him. His eyes are cold and admiring. Bjørn Stranger loses his thread and instead asks:

"What was his name?"

The boy answers:

"Jostein Melsom."

"Was he hurt?"

"He can't hear very well."

"That can be fixed."

"And he's a bit odd in the head."

"Then you'd better say hello to Jostein Melsom from Bjørn Stranger and get well soon. Don't forget. 'Stranger'."

Bjørn Stranger turns and walks towards the gates of Frogner Park, where the dogs don't stop barking. It is time to start wearing a coat. Tomorrow he will wear a coat. He doesn't have to be cold. He continues across the Bridge of Sighs. At Frogner square the Disen tram comes to a halt. No-one alights. Outside the house on the next corner he sees a letter poking out of the slit in the post box attached to the fence post. The people living there must be away for the weekend. Bjørn Stranger stops, pretends to tie his shoelace, snatches the letter and quickly stuffs it in his pocket. He walks on. He finds this amusing. It is just a little prank. But perhaps it is a very important letter, which might change a life, turn it upside down, for better or worse. By then it is no longer a trivial matter. It is a catastrophe. Bjørn Stranger has intervened. He likes this notion. Of intervening. He changes the course of events, not for himself, but for others. When he arrives home he sees Olaf in the bookshop with this woman again, Fru Vik. He thought that was over, well, that there was nothing between them. Bjørn Stranger uses the other entrance instead, to the kitchen. There is a smell of food. A pot of lamb is simmering on the stove. In the living room the table is set for two. He hears them on the stairs. They see him. Fru Vik stops behind Olaf, nods, almost blushes. This is the second time today he has seen it. Bjørn Stranger can't bear old women who blush. He hangs up his coat.

"I believe you've met before," Olaf says.

Bjørn laughs.

"Yes. What has she left behind today?"

"I think I should leave," Fru Vik says.

Olaf Hall holds her, but he doesn't take his eyes off Bjørn.

"She was just here to fetch a book I couldn't sell. An animal husbandry manual. Perhaps you may have some use for it?"

"I'm not a vet. I save people's lives."

"And then I invited her to a meal. Would you like to eat with us?"

"I don't think you want me to."

Fru Vik takes a step forward and says:

"Not at all, Bjørn. I would like it. Very much."

Olaf Hall sets a place for his stepson and opens a bottle of wine. They don't say much during the meal. The lamb fricassee tastes good. Fru Vik says so anyway. That the food tastes good. She goes to help them clear the table, but changes her mind. That would be imposing herself. She is a guest. She has to follow the house rules for guests. She doesn't want to appear over-familiar already. While Olaf Hall gets the dessert ready in the kitchen Bjørn sits down again and refills her glass.

"It'll soon be time to wear a fur coat," he says.

"Not until it starts to snow."

"But that could be any time. One morning it'll be there. It happens overnight. Without our knowing."

Fru Vik sips her wine and looks at Bjørn. His hair is unkempt. The receding hairline is visible and makes him look older, or rather he looks like a mixture, an old man's hairstyle and a face that is still child-like.

"It's true," she says.

Bjørn notices her eyes, he realises what she can see and slowly runs his hand over his temple, forehead.

"What's true, Fru Vik? That snow falls at night?"

"That you save people's lives."

Olaf Hall comes in with the dessert, made with plums from the garden.

"This was Ragnhild's favourite. She could never have enough of it."

Fru Vik helps herself to the compote, not much, she thinks, without actually thinking about it, about her weight. She wants to have a trim figure. Actually she isn't hungry anymore. She passes the jug of cream and the dish on to Bjørn, who jumps up.

"May I leave the table?"

Olaf Hall takes the cream and just shakes his head.

"Can I say no?"

Bjørn goes up to his room on the floor above and lies down on the sofa bed. He tries to hear what they are saying in the room below, but the conversation is lost between floors. He takes out the letter. The stamps are American and bear a Washington D.C. postmark. ANNE-KARINE WELT, KIRKEVEIEN 8, OSLO 2. NORWAY/NORGE. What is most visible, an act of goodness or evil? It depends on the consequences. But are the consequences the real yardstick? Killing a bird while no-one is watching? Is that better for that reason? Bjørn opens the envelope and takes out a sheet of lined paper. The writing is feminine, the letter isn't long:

Dear Mother,

You and Peter obviously didn't hit it off last time we were at home. And it bothers him and me that we didn't talk this through. I've tried to call you, but you don't answer. Anyway perhaps it's best to write. I can see you're against us settling down here, so far away, but that's the way it is. It's my decision. And you have to accept that. And that's why you have to accept Peter, too. And you should be in no doubt that I miss you every single day. But when we have more money (Peter's been promised a higher post in the department or whatever they call it) we can also return to Norway more often. Now I'm going to tell you why I'm really writing and want all our disagreements behind us. You're going to be a grandmother! I'm expecting and the baby's due in February! We're so happy! I hope you'll write as soon as you can (or ring). Then I'll hear from you anyway! Lots of love, Helene. (Peter says hi too. He's at work. It's half past nine in the morning here) . . .

Bjørn Stranger has to laugh. So banal. But Helene is linguistically sloppy and her mother is bound to notice. In just a few lines *home* becomes *Norway*. The daughter has already lost. Perhaps it was just as well that Anne-Karine Welt didn't get to read this letter. He scrunches it up and tosses it into the wastepaper basket. The idea thrills him: letters that are lost in transit, messages that don't arrive. Above the desk, on which the last lecture folder still lies, an adornment, hangs a Royal Dramatic Theatre poster, Ragnhild Stranger starring with Gösta Ekman in "Peer Gynt", Stockholm, 1931. Was that the pinnacle? It was one of the peaks. Bjørn was three years old then, or four. He remembers that his mother was often absent. More often than not she was absent. So much greater the joy, whenever she returned. He sleeps lightly, just a doze, which for a while torments him with a series of images, or moments, each one giving way to the next, blending and fading: the hoisted stage, the curtain, the auditorium, snow falling from the chandelier, the dead woman in the seat, a bright light and masks in a never-ending mirror, a bus braking, the boy hanging in the air for a second, will he fly or fall? Bjørn is woken by a car pulling up outside. He already has a cold on the way. There is no easier place to catch a cold than in a cemetery. He walks over to the window. Olaf Hall holds open the rear door, helps Fru Vik into the back and closes it again. She peers out, waves and catches a glimpse of Bjørn on the top floor, standing still, his hands behind his back, it seems to her. Olaf Hall also raises a hand and bends down, his face suddenly close to hers. Fru Vik tells the driver the address: the corner of Jonas Reins gate and Kirkeveien. She doesn't want anyone to see her coming home in a taxi. She leans back, closes her eyes and hears the rapid swish-swish of the windscreen wipers. They arrive, she pays with coins, gets out and unlocks the door to the yard. She hurries through the rain to the rear entrance. There is a light on in Maj's kitchen. Otherwise it is dark, curtains are drawn. Fru Vik stops on the first floor, hesitates, knocks. Maj opens the door shortly afterwards.

"I was just wondering if everything was alright with you."

"Yes. Everything's fine. How . . .?"

"I saw the light on, so . . ."

Maj has ink on her fingers, her smile is tired:

"I have to finish the accounts. There are so many numbers.

First we're in the black, then I find a bill and we're back in the red. Helping comes at a cost, I can tell you."

"Don't wear yourself out, Maj."

"That's what Ewald says."

"So there are two of us telling you."

Maj wipes her hands on her apron and looks at Fru Vik in surprise.

"Are you crying?"

"Crying? What makes you think that? It's raining."

"We can't hang the washing out now then."

"Promise me you'll say if you need any help taking your washing to the drying loft."

"Jesper will help me. Ewald has started to give him pocket money. He could help you too, by the way."

"I don't know if I can afford him."

Both of them laugh. Maj goes to stroke Fru Vik's cheek, she seems so sad, almost unhappy, but sees all the ink and refrains.

"Is it still as difficult?" she asks.

Fru Vik just nods. They stand for a while without speaking. Then Maj closes the door and Fru Vik holds on to the banister. The back stairs are a lot narrower and steeper than the main staircase.

Our next meeting after the bazaar was held at the chairman's flat. We filled and stuffed dolls we are going to sell privately for 2.50 kroner apiece. Also we're going to raffle a Christmas doll that Fru Lessund is sewing for us, and one pram with a little doll, a pillow and blankets Fru Endresen is making.

Otherwise we had two applications to discuss. Kåre

Solendal, Thereses gate 12, born 2/3/1934, sixteen years old, had lost his right leg; he was applying for a loan of 360 kroner towards an invalid carriage. We don't lend money of course. But after Fru Lund went down to talk to his mother and heard how they were struggling financially – the mother was ill and on disability benefit – we decided to give him the 360 kroner. Great was the joy!

The second application was from Frøken Hansen in Stensgate. She had also lost a leg many years ago and lived with an ailing aunt who'd had pneumonia three times. She has almost no clothes and has got into debt because of her aunt's illness. We bought her a dress, Frøken Skancke gave her a good coat, Frøken Lessund some clothes she no longer wore and we gave her a hundred kroner in cash. To be frank, we had expected a little more gratitude from them.

OUT OF PROPORTION

Jesper decides he will never be fat. He does this after seeing his father naked in the bathroom. It happens by accident. It would never have occurred to Jesper to see him like this of his own accord, and Ewald probably wouldn't have wished to reveal himself in the buff to his son's eyes either, that honour falls to Maj alone. But Jesper's father forgets to lock the door, or Jesper forgets to knock, and in he goes to wash and his father is standing there without even a towel around him. Most fathers are quite fat. Jostein's father is quite fat. But this is something else. Jesper stops in his tracks and cannot move. The sight is too overwhelming. In some way or other he has to rid himself of it. He just doesn't know how. The last thing he should do is cry. Jesper doesn't. He clenches his teeth. They don't know how long they remain rooted to the spot, Jesper in his pyjama trousers and Ewald in nothing, but it isn't long. It is impossible to stand there for more than a few seconds. It is also hard to say who is more ashamed. Perhaps I ought to be relieved, Jesper thinks. If Pappa is that fat he can hardly be ill, can he? I should say something or run away, preferably the latter. His father is the first to move.

"Right, Jesper. Now you've seen this, too."

Ewald Kristoffersen coolly walks out, still naked, and Jesper spends an age in the bathroom this morning.

When they have breakfast, Jesper isn't hungry. Maj is concerned, but Ewald says that scientific research shows that the appetite of eight-year-olds is particularly low on Wednesdays and increases gradually towards the weekend. It is Wednesday today. And, besides, it isn't she who should be concerned about Jesper; it is they who should be concerned about her. To which Maj says that they don't need to be, while putting Jesper's packed lunch at the top of his satchel. The Kristoffersen family have nothing at all to be concerned about. But for a second, and that is more than enough, Ewald has a feeling that Jesper can see right through him out to the other side, like an X-ray machine. Whether he had been wearing a dressing gown, armour or full evening dress, the result would have been exactly the same. From now on he will have to remember to lock the door. From now on he will have to lock all the doors. He looks at Jesper, who avoids his gaze.

"Let's not blow this out of proportion," Ewald says.

Jesper has to wear a scarf, but refuses to wear a hat. The wind in Kirkeveien can flip your ears inside out and he regrets not taking the hat, but he has other things on his mind. At Ole Vigs gate he stops, takes off his satchel, opens it, there is no-one in the vicinity, and he throws his packed lunch into the litter bin there. He is never going to eat again. Then he puts his satchel back on – it feels a lot lighter now – runs and catches up with Jostein, who couldn't be bothered to wait for him any longer.

In the big break Jesper already starts to get hungry. He grasps the wire fence like a prisoner in Belsen. Jostein comes over to him. He is wearing ear-warmers today. He lifts one flap and wants to know if Jesper has forgotten his packed lunch. If so, Jostein has plenty of food and would be happy to share. This conversation consists of fewer words than gestures. Actually the verbal element is not that important. Eventually Jesper shakes his head. He doesn't want any of Jostein's packed lunch, even if that is precisely what he craves. The bell rings. Jostein stuffs the last slices of bread, probably with a liver-paste spread on them, into his jacket pocket and they walk back to the classroom together. In the fourth lesson Jesper has a headache. Hunger isn't on the syllabus. You don't get hunger homework. Hunger is something you have to learn about on your own. In the fifth lesson he can't take any more. He can't sit still. His restlessness increases. It is worse than falling. He is disappointed in himself. Hunger is his weakest subject. The only positive side of it is that he forgets the image of his father in the bathroom and prefers to imagine the flattened but juicy sandwiches in Jostein's jacket hanging on a hook in the corridor. He raises his hand. Løkke is finishing the letter G, which in his opinion occupies a special position in the alphabet, so he asks the pupils to pay particular attention to it. Then at length he addresses Jesper.

"I suspect I know what you're going to ask, but say it anyway."

"I need the bog."

"What did you say?"

"The lavatory."

"Exactly. That's better."

"Thank you."

Jesper makes a move to get up, but Løkke places his pointer on his shoulder.

"And I'm sure you can restrain yourself until the lesson has finished. Then you can go home to the lavatory for as long and as often as you wish."

Løkke sits down behind his raised desk and flicks through an exercise book. Jesper lowers his gaze and mumbles *You cackbag*. Løkke is on his feet so fast the class thinks he never sat down. At any rate he swoops in front of Jesper's desk, his chin quivering.

"*What* did you say?"

Jesper still mumbles:

"Cackbag."

"Louder, Jesper Kristoffersen."

"You cackbag!"

Løkke slaps him so hard that for an instant both of them are on fire, Jesper's cheek and Løkke's palm. No-one has ever hit Jesper before. The surprise is greater than the pain. Actually it doesn't hurt at all. He is just amazed. And it is the first time Løkke has hit anyone. He hasn't laid a hand on even the toughest louts from Aleksander Kiellands Plass. His voice is strangely meek when he has collected himself.

"Go to the corridor, Jesper."

Jesper goes to the corridor, locates Jostein's jacket and eats the last two sandwiches. He was right. It was liver-paste. It has seldom tasted better. When the bell rings, the class walks quietly past him. Usually they grab their coats and run. Jesper sees something in their eyes, admiration in some, scorn in others. Jostein stops and points to his mouth. Jesper doesn't quite understand what he means. Is he referring to the word he used, cackbag? Jesper mouths the word; he daren't say it out aloud. Jostein shakes his head and keeps pointing. Jesper wipes his lips with the back of his hand. It is sticky with liver-paste. Jostein smiles. Then he nods towards the open door. Jesper wipes his fingers on his trousers, goes back into the classroom and closes the door behind him. Løkke is sitting at his desk. He isn't meek any longer. Ashamed is more how he seems. He doesn't say anything until Jesper has packed his satchel.

"I've never struck a pupil before."

Jesper chooses to remain silent until he is forced to answer. Løkke gets to his feet and comes down to him.

"I'm afraid you're the first, Jesper."

It isn't a question. Jesper is silent, head bowed. It is best like that. Løkke continues:

"And I'm sorry. Because you're a good boy."

These words are so deep inside the hardened man that they barely reach the surface with the meaning intact. They are silent again. Jesper wonders why he is a good boy. Then Løkke says, and his voice is firmer now:

"Are *you* sorry, Jesper?"

"I am."

Løkke lingers before returning to his desk. Now he just seems lonely. It is a sad sight. In the empty classroom between the board and the desks Løkke appears lost. One day he will disappear in the chalk. One day the writing on the board will say: *Free!* It strikes Jesper that everyone seems lonely, not all the time, but for moments, in turbulent or perfectly still moments. Grandpa does, Mamma, Jostein, Dr Lund, Fru Vik, especially Fru Vik, Pappa, no, he can't bear to think about

Pappa, but he too has loneliness lodged somewhere in his blubber. Jesper shrugs on his satchel, bows and opens the door. Løkke's heart is heavier now.

"I've noticed, you see, the way you take care of Jostein," he says.

Jesper turns. Løkke shouldn't have said that. Jesper doesn't take care of anyone. Jostein is his friend.

"Jostein's my friend," he says.

"And I hope he continues to be when he finishes with us."

Jesper suddenly feels his own loneliness. It shows.

"Is Jostein going to finish?"

"He's going to a special school. For the deaf."

"Jostein isn't deaf."

"His hearing's getting worse and worse."

"I hear for him."

Løkke raises his arm.

"That's what I keep saying. You're a good boy. Off you go now."

When Jesper emerges in the playground Jostein is waiting for him by the gates. Jesper slows down. Why didn't Jostein say anything? A thought strikes Jesper: Perhaps Jostein doesn't know himself? Jesper stops.

"Did it hurt?" Jostein shouts.

Jesper leans towards his good ear.

"May I ask your father about something?"

They walk together up Kirkeveien. Jesper goes into the shop with Jostein. A customer has to be served first. She wants some minced pork and smoked sausage. The butcher adds and takes away until he has the precise weight the customer has asked for, neither too much nor too little. Then Jostein's mother takes payment at the till and goes with the customer to the door. Jostein turns to Jesper. Jesper prepares himself, changes his mind at the last minute and instead asks:

"What does "to blow out of proportion" mean?"

"Blow out of proportion? Where have you heard that?"

"Oh, somewhere."

The butcher washes his hands and leans across the counter.

"To blow out of proportion means not to see things as they really are. The exact opposite of what we do here. To be inexact, it means. Doesn't it, Mother?"

His wife goes back to the till, pushes in the cash drawer and looks at Jostein, who is watching her mouth.

"Which of you two was kept in? Or were you just dawdling?"

Jesper puts his hand in the air.

"Me."

The butcher shakes his head and smiles:

"Or if someone tells you not to blow things out of proportion, it can mean don't worry too much about how things are," he says.

Jesper has enough to think about as he walks the last weather-beaten part of Kirkeveien on his own. Is this exactly what Pappa is doing, isn't he worrying about how things are? Does he want Jesper to do the same? Does it mean that nothing is clear-cut? The thought is absolutely terrifying. Yet it is a kind of comfort, too. And this is even more terrifying, even if he has suspected it all along: that something can be both terrifying and a comfort. Jesper decides to use the back stairs. This is a day for back stairs. And he has his own key for the yard door. He has a bunch of keys. That means something.

Keys are freedom. Keys can open and close. His mother is sitting in the kitchen crying. She is holding her face in her hands and her whole body is shaking. She doesn't even look up when Jesper bursts in. He comes to an abrupt halt and leaves the door open behind him. A strange noise is coming from the cup on the table. It is the teaspoon, emitting a shrill sound that eventually fills Jesper's head to the brim. The teaspoon is crying. Then his mother looks up. Her eyes are dry now. Her gaze is stern and unwelcoming. Another person has taken her over.

"How could you?" she says.

Jesper's first thought is that Løkke has been here. But he can't quite make that tally. He will have to grope his way forward.

"When do we get the telephone?"

His mother stands up and Jesper braces himself for the second slap of the day. It doesn't come. She sits down again, holding her hands over her belly now, though with her eyes still fixed on him. Then she looks out of the window, and the spoon on the yellow plate is quiet.

"Ingrid Foss has been here," she says.

"Who?"

"Ingrid Foss from the Red Cross. The woman who lives down in Ole Vigs gate."

Maj doesn't say anything for a while and Jesper finds no reason to say anything, either. He has a hunch. He has a hunch he knows what is coming. He prays for something to prevent it. A bomb falling. Who cares who drops it? Maj scratches her neck.

"Don't you like my food?"

"Yes, I do."

"Why do you throw away your packed lunch then?"

She gets up before Jesper has a chance to answer and this time she intends to stay there.

"You *threw* away your packed lunch! Which I made for you here in the kitchen! And you throw it away in full view of everyone living on the corner of Kirkeveien and Ole Vigs gate."

"I—"

"Don't you even dare! Don't you even dare to dare! Ingrid Foss saw you. Ingrid Foss from the board of the Fagerborg department of the Oslo District Red Cross saw you throw away your packed lunch!"

Jesper realises at once that it is impossible not to worry, whichever way you look at it. What can he say in his defence? He can say he saw his father naked in the bathroom. He would prefer not to bring the matter up. Besides it would be telling tales. That is the last thing he wants to do. Telling tales? This is how Jesper thinks. The thought occurs to him without any reflection and it comes instantly. It is like an electric shock. He'd rather say that he is falling. But he has already fallen. He has fallen as low as it is possible to go. Jesper says nothing. He has nothing to say. His mother has:

"And while other children are starving! And while lots of children would've been happy just for the topping. For the very *crust* of the bread!"

"Sorry."

"Why, Jesper?"

Neck bowed:

"Sorry, Mamma."

"That's not good enough. It's no good just saying sorry."

"What should I do then?"

"Perhaps you'd like to meet the Jewish children from Germany? Would you?"

Neck bowed even lower:

"Not really."

Maj opens the pantry door with a bang, takes out the jettisoned packed lunch and slings it onto the kitchen table.

"Eat it," she says.

Jesper sits down and opens the lunch. The cheese has gone hard at the edges. Every bite grows in his mouth. The crusts are soft and disgusting. The sandwiches are bigger than he is. What good is this supposed to be doing? Will the starving have full stomachs now? Will the starving be happy to know that Jesper is being made to suffer? Will he fill all their mouths? His mother stands with her arms crossed and her eyes fixed on him.

"Is it good?" she asks.

Jesper understands. He understands the calculation of punishment. After the act and the words comes the punishment. This is punishment. This is Mamma's slap. It is worse than Løkke's. It is a slow, protracted slap. Once he has finished eating, Jesper goes to the loo and spews up. He is sure his mother hears, but she says nothing. He pulls the chain, goes into the sitting room and pretends to do his homework. When Ewald comes home Maj is unusually quiet and walks on her toes. Jesper senses it. The slightest movement beyond the norm affects him too: his father's vigilance, his mother's voice, which is occasionally heard, short words, lower-case. Jesper goes to bed early. In the end the world is no greater than the vestibule he cannot sleep in. He can hardly breathe. This is how it must be for Jostein, locked into silence, into what soon will be without any sound, only gestures, looks, slips of paper. Pappa comes in wearing pyjamas and squats down by his bed.

"You lost your appetite when you saw me this morning, didn't you?" he says.

Jesper rolls over. He doesn't cry. Ewald spreads the duvet over him.

"Mamma's sorry she forced you to eat the packed lunch."

"She didn't force me."

"But you have to understand this was awful for her. The Red Cross seeing you. The Red Cross of all people. You were terribly unlucky, Jesper."

"Yes."

"But we won't be ungrateful, Jesper. And we won't make demands on you, either. By the way, I'm going to lose some weight."

"Me, too."

"You're already double Belsen."

Jesper turns to his father.

"What does cackbag mean?"

"Cackbag? Where on earth did you get that word from?"

"You."

"Have you called someone a cackbag, Jesper?"

"Løkke, my teacher."

"Oh, no. I suppose you got a slap?"

"Yes."

"Cackbag means, and I'll whisper this so that Mamma can't hear, cackbag means a shit. And not just that. It means a real shit. The worst kind."

Jesper turns away again.

"Then I'm a cackbag," he whispers.

Ewald pats his son on the shoulder.

"No, you aren't. Today we're not worrying, right, so we'll forget everything that's happened."

"Can we do that?"

"Oh, yes, that's what's so good about us humans. We can put things behind us."

Ewald straightens up and goes back to his bedroom. Jesper dreams. In his dreams nothing is out of proportion. Everything is absolutely as it should be. If Jostein moves to the school of silence, loneliness will remain at his desk and loneliness will accompany Jesper every single day. Loneliness also has a father who is a butcher.

———

The board meeting was held on 31/10/49 at Fru Lessund's. Those present were: the chairman, Fru Berit Nordklev, Fru Ingrid Arnesen, Fru Maj Kristoffersen, Fru Lessund and Fru Ingrid Foss. The chairman read out circulars re.: the training of hospital friends and volunteer nurses. In addition, the minutes of the working committee on 28/10/49 were read out. The chairman, Fru Nordklev, expressed her appreciation of the accounts presented by our treasurer, Maj Kristoffersen, whose work was described as exemplary by the board of the Norwegian Red Cross.

The chairman had ordered a hundred Christmas comics and 10,000 charity stamps, which we hope to sell for Christmas.

The allocation of material and yarn was agreed and the board decided to buy fifty metres of coloured cotton cloth and a quantity of linen sheets.

The chairman gave an update on the crèche we would like to set up.

It was decided to hold a members' meeting in Fagerborg parish hall on 23/11/49. Entertainment will be in the form of a talk, a film and possibly the "Nurses' Choir".

It was noted that a letter of thanks had been received from Fru Ingrid Nyhaug for baby equipment.

1/11/49 Ingrid Foss

THE SNOWMAN

Ewald Kristoffersen wakes up alone. A bare white light makes the bedroom seem unfamiliar, his first thought: hotel. He has never stayed in a hotel, yet this is what he thinks, hotel. He lies there for a few moments, once again stretching out a hand to be sure that Maj isn't there. She isn't. She has left him. No, he has left her. He has detached himself. That is the size of it. Ewald Kristoffersen gets out of bed. He opens the vestibule door. The blanket is tight over Jesper's bed. He can't hear anyone. He calls their names and can't hear his own voice, either. He has seen this furniture and these lamps before. He has also seen the wall clock before. Yet everything is unfamiliar. He is in a hotel. Are there more guests here? He goes into the kitchen. No-one is sitting at the table. No-one is standing by the stove. He remembers something from his previous life, the telephone. It is annoying that they still don't have one. Then he could have rung home and said he was dead. They mustn't worry. They can come and visit him. They don't need to bring anything. It is enough for them to come. Ewald Kristoffersen stands by the window. The light is getting whiter and brighter. He has to hold his hands in front of his eyes.

The darkness is in his skin, fingers, under his nails. Then he can see. It has snowed during the night. The first sound he hears is the church bells. It is Sunday. Maj is sitting downstairs in the yard, wearing a winter coat and hat. Jesper is standing behind the washing lines; there are only pegs on it now. He is also wearing a hat. He is looking at the other children who are making a snowman. This sight, of Maj and Jesper, makes Ewald Kristoffersen despise the freedom he once tasted. He doesn't want to be detached. He wants to be attached. He is filled with enormous love and sorrow. Then Jesper ambles over to the children, who are younger than he is, and helps them with the snowman. But there still isn't enough snow, just a thin coating and it doesn't stick, either. It occurs to Ewald that he will never see the snowman finished. And if he does, he will never see it melt.

———

Since the previous board meeting on 31st Oct. Fagerborg department has had its hands full feeding the German children from the Mission of Israel, the members' meeting and the board meeting.

The children were the same ones who came to Norway in the summer and were now in Oslo on their way back to Germany. They arrived here early on the morning of 22nd Nov. and had breakfast, lunch and tea in Fagerborg parish hall. The catering was taken care of by members of the Fagerborg board along with some other volunteers who helped to cut sandwiches the night before the children's arrival. The children had recovered very well in Norway and were travelling home well clothed. The leftover food was given to the needy in the parish.

The members' meeting was held in Fagerborg parish hall on 23rd Nov. The turnout was unfortunately rather poor, only fifty, probably because of the unusually bad weather that day. The entertainment consisted of an update on the department's work since the last meeting, given by Fru Berit Nordklev, a talk by Fru Koldrup Lund about South Africa with a film, singing by the Red Cross nurses' choir, directed by Fru Fanny Elstø, and a film about Bakkebø Mental Institution, borrowed by Fru Heddy Astrup, with a talk by its director, Herr Tveit. Olaf Hall, an antiquarian bookshop owner, talked about his life with rare, old books and rounded off by a reading of his poetry. He could have omitted the latter. A two-litre jar of coffee and a two-litre jar of sugar were raffled and sales of Christmas stamps, advent calendars and Christmas comics were brisk. Due to the poor turnout the accounts for the meeting showed a loss of 121 kroner.

The board meeting was held at Fru Ingrid Arnesen's on 28th Nov. and well attended. The treasurer, Fru Maj Kristoffersen, reported back on the department's financial position. Income from the Red Cross bazaar was 583.50 kroner and the sale of stamps, 2,969 kroner. Budget proposals were put forward and discussed. Maj Kristoffersen urged us to caution. It was decided that we would allocate 400 kroner to twenty packed lunches, at 20 kroner each, to be given to the needy, as well as money for two chairs in the nurses' home, probably 250 kroner. It was also decided that we would put aside the following sums: 1,000 kroner for the children's holiday camp, 1,000 kroner for the crèche,

1,000 kroner for running expenses and 500 kroner as a
reserve fund.

Fagerborg department has been allocated twenty pairs of
new children's shoes by the Oslo District Red Cross at fifty øre
per pair plus transport costs. The shoes, each pair containing
a Christmas card from the Fagerborg department of the
Norwegian Red Cross, will be distributed via the parish nurse
to those in financial need.

The board had also received the Christmas stamps and
was pleased to be able to report that many volunteers had
come forward to sell them this year.

Incidentally this was Maj Kristoffersen's last meeting
before she goes on leave to give birth. She said she was
willing to continue as treasurer as soon as advisable and we
therefore had no reason to elect a new one. All the women
present expressed their pleasure on her behalf and of course
offered any support or help they could.

THE CRUSTS

Jesper is standing on Majorstua steps selling Christmas stamps. This is the continuing punishment. But it is better than having to greet the Jewish children from Germany or helping to make a thousand packed lunches for the starving people of Fagerborg. The stamps are displayed in a cardboard tray hanging from a string around his neck and they cost fifty øre each. It is Saturday after school. The tram has to wait in Bogstadveien because the milk vehicle has parked on the rails outside Smør-Pedersen. Young couples wearing knickerbockers and anoraks appear with skis over their shoulders to catch the train up to Frognerseteren. The weather reports were able to announce optimum snow conditions. Jesper's hands are freezing. But he can't wear gloves if he has to give change. He can barely move his fingers. He has sold two stamps, both to Løkke, who had been to the vinmonopol. You could see that by the bag. What can you do with two Red Cross stamps? Give one as a Christmas present? The deal is that Jesper has to stand on Majorstua steps for an hour and a half. One more hour to go. The driver has finally finished his milk deliveries to Smør-Pedersen and drives on to Vinderen. The tram pulls in to the stop and is late, but not so late that it can't catch up before the next stop, especially if there is a tailwind down to Frogner square. Sales are not going well, in other words. The clock on Vinkelgård shopping centre is even more dispiriting. The hands are moving so slowly that time is almost standing still. Jesper will have to be here for the rest of his life. He is sure about that. It is also the punishment. He has a horrible feeling: no-one likes him. People give him a wide berth when they see him. They lower their gaze and rush past. They turn and head off in a different direction. Perhaps it would have been better to greet the German children after all. Jesper makes a decision. He will never sell anything again, no matter what. Then Fru Vik comes along. At any rate she stops and buys a stamp. She asks if sales are going well. Jesper has to confess they are not. Fru Vik buys another one. Then she scurries into Samson the bakery. She has a bad habit which she herself considers a virtue. Besides, it is good for your teeth. She likes stale bread and especially the crusts. So they keep the loaves they haven't sold during the week for her. Some say Fru Vik is just cheap. She gets them for less than half the price. A man without a hat doesn't manage to get to the vinmonopol on time and is hammering on the door. The light above Majorstua is changing colour. December is putting on its evening gown early. Then Jostein appears. He stands on the step below Jesper and counts how many stamps he has sold. Four. Jostein shakes his head. Jesper does, too. The wind picks up. They look for shelter in the passage, but there is a draught and it is even worse. Jostein has an idea. He can sell the stamps for a while instead of Jesper. He removes the tray from Jesper's neck, hangs it around his own and stands on the steps. Jesper sticks his hands in his pockets and watches.

Jostein appears even more helpless than before. His head hangs at an angle. His jaw hangs open, too. All in all he resembles a pitiable sight. Jesper doesn't like to see Jostein in this state. He is putting on an act. But he does sell stamps. When people catch sight of him it is as if they can't restrain themselves. The stamps sell like hotcakes. He has sold out before the one and a half hours are up and strolls back contentedly to Jesper and gives him the empty tray. But when they have counted up the money it is too much. Jesper does a recount. It is right. It isn't right. The sum is twice what it should be. He eyes Jostein.

"What price did you sell them at?" he asks.

"What?"

Jesper lifts Jostein's bobble hat and shouts:

"The stamps!"

"A krone."

"They cost fifty øre!"

Jostein gawps and looks so stupid that Jesper has to put his hat back on. They look around. No-one has heard them talking. They walk across the Tørtberg field so that no-one can see them, either. The wind drops. Everything is still. If Jostein has sold 26 stamps for a krone each instead of fifty øre that means they have thirteen kroner extra. Jostein works this out. It is a fortune. What are they going to do with it? Should they hand all the money to the Red Cross, who can then trace the various buyers? They know very well what they are going to do with the fortune, but don't want to admit it. Jesper writes *6 and a half* in the snow. Jostein nods and adds: *each*. They stand looking at the letters. The field is the world's biggest sheet of paper. Then it starts snowing. The snow is a rubber erasing all the evidence. They have learned English and Jesper doesn't need to shout.

"Hokey dokey," he says.

"Of kors," Jostein says.

They share the money, agree not to spend any before Christmas and go their separate ways. Jostein takes a detour around Frøen and Frogner Park just to be on the safe side. Jesper decides to walk through Blindern, but as he approaches Kirkeveien he regrets going that way. He should have come from Majorstua. That was where he had been selling the stamps. If he hasn't done anything wrong he doesn't need to change plans. So Jesper has something else on his mind. Outside their house entrance there is a taxi, ready to leave. He can make out his parents on the back seat. Pappa manages to roll down the window.

"The moment has come, Jesper!"

Fru Vik is waiting on the stairs and Jesper has to go with her. He would have liked to avoid that. He has his own key and can manage without help. Fru Vik is in a tizz. She helps him off with his snow boots.

"It might not happen until tomorrow and, if so, Ewald will probably come back this evening," she says.

"Does it hurt?"

"Does what hurt?"

"Having a baby."

Fru Vik straightens up, holding his snow boots in her hands, they are dripping and she doesn't notice.

"I don't know. I suppose it does. But it hurts horses more."

"Horses?"

"Maj will be fine. She's done it before, hasn't she. Now let's not talk about it anymore and enjoy ourselves."

Jesper goes with Fru Vik to the kitchen. He just hopes she won't butter any crusts of bread for him. As they go past the sitting-room door he glimpses a man inside. He is sitting in the armchair by the radio and has grey hair and a tweed jacket. For an instant Jesper thinks it is the ghost of Herr Vik, although he can't really remember what he looked like. But he definitely used to sit in that chair. Jesper shivers. Fru Vik is buttering him some crusts. They look like round rocks. He warms his hands over the stove.

"So you sold all your stamps," she says.

Jesper looks down at the glowing hotplate. How close can he hold his hands without burning himself?

"They went like hotcakes."

Then Jesper sits down at the table and Fru Vik leaves him in peace for a while. He hears muted voices from the sitting room. Shortly afterwards the front door closes. He doesn't want to ask who that was. It is none of his business. If it was the ghost of Herr Vik, then it was her business. At half past five Ewald returns from Wergelandsveien Clinic. The birth will take time. The baby is stubborn, it seems.

The first board meeting of 1950 was held at Fru Else Larsen's on January 12th. Those present were: Fru Berit Nordklev, Fru Ingrid Foss, Frøken Vanda Aasland and Fru Else Larsen.

The chairman, Fru Nordklev, read out a number of thank-you letters from recipients of packed lunches and shoes as well as from the nurses' home who bought two chairs with the money they were given. Melsom the butcher, who facilitated the sale of fifteen packed lunches in the Fagerborg department, refused to take anything for himself and donated an extra packed lunch, which was assigned to the Vestly family, Vibes gate 16.

Fagerborg department had, since the previous board meeting, received twenty pairs of shoes, of which sixteen, each containing a pair of knitted socks or gloves, were presented to social security. The remaining pairs were given to Fagerborg parish for distribution.

CROWN CORK

Jesper gets both. He gets a piano and a little sister. At 16.30, on January 6th, 1950, a girl comes into the world at Wergelands-veien Clinic after wearing out her mother over several days. It hurt. The same evening four men from Majorstua Transport Agency carry a piano up to their flat. Ewald Kristoffersen bought it for a song at Cappelen Instrument Makers. Jesper stands on the landing, close to the wall, and watches the men, who have straps attached to hooks over their shoulders, getting closer step by step. The piano sways between them. Ewald walks behind shouting. Then he squeezes past. He doesn't want the piano to fall on his head if they drop it. Mamma has given birth to a piano, Jesper thinks. So Jesper will always have his little sister in his thoughts whenever he plays, wherever he is. He decides to buy something for her from the money he and Jostein made from the Red Cross.

But where should the piano go?

The vestibule is too small. Anyway Jesper would have to sleep somewhere else and that is not on. It has to go in the sitting room. That is where a piano belongs. In all paintings the piano is in the sitting room. Ewald knows that. But a piano is a vexatious piece of furniture. It demands its rights. The wall facing Gørbitz gate is too short. On the other side the fireplace is in the way. And the balcony doors take up half the room when they are open. The piano has to go in the dining room, in the corner under the clock. Then Jesper can play every Sunday after dessert, just like in the old days at the Bristol. The removal men finally coax the piano into position. Ewald fetches a beer from the kitchen for them. He glances down into the yard. The snowman is finished. Someone has placed a hat on top. Now the snowman is only waiting to melt. Ewald doesn't want to think like this, not on a day like today. He doesn't deserve it. He goes back to the sitting room and gives the guys an export beer each. They knock it back in one swig, apart from the driver who sticks the bottle in his pocket. After they have gone Jesper can choose between Isi-Cola and Solo. He can't make up his mind and wants both. As this is that sort of day Ewald agrees. He pours himself a glass of brandy and lights up a Gitane. All the employees at Dek-Rek were given Gitanes before Christmas by Rudjord. He slumps into a chair exhausted and content and says *skål*. Yes, so long as he doesn't think too much about Oslo's 900-year jubilee, the snowman and that he is going to die within a certain time, he could, hand on heart, say he was a happy man.

"You can have whatever you want, Jesper."

Jesper shrugs and finishes the Solo first. Then he fetches the Isi-Cola. Ewald wonders how this will work. He takes the bottle from Jesper and points to the cap.

"Do you know what this is?"

"A cap."

"A crown cork bottle cap. This is a very important inven-tion. You have to flip it off with a purpose-made device. You can even use your fingers if you're strong enough. Years ago there used to be a padlock on bottles and you needed two keys to open them. But now there's a crown cork seal on all bottles the whole world over.

"On Solo, too."

"Yes, that's what I said. All over the world."

Ewald places the bottle cap against the edge of the table and thumps it, then gives the bottle to Jesper.

"Her name's going to be Stine. After Mamma's grandmother. What do you reckon?"

Jesper takes a swig and puts down the bottle.

"I like Solo better."

"That's good. Oranges are healthy."

Ewald pours more brandy in his glass, but not quite as much as before. Jesper finishes off the Isi-Cola anyway. He can't leave it even if it does taste horrible. The second hand on the clock above the piano goes round making little ticking sounds followed by a dry click.

"Aren't you going to try it?" Ewald asks.

"I can't play."

Ewald goes into the kitchen, is gone for a while, then returns with an old newspaper and a pair of scissors. He flicks through until he finds what he is looking for and cuts out a piece no bigger than a stamp. He turns to Jesper and reads aloud:

"Enzo Zanetti. Private piano lessons. Every day except Monday."

Jesper goes closer.

"Enzo Zanetti?"

"He's Italian, you see. I know him."

273

Jesper is about to say he knows Enzo Zanetti too, but refrains. There is too much to explain. Besides he doesn't understand it himself. And there might be several people called Enzo Zanetti who are Italian and play the piano in Oslo. However, he doubts it.

"How?" Jesper asks.

"He used to play for us when we had important meetings at work. But now he teaches. Shall we ring him and book a lesson?"

"We haven't got a telephone yet."

"We definitely have a piano though, Jesper."

They go up to Fru Vik, who opens the door before they have time to raise a finger.

"We have a foo-foo-child," Ewald says.

"Talk properly!"

"A perfectly formed baby girl."

Fru Vik claps her hands and it resounds down the whole of the stairwell.

"And Maj?"

"Just fine, thank you. She had a girl, too."

They both laugh while Jesper takes a step forward and interrupts them.

"We need to use the telephone."

"I can imagine," says Fru Vik.

Ewald goes into the hall, stops by the dresser and looks around for a moment. Isn't that a gentleman's coat hanging there? Then he puts the receiver between shoulder and cheek so that he has both hands free and can dial the number in the advert. They take their time. Eventually someone answers at the other end. Ewald holds the receiver properly and asks:

"Which key are you in today, major or minor?"

Ewald, at any rate, laughs and immediately introduces himself with his full name and address, but as that doesn't seem to help either, he starts getting impatient:

"I saved you after the assault. Elling Duketon."

Jesper smiles and is confident. He also knows Enzo Zanetti. Now he knows which tune he is going to learn. This city is so small everyone has the same shadow. Fru Vik leans down and whispers:

"That's not Maj he's talking to, is it?"

Jesper shakes his head and is still smiling.

At last Ewald states what he wants. He has a son of almost eight years and three months who would like to learn to play the piano. No, he can't play. That's why he wants lessons. That's why he's ringing. Is there something wrong with the telephone? Ewald listens for a moment. Fru Vik pulls Jesper closer and he lets her. It was here, in her flat, that he heard the sad, laconic tune that gives him a certain calm, a certain balance, just thinking about it. Ewald finishes the conversation, cradles the receiver and turns to Jesper.

"You've got a lesson on Monday, January 30th, at five-thirty sharp in Jørgen Moes gate 4. And woe betide you, if you're late."

Jesper is uneasy.

"He doesn't work on Mondays."

"He's changed his mind. Now he doesn't work any days except for Mondays."

Fru Vik opens the door for them and pats Ewald on the back.

"You've got lots of irons in the fire, you have," she says.

"And you too, it seems, Fru Vik."

Ewald and Jesper go back downstairs. They are as tired as each other. For a moment the veil is ripped aside and everything is revealed as it is. It is impossible to forget such moments. On the scullery bench is the Norwegian Red Cross magazine: *For Safety's Sake*. In fact, most accidents take place in the home. There is a hole in the corner of the magazine so that you can hang it somewhere which is easy to find.

Twice in the night Jesper has to get up for a wee, first the Isi-Cola, even though he drank it last, then the Solo. They are the same colour. But the Solo was yellow anyway. When he gets up for the third time he doesn't want to have a wee. He tiptoes into the dining room. It is quieter than he has ever known. The whole building is asleep. The floors lie cheek to cheek. The walls don't talk. Even the clock rests between clicks. He switches on the table lamp. There is a greenish light from the lamp shade. It is ten minutes to three. He pushes a chair over to the piano and sits down. The chair is too low. He sits there anyway. He raises his right hand, changes his mind, then lifts his left. Suddenly he doesn't know what to do with the other one. It is in the way. He puts it between the buttons of his pyjamas and keeps his left hand in the same position, directly above the keys. He can just make out his reflection in the shiny black lacquer. The music rack is empty. The candelabra on each side are also empty. Only hardened wax is left. The keyhole is empty too. The piano is a Bluthner. All the silence collects in his mouth. Then Jesper carefully lowers a finger. He doesn't know which note he hits. Ewald sits up in bed. The sound has moved him. He thinks: We'll get through this. He hears Fru Vik walking across the floor of her bedroom.

She stops and listens. There is nothing but this one note, a sound waiting to become music. She is cold in her nightie. She should put some socks on. Then she drops something. She can't understand it. She isn't holding anything to drop. It is her ring. It just slipped off her finger. A circle of white skin is all that is left. The ring rolls under the bed. Fru Vik crouches down and stretches out her hand into the darkness.

———

It was agreed that two bundles of baby clothes (the remainder of the gift from the Norwegian Women's Association in Washington) would be transferred to the stock of hospital resources to give to those in need.

Flowers and cards have been sent to our treasurer, Fru Maj Kristoffersen, to congratulate her on the birth of a daughter. Fagerborg has another inhabitant!

AN EAR

Jesper thinks she is ugly. She is lying in the cradle in her parents' bedroom drooling from both corners of her mouth. Her hair is black and hangs in thin strands over her wrinkled skull. Her hands are like two pale meatballs. It is impossible to see where her hand finishes and the fingers start. It is the same with her feet, but they look more like two fish balls. She has kicked off the little duvet. Incidentally these feet came into the world first. That is why she took such a long time. Usually the head comes first. Even Jesper knows that. How could you be so stupid? That is why she might be lame or at worst have a club foot. In Jesper's eyes she already has, two of them what is more, and it is her fault. Where is she going to sleep when she gets bigger? In the vestibule? Where will he go? There isn't room for both of them. She will take his space. It doesn't matter. When she is big enough to sleep on her own Jesper will be over the hills and far away. He leans closer. She looks at him and laughs. At any rate the mouth emits a sound. She isn't laughing. She is just gurgling. Can she see him? Can she see her big brother and is she forming an opinion of him? Perhaps the relationship between them is already formed? Or is there anything at all happening inside the podgy creature intended to resemble a human and not too big for Melsom to weigh on the scales? Jesper is dubious. He puts the little packet on the pillow.

"You haven't woken her up, have you?"

Jesper straightens up like a shot. Maj comes in, pushes him away and lifts Stine. Stine starts crying. Maj is pale and impatient.

"Look what you've done," she says.

Jesper shakes his head.

"She was awake."

"And now she's crying. It's your fault."

Maj walks over to the window and stands there with Stine. Jesper turns to the door. His grandparents are in the doorway and don't say anything. Grandma in front. Grandpa behind, digging in his pipe. Grandma nods and Jesper follows them into the kitchen. She has some home-made apple cake for him. It is made with apples from Hurdal. There aren't a lot of apples in Hurdal, but they are good. Hurdal is in the country. Jesper vaguely remembers a brown, nearly black, house on the edge of the forest, a woodshed and a lake nearby where they fished for perch. They were there a few times during the war. Jesper might think it is only a dream, it is so far away in every way, but his grandparents do exist at any rate. They are as old as Stine is new and perhaps we are quite similar when we are at the beginning and end of life?

Grandpa lights his pipe and goes away. Grandma puts another piece on Jesper's plate.

"It wasn't your fault," she says.

Jesper doesn't want any more. It has almost slipped his mind that he never wants to become fat. He pushes the cake away.

"She always says that."

"She doesn't mean it."

"Why does she say it then?"

"Because she's exhausted, Jesper. Have you never said anything you don't mean?"

Jesper ponders the question.

"Actually I haven't," he says.

They hear Grandpa's laughter, but they can't see it. At that moment Maj ploughs through the fog and opens the window wide.

"If you absolutely have to smoke, go on the balcony."

Grandpa appears.

"Doesn't Ewald smoke?"

"He smokes French cigarettes, Pappa. Not old pipes."

"I can't stand outside smoking in the middle of the city, can I now?"

"We go outside to smoke."

Grandpa puts his pipe on the edge of a plate and doesn't say another word. Maj closes the window and looks at her mother.

"Hasn't Ewald come?"

"Not to my knowledge."

For an instant it's as if Maj's about to implode. This is too much. This is suspicious. Her whole body is shaking, her knees too. Jesper gets up first.

"I can go on my own," he says.

"You certainly can not."

At length Maj calms down, at least she acts as if she does, and looks at her mother again.

"Can you cut and clean his nails while we wait? And he should put on his white shirt and grey trousers."

"Where are you going?"

Maj runs up the back stairs to Fru Vik and knocks on the door. She opens quite quickly. Maj walks straight past her, to the telephone and dials the Dek-Rek number. She gets the secretary on the line and asks to speak to Ewald. Everyone's gone, Ewald too.

"When did he go?" Maj asks.

"Several hours ago."

"Several hours?"

Maj rings off and almost falls into a chair. Fru Vik is close at hand.

"Something the matter?"

"No. Only that Stine won't sleep, Mamma and Pappa are never going to leave, the Red Cross accounts have to be ready in two days, Jesper has his first piano lesson this evening and the nitwit I'm married to hasn't kept his word."

Fru Vik shakes her head.

"And I'd wanted to ask you about something."

Maj looks up at her.

"Is it very important?"

"Yes, it is, but it can wait."

Maj scampers downstairs again. Jesper is ready. He looks nice in his clean, freshly pressed clothes, almost too nice. Grandma shows her his hands. They are also impeccable. Then she helps him into the new duffel coat, which is much too big; he could go hiking inside it. Maj delivers her final admonishments and just has time to throw a coat over the clothes she is standing up in. The snow is blowing along the walls in Kirkeveien. The clock on Broadcasting House in Marienlyst says a quarter to six. They take the tram from Majorstua. Inside the windows are misted up. Soon they can barely see where they are going.

"You should've put gloves on," Maj says.

"Why?"

"So that your hands don't get cold. You can't play with cold fingers, can you."

"Then I should've worn a hat as well."

"Why?"

"I can't play with cold ears."

Maj pulls the hood over his head and laughs, but in a slow, tired way, it sounds more like a yawn.

"Do I look terrible?" she says.

"We've been to see him before, haven't we? With a Christmas box?"

Maj nods and is quiet for a few moments. The tram makes a sudden turn, they must be in Holtegata. Jesper wipes the window and can see an old Christmas tree in a gateway and a dog disappearing behind a refuse bin. Maj takes out another present.

"Was it you who gave this to Stine?"

Jesper's turn to nod. He is suddenly shy.

"We have to get off at the next stop," he says.

"No, there are two more. What did you buy it with?"

"Money, of course. What else?"

"Don't you be cheeky. What money?"

"Money I'd saved. From my pocket money."

Maj feels the paper and looks at the card with the clumsy, crooked writing: *To Stine from Jesper*.

"Is this a present we have to open at once or can we wait?"

Jesper looks out, but the window has misted up again. He shrugs.

"It can easily wait."

"Perhaps we should wait until Stine can open it herself? What do you think?"

"Fine by me."

Maj lays a hand on his cold fingers.

"I'm very happy you're being nice to Stine," she says.

They get off at Uranienborg School and then it is only a stone's throw to Jørgen Moes gate. The clock at the top of the church tower says two minutes to six. They wait a moment outside, then Maj rings. It takes at least a minute before the door buzzes and they can push it open. On the first floor Maj stops, pulls Jesper closer and whispers:

"Do I really look that bad?"

Jesper is reminded of what Grandma said about speaking your mind. He appraises Maj and almost feels sorry for her. Sleep, or the lack of it, is clear from the sagging black bags beneath her eyes. Her forehead is pale and dry and she has split ends. And her mouth is like a round bracket facing downwards.

"Yes," Jesper answers.

Maj takes out her lipstick and pocket mirror from her bag and tries to repair her face as best she can. Yes, Jesper feels sorry for her and he hates that. She will have to go to a repair shop for at least a week to be as she used to be, if she ever will. Then there is only one more flight of stairs. Enzo Zanetti is waiting for them in the doorway. He looks at Maj in surprise and hesitates before offering his hand.

"Nice to see you again," he says.

Maj nods and sends him an appraising glance, he has obviously been busy in the meantime, his hair is combed, his white shirt is ironed, ditto the trousers, and his shoes have been polished. But she can detect a waft of alcohol, faint, mixed with aftershave, which he clearly hasn't skimped on. She shakes his hand.

"It'll be nicer this time," she says.

Enzo Zanetti smiles and glances at her, this still young woman who will soon be middle-aged anyway. She seems both worn out and in high spirits, and a little unkempt. She reminds him of the temps in the cloakroom at Hotel Bristol, the kind that had to be called in at the weekend and the regulars liked to call a *pocket Venus*. He lets go of her hand and turns to Jesper. The boy is good student material. But he is difficult to work with. He can break as easily as he can produce the most beautiful sounds. Enzo Zanetti has already noticed. They follow him into the flat. The sliding doors to the room where the piano is situated are open. A candle on the windowsill has been lit. The flame flickers for a moment. Enzo Zanetti helps Maj off with her coat.

"You can wait here," he says.

"Wait?"

"I prefer to be alone with my pupils."

"Couldn't I—?"

He cuts her off.

"This is how I work. You can go for a walk in the meantime."

"A walk?"

"The first lesson is for half an hour. The next one, if we get that far, will be for an hour."

Maj has to collect herself. Suddenly she doesn't know if this is right. She doesn't know what is right any longer.

"Have you got a lot of pupils?" she asks.

Enzo Zanetti puts his arm around Jesper.

"Only a few select ones. So let's see if Jesper is one of those. May I bring you anything?"

"No, thank you."

"The bathroom's down the corridor on the right."

Enzo Zanetti takes Jesper into the sitting room and closes the sliding doors. Maj sits down on the only chair there is, places her hands and her bag in her lap and listens. She can't hear anything. Why aren't they playing? Why isn't Enzo Zanetti showing Jesper how it is done? Why doesn't he play for Jesper, a scale for example or an easy tune? Instead there is total silence. She tiptoes over to the sliding doors. There isn't a keyhole in them. She can't see anything, either. Ah, she can hear something. They are breathing. First Enzo Zanetti takes a deep breath; it must be him because there is a deep gurgling sound. Then it is Jesper's turn. He inhales quickly, in short wheezes, then his breathing becomes calmer and calmer. Enzo Zanetti also starts to breathe again and soon they are breathing in harmony. Should she interrupt them? Maj stands there, mesmerised and nervous. Afterwards they laugh. It is a different laughter. Jesper is already laughing in Italian. She has to go to the toilet. She moves as quickly and quietly as she can to the corridor, takes the wrong turning at first, it is a bedroom, a double bed, made, a few drawings on the wall, a glass on one bedside table, where there is also a pile of music books. She closes the door, finds the toilet, hooks the door to, but feels a sudden reluctance to sit on the loo. It isn't dirty.

It isn't that. Everything is generally clean and tidy, unusually so for an old bachelor. Bachelor? On the shelf above the bath there is a bottle of eau de cologne between a deodorant and shaving cream. And there are two toothbrushes, one white and one yellow. But that is not enough to be married. Enzo Zanetti probably makes his arrangements in other ways. Maj looks at the mirror and feels like crying. She is going to look awful for the rest of her life. That is just how it is. She walks back to the hallway, sits down and puts her hands and her bag in her lap. A thought strikes her: There isn't a single memento here, apart from the perfume, but that isn't a memento, just something that has been left here. Then Maj hears a note. It is a single note, pure and clear, which resonates, then fades and leaves a different kind of silence. Maj doesn't understand a lot about music, she likes a happy rhythm best, but the note has given her goose pimples. That could of course be because her son played it. Can one note also be music? Immediately afterwards, Enzo Zanetti and Jesper come out. Jesper is silent. This is not unusual. But he seems surprised, not uneasy but surprised, almost frightened. Maj gets up stroking the goose pimples from her lower arms. Enzo Zanetti looks at her, lights a cigarette and smiles.

"Can we drop the formality in the future?" he asks.

On the tram Jesper doesn't say anything either and Maj doesn't want to nag, now that everything is going so well. This much she knows about her son. But walking up Kirkeveien she can't restrain herself any longer.

"Did you learn anything?"

Jesper nods, hands in pockets.

They walk a bit further.

"What?" Maj asks.

"He said I was one of his select pupils."

Maj stops and places her hands on his shoulders.

"Now I don't want this Italian putting ideas into your head, Jesper."

"And I have to wear gloves."

They continue past Broadcasting House. The clock says ten minutes to seven.

"I didn't mean it like that," Maj says.

"What did you mean then?"

"It's sensible to wear gloves. At least thick gloves. You mustn't get cold."

When they arrive home Grandma is sitting with Stine. Stine is asleep. They let her sleep and tiptoe out. Grandpa is still in the kitchen. That is the place he likes best. All kitchens look alike. He has his cold pipe in the corner of his mouth. Maj feels sorry for him and puts on some coffee. There is some apple cake left too and they can whip some cream, if there is enough. But Ewald still hasn't made an appearance. Maj tries to act unconcerned. Ewald has a lot to do at work. He is preparing for the 900-year jubilee. The grandparents want to know how the piano lesson went. Can Jesper play anything for them? Can he play some dance music? Jesper shakes his head. He doesn't want any cake.

"The piano teacher said Jesper was one of the chosen ones," Maj said.

Jesper goes to bed early. There is too much to think about. He has to be alone with his thoughts. He has to get them in the right order so that they don't trip up over each other: Jostein, Stine, the piano, the present, Mamma, Pappa, his grandparents.

After a while he swaps them around and puts the piano first and moves Stine in front of Jostein. There is probably more to think about on top of this, but he hasn't got any more space. Time is doing a lap in his head. He can feel it. It is exactly like the vacuum cleaner Fru Vik has, when he puts his palm against the nozzle and feels the pressure on his skin. He hears Maj go into the bedroom. Stine cries for a few minutes. Incidentally she has a strange way of crying. It is not how you cry if you are fed up or have done something wrong. It is crying for no reason. Or perhaps she is crying because she exists, she is human. However, her crying frightens Jesper. He turns over in bed. Then it is quiet again, as quiet as it is possible to be in a block of flats. Then he hears the low voices of his grandparents. They are better to listen to, a mumble, as incomprehensible as Stine's wails, but gentle, soporific. He dreams. Jostein is standing in the middle of Kirkeveien directing the traffic. The bus runs him over and after it has passed, Jostein is sitting on the seat at the back waving. Then Jesper wakes up. Ewald is crouching by his bed. There is a bloodstain on his shirt collar. His face is white and lights up the whole vestibule.

"We have to move the clock," Jesper says.

"Shhh. Which clock?"

"Above the piano."

Ewald nods.

"I'm sorry I couldn't make it today."

"Never mind."

"Did you learn anything from our man on the ivories?"

"He said you can make people cry by playing just one note."

"One note?"

"Yes. He says that's the aim."

Ewald listens. There is something anxious about him. That is what is making his face light up the way it does. He gently places a hand on Jesper's forehead.

"That's a bit like what I try to do."

"I know," Jesper says.

"Go to sleep now."

Ewald gets up and walks quietly into the kitchen. His in-laws are sitting there. Esther looks at him, sternly. Halvard has his pipe in his mouth, but it isn't lit. He says hi, but looks in another direction.

"Why haven't you gone to bed?" Ewald asks.

Esther lifts the coffee jug.

"Would you like a drop of coffee?"

"No, thanks. Why are you up?"

"The train goes at half past six. We don't want to oversleep."

Ewald turns to Halvard.

"Haven't you got any more tobacco, Halvard?"

"Maj said I wasn't allowed to smoke here."

"What nonsense. You—"

Esther cuts him off:

"He can smoke when we're at home."

Halvard stuffs his pipe in his pocket.

"Have you got enough wood for winter?" he asks.

Ewald nods, stands lost in thought and hears the clock in the dining room. Jesper's right. It has to go. He looks at Esther.

"You can have a nap with Maj," he says.

"No, you should be asleep with her."

Ewald stays on his feet a little longer. He would like to sit here for the rest of the night. That is what he would like most.

There is so much he would like to ask about. He wants to get to know Maj better. After all, he barely knows her. He hasn't known her for most of his life of course. Suddenly he is gripped by profound despair. He wants to know more. He wants to know everything. Is it true that she knows how to slaughter a lamb? Was she really a soloist in the girls' choir at middle school? Did she go jig-fishing for perch in the winter? Did she like to read Johan Falkberget? Ewald says goodnight and gets ready for bed in the bathroom. He notices the little bloodstain on his collar. How did that happen? You have to be so careful. He pushes the shirt down to the bottom of the laundry basket and goes into the bedroom. Stine is asleep. At any rate she is quiet. There is only the sound of her breathing. Her breathing moves the curtains. Her breathing moves Ewald. He lies down beside Maj. She is asleep as well. With her back to him. She isn't asleep. She feels like giving him an earful. She feels like giving him both barrels. He deserves it. But she hasn't the strength. Maj hasn't the strength to be angry. The day passed anyway. It came to an end. She got through it. Here they are in bed.

"Where have you been?" she asks.

"At the Bris."

"Thought so."

"I'm sorry . . ."

"You're waking Stine."

"Sorry."

They lie awake and silent for some seconds, in the same bed, each in their own world.

"Jesper gave Stine a present," Maj says.

"Did he? What was it?"

"We haven't opened it yet."

"That was nice of you."

"Nice of us?"

"To wait until I got back."

"We're going to wait until she can open it herself."

"Of course."

"Shh. I'm going to sleep."

They don't say any more. Maj hears Ewald eventually fall asleep. His breathing becomes heavy and regular, at least three octaves below Stine's. Maj turns to him. His face is close. At first she doesn't know what it is that has taken her aback. Something doesn't add up. Then she realises. He doesn't smell of beer, or spirits, not in the slightest. Not even of tobacco. Has Ewald been to the Bristol until midnight and he hasn't drunk and he hasn't smoked? He is lying. She wants to ask. She wants to shake him until he wakes up and ask what he was doing. She doesn't. She turns back the other way, looks at the alarm clock, which is set for a quarter past five. Maj is sure. Ewald has someone else. That is why he has been so different recently, so thoughtful, so nice. The only way of hiding that you are bad is by being good. Maj begins to doubt herself. She knows Ewald has always been good. She wakes just before the alarm clock rings. She switches it off and gets up, takes Stine into the bathroom and changes her nappy. Maj's parents are still sitting in the kitchen. Her mother has made coffee and prepared a packed lunch for the journey, even though it doesn't take more than two hours. But they may have to wait at Dal Station if the bus is delayed and then it is nice to have something to eat. Her father nods. Their suitcase is ready at his feet. Thank you for everything. They don't need to wake Ewald. He is busy and can sleep a little longer. But Jesper is awake and says *see ya* to these strange grandparents who are slow at everything they do and he can't help liking, perhaps precisely because of their slowness. Maj corrects him: Not *see ya* but *goodbye*. Jesper says *goodbye*, it sounds strange, and goes into the bedroom. Ewald is already up and by the window, fortunately wearing both parts of his pyjamas, but he seems thinner than last time anyway, and bent. Jesper stands beside him. Soon Maj emerges from the building with the pram. Esther is behind her, carrying the net bag with the packed lunch, and Halvard brings up the rear, dragging the suitcase. Ewald laughs.

"They always walk in single file," he says.

Jesper leans forward and watches this procession rounding the corner of Kirkeveien towards Majorstua and from there they catch the tram to Olso East Station, where Maj can safely see her parents off on the right train.

"Who does?" Jesper asks.

"Grandma and Grandpa. They've only walked beside each other once and that was in the church when they got married."

"Why?"

"Because roads are narrow in Hurdal. They're like paths. There's no room for more than one person."

"But they don't have to follow each other in town?"

"Old habits die hard."

"But Grandma goes first," Jesper says.

"Always."

When Esther dies four years later – she just doesn't wake up one morning – Halvard follows the very next evening, right behind her, on the same path into eternity.

Just before Maj rounds the corner she turns and looks up

at Ewald. He is shocked. Her gaze is accusatory, embittered. There is no mistaking it. He can see it all the way from here, her darkness. Ewald raises a hand. By then Maj is out of sight and he waves to Halvard instead, who is putting the suitcase into his other hand, he waves back. Ewald looks at Jesper. Has he also seen his mother's gaze? No, it was for him, Ewald and no-one else. And he suddenly thinks of the present Jesper has bought for Stine and he will never have a chance to see.

"Who's more in a hurry, you or me?"

Jesper dashes into the bathroom so as not to see his father there. Ewald puts on his dressing gown, sits in the kitchen and drinks the rest of the coffee, it is lukewarm and bitter. He makes some more and sets the table for two, no, for three, because Maj will probably be back soon. He has to do everything right. He mustn't be sloppy. That is imperative. He hasn't done anything wrong, but he must do everything right. He makes a packed lunch for Jesper. How many slices of bread does he usually have? Two should be enough. No, today he'll have three. The boy is too thin. He can't find the greaseproof paper. Why isn't the greaseproof paper where the food is?

"What are you looking for?"

Ewald turns round. Jesper is in the doorway, dressed, his hair wet and combed, he can barely recognise his son. For a moment Jesper is a grown-up, soon as old as his father. Is this how the disease develops? Is he going to see flashes of all he is going to miss? It is no comfort. It makes things worse. Ewald has to lean on the windowsill. Down in the yard the snowman is still waiting. Someone has put a black hat on his head and two lumps of coal have become the eyes.

"Greaseproof paper," Ewald says.

Jesper finds it at once, behind the bread bin and wraps the sandwiches himself.

"The bathroom's free."

Ewald goes out and fetches the newspaper instead. On the doormat there is an envelope as well, a little envelope, the type used with thank-you cards. He picks it up. It is for Maj. *Maj* it says. He closes the door. It must be from Fru Vik. Ewald becomes anxious. What does Fru Vik want? What does she know? Does she know anything? Ewald becomes anxious so easily. He has to be careful. Should he open the envelope? No, he might be doomed, but he still has integrity. He puts the envelope in his dressing-gown pocket, leaves the newspapers and goes back to the kitchen. Jesper is rinsing the milk glass in the sink. He does everything correctly too. They have to maintain norms. It is decisive. That is the rule they have to hold on to. But why does Jesper do everything correctly? Does he also know something? Does he know his father is going to die? Jesper puts the glass on the worktop, upside down, so that the water can run out. Ewald has never felt so close to his son.

"Where shall we hang the clock?" he asks.

Jesper turns.

"In the sitting room maybe?"

"Or should we just get rid of it?"

"Chuck it?"

"No, no. We don't chuck things away. We give them to the Red Cross bazaar."

At that moment the doorbell rings. It must be Maj who has forgotten her key. Jesper throws on his satchel and runs to answer the door. Shortly afterwards he calls his father. Ewald goes through the hall to the hallway. It isn't Maj. Two men in identical overalls are standing outside, one holding a four-sided carton, the other a toolbox plus a roll of thin, black cable over his shoulder. The man with the carton speaks.

"Are you Ewald Kristoffersen, date of birth September 4th, 1911?"

Ewald nods.

"Yes, that's me. What's this about?"

"Telephone."

"Telephone? Now?"

The second man says:

"We tried ringing you to tell you we were coming, but no-one answered."

They are quiet for a moment, silent, then they burst into laughter, Ewald does the same and lets them in. Jesper removes his satchel. He can't miss this. And Ewald has forgotten everything called work or school. He has forgotten Maj and Stine. He has even forgotten death. They are going to get a telephone. It is the same problem as with the piano, only smaller, but just as big: Where to put the telephone? It can't be in the dining room. That is where Jesper will play and Ewald doesn't want to be disturbed while he is eating his Sunday lunch, either. The kitchen is out of the question, no-one has a telephone in the bathroom and the scullery is too cramped for a conversation. It has to be the sitting room. The engineers are very serious again and don't make another joke that day.

"It's usually in the vestibule," one says.

Ewald isn't sure.

"My son sleeps there," he says.

Jesper takes a step forward.

"It doesn't matter."

Ewald shakes his head.

"Do you want to be woken up every night by the telephone?"

"Who rings at night?" Jesper says.

"Who? You can't know until you've answered the telephone."

It is to be the sitting room. The telephone will be on the little table between the sofa and the sideboard. There is enough light and you can sit while you are talking. The engineers ask to be left in peace to work. Ewald and Jesper sit in the kitchen waiting. It takes time. Waiting is the least they can do. The Kristoffersen family is going to be connected. What has happened to Maj? They don't give her a thought. They say nothing. They don't want to disturb. Sitting here is pleasant. This evening they can light the fire and talk on the telephone. Then one engineer comes out. It is finished. They follow him to the sitting room. There it is, black and shiny. Ewald hasn't seen anything more beautiful. It is the most attractive item of furniture in the whole flat. He puts his arm round Jesper. Maj should be here now. Ewald feels a lump in his throat, swallows twice and is embarrassed. This is how it is. He has become sensitive. Impressions make a greater impact. The second engineer hands him a card. On it is a number, their new personal number: 551430. The second man leaves a telephone directory on the sitting-room table. Finally Ewald has to sign three documents, he can keep one. The engineers say their goodbyes and leave. Ewald and Jesper are alone with the telephone.

"Don't touch it!" Ewald shouts.

Ewald reads the number out loud: 551430. This is now the most important number in their lives. He explains – he has gone into this you see, it is child's play for anyone in advertising: you stick your finger in the number you want, turn the dial to the right as far as you can, *clock*wise, and let go. Then the dial goes back to where it started. Then you do the same again, with the next digit in the number, and then the exchange in Tollbugaten knows which part of the country you are after. But it is only when you have dialled the whole number that what are known as selectors start, and a selector isn't someone who chooses who plays in a team, no, this selection is on a higher plane, in fact it is an electromagnet that makes an arrowhead travel along a load of cables and stop at the correct number. Why so laborious? Well, that is because if we change our minds and ring off before we have finished dialling, valuable lines have been busy for absolutely no purpose. This is how society works. Now shouldn't Maj have been here some time ago? And then Jesper has to learn the number by heart. It is vital.

"551430," Jesper says.

The telephone rings. They both jump. Ewald steps forward, hesitates, carefully lifts the receiver from the cradle and says in a tremulous voice:

"This is the Kristoffersen household, hello."

He hears a woman speaking fast.

"Ewald Kristoffersen, date of birth September 4th, 1911?"

"That is indeed the person you are talking to at this moment."

"This is the telephone switchboard. You're registered. Thank you."

The conversation is broken and Ewald carefully replaces the receiver. He thinks: I exist. They exist. We exist.

"Who was that?" Jesper asks.

Ewald turns to him, running the back of his hand across his eyes.

"That was the world."

They stand at the window looking for Maj and Stine. It is snowing lightly, so lightly that the snowflakes don't land. They swirl around in a slow maelstrom. Jesper flicks through the telephone directory. There are lots of Kristoffersens in Oslo, but there is no Ewald, Maj, Jesper or Stine. Perhaps he hasn't read it properly? Is there no space for them? What use is the telephone if they are not in the directory? Ewald laughs. Next year it will be completely different. Then their names will be there in capitals. At last Maj comes into sight. She pushes the pram around the corner. A shopping bag hangs from one handle. Ewald watches as Jesper puts a blanket over the telephone and hides the directory behind the radio. But Maj doesn't look up to the window this time. She doesn't even send Ewald as much as a glance. She just pushes the pram into the entrance and puts it under the stairs. She has a bad conscience. She is happy her parents have finally gone. She has gone wild and bought a blue shawl at Franck's in Bogstadsveien and it wasn't even on offer. It is Ewald's fault. She will go wild for as long as Ewald does. She has heard him talking about it, but then it is always the others who do it, who have a bit on the side or double-park or whatever the disgusting expressions are they use. Maj lifts Stine, she opens her eyes a fraction and closes them again. Then she hooks her shopping bag onto her wrist and carries her up two floors, lets herself in and comes to a halt. Jesper's satchel is on the floor. She calls: *Jesper!* No-one answers. Stine starts to cry at once. Maj kisses her on the forehead. The heat from her daughter goes through Maj like an electric shock, she also notices that Ewald's coat is still on the hook and his shoes are on the rack. She is gripped by this sense of heaviness, it is like a dream: of letting go, of falling. She puts down the shopping bag, holds Stine tighter, walks through the hall and stops in the sitting room. There they are, Ewald and Jesper, bursting with excitement like two small children, one no older than the other. They beckon her closer. Maj takes two steps towards them. Ewald puts his arm around her. Jesper stands by the sofa, counts down to zero and pulls away the blanket, an unveiling of the temporarily hidden number for Kirkeveien 127, Fagerborg, Oslo 3: 551430, their code in the Great Conversation. Everything is forgotten. Everything is forgiven. Everything is fine. They have a telephone! Maj claps her hands and almost drops Stine. She even lets Ewald have a kiss, a little one, while Jesper takes out the directory. Then she comes to her senses. Doesn't Jesper have to go to school? And Ewald? Can he be absent from work like this? Ewald sighs good-naturedly: In life they have to be able to take a day off, even if it isn't one. Maj goes into the bedroom, puts Stine in the cradle. When she wakes up again, she will have to be changed and fed. Then she has to wash the stairs in the entrance because it is her turn this week. A day off, she thinks. The phrase is bigger than she is. It is so big there is no room for it in the flat, it doesn't even have any room in her life. When she goes back to the sitting room Ewald and Jesper are waiting. Who shall they ring? The school? No, that is a waste of money. Jesper can take a note with him. Rudjord and Dek-Rek? Ewald is against this as well. For a moment he gets himself agitated. Isn't he his own boss? He is working at home and doesn't have to inform anyone. He doesn't need an absence note! What about Ewald's father? At Tåsen old people's home you can only ring between three and a quarter to four. Jesper has a suggestion: Jostein. He can call Jostein. They have a telephone in the shop. But Jostein is at school of course. They stand looking at each other, stumped. Maj knows: she can ring the Red Cross chairman, Fagerborg department, Fru Berit Nordklev, to inform her that they finally have a telephone. Ewald is not in favour. Red Cross didn't get them the telephone; they got it through Ewald's own efforts. They mustn't forget that using the telephone has a cost. So you have to choose who you ring with care. What about Dr Lund? Ewald is immediately on his guard. Doesn't Maj feel well? Yes, she does, but isn't it important that Dr Lund knows how to get hold of them? Ewald strolls over to the window. The snow has drifted. The air is cold and seems hard to the touch. Would Dr Lund call to ask if we are well, eh? Surely that's not necessary. Jesper has another suggestion: they can ring for a taxi. Ewald turns to him and laughs. He can still change mood as quickly as the weather. Is Jesper planning to go anywhere? No, he isn't. They look at each other. Ewald goes into gloomy mode: perhaps they will never have a use for the telephone? Perhaps it will just stand there as a reminder of loneliness and everything it is impossible to talk about? No, that isn't how it is. The next time he is at work he can ring Maj at home and tell her he loves her. He loves her and Jesper and Stine. That is what he will do.

"Have you received a letter?" she asks.

Maj points to his dressing gown. The envelope is poking out of a pocket. He gives it to her, ill at ease, and it really surprises him that such a small envelope can disrupt a day like this. The in-laws have gone and they have a telephone. It is a nuisance. Maj opens the envelope, takes out a little card and looks at it. Then she turns to Jesper.

"Get your satchel and go to the kitchen."

"Why?"

"Because I say so, Jesper."

Jesper is ill at ease too, because he, too, has something on his conscience. Everyone has something. He hesitates, then obeys and drags his feet through the flat. They hear him stop in the bathroom and have a wee, a long one. Maj glances at Ewald, who stamps the floor.

"Tell me then!" he demands.

"That was violent."

"Mm? Violent?"

"Are you so inquisitive?"

"I'm not inquisitive."

"Is there something you're afraid of?"

Ewald doesn't stamp on the floor again. On the contrary, he takes a step back.

"Afraid of? What would I be afraid of?"

"Fru Vik's getting married."

"What on earth . . . ?"

"Fru Vik's going to marry Olaf Hall."

It is a long time since Ewald has laughed so much. In the end he has to lie down on the sofa.

"And so she sees herself honour-bound to inform us via a letter on the doormat? Well, well, the Lord does indeed work in mysterious ways, as the city treasurer said."

Maj sits down beside Ewald.

"She wants me to be her chief bridesmaid."

Ewald mulls this over.

"Bridesmaid? Does she really need one at her age?"

"They're getting married in Fagerborg Church."

"You're kidding? In church? Can't they do it at the registry office?"

"And Olaf Hall wants you to be his best man."

Ewald has to get to his feet.

"Have they rented the royal balcony so that they can come out and wave to the populus?"

"Ewald, please."

"I've never heard the like of it."

Ewald sits down again and is actually not displeased. He is happy to be the best man for the ponce in tweed and wishes the ageing bride and groom the best of luck. Maj places a hand on his knee.

"We can't say no, can we."

"Can't we?"

"Think about everything she's done for us. Looking after Jesper. Taking messages."

Ewald thinks: What if I die before the wedding? There is always a time limit. The whole of life is a time limit. But so what? If he dies they can just find another best man. He can be replaced. He can be swapped. Most things can be replaced. These thoughts are depressing.

"We'd better say yes then," Ewald says.

Maj opens the telephone directory. But that is a step too far. Ewald draws the line right there.

"Are you going to ring?"

Maj laughs.

"Yes. Isn't that fun?"

"Can't you just go upstairs and talk to her? Then we save money, too."

"Now you really are being mean, Ewald."

"So Fru Vik will be the first person we call from our own telephone?"

And suddenly the mood changes again. Maj closes the directory and glares at Ewald in the same way she had done from the street corner.

"Yes, I can imagine you have lots of calls to make."

"Lots of calls to whom?"

"Others, not Fru Vik."

"What do you mean?"

"Oh, you know right enough."

But Ewald doesn't know. He doesn't understand her. She is out of balance. Wasn't she like this after Jesper's birth as well? She is in a spin. The best is to keep quiet and wait or change the subject. Ewald isn't good at keeping quiet.

"Did Esther and Halvard get off safely?" he asks.

"Yes."

"The train goes all the way to Trondheim, doesn't it?"

"No, only Eidsvoll. It was a regional train."

"But they had a seat, did they?"

"Yes, it wasn't very full."

"What did you buy?"

"A shawl. It was on offer."

"A sale now? In March?"

Maj turns to Ewald, takes a deep breath and lets it out slowly. Ewald would like to hug her, but dare not.

"I'm going up to see her," she says.

"No, you can ring. Why else have we got a telephone?"

"I'll go up anyway."

Maj gets to her feet, pokes her head in to see Stine first and soon Ewald hears the front door slam and even from inside he can hear her footsteps on the stairs. The walls are too thin. Jesper stands in the doorway looking at him. He seems sad.

"Well, that was a bit of a macaroni," Ewald says.

Jesper's sadness changes to anxiety.

"Macaroni?"

Ewald laughs.

"Fru Vik is only going to get bloody married."

At last Jesper smiles.

"Get married? Can she do that?"

"It seems so, Jesper. And do you know what we learn from that? Some people never learn."

They manage to move the clock before Maj returns. They hang it on the wall above the telephone. So that you know how long you have been on the phone. Later that evening, when Jesper has gone to bed, Maj puts on the blue shawl and goes into the sitting room where Ewald is reading the telephone directory. He looks up. It suits her. Blue suits her. She moves like a model. But she is making too much of it. She is overdoing it. It is only a shawl. Ewald sees something else, something that he hasn't seen since they met at Rondo Restaurant in the autumn of 1937 and she was a newcomer in Oslo and he had a roving eye and knew all the tricks. Ewald sees shyness. And isn't shyness one of our truest faces? Ewald thinks: it was shyness he felt first when he was told he was going to die. But it wasn't death that made him feel shy. It was the thought of Maj. He says she should have bought two shawls, one for inside and one for out. Maj explains it can be worn inside and outside, all according to what season it is. That was why she bought it, to save money. They sit next to the telephone for the rest of the evening. However, no-one knows their number, apart from Fru Vik, but Maj has already spoken to her.

"They're getting married on May 13th," she says.

Ewald goes into the bathroom first. He looks at himself in the mirror. Can he see any difference? He can't. It probably comes so slowly that he won't notice it until it is too late. And when it is too late who cares. He turns away when Maj comes in, so that she can't see the marks from the blood tests on his left arm, the bruises that are blue at first, then go green and soon are the same colour as his skin. Then his illness has a natural appearance. Ewald leaves the bathroom to her and tarries for a moment by Jesper's bed. He is asleep. He is pretending to be asleep. It is easy. You just close your eyes. He can see through his eyelids. When his parents finally go to bed and the last light has been switched off, he gets up and tiptoes into the sitting room to the telephone. The clock on the wall says ten minutes past twelve. If he had his way there wouldn't be a single clock on the walls. He lifts the receiver and listens. The whole of this day, the whole of these twenty-four hours collects in the dialling tone, this continuous sound, so full of promise, waiting only to be interrupted and to metamorphose into conversations, confidences or silence. It is an A. That much he can hear. If there is a note that can make people cry, there must also be one that can make people laugh, Jesper thinks. He doesn't know yet that it is the same note, just played in a different way.

———

An extraordinary board meeting was held at the chairman's house on March 6th, 1950. Those present were only the vice-chairman Fru Lund, the secretary Else Larsen and of course Fru Berit Nordklev, as a result of the short notice. The treasurer Maj Kristoffersen is still on leave. She now has a telephone, we were informed, and the number was given to committee members.

The chairman presented the issue: a complaint had been received from two persons in the district (independently of each other) in connection with the sale of Christmas stamps. The seller charged one krone instead of 50 øre per stamp. Apparently this incident took place on the Majorstua steps. As the accounts for the sales tallied, the seller in question must have pocketed the "surplus". The board takes this matter very seriously and will immediately start investigations to get to the bottom of it, otherwise confidence in our activities will be jeopardised. The matter has also been reported to the working committee in the Oslo District of the Red Cross.

I should add that there was a sad, dismayed atmosphere at the meeting.

GUILT

Jesper already knows: Jostein has gone. He can see by the unused hook. And the desk at the head of the middle row is empty. How long will it be like this? Until a new pupil starts or the caretaker moves the desk to another classroom? By then Jostein, the boy who could barely hear at all and walked with his head at an angle, will have been forgotten. Jesper sits down. He won't forget Jostein. He promises he won't. It must have happened yesterday. Yesterday Jostein stopped and Jesper wasn't there. Løkke glances at Jesper and leaves him in peace. But when the bell rings he has to stay behind. Løkke walks down to Jesper.

"As you can see, Jostein has started at a school where he can be helped better."

Jesper nods.

"Have you got an absence note?"

Jesper gives the note to Løkke, who first runs an eye over it and then reads aloud:

"Jesper Kristoffersen was absent from school yesterday, March 2nd, 1950, because of the telephone. Yours sincerely, Ewald Kristoffersen."

Løkke folds the note, laughs all the way to his desk and

puts it in the drawer, with his grade book. He stops laughing.

"Well, well, Jesper, give my respects to your father and tell him I've read many absence notes in the course of a long life of service to this school, but this one was a first."

Jesper looks down and can't get the sight of Jostein's empty desk out of his head.

"Alright."

"Tell me, Jesper, was it you or your family who got the telephone?"

Jesper has to give this some thought.

"We got a telephone."

"Good. Can you remember the number as well?"

"55 14 30," Jesper says.

Løkke takes out a planner and writes the number there. The bell rings. Soon everyone is back. It all happens in this lesson. They are up to the letter L. In the book there is a drawing of a girl laughing. Jesper imagines it is Stine, except that the girl in the book has blonde hair and a blue ribbon. Underneath it says: *l – leaf – loaf – we all have to laugh.* Then the door opens, although no-one knocked. It is the Deputy Head. The Deputy Head doesn't knock. He is feared. The pupils stand up and stand so erect their spinal columns could be used as flag posts. Of the Deputy Head it is said he once locked a third class in the broom cupboard in the cellar for a whole day. That was just before the war. A boy had raised his arm in an inappropriate way. This came to cost the Deputy Head dearly. He was in Grini concentration camp and later, in 1941, sent to Germany, to Bergen-Belsen. When he came home he weighed 41 kilos. Løkke, who is as subservient with the Deputy Head as the pupils, goes to meet him. The line between awe and fear is sometimes no greater than a line of chalk on the blackboard. Something is said. It is impossible to hear what. That makes it only worse. Everyone has something on their conscience. Everyone has done something. Everyone has something to answer for. No-one is innocent. Løkke turns to Jesper. This time he is the one. The others can breathe a sigh of relief, but they don't. They keep their relief to themselves. One day the door will open and it will be their turn. Jesper has to go with the Deputy Head. They walk through the empty corridors, where coats hang and give off a damp, musty smell. They ascend a staircase and go down another corridor. A cleaning woman turns to watch them. Jesper walks behind the Deputy Head and can barely keep up. The Deputy Head stops outside a door. Jesper stops, too. The Deputy Head places a hand around his neck, at first it feels like a comfort, a gentle assurance, then he squeezes, for a moment Jesper's breath stops and he feels only that he is being lifted from the floor. Then the Deputy Head lets go and they go into the office of the Principal, who is the school's supreme authority and even the Deputy Head has to obey him. The Principal always wears a suit with a waistcoat and a clock chain. He nods to the Deputy Head, who withdraws. There is one more person in the office. Jesper recognises her. It is Fru Nordklev, the harridan, the one who runs the Red Cross. Jesper immediately knows what this is about and starts to concoct a story, but his head is empty, the Deputy Head emptied it. Fru Nordklev stays seated. The Principal comes around the desk and halts in front of Jesper.

"Did you sell Red Cross stamps on the Majorstua steps before Christmas?" he asks.

"Yes."

"Did you sell them for a krone instead of fifty øre?"

"No."

"No? Are you sure about that, Jesper Kristoffersen?"

"I sold them for fifty øre."

"I think you're lying. Which compounds the matter."

"I am not lying."

The Principal hands over to Fru Nordklev. "Was anyone else selling stamps with you?" she asks.

Jesper looks down.

"Jostein."

Fru Nordklev gets up.

"But he wasn't selling stamps for us?"

"He was selling stamps for me."

"Why?"

"He wanted to try."

Fru Nordklev appears to be unhappy, at any rate she heaves a deep sigh, and she turns to the Principal, who puts his hands behind his back.

"Did you know Jostein sold the stamps for a krone each?"

Jesper shakes his head.

"No."

"And you didn't see any of the money that was, how shall I put it, left over?"

Jesper's head sinks further.

"No," he repeats.

The Principal takes a seat behind his desk, takes out a sheet of paper and writes something. Only the sound of the nib moving across the paper can be heard. Then he looks up.

"I appreciate your honesty, Jesper."

Fru Nordklev places a hand on his shoulder.

"We do, too," she says.

The Principal hands the sheet of paper to Fru Nordklev and looks at Jesper.

"I know how much it hurts when you're let down by someone you think is your friend. But you've done the right thing. You can go now."

The Deputy Head is waiting outside. They walk down the corridor together. Jesper's shoes are heavy. He drags behind. It isn't Jesper who has been betrayed. It is Jesper who has betrayed Jostein. The Deputy Head stops at the top of the stairs.

"I was in Grini," he says.

Jesper nods and studies his shoes. One shoe lace has come undone.

"It was December, 1941. There were six hundred of us in the camp. Do you know who arranged for us to be given clipfish, butter, sugar, sardines, caviar, honey, vitamins, pork, stock cubes, pearl barley, scouring cloths, liver oil and underwear? Do you know, Jesper?"

"No. Who?"

"The Red Cross. And later, when I was in Belsen, do you know who sent a parcel of food, tobacco, books and toiletries every month?"

"The Red Cross."

"The Red Cross saved my life, lad. Do you know how much I weighed when I came home?"

"41 kilos."

"And had it not been for the Red Cross I would have weighed nothing. I would've been dead. And the dead don't weigh anything. I've seen them. Look at me, Jesper."

Jesper looked up; this is as heavy as both shoes put together.

The Deputy Head is still lean. He can't rid himself of what he lost. The lines in his face are deep and straight. With him he carries a shadow that can change into bright light at any moment.

"But do you know what was the most important thing they sent?" he asks.

Jesper is afraid of giving the wrong answer.

"Underwear," he says.

The Deputy Head laughs and an unusual sound comes from this man; his laughter doesn't suit the geometrical mouth.

"The thought, Jesper. The knowing that we weren't forgotten. That someone remembered us."

Jesper bends down and ties his shoelace. It won't be long before the bell rings. He can hear the unrest in the classrooms, not much, just a chair being carefully moved backwards, the crinkle of greaseproof paper, a pencil case being zipped. Then Jesper goes back to the office, and this time there is no weight, he feels light, he can almost fly. He meets the Principal and Fru Nordklev in the doorway.

"We shared the money," Jesper says.

Both stop and stare at him, then at each other. The Principal takes over:

"I beg your pardon?"

"Jostein and I shared the money that was left over."

"You don't need to protect Jostein."

"It's true. We—"

The Principal interrupts Jesper:

"We've spoken to Jostein. He's confessed. One sinner is more than enough in this business. Is that clear?"

Jesper doesn't answer.

"Is that clear?" the Principal repeats.

It isn't clear. It isn't clear at all. If he had said it the first time, they would have believed him. Or is it because they don't want to believe him, that what the Principal said is true, that they don't want any more sinners? Jesper nods anyway. Fru Nordklev holds her little bag with both hands and her eyes roam the room; she looks anywhere but at Jesper. The bell rings. It is a short break. The bell rings for class. And in the course of the day a new expression comes into use at Majorstua School, and it spreads across the whole city, first to other schools in Oslo West – Uranienborg, Midtstuen, Slemdal, Tåsen – and from there north to Lilleborg, Sagene, Bjølsen, to take root in Oslo East – Grünerløkka, Gamlebyen, Sinsen – and finally to stop in Ruseløkka, which lies between everything, east and west, with its back to the fjord: *Are you stone deaf or what?* It isn't exactly meant as a statement, but it isn't meant that badly either. There is more a kind of resignation in the expression. At any rate it isn't as bad as cackbag.

Today Jesper takes a different way home. He doesn't want to meet Jostein in Kirkeveien. He would prefer not to meet him at all. He won't say *Are you stone deaf or what?* again either. He walks across Tørtberg, behind Fagerborg, he sneaks off and has a wee in the bushes down from Marienlyst. There are other yellow stains in the snow too, but they are from dogs. Jesper is a dog today. When they have lunch, and Maj has made fishcakes, he has no appetite. He doesn't want to be as thin as the Deputy Head was. He flicks through his reader even though he is actually not allowed to do anything but eat at the table. But you can make an exception for homework. He doesn't take in a single letter. Ewald isn't hungry, either.

He just chases food around his plate with the fork. Maj looks at him with surprise.

"Don't you two like my cooking?" she asks.

Ewald immediately helps himself to more, despite his plate still being full. He is so keen to be exactly as before – hungry, gentle, straightforward – that he knocks over Jesper's glass and water runs across the letter M, M for meal, for mistrust, for misunderstanding. Jesper can't help himself:

"Are you completely deaf or what?"

A moment passes, a moment of profound silence and surprise, almost reflection. Then Ewald bangs the table and knocks over more glasses. He is angry, unusually so. He shouts:

"What did you say? What *was* it that you said?"

Jesper cannot comprehend what made him say that.

"I just . . ."

"Did you say I'm dead? Did you say your father was *dead*?"

"No, I just said . . ."

"Just said? Just said what?"

"That you're deaf."

Ewald glares at Jesper. Maj decides to leave the table. Stine has started crying. It is Jesper's fault. Then Ewald laughs. It is a long time since he has laughed in this way. He laughs until his appetite returns.

"Deaf, Jesper? I'm not deaf."

"I didn't mean it anyway."

Where did you get that language from? I haven't heard it before and I've heard most things."

"School."

Ewald crushes a potato with his fork.

"I see. Jostein."

314

Maj returns with Stine in her arms. She sends Jesper a look and is not pleased with him.

"Don't talk like that anyway."

Ewald wants to agree with her.

"Mamma's right, Jesper. It's not nice. Don't talk like that."

Maj turns to Ewald and apparently isn't pleased with him, either.

"You're a fine one."

"Fine one? What do you mean?"

"What about all those dirty words you bring home from the Bristol. Cackbag!"

"So you've become refined now, have you?"

"Or wherever it is you come from now."

Maj goes back out with Stine. A few doors slam. Ewald looks at Jesper.

"I think we'll do the washing-up today," he says.

Afterwards they hang Jesper's reader up to dry over the stove.

At eight the telephone rings. It is the first proper telephone call they have received. This time it isn't a test. The ringtone is shrill and fast and can be heard in all the rooms. Ewald gets up from the mattress in the dining room, Maj straightens up over the cradle in the bedroom, Jesper gives a start sitting over the narrow desk in the hall. They collect in the sitting room. The telephone continues to ring. Ewald takes the receiver. He speaks in a loud, clear voice, like last time:

"This is the Kristoffersen household, hello."

Then he listens for a moment, seems disappointed, almost offended, and turns to Maj.

"It's for you."

Maj goes closer, whispers:

"Who is it?"

"The Red Cross! Who else?"

Maj takes the telephone, holds the receiver with both hands in an oddly awkward way and puts it to her ear. Ewald takes Jesper with him from the sitting room and closes the door. The person talking should have some quiet. This is a private matter. It annoys him that Maj should be the first to receive a call. Then he is relieved after all. It could have been bad news. Ewald listens and is already getting impatient.

"The women are yodelling on the line," he says.

Jesper listens too, but hears nothing. Which means it is the other person speaking, from somewhere else. That makes him ill at ease. He also suspects the telephone can spell danger. Ewald pulls him away from the door. You're not supposed to eavesdrop, either.

"You must never say 'Are you deaf' to Jostein," Ewald says.

"Why not?"

"Because he *is* deaf, Jesper."

Finally Maj puts down the receiver. Ewald opens the door. She looks at the clock above the telephone and says nothing. Ewald can see by her neck that something is wrong. A terrible thought strikes him: Dr Lund has broken the Hippocratic Oath and told his wife that Ewald Kristoffersen has an incurable disease and she couldn't control her tongue at a meeting and now it is generally known in Fagerborg that he will die within a certain period of time. He feels impelled to ask:

"Was it anything important?"

"It was Jostein who cheated us over the stamps."

"How did he manage that?"

316

"He sold them at a krone apiece and put fifty øre in his pocket."

Ewald laughs, but realises at once this is inappropriate.

"So the Red Cross didn't lose any money and no good causes were damaged."

"We lost trust, Ewald. That's even worse. Trust. As an adman you should know that."

Ewald looks down and wonders if this is the right moment to show Maj the marks on his arm, lay all the pills he has to take on the table – and always carries in his pocket – unbutton his shirt and let her see right through him, apart from the black spot that grows and grows and blocks the view. He doesn't. Again this shyness. He can't bring himself to do it. He blushes. He is ashamed and puzzled.

"The Red Cross is robust enough to take a knock," he says.

Now Maj stares straight at him and he has to look away.

"Are you sure?"

Jesper scurries into the kitchen. He can't bear the atmosphere. It jars in his ears. It jars in his heart. He can't stand himself. The pages of his reader are dry and wrinkly, but he can easily read what is written. He doesn't like the illustrations: a cat slinking up to a dog's bowl of food, another cat chasing a mouse, a goat butting a girl, who falls into a stream, a naked child sitting on a cushion shaped like a cloud and a brother and sister planting a tree. Is it in a cemetery? Worst, however, is the snowman holding a broom. *Our snowman stood for a day or two and the sparrows were afraid of him, as you can imagine. But when the sun shone the big man turned to water.*

Jesper goes over to the window and looks down at the yard. He sees only shadows. He doesn't hear any more voices from the sitting room. When he has gone to bed, his mother comes in and stands by him. She doesn't say anything for a while. She swallows several times.

"Stine's present?" she asks at length.

Jesper refrains from saying anything yet. His mother leans closer.

"Did you buy it with the money you got from Jostein?"

A lie now wouldn't hurt anyone. It was the lie in the Principal's office that hurt someone. It hurt Jostein. Almost mortally. It hurt Jesper too because he realises what kind of person he is, what he is capable of, and it is too early when you haven't yet turned nine and are behind with most things.

"No," Jesper says.

"Are you sure you're telling me the truth?"

"Yes."

Maj takes a step back and stops in the semi-darkness.

"I'm going to throw it away anyway," she says.

She closes the door quietly behind her.

This is Jesper's mortal wound: his mother no longer trusts him. He can never be completely happy again. Neither of them can. If he tells the truth, would both of them be happy? Jesper thinks about music, of the sad, laconic melody that he has learned off by heart, but still cannot play. There is a certain kind of happiness after all.

———

On March 19th the board meeting was held in the parish hall. All the members were present. Treasurer Fru Maj Kristoffersen was welcomed back after her leave. She thanked the board for the bouquet of flowers.

The parish nurse in Fagerborg has applied to Fru Nordklev for more pairs of shoes, if possible. The shoes will be made available by Oslo District. A card-index file is kept on the families or individuals who receive help in the form of a packed lunch, shoes or whatever.

Via Fru Esther Andersen the department has received an application for financial support to pay the wages of a kindergarten teacher at the newly established children's clinic at the Rikshospital. After some discussion it was decided to donate sixty kroner a month during the current year.

The autumn bazaar was discussed and it was agreed we would try to acquire the following prizes: two sets of bed linen, a table lamp with a shade, a doll with a bed, coffee (and perhaps sugar) and possibly ladies' underwear.

The chairman, Fru Nordklev, received 32 pairs of children's shoes from Oslo District. Fru Stubberud, Holbergsgate 27, was given some second-hand clothes by members of our department.

We discussed a proposal, also put forward by Oslo District, about departments arranging joint trips into the country for the elderly. The Fagerborg board, however, would prefer to organise such trips in its region independently of others. The finance for the children's holiday camp and the old people's trip, originally set at 500 kroner, will probably be reduced to 465 because of expenses: the department will have to reimburse those who paid a krone for a Christmas stamp. The perpetrator, incidentally, has confessed. The matter will not be pursued. It was a strain for all parties. We must have stricter guidelines next time. However, we see the case as terminated now.

March 21st, 1950

REPAIR

Enzo Zanetti drains the little glass and turns to Jesper.

"No, you'll have to wait for this Satie for a lesson or two."

"Why?"

"Because you have to be able to do all the other stuff first."

"Such as what?"

Enzo Zanetti sighs:

"Such as playing the piano, Jesper. By the way, isn't your mother with you today?"

"No."

"You can find your way home alone as well?"

"Yes."

"Play me a C."

Jesper lifts his hand, the left one, and allows his middle finger to fall on the correct key, holds it, then let's go. Enzo Zanetti listens in amazement to the sound hanging in the air.

"Which hand do you write with?" he asks.

Jesper has to mull this over.

"My right hand."

"Then play the same note with it."

Jesper does, but uses his index finger this time. There is no resonance afterwards. The note has gone the moment he takes away his hand. Enzo Zanetti sits down beside him on the stool, plays a scale and tells Jesper to do the same. He manages it without much difficulty. Enzo Zanetti only has to adjust the position of his fingers and explain how the thumb is the real secret in the sequence. Then he tells Jesper to play the scale with his left hand and Enzo Zanetti is even more astonished. The boy plays it easily and without any strain. There is a depth in all the notes which gives them space and it doesn't appear to cost him any effort. It seems, if anything, too easy.

"Most things in life are boring," Enzo Zanetti says.

"Why are we doing this then?"

"Because the humdrum will lead us to happiness, Jesper."

Enzo Zanetti is about to get carried away by his own words and pours himself another glass, which he drains again and re-fills.

"You're thirsty," Jesper says.

Enzo Zanetti shakes his head.

"Repairs."

Jesper wonders what is broken in Enzo Zanetti since he has to repair it so often, but he doesn't ask. He can keep it to himself if he doesn't want to tell. Jesper plays the scales, with both hands this time. Enzo Zanetti pushes a chair closer to the piano and sits down.

"Try the other way," he says.

Jesper does that too, as fast as he can. Afterwards Enzo is quiet for a good while. Perhaps he is already broken.

"Didn't you like it?" Jesper asks.

"Are you trying to impress me?"

"I don't know."

"You should never try. You should never try to impress anyone. And you should never rush, either."

"What should I do then?"

"You should just try to move people. What did I tell you last time about a C?"

"That I should play a C to make people cry."

"Exactly. That's what you will learn from me."

Jesper doesn't quite know if he understands this, but he senses a context anyway, a mysterious connection between what Enzo Zanetti says and all his repairs. Jesper plays an A.

"The dial tone," he says.

Enzo Zanetti laughs.

"The dial tone doesn't impress anyone. But think of everything that's waiting afterwards."

"No-one's at home."

"No. God himself answers. Think about that a little. And now you can play the engaged tone."

Jesper hits the same note again and again and keeps the rhythm until he rings off. When the lesson is over he is given a pile of sheet music, the activities he can do at home.

"Give my regards to your mother," Enzo Zanetti says.

Jesper goes downstairs and out into Jørgen Moes gate. The clock on the spire says ten past six. He hears the tram whining round the corner on the Holte bend. It sounds like a whole orchestra playing on untuned saws. For a moment he wonders which way to go. He only knows he shouldn't rush. Or did that only apply to music? He could, for example, go to Bislett and past Fagerborg Church, but he doesn't like the public urinal down there, not only does it smell foul, but there are also elderly men hanging around and it is impossible to work them out. So he chooses the road past Vestkanttorget which, in the winter, when it is cold enough, is usually turned into a skating rink, mostly for girls. Now the ice is melting and no good for anything, it is just slush and deserted. The kindergarten by the yellow timber house is equally deserted and abandoned at this time of day. The unused children's climbing frame resembles a skeleton of a rectangular prehistoric animal that went extinct before the war started. Jesper suddenly feels like an adult, not old, but grown up, with this music under his arm he is an adult. He is coming from the office. No, he is coming from the workshop where everything is repaired. He will have to get himself a bag for this music. He can't be seen carrying the music like this. Should he take Jacob Aalls gate or Kirkeveien? In Jacob Aalls gate he risks bumping into the Stenspark gang and that isn't a good idea. Jesper takes Kirkeveien. The sky is completely black and yet there are no stars. Light falls in clusters from the street lamps. He stops outside Melsom the butcher's. Inside the shop is Jostein. He is sitting on the floor in the corner under the hams hanging from hooks. He is wearing a stained white coat that is much too big for him with his arms wrapped around his knees. Jesper knocks on the window. Jostein doesn't hear, nor the next time Jesper knocks. Jesper becomes nervous. He rolls up his sheet music, stuffs it into his pocket and waves his arms. Then Jostein gets up, comes over to the door and lets Jesper in. Jostein locks the door again and puts out a hand. Jesper shakes it. Suddenly they are both adults. Jesper is a pianist. Jostein is a butcher. Jostein laughs. His laughter is different from before. Perhaps they teach them to laugh like that at deaf school. Jesper is overwhelmed by his bad conscience and starts to cry. Jostein lowers his head like a bull, runs towards Jesper and butts him. They tumble over one another and push each other.

"I didn't mean it," Jesper shouts.

"What?"

"I didn't mean to blame you."

Jostein holds his ears, as though that were necessary, and he shouts too, it sounds like a song:

"I can't hear! I can't hear!"

They lie still panting. Then they get up. Jostein looks stupid in his coat, which covers his shoes and is twice as long as his arms.

"What are you doing here?" Jesper asks.

Jostein watches his lips, but it isn't until afterwards that he understands. Everything is delayed.

"Grounded. Punishment. I have to wash the basins."

"I can help you."

"It could be worse though. I could be blind, too. Lots of people are."

Jostein finds a knife, cuts two slices from a mutton ham and gives one to Jesper. They chew for a few minutes. It doesn't taste particularly good, but it is good to have something else to do.

"I told the Principal that we shared the money," Jesper says.

Jostein stares at him and nods.

"And then?"

"He didn't believe me."

Jostein laughs again. He has obviously adopted that laugh. It is like coughing into a bread bin. At any rate it doesn't sound healthy. He should get Dr Lund to look at it, or at least listen to it.

"Doesn't matter," Jostein says.

"How come?"

"I have nothing to lose anyway."

Jesper walks home, relieved, though still uneasy, and puts the music on the little rack above the keys. Ewald stands in the doorway, in a white shirt and braces, even though strictly speaking he doesn't need to wear them anymore.

"What have you learned to play today?" he asks.

"The dial tone."

"The dawdle tone? Am I paying money for you to learn the dawdle tone, which we already have on the telephone?"

"And the engaged tone."

"Which do you like better?"

"The engaged tone."

Ewald isn't satisfied with the answer at first, not at all, but soon changes his mind. If the tone is engaged then at least there is someone at the other end, however long it takes. He shrugs and there is more he wants to say. He asks in a low voice:

"You didn't have anything to do with the stamps Jostein was selling, did you?"

Jesper thinks: This will never end, this will carry on for the rest of my life, although he cannot imagine what the rest of his life means.

"No, Pappa."

Ewald looks around, then takes a little packet from his pocket.

"Mamma threw this in the rubbish bin. And I went downstairs and retrieved it. Do you think I did the right thing?"

Jesper just nods. His father gives him the packet. Where

can Jesper hide it? He puts it in his satchel. If his mother finds it he can at least blame his father. Then he will immediately lie and say Pappa fetched the packet from the shed where the bins are. Then he will be held to account. He goes to his mother, who is sitting at the kitchen table with the Red Cross ledger. Ewald checks to see if Stine is asleep and comes back soon after. They stand in silence beside each other, not wishing to disturb her. They do anyway. Maj looks up, sees her two men, both standing with their hands behind their backs, and she hasn't the heart to tell them to go somewhere else and leave her in peace. On the contrary, Maj wants them to stand there for the rest of their lives and she will soon have got to the point where she understands what the rest of life means.

"There's something I don't understand," Maj says.

Ewald and Jesper say nothing. They just take a short pace backwards and they do it in step. Their movements are bound together by a bad conscience. What is it that she doesn't understand? Doesn't she understand them? Are they impossible to understand? Maj looks down and adds the figures once again. They can see her adding silently and at the bottom of the page she draws two thick lines: *Total*.

"What don't you understand?" Ewald asks.

Jesper also ventures a step forward.

"Perhaps we can help you?"

Maj sighs:

"How many stamps was it Jostein actually sold for you?"

"Twenty-six, Mamma."

"And now thirty-one people have contacted us asking for their fifty øre back. The number's rising and rising. Can you understand how anyone can be so petty?"

Maj looks at them again, her boys, and all the hardness inside her, the numbers and the suspicions, even the fury, moves to one side and the space vacated is filled with love, or at least gratitude.

"Enzo Zanetti sends his regards," Jesper says.

———

The board meeting was held on April 14th at Frøken Vanda Aasland's. Those present apart from the host were: Fru Nordklev, Fru Arnesen, Fru Larsen, Fru Lund and Fru Kristoffersen.

Fru Arnesen read the minutes from the working committee meeting on April 2nd. As mentioned in the previous board meeting a joint trip for the elderly was proposed. The decision was taken to go ahead with it and the trip was scheduled for June 20th.

Fru Nordklev had received a request from Oslo Children's Aid for parcels of babywear. Children's Aid was given two parcels and one parcel was given to Seaman Oswald Hansen from Porsgrunn, who was in Oslo for medical treatment.

It was agreed to change one of the prizes for the bazaar, from a doll with a bed to a travel alarm clock.

Fagerborg department stock as per April 14th, 1950, is as follows: 35 metres of coloured cloth, 24 pairs of children's shoes, 7 parcels of babywear, one ceramic dish with six plates plus a variety of medical equipment.

The treasurer, Maj Kristoffersen, made an ominous announcement. According to the accounts for stamp sales more people had contacted the Red Cross for the reimbursement of fifty øre than her calculation of the correct figure. It was discussed how the board should react to this and we decided to pay up whatever to bring this sorry business to an end. All members of the board expressed their disappointment that there were such rotten apples on all sides of our district willing to exploit a difficult situation.

RESONANCE

Many eager spectators have come to Borggården, the square in front of the City Hall, this morning, mostly men who have taken a break from work or are on their way to a meeting, some newspaper boys on bikes, a few women who are shopping, two classes from Oslo Commerce School close by, the odd tramp and in addition four police officers making sure that everything passes off as smoothly as possible. This is serious: the 49 bells that should ring every quarter of an hour and chime every full hour in the City Hall arrive on lorries, there is room for three on each, sixteen lorries are needed. Then they have to be hoisted up to the towers. There is an ingenious system of wires, pulleys and hooks and machines. The police ask the spectators to move back. This could be dangerous to life or limb. Also a way to die, Ewald Kristoffersen thinks, getting one of those bells on your head. That would resonate. He stands at the back and follows events. He isn't really interested. Everything is impressive, brilliant and historic. But he doesn't let himself get carried away. He has lost interest. It is just happening. He had thought it would be the opposite: that his senses would be heightened and for that reason he would feel the merest bump as an assault. It wasn't like that. He watches the Dek-Rek team enter the main door. They are going to check if their decorations have been handled correctly and are in the right order. Ewald strolls back to the office. It surprises him: now that he is going to die soon he has plenty of time. He thought this too would be the opposite: that everything he did he would have to do at a certain speed. It isn't like that. He does a round of Karl Johans gate. Some people are already in spring clothes and are regretting it. It is April. The old season hasn't let go yet and the new one hasn't established itself. Ewald is reminded of the snowman in the yard. He forgot to check. At Dek-Rek only Frøken Bryn is at her place. She looks up at him with concern.

"Aren't you with the others in the City Hall?" she asks.

"They'll have to manage without me now."

"Do you think they can?"

Ewald is forced to give that some thought.

"Yes, I think they already are."

"I'm not so sure about that."

Ewald looks down at the loyal secretary and is moved and nervous. What does she know about him?

"It was nice of you to say that. But when I've drawn it the way they want it, they don't need me anymore."

"You should be an artist, you should, Ewald."

"Nonsense. Things aren't that bad."

Frøken Bryn laughs and gets up.

"I have to go on an errand. Is there anything you need?"

"Nothing except faith, hope and love."

"I can buy you a cinnamon bun anyway. So that you can put some weight back on."

"I'm dieting, my dear."

"But you don't need to vanish in front of our eyes. I'll buy two!"

"But you eat one of them."

"If you're going to be difficult, OK."

She passes Ewald a letter. It is from the Rikshospital. Frøken Bryn pauses a little before letting go.

"Is it alright if they send letters here?" Ewald asks.

"The question is if it's alright with you."

"So Rudjord hasn't said anything?"

"No."

Ewald sticks the letter in his pocket and sits at his drawing board in the empty design office. Soon he hears the door closing behind Frøken Bryn. He waits a bit. Then he opens the letter, reads it, folds it and puts it back in the envelope. After a while he goes to the telephone, lifts the receiver and rings home. Maj answers at once. Her voice is deep and serious.

"Kristoffersens here."

"It's me."

"Ewald? Is something wrong?"

"Wrong? Surely there doesn't have to be something wrong if I call."

"Why are you ringing then?"

"I just wanted to say . . ."

Ewald turns away although he is alone. Only death and love make him shy.

"What did you want to say, Ewald?"

"That I love you."

There is silence for a few seconds. He hears only her breathing.

"Why are you telling me on the telephone?"

"I can say it when I get home, too."

"Yes, that would be nice."

"Is Stine asleep?"

"She's slept all day. And I've spoken to Fru Vik about the wedding. There'll be a party after the ceremony at Sim. Solberg's."

"Yes, that fits. A wedding party at a bakery-cum-café."

"You'll probably have to give a speech."

"I probably won't."

"Yes, you will, Ewald. Now that we've said yes to . . ."

"I'll be back late by the way. Don't count on me for dinner."

There is another silence. Her voice is different when she continues.

"So that's why you ring to tell me you *love* me?"

"What do you mean?"

"You know very well."

"We're setting up the exhibition in the City Hall. Everyone's working overtime."

"You can come home as late as you like."

"No, I'll come as quickly as I can. I—"

Maj rings off before Ewald can finish, regretful at first, but then she catches herself. She is in no doubt. He rings to tell her he loves her. That says it all. She is on the verge of tears. He doesn't deserve them. She cries anyway. Then she hears Jesper in the hallway. She wipes her eyes, blows her nose and goes to see him.

"Could you look after Stine for a bit today?" she asks.

Jesper looks up at his mother and smiles.

"I suppose I can."

"She's asleep. Don't wake her. And if you need help, then go and see Fru Vik."

"Can't I ring?"

"You can do that too, yes. I'll be back in an hour or two. At the latest."

Maj puts on her winter coat, hurries down to Majorstua, takes the tram to the National Theatre, walks to the corner by the travel agency and waits. She feels wretched. She doesn't want to feel like this. It is the last thing she wants. She despises herself. But it is Ewald who has made her feel wretched. That is perhaps what angers her most. Then Maj sees him coming out of the Dek-Rek offices in Rosenkrantz' gate. He is alone. He is walking towards her. She turns away. In the window there are pictures of wonderful holiday destinations: Copenhagen, Paris, Rome, even New York. Ewald doesn't see her. His mind is probably elsewhere. Is he going to the City Hall? He goes into the Grand Hotel. Is this where it happens? Does he rent a room at the Grand right around the corner to be with his lover? He has no shame. Maj, feeling sick, follows him. The doorman bows and lets her in. Ewald isn't standing at the desk waiting impatiently for a key. Instead he is sitting in the hairdressing saloon. The hairdresser throws a gown around him and takes out a comb and a pair of scissors. Ewald has to make himself look good first. That is the connection. Maj feels like going over and laying into him. She stands in the foyer. Ewald finally has what he wants: his hair is as thick as lacquer across his head. He pays and walks back the same way. Was that all? But he's not going back to the office. He walks on. Has he got a room waiting for him in Bondeheimen Hotel which he considers the perfect bolt hole? Then he'd better think again. He isn't going to the Bondeheimen or the Bristol. He has other plans. She follows him. How could things end like this? With her having to snoop on her husband. She continues down Pilestredet. Cars splash dirty water across the pavement. She keeps her distance. But if he suddenly turns he will see her. For a second she hopes he will. He doesn't. He seems determined, almost obsessed, she struggles to keep up. Where is he going? Who is he going to meet? She feels like screaming. She feels like running, catching him up and slapping him across the face. She doesn't. But what will she do when she catches him in flagrante? She hasn't thought that far ahead. She can't. Ewald turns into Langes gate and stops outside the entrance to the Rikshospital. Maj stops too, behind a cart full of cobblestones. Is he waiting for someone? Is this where it will begin, the break-up, is he going to a rendez-vous with a nurse? Is Maj the bit of fluff on the side now? What is it that his colleagues say? Have you got a fancy woman? Has Ewald got a fancy woman? Suddenly she hears a strange sound, a sound she hasn't heard before in this city. A bell rings in the City Hall tower. It must be a test. Ewald hears the same. He stops and looks around. When it is quiet again he catches sight of Maj. She is standing by the corner of Pilestredet, half-hidden behind a cart from the Highway Authorities, he can't understand it. Neither of them makes a move to meet the other. In the end Ewald goes down to her. There is this shyness again. He finds it difficult to speak. She doesn't say anything either and doesn't look at him.

"What are you doing here?" he asks.

Maj has to continue to be angry to manage this situation. She raises her gaze.

"I think it is me who should be asking you that. What are *you* doing here?"

"Have you been following me?"

"I just want to know what you're doing. And don't try to deny anything. I know enough."

Ewald has to hold on to something.

"What do you know? Who told you?"

"So I'm the last to know, am I? The last to find out that you have someone else?"

Ewald can hardly look at her.

"Do you think I've got someone else?"

"I don't know any longer what I think!"

He tries to put a hand on Maj's shoulder, but she doesn't let him near her, she pushes him away.

"I'm going to die," Ewald says.

"What?"

"I have a lung disease. I didn't want to frighten you."

Maj stares at him, still in doubt. She can't believe it.

"Is that why you've lost weight?"

"Yes, it's a fantastic diet. You'll have to take in all my trousers."

"If you're trying to trick me now, you've had your chips, Ewald Kristoffersen."

"I have an appointment with the doctor five minutes ago. I want you to come with me."

Maj has no strength left and rests her forehead on his chest. Ewald gently places his hands around her neck.

"I'm so happy," she says.

She becomes conscious of what she has said, she is ashamed and desperate.

"I didn't mean—"

Ewald interrupts her:

"It's an ill wind that blows nobody any good. Are you coming?"

They walk into the hospital grounds, to Building 4, and take the lift to the second floor, the radiology department. The doctor, a modern young man, greets Maj and tells her that relatives are affected by the illness too, sometimes perhaps they are the ones who suffer most because they can feel helpless, inadequate, and as a consequence a bad conscience can make them ill. He has seen cases where the patient has to console their nearest and dearest. It isn't unusual. So he is very glad that Maj has come this time. When they talk about hospitalisation, Ullevål Hospital is the one in question. Otherwise there isn't much to add. The recent tests and X-rays speak for themselves. Death is spreading: this is Ewald's way of expressing it, not the doctor's. He is given his medicines and no longer has to hide them. Maj puts them in her bag. It is enough to stock a chemist's. Does she have any questions? She has lots, but is incapable of asking them. Ewald asks instead, even though he isn't interested in the answer, he does it for her sake.

"How much time have I got?"

The doctor stands up and put his hands behind his back. They always put their hands behind their backs when it is a serious case or they don't know the answer. It must be something they have learned at medical school.

"May I put it this way? You should use your time well."

Ewald and Maj walk home hand in hand. They say nothing. They don't need to. Maj is happy that she has brought her winter coat. The wind is chilly. But the roof gutters are dripping. How do you use your time well? When they reach the entrance to the flats they hear someone playing the piano. It is Jesper. They stop outside their door. It is a simple tune. It is well known, they have heard it before, but can't remember where. Jesper plays with only one finger, but now and then they also hear a chord, or just a resonance.

"He should play that one at my funeral," Ewald whispers.

Maj lets go of his hand and takes out the key.

"There isn't a piano in the chapel, is there?"

"There's an organ. I suppose he can play it on an organ as well?"

"Give over. You're not going to die."

Ewald speaks softly:

"Did you really think I had a fancy woman?"

"Don't speak like that."

Only now does Maj start to cry. She has to borrow Ewald's handkerchief. Then they quietly unlock the door. Jesper stops playing at once. He knows you aren't allowed to play between four and five on weekdays. Stine is asleep. Down in the yard the snowman melted long ago. Only the hat is left and the lumps of coal that once were eyes.

The board meeting was held on May 4th at Fru Lund's. Everyone was present. Fru Nordklev has received a request for help from the Mission of Israel to provide board for Jewish children in the third week of July. Because of the holidays it is impossible to help at this particular time. This was unfortunate and we promised to redouble efforts from our side.

The Red Cross, Oslo District, has asked Fagerborg District to help Hulda Engen, a resident of Fagerborg, now in Eugen Hansen's old people's home, with money for fuel, among

other things. Fru Lund promised to talk to her to assess
her need for help.

Fru Lund informed the board that the hot-water bottles
used by the Red Cross were not furnished with screw tops
but corks, which had come out on two occasions and soaked
the bed. She would take the matter up with Plesner, where
the bottles were bought.

It was suggested that we send flowers on the occasion
of Olaf and Margrethe Hall's wedding. The proposal met
some resistance, but was passed with the smallest majority
possible.

Maj Kristoffersen, the treasurer, brought up the 1948
Patient Friends scheme and said that Fagerborg District
should involve itself more, with regard to training and
activity. After all, we have Ullevål Hospital in our district and
furthermore the Rikshospital, Betanien and the women's
clinics (Josefines gate and Wergelandsveien) in close vicinity.
The chairman promised that the matter would receive more
attention and thanked her for her contribution.

It should also be mentioned, as we were all so upset, that
Fru Kristoffersen fell ill and collapsed after making her appeal.
Fortunately the host's husband, Dr Lund, was at home. He
immediately came to the rescue and was able to confirm that,
luckily, Fru Kristoffersen had not had a heart attack, cerebral
thrombosis or something worse, only a nervous breakdown,
probably caused by intense strain over time. It wasn't a matter
of life and death and so an ambulance wasn't required. When
Fru Kristoffersen recovered she apparently felt a need to
explain, or apologise, which really wasn't necessary. We are all
aware of women's daily burdens. Fru Kristoffersen insisted,

however. Her husband, Ewald Kristoffersen, has terminal cancer and there is no hope. We recommended she take leave again from her post as treasurer, which she opposed. Dr Lund supported her decision. To use his words: it is important that life, when it manifests itself at its most difficult, such as during war or illness, carries on as normal, as far as is possible.

At various junctures I have pointed out that personal and private matters do not belong in our minutes. On this occasion, however, I am making an exception as this episode demonstrates with the utmost clarity the sacrifice, loyalty and strength of Red Cross women.

DIVING BOARDS

Bjørn Stranger is sitting in the back seat of a taxi parked in Sporveisgata below Fagerborg Church. From there he can see the guests arriving. There are not many. He recognises a few customers from the antiquarian bookshop, bibliophile collectors, old men with dust in their hair. None of his mother's colleagues – actors – appear. That was all that was missing. Bjørn Stranger is pleased. However, he doesn't know who most of the people are, probably they are his new stepmother's little circle of friends. Bjørn Stranger almost laughs aloud. His new stepmother! The taxi driver turns round for a second, but says nothing. Instead he rolls down the window on his side. The sun is high; it must be close on twenty degrees. The delicate, green veil over the trees in Stenspark is beginning to take shape. Mothers push their prams along the narrow paths in the grass while fathers stand at a distance smoking. Two girls dressed in light clothes sit on a bench laughing. Some young boys are on their way into town, sniggering and impatient. They wave to the girls and shout something. The girls laugh with their eyes closed, but stay where they are. It is Saturday morning. Everything is worthy of envy. Bjørn Stranger tightens his tie, runs a finger over his left shoe and combs his hair.

He notices the blond wisps of hair in his comb. Then the church bells start to ring. It is a sound that doesn't belong in this light. It scares the birds away. He pays the driver, adds an extra banknote and gets out. He sees the verger closing the doors. Bjørn Stranger thinks: unfortunately he has arrived late. He walks up the hill anyway. The verger opens the door for him. He finds a free place in the back row. It isn't difficult to find a free place. But no-one knows where to sit in a church that is almost empty. Bjørn Stranger feels like laughing. They have no shame. They would have been better off marrying in a storeroom. They are sitting by the altar, together with the best man and chief bridesmaid. He recognises them from the cemetery, the woman at least. The man could be someone else. He resembles a skeleton. Actually that fits perfectly. His stepfather's best man is a ghost. Then a boy in the third row turns around. His head is at an angle, his cheek is resting against his hand and he stares at Bjørn Stranger. His eyes are nondescript, they just move, in a combination of anxiety and indifference. It is the boy whose life he saved. At that moment the organ strikes up and the priest comes from the side-door. Everyone stands up. Bjørn Stranger stands up too, lowers his head and hurries back out. The sun blinds him. He raises a hand to provide some shade. The girls are still sitting on the bench. They are sharing a cigarette and he hears their laughter. They wave to him. He walks down to the public urinal, stands by the trough along the wall, unbuttons his trousers and pisses. Now he can laugh aloud. He is pissing on them. He closes his eyes and pisses on them. It is wonderful. He feels like crying. A man comes in. He is wearing a beige coat. He stands with his back to Bjørn. There is a smell of aftershave, a cool waft of fragrance that mutes the stench of stale urine. Bjørn Stranger finishes. He would have liked to stand here pissing for the rest of his life.

"You have to be careful with your hair."

Bjørn Stranger turns and sees it at once. He is one of them. They have many names, but look like one another: queer, bum-boy, fudge-packer, poofter.

"My hair?"

"Never use a wet comb. You'll lose even more."

"Thank you for the info. I didn't know that."

The bum-plumber takes a step closer, opens his coat and lays his hand gently on Bjørn's shoulder while looking down all the time.

"Have you escaped from the wedding?"

"You could say that. It was nothing for me anyway."

Both of them laugh. The man, the fairy, who is middle-aged and very pale, perhaps he wears some kind of powder, plucks up courage and strokes his hand across the hips of Bjørn Stranger, who lets him do it, it is a strange feeling, intimate and revolting, and yet tempting, boundless. He feels the fingers opening the buckle of his belt and the top button. Now he is putting the ring on her finger, thinks Bjørn Stranger. He rams his elbow into the man's jaw with all his strength. He hears it break. The man collapses onto the wet floor, moans and gurgles. Bjørn Stranger stands over him. The man looks up, blood is running from his mouth, his tongue is split, several teeth are loose. But his eyes are still gentle, searching; the pain hasn't reached there yet. In the eyes of this affected fudge-nudger seduction is still alive. This is just an interruption, a misunderstanding. Soon they will continue where they left off. Soon he will be on his knees sucking off the young man and making everything right again. Bjørn can see his erection pressing against the thin material. He kicks the man in the crutch. He does it again. The pain reaches his eyes, but manifests itself only as sorrow. Bjørn Stranger becomes even angrier and stamps on him. Then he hears the church bells again. It is strange: the sombre sound makes everything go absolutely still. Bjørn Stranger leaves the man lying on the floor, rushes over to the branch of Creditkassen in Thereses gate and gets there in time to take out enough money from the account his mother, Ragnhild Stranger, not Hall, opened for him the year before she died and he started to study. He also asks for five hundred kroner in Danish currency. The cashier studies his passport for a long time. Then Bjørn Stranger goes to Rosenborg, the restaurant, directly opposite the cinema, finds a free table and orders coffee, a glass of water and an open shrimp sandwich. The waiter eyes him and hesitates for a moment, then nods and writes the simple order on his pad. Bjørn Stranger goes to the toilet, looks at himself in the mirror: there are some bloodstains on his shirt. He tries to rub them off with soap. His hair is hanging the wrong side, it is messy and thin. The high receding hairline shoots up from either side of his forehead. What was it the poofter said? Never use a wet comb. He combs carefully. There is blood on his shoes, too. He washes it off with toilet paper. When Bjørn Stranger returns to the table his sandwich and coffee are there, but not the water. He calls back the waiter, who is slow to appear. Bjørn Stranger asks if he can have a piece of paper from his pad. The waiter tears off a sheet and puts it on the table cloth. And maybe a biro? Bjørn Stranger adds. You wouldn't have a typewriter as well, would you? Only Bjørn Stranger laughs. The waiter gives him a pencil, leaves the table and serves beer and port to this morning's men. This is the late Oslo breakfast. Rosenborg is full of trembling hands. Bjørn Stranger drinks the coffee, it is lukewarm. He has no appetite and leaves the sandwich. A dark membrane lies over the mayonnaise. The shrimps are nearly grey. Bjørn Stranger's hand doesn't tremble. He writes the speech. He has thought about it for a long time. It isn't too late. *At some point everyone has taken a bite of an apple and then left it.* When he has finished he beckons the waiter over and asks for the bill. The waiter glances at the untouched shrimps. He can probably sell the sandwich again if someone orders the same soon. Bjørn Stranger tips more than he needs to, he owes that much to the waiter. He would like to show his goodwill. He looks at his watch. He lets them have a bit more time. Now they are cutting the cake. Now they are drinking a toast. He thinks: It shouldn't be like this. Then Bjørn Stranger goes downstairs, he has to stop on one step and squeeze against the wall to let a group of cheery people pass on their way up. It is only a short distance to Sim. Solberg's patisserie. Just before he arrives his courage fails him. The streets are crowded this Saturday, perhaps the first day of spring this year. No-one notices a young, fair-haired man, elegantly dressed, otherwise ordinary in every way, suddenly stop and take a deep breath. It is just one of many movements that go unregistered, which aren't recorded in a ledger but just slip into place in the city's choreography, an apparent chaos that is still meaningful, unpredictable and purposeful. But Bjørn Stranger's courage fails him. It is his nature. He has plans he has abandoned. He

344

has dreams he hasn't fulfilled. He gives up. Anger is the sole lasting quality in Bjørn Stranger. He tears himself free, pushes a man away, omits to say sorry, continues over the crossing and stops again, outside the window of Sim. Solberg's patisserie this time. He can see them in the function rooms that face the back. A waiter is pouring wine for one of the few guests. The bride and groom are sitting at the end of the table. Bjørn Stranger has no more to do with them. He has only this speech. Fru Vik, or Fru Hall as she is probably called now, turns and meets his gaze. She says something to Olaf Hall, gets up and instead of going to the toilet on the lower floor she comes out to him. Fortunately she isn't dressed in white. They have some shame anyway. She is wearing a long, green dress that is more appropriate for the season than this occasion. Bjørn Stranger drags himself away from the window. She stops in front of him.

"Aren't you coming in?"

"No, thank you. There's no time. I . . ."

He doesn't complete the sentence and looks away. He is wearing a grey suit with striped trousers. He has dressed up. He had been intending to come. She places her hand gently on his arm.

"You don't like this, do you."

"That's neither here nor there."

"Yes, it is. For me."

"I just wish you all the happiness you can find."

Fru Vik, she still can't think of herself as anyone else, is surprised by the words. They seem so formal, almost threatening.

"You mean *both of you*," she says.

Bjørn Stranger pulls his arm away, inclines his head

perfunctorily and strides past the window of Sim. Solberg's patisserie. Fru Vik, or Fru Hall, doesn't move, she is also a pause in the city's movement, more visible, more noticeable because of her dress, the pearl necklace. Maj, equally dressed up – you look just like a Gregorian bride, ready to go begging for alms, Ewald had joked this morning – comes out to join her.

"We're waiting for you," she says.

"Waiting for me?"

"You have to cut the cake, my dear."

Maj laughs, but stops when she sees Margrethe's face change, she is distant and pale and her eyes are fixed elsewhere. Maj goes closer.

"Is something the matter?"

"There's so much I haven't thought about. The flat. My name. The rumours."

"Really, now you have to stop it. Honestly. Everyone's happy for you."

"I've just allowed myself to be carried away."

"But isn't that quite wonderful?"

Margrethe takes out a handkerchief.

"For a while maybe."

Maj turns and sees the same as her. Bjørn Stranger, Olaf Hall's stepson, is he Margrethe's stepson now too, rounding the corner of Parkveien. He is pleased he didn't turn round. If he had, he might have gone back. He is good at something. No-one runs after him anyway. He gets into the only taxi in Riddervolds Plass. He tells the driver to take him to Filipstad Quay, to the ferry for Denmark, he can still make it. In the departure hall he asks for a first-class ticket. The clerk asks him if he has any luggage. Bjørn Stranger shows him his passport. Then he boards the *Kronprins Olav*. He finds his cabin, sits on his bed thinking nothing. Yes, he does think about something: he wants to buy a moped. Soon he hears the City Hall bells strike four and for a moment feels the boat vibrate under him. Bjørn Stranger goes up onto deck and stands on the port side. The *Kronprins Olav* glides out of the harbour, past the closest islands, Langholmen, Hovedøen, speeds up past Dyna Lighthouse, pitching slightly. The seagulls are already gathered around the wake. Bjørn Stranger can't hear them. Some of the passengers take photos of a yacht. Then they photograph each other. The light takes on a hint of blue. It comes from the west, from Kolsås ridge behind him. The waves beat against the greenish jetty posts of Nesoddtangen. Bjørn Stranger sees their country house, directly opposite Hornstranden Beach. It is his mother's house, even though she is dead. The shutters haven't been removed yet. He sees all the bathing huts and the steps going into the water, the unending steps. He sees the diving boards built into concrete on the rocks. It is especially them Bjørn Stranger sees, the diving boards. A seagull lands on one and the spring in it makes the revolting, obnoxious bird take off again.

On May 11th the board meeting was held at Fru Ingrid Arnesen's. Fru Nordklev, Fru Lund, Fru Arnesen, Fru Kristoffersen, Fru Larsen and Frøken Aasland were present.

Fru Nordklev has received another application from Hulda Engen (see earlier minutes) for help. Fru Lessund has repeatedly tried to meet Hulda Engen, without success. Fru

Lessund will try again, but initially it has been decided to give the applicant fifty kroner for fuel after the summer.

The hot-water bottles mentioned in the previous minutes have been replaced with new ones by Plesner.

Fru Nordklev informed the meeting that she had received a thank-you card from Olaf and Margrethe Hall.

May 12th, 1950. Else Larsen.

POETRY

Maj has taken in all Ewald's trousers although he said it wasn't necessary. It would have been easier to make new holes in his belt. He has braces, too, by the way. Maj, however, doesn't want him to walk around like a barrel. Ewald doesn't mind looking like a barrel. He loved Maj when she mentioned walking around like a barrel. Because he realised she wasn't taking in his trousers only for his sake, but also for hers. She doesn't want to walk arm in arm with a barrel. Now they are on their way down the hill from the Royal Palace. Fru Nordklev is looking after Stine in the yard below their block of flats. Jesper is walking directly behind them. It is Saturday, May 20th, and the City Hall is open to the public. Norwegian flags are still flying all along Karl Johans gate. They pass by Pernille, where the waitresses carry mugs of foaming beer in the open air, and around the National Theatre. The statues of Ibsen and Bjørnson are also decorated. School-leavers have been out and about and have dressed them in red hats and scarves. There is already a queue outside the City Hall.

"Aren't we going to have something to eat?" Ewald says.

Maj looks at him in surprise.

"Are you hungry now?"

"Not really."

"Then let's eat afterwards. I'm looking forward to this. Aren't you?"

"I don't like queueing."

Maj is still surprised.

"Aren't you looking forward to showing me your exhibition?"

Ewald takes Jesper's hand.

"Mamma decides," he says.

And while they wait their turn it occurs to Ewald Kistoffersen that he doesn't care. This frightens him. He had thought that everything was at stake. It isn't. At first he thought he wouldn't have enough time. He does. He has plenty of time. He doesn't care. This frightens him because he doesn't understand it. Then they are admitted into the hall. It is bigger than a church. It is bigger than the docks in Akers Mekaniske Verksted. Everyone lowers their voices or goes quiet. The hall has been decorated by the country's best-known artists. They have chosen grandiose motifs from the history of the nation and the capital, from the Constitution to industry, from a cairn to the telegraph line, from the shield to the cross. Here the fisherman, the worker, the smithy and the logger appear, men, and mix with the general public, who are also part of the same history. On the back wall, however, it is different. Ewald smiles and is about to say something, but discovers he is on his own. He can't see Maj or Jesper. He is alone in the quiet, slow-moving stream of people around him. How long has he been like this? Ewald doesn't know. Then, finally, he catches sight of them. Maj and Jesper are coming down the broad staircase from the gallery. Maj seems disappointed, or rather concerned, and tries to hide it.

"What happened to you?"

Ewald laughs.

"I didn't go anywhere."

"We couldn't find your exhibition."

"That's not so strange. Because it's here."

Ewald points to the back of the hall, where Henrik Sørensen has painted straight onto the wall, the city's biggest canvas, 24 × 12 metres. Everyday life, life as it is lived every day, has been portrayed in various phases, all in balance with the rhythm of the day and the course of the years. Everything is taken in turn. And in the centre is the child, who stands for hope and the future, but first and foremost woman, who is the form and essence of love. It can't be simpler. And it can hardly be more beautiful. They step closer.

"Did you speak to Henrik Sørensen?" Maj whispers.

Ewald shrugs.

"Did I? Perhaps not exactly to him, but I put in a good word or two."

"It's fabulous. And so big."

"It could've been better actually. If he'd listened to me more."

Maj takes Jesper's hand. He is getting restless.

"Isn't it good?"

Jesper shakes his head. Maj looks at him.

"Don't you like it?"

"No."

Ewald smiles. He doesn't like it, either. It is four-sided and lifeless. It is magnificent and boring. The women don't carry washing, they wear halos. They don't mend clothes, they dry tears. It is a school book, a Bible, of 300 square metres.

"One day I'll take you up the bell tower with me," he says.

And Ewald realises it is so easy to make promises when you are going to die. He can promise the moon. He can promise everything. And if he doesn't manage to keep the promise it isn't his fault. Then a liveried official hits a gong and a hush falls over the assembled crowd. Everyone focuses on the woman who appears on the gallery. A sigh runs through the hall. It is the actress Aase Bye. She reads the prologue that the poet Olaf Bull wrote at the laying of the foundation stone of the City Hall, which he never saw finished as he died shortly afterwards, in 1933.

In the summer haze and winter fog,
in balmy spring sun and autumntimes
the town's largest building stands agog
boldly facing four different climes!

The applause is thunderous, it is never-ending, and when the public emerges, "in balmy spring sun", they see the building with new eyes and no longer name it after a goat cheese. They are proud of it. The poet achieved what the architects were unable to do. The City Hall is theirs.

They also walk home through the Palace Gardens without stopping for something to eat. A red lorry has parked, or broken down, in the middle of the Majorstua crossing. The red-clad school-leavers are on the back waving their bamboo sticks, exhausted and excited. The sight does something to Ewald. The exaggerated and genuine pleasure, or happiness, creates a deeper layer in his own indifference, changing therefore into another material, harder, not sorrow, but anger, anger at everything he won't be able to experience. Inside his head he says: *everything he won't be able to be part of*. A police officer strolls over to the driver and asks him to drive on. The trams have to keep to a timetable. There are no riled faces. There is good humour on all sides. This is life as easy as it can be in the irresponsible, unconditional moment between festivity and official disapproval. Maj rushes along Kirkeveien. Ewald and Jesper can hardly keep up. Stine is asleep in her pram in the yard. Fru Nordklev is sitting on the bench knitting.

"I've rarely seen such a good-natured child," she says.

Maj is happy and proud.

"She doesn't keep us awake anyway."

She lifts Stine out and holds her in her arms. Fru Nordklev gets up and whispers as she puts her knitting in the basket:

"How is he?"

"We're taking it one day at a time."

"Hoping there will be many."

"Yes. Many. Many more."

They hear the door slam and Ewald and Jesper come in. Fru Nordklev can't get used to seeing the thin man who only a short time ago was tubby and jokey about everything. Maj lets him hold Stine. He rocks her gently. She opens her eyes and smiles.

"Was it nice in the City Hall?" Fru Nordklev asks.

"No," Jesper says.

Maj laughs.

"He's only joking. You have a real treat in store."

Fru Nordklev nods.

"We've been there already. To the official opening. And do you know what, Maj?"

"No, tell me."

"I saw the Crown Princess dancing with Stokke. Hallvard Stokke. The mayor."

"What was she wearing?"

"A long silk dress. And a diadem. And some magnificent earrings. She isn't very attractive, if I may say so, but she looked really good."

"With accessories like that even an owl can dazzle."

"Owl wasn't my word, Maj."

"No, that wasn't very nice. Shame on me."

The two women laugh. Ewald carries Stine to the kitchen steps and Jesper follows with the pram. Fru Nordklev watches them and leans closer to Maj.

"Do you think Jesper can play for us at the next members' meeting?"

"I don't know. He can't play much yet."

"That doesn't matter. Just something simple. That would be so sweet."

"I can ask him anyway."

"It will have to be before the summer."

"Do you know what we saw? Aase Bye reading Olaf Bull's prologue. She was so beautiful."

Fru Nordklev looks up at the windows on the second floor where the blinds are down now.

"Yes, Aase Bye read at the opening, too. And do you know what I thought? I thought it could well have been Ragnhild Hall doing it. If she hadn't committed suicide in the way she did."

Maj falls silent for a moment, thanks Fru Nordklev for her help, fetches the duvet and pillow from the pram and joins the others. Ewald and Jesper are sitting in the kitchen waiting. Stine is screaming and they don't know what to do.

"So you managed to tear yourself away from that old biddy, did you?" Ewald says.

Maj gives Stine some lukewarm milk and puree and she is soon quiet and compliant.

"You shouldn't talk like that about Fru Nordklev. She helps us."

Ewald snorts and bows.

"Oh, yes, pardon me. She's a merciful Samaritan with dimples in her knees."

"Shh! Why are you so bitter?"

"'The Crown Princess dancing with Stokke, the mayor, you know.' Ugh. Doesn't she think I know who the mayor is? Eh?"

"I don't suppose it was meant like that."

"I've shaken hands with Stokke, 'the mayor'!"

Maj stuffs the spoon in his mouth and Ewald slurps at the tasteless mush and softens. The dying man just needed a vent for his anger and is indifferent again. The dying man is a child. Jesper can't bear to witness this. He'd prefer to go, to be as far away as possible from here, but he sits and studies the ceiling instead. Maj and Ewald also look there. The silence is different at once. The building is holding its breath. Maj puts Stine in the bedroom and together they walk up the back stairs. The door is open. Maj knocks, to be on the safe side. No answer. They walk in. The flat is empty. The place that was once nice and tidy seems neglected and run-down now. There are discoloured patches on the walls where pictures used to hang. The wallpaper bulges in several places and is beginning to develop cracks. In the corners, which previously were hidden by a stove, a refrigerator and a writing desk, the mouldings have come loose and clouds of dust rise and fall in the light that will also soon leave the room. Cables stick out from holes in the ceiling. Everything is revealed. Jesper feels like crying, not because he misses Fru Vik, but mostly because he is thinking about his father, Ewald, and already misses him. Then they smell a waft of tobacco, pipe tobacco, the only reminder of a person here. They continue through the scullery and stop. In the sitting room there is still the armchair, the last piece of furniture in the whole flat, veterinary surgeon Vik's smoke-impregnated armchair.

Jesper has to pee. Maj is resigned. Can't he hold it for a bit longer? Jesper has to go. And when he has to go, he has to go. He runs into the bathroom. It is bare as well. Only the toilet is left. Isn't the toilet a piece of furniture as well? Don't you take the toilet with you when you leave? If Jesper ever moves house, he will definitely take the toilet with him. The toilet is the first item he will take. He lifts up the lid and wees for a long time. Now it is he who is emptying himself. The pee flows out. It is wonderful. The water in the bowl slowly turns yellow, at first light yellow, then darker and darker, until it is almost brown. Jesper shakes off the last drops, does up his flies and flushes, but nothing happens. He tries again, pulls the string hanging from the cistern in the ceiling, with precisely the same result. Nothing happens. His pee remains in the bowl. Jesper finds this embarrassing. He is ill at ease. Will his pee stay for ever in Fru Vik's flat? He hurries back into the sitting room. Ewald is about to sit down in the armchair. Then the telephone rings. But they can't see it anywhere. Maj clasps Ewald's hand. It is spooky. Has Margrethe left her telephone, or hidden it somewhere for safety? Where might that be? There is nowhere to hide it. Ewald is getting uneasy, too. After all they are here without permission. They have trespassed. It is like being caught red-handed. Maj looks in the hall again, where the telephone used to be. It isn't there. And it can't be just anywhere. It must be next to a socket. Otherwise it can't ring. A telephone doesn't ring from nowhere. Ewald looks high and low anyway. Jesper can't restrain himself any longer.

"It's ours," he says.

Maj and Ewald turn. Jesper points to the floor. It is ringing in their sitting room. It is for them. Ewald rushes downstairs and just catches it in time. Televerket is on the line. They want to know if Ewald Kristoffersen wants his name in the telephone directory. Ewald Kristoffersen certainly does. Maj hears him say so, loud and clear. Then she spots something sticking up between the floorboards in the bedroom. It is Fru Vik's wedding ring. She takes it and pushes Jesper back to the kitchen while reacting with alarm at how thin the walls are here.

———

The board met on June 14th at Maj Kristoffersen's. Those present were: Fru Nordklev, the chair, Fru Arnesen, Fru Larsen, Frøken Aasland and Fru Kristoffersen.

Fru Nordklev said that she had been present, on behalf of the Fagerborg department of the Norwegian Red Cross, at the unveiling of the Franklin D. Roosevelt statue by Mrs Eleanor Roosevelt and the American Ambassador in Skansen on June 7th.

Re.: the autumn bazaar she was able to tell us that Olaf Hall had given most of the inventory of Fru Hall's flat — formerly Fru Vik — to the draw. This, however, is problematic as it is very difficult for us to raffle such big items as furniture. Fru Arnesen and Frøken Aasland thought the board should reject the gift. Fru Nordklev suggested initially conferring with the management of the Oslo District of the Red Cross, possibly to make a selection thereafter. There might be some interest in selling the contents of the flat assembled in a different part of the country.

On the same theme, Fru Larsen said that an alarm clock bought for the draw was found to be defective and will be exchanged for another prize, perhaps a doll and some nylon stockings.

At the end of this last meeting before the summer Jesper, the treasurer's son, was going to play the piano for us. Unfortunately he didn't get that far as when he played the first note his little sister started to cry. Fru Kristoffersen decided therefore to cancel the concert and organise a little visit to Stine instead. She was quiet again when we tiptoed into the bedroom one by one. The ladies were enchanted.

Now we have to summon up our strength for the autumn.

THE BLACKBOARD

Maj and Ewald Kristoffersen are waiting outside the classroom where they had been told to go. It is Saturday, not only after school but also after the first school year. They have smartened themselves up. They want to make a good impression. Ewald, however, is not in the mood. Maj could have gone alone and talked. He has nothing to add. But Maj wanted him along. After all he was the one who answered the telephone call from Løkke, who finally opens the door, shakes hands and lets them in. All over the blackboard the pupils have written, in upper and lower case: *Have a good summer!* Løkke has put three chairs in front of the desk so that they can sit on an equal footing, so to speak. Won't be long before he lights a candle, thinks Ewald, who gets straight to the point, this has become part of his indifference.

"Has Jesper done something wrong again?"

Løkke looks at him.

"Again?"

"I was thinking about the Christmas stamps."

Løkke is about to say something, but is interrupted by Maj:

"Jesper didn't have anything to do with that."

Ewald tries to count how many pupils have written *Have a good summer!* on the board.

"Are there twenty-seven pupils in the class?" he asks.

Løkke puts the register on his lap and looks up.

"Yes, there were twenty-eight until Jostein moved on."

Maj giggles.

"And there was me thinking it was enough with one."

"Two," Ewald says reprovingly.

Then Maj joins in:

"Three," she says.

Løkke laughs as well and looks at Ewald, who is losing patience:

"Jesper's not without ability," he says.

"No, he certainly isn't. On the contrary, he is very able."

"Do you hear that, Maj? Why are we here then?"

"Because I'd like to talk to you about him nevertheless."

"If he hasn't done anything wrong and doesn't lack ability, I suppose we can make this a short conversation."

Løkke turns to Maj. She is embarrassed and angry. She should have done as Ewald said, come on her own.

"Jesper's a good boy," she says.

Ewald is on the point of standing up.

"Of course he's a good boy! He—"

"Now you let Herr Løkke say what he has to say, Ewald!"

Ewald stays put, almost clinging to the chair, feeling he deserves to be sent into the corridor.

"Sorry."

Instead Løkke gets to his feet.

"Jesper's not without ability."

Ewald can't let that go:

"We know that already. Jesper doesn't lack ability. Tell us what it is he does lack."

"Concentration. He's restless. He—"

"Who isn't at that age?"

Løkke sits down again.

"He disrupts the rest of the class. For example, he is constantly disturbing the lesson because he has to go to the toilet."

Maj looks up.

"Yes, he pees a lot."

"Is there something he's nervous about?"

Ewald puts up his hand.

"I'm ill, Herr Løkke. I'm going to die soon. I can live with that. But it's worse for Jesper."

It takes time for Løkke to find the words.

"I'm sorry to hear that, Herr Kristoffersen. I really am. But Jesper's been like this all the time."

They say nothing for a few moments. Ewald thinks: The bell must ring soon. Then he will realise that summer has started and the bell won't ring again until autumn.

Maj asks, in a tremulous voice:

"You're not going to send him to another school, are you? That's not why we . . ."

Løkke closes his register.

"No, no, he'll get another chance."

"He's started to play the piano."

Løkke nods, opens the register again and makes a note.

"Piano?"

"Classical."

"That could be good for him. Where?"

"With Enzo Zanetti. He has private lessons with him."

Ewald gets up.

"We've said enough then, have we?"

Løkke looks up without moving from his chair.

"Incidentally, what's Jesper going to do this summer?"

"We'd decided he should be with his grandparents for a bit. In Hurdal."

"That seems like a sensible idea."

"Why?" Ewald asks.

"Why? Because living in the country is healthy. Because a holiday should be a change."

Ewald glances at Maj and nods.

"Of course. And then he comes back home as fat as a farmer."

Maj wants to talk about the visit to Dr Lund, who said there was nothing wrong with Jesper, he was just *sensitive*, but suddenly remembers she hasn't told Ewald about this. Løkke gets up at length, Maj follows suit. They put their chairs in their places, on top of the desks, to have something to do while not knowing exactly what to say before they take their leave. They shake hands again.

"Jesper misses Jostein," Løkke says.

Ewald lets go of his hand.

"I'd imagine Jostein misses Jesper more."

"Possibly. Jesper was a great support for him."

"See. I still don't know why we're here. Although it was nice to talk to you, Herr Løkke."

"Because I want you to keep a close eye on Jesper."

As they leave, the cleaner comes in and wipes the board, all the summers, 27 *Have a good summer*s, and the black, shiny surface opens for a second for Ewald, it is a well with the autumn, or nothing, at the bottom. He doesn't say a word until they are in Majorstua.

"That went well then," Ewald says.

"As fat as a farmer!"

"I was just trying to liven up the atmosphere."

"Well, you managed that alright."

"Herr Løkke isn't exactly a firework. I can imagine getting restless in his lessons."

Ewald laughs and they walk over the last pedestrian crossing. Maj stops on the corner and grips his arm tight.

"Don't you take anything seriously?"

"I do."

"Why don't you care then? Aren't you worried about Jesper, too?"

"How could you believe anything else?"

"Then show it!"

"I'm trying, Maj. I'm trying as hard as I can."

Maj looks at him, the reflection of the blackboard is still in his eyes and she leans her forehead against him.

"Forgive me," she whispers.

"You don't need to say that."

"I mean it."

Ewald places his hand on her neck.

"Don't turn round, but Jesper and Jostein are outside the butcher's."

"Has he seen us?"

"Don't think so."

"Shall we go over to them?"

"I think we should leave them in peace."

Maj glances over her shoulder anyway as Ewald lets go

of her and they walk to Jacob Aalls gate, which is a nicer way home at this time of the year, probably any time of the year, and she sees Jostein also turn and nudge Jesper.

"That was your parents," Jostein says.

Jesper looks in the direction of Majorstua, but doesn't see them. He shakes his head.

"You're fibbing."

Jostein laughs in his weird way.

"It's true. They were snogging."

Jesper goes a step closer and shouts:

"They were not!"

"I'm not blind. They were standing on the corner and snogging."

Now it is Jesper's turn to nudge Jostein, but he does it harder, with greater force. Jostein falls over, Jesper sits on top of him and begins to punch. Melsom comes running out of the shop, separates the two fighting cocks and keeps them apart, one in each hand.

"If you have to fight, do it elsewhere."

"We were only messing about," Jostein says.

The butcher eyes Jesper:

"Don't frighten away my customers! Do you hear me?"

They walk over to Marienlyst and sit down there among the pigeons and the darkly clad pensioners. It is ten minutes to three. The sky seems smooth and empty. There is no shade, not even beneath the trees along Færdens gate, which leads up to Vestre Aker Church, which has the steepest cemetery in Oslo, maybe in Scandinavia. Jostein straightens his shirt. A button has come loose. It doesn't matter.

"What are you going to do this summer?" Jesper asks.

Jostein stares into the air.

"They think I'm stupid."

Jesper wonders for a moment what it would be like to have a pal who can't hear for the rest of his life. He tugs at Jostein, who turns slowly towards him.

"Who thinks you're stupid?"

"The school."

"Why?"

Jostein looks down at his shoes, where the laces only go through half the eyelets. There isn't enough meat to sell. People still mostly eat fish, that is what his father says anyway, even if they prefer meat.

"Going to a holiday camp."

"Where?"

"By bus to Egersund. With only deafies. Apart from the driver."

They wait before saying any more and Jesper thinks differently this time: how great would it be to have a pal for the rest of his life he doesn't need to talk to all the time? People around them are moving at a particular speed. They are not going anywhere. They are just outdoors. There is a sudden whiff of petrol from the Esso garage up by Ullevålsveien. They take a deep breath and enjoy the distinct tang, which seems chill, almost stimulating in the heat. Jesper leans forward.

"I'm going to my grandparents. They live in a place called Hurdal. By a forest. Have to catch a train. And they pick me up there. Have to chop wood. Grandpa chops wood all the time. And Grandma bakes bread. But I know why I'm going there. I'm going there because Pappa's dying and he doesn't want me to see."

Jesper stops speaking and sits in silence. When he turns he realises that Jostein hasn't heard a bloody thing. It doesn't matter. Actually it doesn't matter. Jesper can hear for Jostein.

———

On August 14th the Fagerborg dept of the Norwegian Red Cross, at the Mission of Israel's expense, took responsibility for feeding approx. 50 German Jewish children. The evening before, volunteers had made open sandwiches and prepared in a variety of ways to feed them. The children were on their way back to Germany.

ABSENCE

Jesper can see straight into the windows of the tenement blocks alongside the rails as the train approaches Oslo East Station. He wonders what it is like to live there. Every quarter of an hour, perhaps more frequently, a train goes past, and someone can see into your flat. He sees an old lady sitting alone at a kitchen table. He sees the back of a girl standing and combing her hair. He sees a man opening a bottle, it looks like beer. Jesper sees them just in brief glimpses, as he passes by, but it is enough. The sights stay in his mind's eye and he doesn't know what to do with them. He should forget them or translate them into something else. He should translate them into music. He thinks he can hear them too, the girl, the old lady, the man with his chest bared, a sigh, a peel of laughter, a groan. Everything around him is a mood. Then he hears the bells in the City Hall too, they chime four times, and he closes his eyes, he is tired. He remembers what his father promised him: that they would go up the bell tower. Jesper dreads it, not seeing the bells but seeing his father. Perhaps he isn't there. What do the others do when you are gone? What happens while you are not there? It is impossible to imagine. We grasp so little at any one time that it is less than a drop in

367

the ocean, barely that. The other passengers in the carriage, however, are happy. The holiday is over and they are looking forward to going home. Before the holiday began they were happy to be leaving and could hardly wait to get away. Now this is an excited, almost nervous happiness, and still impatient. The luggage has to come down from the racks: suitcases, boxes, rucksacks, packets. The train pulls into the large, grey station. Jesper remains seated until the carriage is empty. He is never going to wear shorts again. There are midges and nettles in the country. He is not going to wear long underpants again, either. They itch and prickle. A conductor comes over to him and says, with a smile, that unfortunately the train doesn't go any further, in which case he will have to go back with him, and that of course is a different matter entirely. Jesper gets up, the conductor helps him with the little suitcase, but he wants to carry it himself. Jesper stands on the step for a few seconds, nervous, holding his breath. Then he alights onto the platform. His mother calls his name. He turns. She comes running towards him while his father waits with the pram beneath the big clock, which says eight minutes past four. She hugs Jesper from all sides and he is embarrassed and happy. It could equally well have been him who had run to meet her. His mother takes his suitcase, he lets her, and they walk along the platform, which smells of tar, to his father and Stine. Jesper's pace slows right down. Only now can he see how thin his father has become. He could have an elastic band around his waist instead of a belt. Soon there will be nothing left of him. He is different from when Jesper departed and yet he is still his father. At that moment a throng of children emerge onto the platform next to them, both girls and boys, Jesper's age, although that isn't easy to see. They seem different, darker, heavier, not fat, just heavier, a kind of sad weight, despite the fact that some of them are smiling. Jesper stops, his mother stops, too. The children board a longer train, the train to another country. Three women make sure none of them are lost, one waves to Jesper's mother, it is Fru Larsen from the Fagerborg department of the Oslo Red Cross. This is also a sight, which for some reason or other chills Jesper, makes him tremble, these foreign children boarding the long international train. The world is full of sights. There are too many. A metallic voice fills the station, *Hamburg, departure, platform 1.* Jesper wants to carry his suitcase. His mother lets him. They walk towards his father, who tries to lift both Jesper and his suitcase, but he can't. It was a bad idea anyway. Ewald laughs.

"Have you got logs in your suitcase?"

"No, just clothes. And a few comics."

"Then they must've fattened you up. Did you have sour cream porridge for breakfast?"

"Bread."

"Homemade bread, yes. With jam, I imagine. While I've been on lye and cold water, as we say. Can't you see how slim I've become?"

Jesper shakes his head, moves away slightly and peers into the pram. Stine will soon be bigger than her father. And all of a sudden, for an instant, also fleeting, Jesper sees who she resembles, it is her grandpa, she has his features, the straight mouth, the narrow chin, the grandpa who taught him how to chop wood this summer. Then she doesn't resemble anyone anymore, just who she is, or will be. Maj takes the pram and looks at Ewald, who nods for some reason.

"Thank you for the card," he says.

"Did it arrive?"

"Straight to the door, Jesper. It was a nice card."

They go out to Jernbanetorget and take the tram up to Adamstuen. It wriggles through the city, where summer is not yet quite on the wane. It is just a different colour and has a different rhythm. People are preparing to go back to what Maj calls *sackcloth shirt and oat grain*. The daily grind. Fortunately Jesper has never seen the one or eaten the other. Well, Grandpa used to wear a sort of shirt on the rare occasions he sat in the sun that might have been sackcloth, at least it looked like it. Nor has he ever seen anyone drink lye and cold water. It sounds more like a detergent, or perhaps something to remove fungus or warts. Jesper is full anyway. He has eaten enough for the rest of his life. He doesn't need to eat anymore. Then it is not far to Kirkeveien, but Ewald starts to lag behind and they have to keep stopping to let him catch up. Maj stows the pram under the stairs and lifts Stine out. Fru Vik's name is still on her post box. Her flat is still empty. It is like with telephone directories. The names remain. The names are behind schedule. There is perhaps some meaning in this. It offers an opportunity for remembrance. When they reach their flat Jesper sees, indeed notices at once, that something has changed. He thinks for a moment that Stine has taken over his vestibule, but she has been given a corner in the dining room. She has a cot there. She no longer sleeps in the cradle in his parents' bedroom. Now I can't play the piano anymore, he thinks. Or the piano has to be moved. Maj grasps his shoulders at once.

"You can practise whenever you want," she says.

There is something else too: a refrigerator. They have a refrigerator in the kitchen. It is Fru Vik's, the former Fru Vik's old refrigerator. Her frost has moved down a floor. The summer is over anyway. This signifies change. Jesper feels some distaste, no joy, although he can see that his mother is pleased because she is the one who needs the refrigerator most. Previously she had a larder, now she has a treasure chest. But Jesper doesn't like change. It doesn't fill him with happiness. On the contrary, it is a foreboding. It is a foreboding of something. His father prepares himself. He adopts a pose. He opens the refrigerator and cold light pours out. He closes the door just as fast with a laugh.

"Did you get cold?"

Jesper shakes his head.

While they have lunch, fishcakes, which Jesper doesn't feel like – he has eaten enough for the rest of his life, as he has said – he has to tell them about everything that happened *in the country*. He can barely sit still and he isn't very informative, either.

"It's in my postcard," is all he says.

The problem is Jostein. Jostein is weighing on Jesper's mind. Why didn't he send Jesper a postcard? Maj sighs and lets him leave the table. Jesper runs off. He runs into the street and down to Jostein's. The shop is shut, but he can see Fru Melsom, his mother, in the semi-darkness, she is cashing up at the till. Jesper knocks. She lifts the flap in the counter, comes over slowly, reluctantly almost, to the door and opens it, but stands in such a way that Jesper cannot enter.

"Is Jostein at home?"

"No, he isn't here yet."

"When will he be back?"

Fru Melsom looks at Jesper and attempts a smile.

"You had a nice summer anyway."

"Did he get my card?"

"He'll get it when he comes home. That was nice of you, Jesper."

She closes the door. Jesper lingers and watches her lift the flap in the counter again and go over to one of the shelves where his postcard lies next to a tin waiting for Jostein. It takes Jesper a long time to walk home. The following day he starts in the second class. Løkke has written on the blackboard: *Welcome back!* His face is tanned, but not his forehead. It is as white as always. Unfortunately his forehead had to stay at home and correct tests. The pupils try to stifle their laughter. Jostein's desk has gone. Jesper notices that everything has become more dangerous.

The board meeting at Fru Lessund's on 23/8 included Fru Lessund, Fru Foss, Fru Kristoffersen, Fru Arnesen and Frøken Aasland.

An application made by Hulda Engen for help to buy wood was rejected on the basis that she had received support on several previous occasions and we thought that others – perhaps in greater need – should have a turn. Fru Kristoffersen said they had more wood in storage than they needed, if things really were tight for Hulda Engen.

Fru Lessund and Fru Foss reported back on the joint trip for the elderly that Oslo District organised on June 20th to the Museum of Cultural History. Twenty-five people from

Fagerborg took part plus Fru Lessund and Fru Foss as leaders. The trip could not be regarded as entirely successful, and we agreed that next year we wouldn't take part in the joint trip, but organise our own again.

With regard to the Red Cross Week, which this year will be held from 8th to 23rd September, Fru Lessund undertook to take charge of the bazaar and Fru Foss the sale of stamps. Frøken Aasland agreed to send cards to the people who sold stamps last year asking if they would like to help this year as well. We emphasised the strict controls that would be in place, bearing in mind the swindle over the Christmas stamps. But we considered it unlikely that anyone would do the same again. Fru Kristoffersen would also be especially vigilant when doing the accounts. We realised that we could not take part in the arrangement in Studenterlunden this time as none of the present board members was able to take on any responsibilities.

Notice was given of an orientation meeting, to be held at Munkedamsveien 80, regarding "the week", and most board members said they would be willing to attend.

Fagerborg department of the Oslo District of the Norwegian Red Cross has asked the working committee to handle the donation by Olaf and Margrethe Hall (formerly Vik) of the contents of the latter's flat.

We have decided on the following as raffle prizes:
Doll with various accessories plus a chair
Nylon stockings
Down duvet
2 white duvet covers
6 ice-cream spoons, possibly a lamp with a shade

REPAIRS

Enzo Zanetti is standing at the window looking at a postcard: there is a picture of Lake Hurdal with something called Mount Mistberg in the background. The colours are matt and pale, only blue water, green forest, a light sky. Nevertheless he can see it is beautiful countryside. He himself grew up near a deep lake surrounded by forest and the sky above, but there is nothing in this photograph to remind him of it. That surprises him. Can forests be so different? Can a sky and a lake also be so different? Can two countries, which despite everything are on the same continent, be so different? Then he sees the difference. There isn't a house in sight. In all this nature there is not one person, nor any evidence of them, as far as the eye can see, neither masts, nor telegraph lines, nor roads. The country hasn't been discovered yet. Or his memory might have been playing tricks on him. There is a void in him, a room that is closed. He turns over the card: *Dear Enzo Zanetti, They haven't got a piano. Regards, Jesper.* Then Jesper comes round the corner below, with a slim briefcase in his hand. He looks like a little office clerk. Enzo Zanetti eventually lets Jesper in. He doesn't need to take off his shoes.

"Who are *they*?" he asks.

"My grandparents."

"On your mother's side?"

"On my mother's? Yes."

"Did you swim in the lake?"

"No."

"Did you go for a walk in the forests?"

"No."

"What did you do, Jesper?"

"I chopped wood."

"My God. Let me see your fingers."

Jesper shows him. They are intact. Then he takes out the music, sits at the piano and begins to play. But the same fingers that were supple and obedient before the summer are now stiff and inflexible. Enzo Zanetti lets him continue until the joints, knuckles and fingertips melt and flow along the scales. It takes half an hour. Then there is only half an hour left. Enzo Zanetti says they are going to lie on their backs. Jesper has no idea why, but does as he says. They lie on the floor looking at the ceiling.

"Close your eyes," Enzo Zanetti says.

Jesper closes his eyes. It is quiet, not completely, because it can never be. The world is not only sights, it is also sounds, which come from outside and inside, the city, blood pounding, everything, for nothing is completely still. He thinks about Jostein. How quiet is it actually inside him? If Jesper hears for Jostein, Jostein can be quiet for him.

"Imagine music, Jesper."

Jesper tries, but doesn't know if he can do that. They lie like this for a good while. What does music look like? What form does it take, round or angular, flat or deep? Is it high or low? Then all of a sudden Jesper sees it. He sees the music. It is a scene from the summer. So the summer wasn't in vain, after all. There is a fish in the river meandering under the little wooden bridge by Vesttjern Lake. Grandpa explains that it is a trout, a fine trout, maybe 1.2 kilos. He talks in a low voice so as not to disturb it. Jesper leans over the railing and looks down into the water, the way he is doing now with his eyes closed, on the floor in Enzo Zanetti's flat. The trout sparkles, its colours are dark, reddish, some almost yellow, others green. The colours merge into one another and become a coat of paint for which there is no name. The fish is absolutely still in the water, against the current. Occasionally it wriggles. It is the fish that moves the water. There is a ring at the door and the scene has gone. How is Jesper going to explain what he saw? Enzo Zanetti gets up, groans, stiff and drowsy, and goes into the hall and opens up. Jesper doesn't move and looks backwards, as far as he is able. It is a lady with long, blonde hair. She is upside down. Enzo Zanetti is also upside down. The world is upside down at this moment. He fetches something for her; it is a white jacket or a blouse. She takes it from him and is about to go, her head bowed, unless she is holding it high, everything is upside down, as mentioned before, but she changes her mind and slaps Enzo Zanetti instead. Jesper hears the stinging smack across his cheek and shortly afterwards the door closing. Enzo Zanetti comes back, sits at the piano and plays something, a simple sonata by Beethoven, but his hands are trembling and the notes come together in the wrong way. He puts his hands in his lap. They continue to tremble there.

"Right after Schubert," Enzo Zanetti says. "Right after

Schubert's finales and Norwegian sausages come jealous women. On my list of things I hate."

Jesper gets to his feet and Enzo Zanetti goes over to the shelves and manages to pour himself a glass, which he knocks back in one swig and fills again.

"Do you know what I'm doing now?"

"Repairs."

"*Anguiferumque caput dura ne laedat harena.*"

Jesper doesn't ask what it means and stuffs the sheet music of Beethoven's sonatas in his bag. He opts for Industrigata, it goes straight to Fagerborg and he has no intention of doing any detours tonight. He has seen enough. Then he sees more. On the corner of Suhms gate Jostein's father, the butcher, is punching a tree. It is a birch. The trunk is white and smooth. The leaves are beginning to go yellow. Jesper stops. Someone opens a window and shouts: *That tree should be tender by now, Melsom!* But Melsom just carries on hitting it. Jesper sees despair rather than fury. Jesper goes over to him.

"Is Jostein home yet?"

The butcher turns and looks blankly, searchingly, at Jesper.

"He came home yesterday."

"Yesterday?"

"Yes, Jostein came home yesterday."

"Can I . . .?"

The butcher looks down at his bleeding knuckles and interrupts:

"What have they done to my boy?" he says.

Jesper takes a step closer.

"Have they done something?"

"Jostein's not stupid."

"Of course he isn't."

"Jostein's just a bit hard of hearing."

"Who's done something?" Jesper asks.

The butcher looks up again and now his despair has found its lowest point: fury.

"That damned holiday camp. They tormented him. They've ... They have ..."

The big man can't say any more and leans against the same tree he has been punching. Jesper takes a step back.

"Can I visit him? Can I see him?"

The butcher shakes his head and smiles. This is almost worse: fury with a smile.

"But I know where he lives, I do."

Jesper has no idea what he is talking about and doesn't want to ask.

"Do you?"

"I do, Jesper. And now I'm going to pay him a visit."

Melsom walks along Suhms gate, down Norabakken and stops at the public urinal to wash the blood from his hands. The sooner, the better. Two men give him a wide berth and leave him in peace. Then Melsom doesn't stop until he has arrived in Uranienborg Terrasse. There he finds the right name, Carl Hvidt, and goes up to the second floor, rings the bell and holds his arms behind his back. A fragile woman in her fifties opens the door.

"Is Carl Hvidt at home?" Melsom asks.

"Yes, that's my husband. What's this about?"

"I'd just like to thank him for this summer. My son was at his holiday camp for the mentally handicapped."

The woman is a little taken aback, but lets him in and goes

to get her husband. Melsom waits. He can wait as long as he wants. He mustn't lose his fury, that is all. He doesn't. He looks around. There is so much furniture here there is hardly any room to move. In the sitting room there is a Venetian chandelier hanging from the ceiling with green pendants and leaves. On the sofa are a boy and a girl, each reading a book. They look up, smile and continue reading. Melsom nods and doesn't like them being there. The married couple return. Carl Hvidt is wearing a blue suit with a waistcoat. He is smoking a pipe. He holds out a hand. Melsom shakes it despite himself.

"Carl Hvidt. Whose father are you?"

"Jostein's. Jostein Melsom."

"I can remember him. Funny boy. You're a butcher, aren't you? You have a shop in Kirkeveien?"

"May I speak to you alone?"

"What's this about actually?"

"I'd like your wife to join the children and close the door. Or perhaps we could go somewhere else?"

Carl Hvidt looks at Melsom and unease grips him, not much, just a firmer bite on the mouthpiece of the pipe.

"Why?"

"Because I'm a considerate man. Unlike you."

His wife is about to go, but Carl Hvidt holds her back.

"Let your heart speak, Herr Melsom."

But the butcher's heart is so heavy that he doesn't have any more words. Instead he punches Carl Hvidt in the face with his fist. The pipe breaks and falls to the ground. His wife lets out a short-lived scream. The children look up from their books and can't take in what has happened. They see only their father with his hand over his nose, spitting blood and looking up.

"That was nothing to be proud of," he says.

Melsom goes home, displeased and ashamed. He owed Jostein more than that. He should have made more of his assault. He should have put more love into the punch, not only fury. Ellen asks where he has been. But she sees the damaged knuckles on his right hand. Before they go to bed she tends his wounds. She doesn't ask what he has been doing. In the middle of the night Jostein comes into their bedroom and lies between his parents, the way he used to do when he was a child, a child he no longer is.

The following day Melsom expects the police to come. They don't. They probably have other things to see to first. There has been a robbery and an attempted murder at a branch of Spareskillingsbanken in Nedre Slottsgate and there is a widespread hunt on to catch the perpetrators. You can hear sirens everywhere. The next day Melsom also waits in vain. The police don't come to pick him up. A week passes. Then another. It is almost unbearable. Life continues what is called its usual course while Melsom the butcher treads water. Only the cuts to his hand heal. He sees Jesper walk past the shop every morning. Jesper turns quickly and disconsolately. He does the same when he returns from school. Occasionally he passes in the evenings, too. He carries a small, creased bag, a briefcase. Then he stops doing that too or perhaps he just takes a different route. Customers come in to buy. They chat about everything and nothing, all things great and small. It is simply part of the hushed tone of conversation that travels the streets, stops for a break, sighs or laughs. Thank goodness the police caught the bank robbers. And in a barn in Eidsvoll! It was no surprise that Sweden beat Norway 3–1 in the international at Ullevål. Apart from the Norwegian goal. What's happening in Korea? Will there be a war? Thank God that's a long way away. And the bus that turned over in Klemetsrud? How many passengers were there on board? Forty-eight, and only three had to go to hospital, yes, the angels were on their side. One Friday Løkke, the teacher, pops in. He wants two entrecôtes, if they have any. Fru Melsom does. She cuts off two fine steaks for him. The fat in the soft, red meat resembles marble. He also asks how long they have to be fried. Two and a half minutes on each side, then they're done but not dry. By the way, did the butcher know that entrecôte was pronounced with a "t" at the end, not without, as many Norwegians say, unfortunately, including waiters? The teacher says the word aloud, first of all *entrecô*, afterwards the correct pronunciation *entrecôte*. Melsom, who has his back to everyone for most of this, as he tidies the shelves, just nods. He knows how the meat he sells should be pronounced, but thank you all the same. Fru Melsom asks if Løkke is expecting a visit, and he can, in all modesty, tell her that a lady is coming to dinner the following day, he met her at Regnbuen. Regnbuen Jazz Restaurant? Yes. A soft sigh. But how is Jostein doing? The class misses him. Especially Jesper misses him. How is it at the new school? Jostein is at home for the moment, Fru Melsom says, while the butcher finds himself something to do in the back room. Is he indisposed? Nothing serious he trusts. Fried potatoes are good with steak, says Fru Melsom, and they have a wonderful béarnaise sauce at Smør-Petersen's around the corner. It is pronounced beahnayz, the teacher says, with a voiced "s", no "e", it is French, you see, just like entrecôte, with the "t". Melsom comes back in and opens the door for him. *På gjensyn* is Norwegian for goodbye, and it is pronounced without the "g".

The police don't turn up this weekend, either. It is the punishment. Melsom knows. Waiting is a punishment. He should have hit him harder and twice. In which case they would have been here long ago. On Monday he can't wait any longer. He wants to walk the whole way to Møllergata 19 and give himself in. Then Fru Melsom puts her foot down. She holds her husband and looks him in the eye.

"I'm proud of you whatever you've done. Do you understand?"

Melsom nods.

"I should've hit him much harder."

"Your knuckles looked as if you'd hit him hard enough."

"That was only from a tree."

"And now let's put it behind us."

"Us? What about Jostein?"

"He'll put it behind him, too."

As Melsom is about to kiss her quickly on the mouth, finally reassured, well, blessed almost, he feels, because it is over, there is a ring at the back door. He gives a start.

"Here they are! Bloody hell."

Fru Melsom goes into the kitchen and returns with Jesper. As usual, he is carrying the little briefcase and already looks like a pen-pusher. He looks so comical that the butcher has to laugh. Is Jesper going to arrest him for punching Carl Hvidt? He can't stop laughing. He hasn't laughed for a month. That is how it feels. He hasn't so much as smiled. In the end

Fru Melsom has to stop him. It is too much of a good thing.

"Can I see Jostein now?" Jesper asks.

The butcher pulls himself together and accompanies Jesper through the scullery and stops in front of the door between the bathroom and the kitchen. It strikes Jesper that he has never been in Jostein's house before, only downstairs in the shop. They have a telephone up here as well. But they have hardly any furniture. Perhaps because the butcher is so big that he needs plenty of room.

"Have you been to your music lesson again?" he says in a low voice.

"Yes."

"What do you play?"

"Beethoven."

"Isn't he difficult?"

"Yes, he is."

At last the butcher knocks on the door and carefully opens it. The lamp on the desk is lit. But the curtains are drawn. Jostein is sitting on the floor leafing through a book. He looks up and smiles.

"Don't stay too long," the butcher says, closing the door.

Jesper sits on the floor too and looks around. Jostein's room is bigger than his vestibule. The wallpaper has a green leaf pattern. If you didn't know any better you might think you were sitting in the middle of a forest one evening in May. It is October. Otherwise, there are lots of books, some of them fat. Jostein hasn't changed since the last time they saw each other, but Jesper has already noted the difference. He saw it at once. Jostein has no scars or bruises. He has no weals from whipping, nor any open sores. It is his eyes. They are downcast.

When Jostein looks up they never lock onto the target. Then he turns inwards.

"Have you been playing the piano?"

Jesper nods.

"What did you play?"

"Beethoven."

"Is he difficult?"

"No."

They say nothing for a few minutes. Jostein pretends to be reading. Then he looks up and the same happens: his eyes don't lock onto the target.

"Do you know what happens every day in Norway?" he asks.

"What?"

"Guess."

"Twenty-one people die."

"How many?"

"Twenty-one," Jesper shouts.

"No, fifty-nine. And 173 are born, seventy-two get married. Three point three million—"

"Million?"

"What? Yes. Three point three million cigarettes are smoked. 20,200 kilos of chocolate are eaten. 560,000 letters are sent. Thirty-nine planes land in Oslo. And guess how many telephone conversations there are?"

"Just tell me."

"One point three million."

"That's quite a lot."

"There's more going on, too."

"Do you know what we call Løkke at the moment?"

"What?"

"Do you know what we call Løkke?"

"No. What?"

"Lykke."

"Why?"

"He's so happy. He lets us play dodgeball in the last lesson every day."

Then they don't say anything for a while, until Jesper asks:

"What happened at the holiday camp?"

Jostein leans forward.

"Can't hear what you say."

"How was it at the holiday camp?" Jesper shouts.

"Dark."

"What do you mean dark?"

Jostein leans against the green wall.

"Just dark."

"In the day-time, too?"

"All the time."

"You can tell me."

"What?"

"I'm going to hear for you."

They look at each other and finally Jostein's eyes focus on the target.

"They locked the door from the outside."

Jesper gets up.

"Ring me," he says.

Jostein stays on the floor. When he closes his eyes sometimes it is lighter. Then he gets up too, goes into the scullery, past the bathroom and stops by the telephone. His parents are standing in the sitting-room looking at their son. Jostein looks at the numbers, the important ones, which are in a special folder on the directory. He rings Information and asks for Jesper Kristoffersen's number. Information can't find any Jesper Kristoffersen. Kirkeveien 127, Oslo 3, Jostein says and presses the receiver to his ear. Could that be Ewald Kristoffersen? Jostein hears the number read out, he has to listen twice and writes it as quickly as he can in the folder because this is also a number it is important to remember. Then he rings. Ewald answers:

"Kristoffersens here, hello, yes."

"This is Jostein Melsom here. May I speak to Jesper Kristoffersen?"

"Jesper isn't home yet. Jostein? Nice to hear from you. How are you, lad? Hunky-dory? Or just dunky-hory?"

"No, it's not raining here."

"You don't say. Then the rain must've moved up here."

"May I speak to Jesper?" Jostein repeats.

"Jesper's not here. Yes, he is. Here he comes. You're lucky. Hang on a moment."

Ewald places the receiver gently on the table and goes to Jesper, who is hanging up his coat in the hallway.

"Telephone call for you," he whispers.

"Who is it?"

"Jostein. Dear me, his hearing's bad now."

Jesper runs to the telephone. Jostein's voice is a long way away:

"Jesper?"

"Yes, it's me."

"You don't have to hear for me."

"What shall—?"

"You have to play for me."

"Shall I?"

"That was all."

Jostein rings off. Jesper stands with the receiver in his hand. Then he cradles the telephone too, fetches his briefcase, goes into the dining room and puts his sheet music on the piano. It is still Beethoven's sonatinas. He is beginning to get the hang of it now, but it bores him, apart from the last three notes. Stine is asleep in the cot. Maj bends down over her. Ewald lights a cigarette, it doesn't matter anymore, and looks at Jesper.

"What have you learned from this Italian of ours this autumn?"

Jesper closes the piano.

"How to carry out repairs," he says.

———————

The board meeting was held at Fru Berit Nordklev's on 11/12/50. Those present were Frøken Aasland, Fru Foss, Fru Arnesen, Fru Kristoffersen and Berit Nordklev. Fru Dagny Hoffmann, who would like to be on the new board, had kindly offered to help with the packing of Christmas parcels.

Fifty-eight parcels of clothes of various types, all new (a present from the American Red Cross, allocated to the department by the District Office), were ironed and packed. With every parcel was a Christmas card from the dept.

Furthermore, ten pairs of shoes and twenty food parcels (twenty kroner each) plus one extra parcel, a present from O. Laache, a merchant, were distributed. Co-operation with Melsom, the butcher, has ceased. The decision is Melsom's and the board very much regrets it. Three copies of the Red Cross Christmas comics sent to: Oswald Hansen, Ullevål Hospital, Frøken Tillisch and Fru Tengelsen, Rosenborg old people's home. The two latter ladies, plus Frøken Else Lange and Fru Lie, have knitted sixteen pairs of mittens and socks, which were placed in the parcels. Christmas greetings were sent to Frøken Lange and Fru Lie, Fru Esther Andersen and both the parish nurses.

The parcels were distributed, half through Fagerborg parish and half through social security. Three parcels for three motherless children. Anne, Aase and Inger Hansen received parcels directly.

Fru Hulda Engen, who had been given wood earlier this autumn, came on December 22nd and asked for a jumper for a nephew who was in dire need. She was given four balls of yarn and told to knit it herself.

THIEVES

Margrethe Hall wakes up alone. She looks at the watch she put on the bedside table. It is nine o'clock, already nine. This is absurd. She should jump up and start the day. She should have been up and about ages ago. But what should she do? She lies in a little longer, listens, the noises are different, they are unfamiliar; there are other objects, not hers. There is the tram in Frogner square, not the bus in Kirkeveien. She can't stop thinking: she is lying in another woman's bed. She feels ungrateful and sad in equal proportion and thinks: at least I've changed the bed. It is my sheet. She goes to the bathroom. There is a shower. The water is only lukewarm and never gets really hot. She showers anyway and is cold for a moment. It feels good. Olaf has set a place for her in the kitchen. She isn't used to his breakfast, which consists of porridge and water. She likes something sweet, not too sweet, but she soon gets used to it, all the non-sweetness. She admires him. She puts on the coffee and closes the window that is ajar. The snow in the garden suddenly seems very cold. Then she takes two cups down to the shop. Olaf is sitting at the desk at the back and doesn't turn. She stops and waits. He is slowly turning the pages of a magnificent, flat book. It is *The Chinese Flute*, number 263 of 300 copies, signed by the poet Eugen Frank. He has finally got his hands on it. The pages are dry and thin, almost transparent. He has to keep an eye on the temperature, so that they don't come loose and disintegrate. What a joy it is to hold. What a joy it is to have in your hands. It will be painful to part with. He won't sell it to just anyone. *The Chinese Flute* will end up in a good home. He already knows who will get it – Høegh Senior. He had ships in the Orient between the wars and sailed there himself for some time. Just the dedication in the beautiful monogram, *To My Wife*, is enough to make you tremble.

"Good morning," Olaf Hall says.

"Is it still morning? Soon be lunch."

He turns and sees Margrethe standing there with a cup of coffee in each hand. Ragnhild never came down here. He laughs.

"And so what? You can sleep for as long as you like."

"I'd like to get up at the same time as you."

"Is that what you and Halfdan did?"

Margrethe seems embarrassed for a moment.

"I've been thinking about something," she says.

"Oh, yes?"

"Could we ask the Kristoffersens here this Christmas?"

"Do you think?"

"I'd like to see little Stine. And Jesper."

"I thought we might spend Christmas alone. Our first Christmas."

Margrethe lets slip a smile:

"You're right. How stupid I am."

Olaf puts *The Chinese Flute* in his lap.

"Now the coffee's getting all cold, I suppose."

"You like it cold, don't you?"

He laughs again.

"I was thinking mostly about your coffee, darling."

Margrethe moves towards him between the narrow shelving and piles of books. Olaf doesn't like this. You simply don't serve coffee around these fragile, precious objects, nor tea for that matter, perhaps spirits, but then only enough brandy to cover the bottom of the glass, to celebrate a successful deal. However, he doesn't let this show. He is tolerant. He loves her. She will learn in time. She is wearing a perfume he likes so much today, although nothing can compare with the aroma of books.

"Have you heard from Bjørn?" Margrethe asks.

Olaf doesn't see how it happens. He just sees a cup falling, from her left hand. He tries to catch it, but is too slow. Coffee splashes over his trousers, over the book lying open in his lap, the dry pages absorb the black liquid at once and the typeface is thinned, concealed, and disappears. Olaf stands up and holds the dripping book as far as possible from his body; Margrethe hides her face in her hands and drops the other cup as well.

"Did you burn yourself?"

Olaf Hall stares open-mouthed.

"Burn myself? Do you think I care about that? Do you really think . . . You . . . ."

His face is set in a scowl. She takes a handkerchief from her dress pocket.

"Go on. Say it. You fool."

She wants to wipe him down, but he pushes her away with his free hand.

"Don't touch me. Please. Don't touch me!"

Margrethe retreats, goes down on her knees and tidies up the broken pieces of the cup and saucer while looking up at him all the time.

"I didn't mean to."

"Of course you didn't! Do you think I'm stupid?"

"No, I'm the one who's stupid."

"Don't keep repeating yourself, please. My God. Do you know what this book's worth?"

Margrethe Vik bows her head, trying to hide her tears.

"I don't know anything."

"Well, you said it."

Olaf Hall walks over to the door; she hears him changing his shoes.

"Where are you going?"

"To cool down."

The door slams behind him and she gets up slowly, wearily, lazily almost. What had he called her at the start? A transfer ticket. Was her time up already? The book is lying on the floor, soiled and stained; she lifts it carefully and puts it on the desk. One of the pages has come out. She tries to put it back. It is no use. She reads the first lines of "The Maiden's Lament", from *Schih-Ching*, a collection of poems from the twelfth to the seventh century B.C.

My Friend, listen to my Prayer!

Don't come to our little Village! Don't cross my Path!
Spare the Willow tree that has grown tall with me
You know I cannot give you my Heart

Then Margrethe Hall carries the shards to the kitchen and throws them in the bin. She wants to rush back down and wash the floor, but she doesn't. She doesn't want to do any more damage. The best intentions don't help. As if she didn't know. Or she doesn't have the strength. She doesn't have the strength to go down to the smell that is reminiscent of mothballs and cowshed. She just stands by the windowsill, for a moment powerless and terror-stricken. Did he raise his hand to her? No, that was just a gesture, an accident. She is unable to visualise the sequence of events, the cup, the book, Olaf. Well, she tripped, he raised his hand to protect himself and the precious book. That is how it was. But afterwards? Didn't he raise his hand then, too? No, she isn't thinking clearly. She is an idiot. It is her fault and she isn't thinking clearly. Margrethe Hall can't be bothered to wait for Olaf any longer. She gets ready again, wraps up well, puts two name tags in her bag and goes outside. It is cold, minus twelve. The snow on the pavements is hard and slippery. It is surprisingly light outside. In Bogstadveien she buys first a doll with a dress at Hagen's and asks the assistant to gift-wrap it. At Øye she finds a little tie, blue with diagonal stripes, and asks for it to be gift-wrapped as well. Then she walks along Jacob Aalls gate and being in old territory – even though she hasn't been away for more than a few months, and not that far away either, Oslo 3 became Oslo 2, a smaller number – feels like coming home. The most difficult part is not getting used to another person, Margrethe Hall thinks, but to their habits and objects, everything that is attached to a person. She should have known that, too. She should have known that a person consists of small movements and nothing is basically new. She reaches the entrance and sees her name on the sign above the post boxes. It is like meeting a ghost. Then she goes upstairs and rings the bell at the Kristoffersens. Maj opens eventually, with Stine under one arm. Margrethe bursts into tears. Maj lets her in, anxious and surprised, and doesn't care that she has just washed the floors.

"But what is it, my dear?"

Margrethe draws breath.

"I need a pen."

"Surely that's nothing to cry about."

Maj finds her an ink pen in Ewald's jacket and Margrethe sits down in the kitchen. She writes on the name tags: *To Jesper from Aunty Margrethe* and *To Stine from Aunty Margrethe*. She ties them to the ribbons on the packets and becomes lost in thought again. Maj comes back from the room where she has laid Stine and sits down.

"You were just so nice, both of you," Margrethe says.

"Do you want anything to—?"

"No, no, I have to be on my way."

Maj looks at the presents.

"You didn't need to."

"Should I put Olaf's name as well?"

"What do you think?"

"I don't know."

"I don't, either. I'll make some coffee anyway. And then you can try my first Christmas biscuits."

Maj heats up what's left in the kettle. They are silent as she sets the table and puts out a plate of syrup snaps. Margrethe looks at the ceiling, sighs and tastes Maj's baking.

"They're good," she says.

"How are yours?"

"I haven't baked this year."

"You haven't baked? Nothing?"

"Olaf isn't used to Christmas bakery."

"But you are. Aren't you?"

"We're adapting to each other, as well as we can."

Maj pours the coffee.

"Lucky thing. I wish I could've given it a miss as well."

They are silent again over their cup of coffee.

"Do you think there'll be time to say hi to Jesper before I have to go?"

"You're not going already, are you?"

"There's a lot to do, even if I don't bake."

"Jesper's going up the City Hall bell tower after school."

"Well I never. The bell tower?"

"Ewald has got permission for three people, but I said no."

"How is he?"

It is Maj's turn to cry. She doesn't.

"The doctors keep saying he hasn't got long. They should be back by now."

"Perhaps they're looking at the decorations in the streets?"

"I'm sure they are. While they're in the city."

"He was so thin at the wedding."

"He's even thinner now. And he's got this idea on the brain."

"What's that?"

"That he's not going to die before his father, Alfred."

"The Alfred in Tåsen old people's home?"

"Yes. And he could keep going until he's at least 120."

"But isn't that wonderful? Then you'll have Ewald for lots more years."

"It's like a competition. It's wearing me out!"

"So let them compete."

Maj hides her face in her hands and cries between her fingers.

"I'm bad, aren't I. Evil, I am."

"You couldn't be if you tried."

"Obviously I don't want him to die—"

"I know. It'll be fine, you'll see."

Maj puts her hands down on the table cloth and for a moment she can feel how everything was before. She looks at the gift tags as soon as this feeling has gone.

"I think you should leave them as they are," she says.

"Just from me?"

"Yes. Just from you."

"That's probably right."

"And you can write from both of you next year."

"Yes, next year they'll be from both of us."

Margrethe gets up. She would like to ask if she can use the telephone to call Olaf. She wants him talking as soon as possible. She doesn't call him. It would appear odd. Instead she wishes Maj a happy Christmas and decides to go straight home to the house in Nordraaks gate and not via Melsom the butcher, as she had planned. When she comes out the earlier light has gone and the shadow causes everything to lose its outline and flow slowly into its surroundings. Maj stands in the window waving to her, but Margrethe doesn't turn around. That makes Maj uneasy, or suspicious. You always turn around and wave to people you have visited, unless the visit has been a failure in some way, and it definitely has not. They had a good chat. Perhaps she talked too much about herself and didn't let Margrethe get a word in? That is the reason. Maj will have to call her later in the evening and say she didn't mean to hog the conversation. The telephone rings and Stine wakes up at the same time, or after the brief pause that allows space for movement, a reaction. It is Ewald. He just wants to say they will be a bit late, they are walking through the graveyard, it seems fitting somehow. Where is he ringing from?

"The telephone booth in Frogner Park. Jesper wants to talk—"

"It'll be expensive, Ewald."

"And I'm paying, Fru Treasurer. He hasn't called from a booth before."

Maj hears a cacophony at first and then Jesper's breathing. She can almost see his breath as rime frost on the lines. Her voice is loud to make sure they can hear at the other end.

"Was it nice up the bell tower, Jesper?"

"No."

Then the connection goes, perhaps the money has run out and there is no time left to talk. Ewald takes the receiver from Jesper, bangs it down and walks out, abruptly and with little reflection. Jesper can hardly keep up with him over Vigeland Bridge. Soon he can't be bothered to try, either. He just straggles behind. Ewald stops, too. Jesper sees his father's back, the black coat the wind lifts by the tails and drops like wings. He turns and walks back.

"Why did you tell Mamma it wasn't nice in the bell tower?"

But Jesper doesn't know how to explain, how to translate the sound, because the moment they were up there the bells rang for half past two, and this sound is a heavy globule of water that won't let go, that won't come out.

"I thought she asked if it was creepy," he says.

"Who's hard of hearing: you or Jostein?"

"Jostein."

Ewald muses and after a lot of ifs and buts approves of Jesper's answer. Of course it wasn't creepy. They walk the last bit to the graveyard and locate Ewald's mother's resting place. On some of the graves nearby there are candles shining like yellow dots in the darkness that falls from the cypresses. Ewald regrets not having brought a torch with him. How feather-brained he is. He takes Jesper by the hand.

"My mother and father are the same age," Ewald says.

"Grandma's dead," Jesper points out.

"Yes, but they can still be the same age."

Jesper gives this some thought.

"Does Grandma get older in the grave?"

"No, not as such. But they were born in the same year, 1884, and no-one can take that from them. However dead they are."

Then they both catch a glimpse of a man dressed much too thinly, only a suit, walking between the graves. They see who it is. It is Olaf Hall. Ewald turns and whispers.

"Now stay perfectly calm and pretend we haven't seen him."

But Jesper is still witness to something bizarre. The man, Fru Vik's new husband, bends down quickly by a gravestone, takes the pillar candle there and strides over to another grave. Suddenly, between two strides, Olaf Hall meets Jesper's gaze, he hesitates, perhaps he is about to say something, then he acts as if nothing has happened and puts the candle he took, or stole, down by a gravestone sticking out of the snow.

"He's already seen us," Jesper whispers.

"Bugger."

Ewald turns and sees Olaf Hall digging in the snow with his hands.

"Are you sure?"

"Yes."

"Did he say hello?"

"He needs some matches."

Ewald lets go of Jesper, takes out his box of matches and goes over to Olaf Hall, who stands up with a smile.

"Aren't you cold?" Ewald asks.

"I'm never cold."

"Lucky you."

Olaf Hall takes the matchsticks and lights the candle, which flickers on all sides for a moment before stabilising in the darkness.

"And you? You haven't stopped smoking?"

"I have nothing to lose."

Olaf Hall regards Ewald, who is barely recognisable.

"Do you need any help?" he asks.

"Help?"

"You seem unsteady on your feet."

"Not at all."

"Sure? I wouldn't like you to fall."

"I won't."

"I can't promise you that I'll be able to get you back on your feet afterwards. In this deep snow."

Olaf Hall is about to grab Ewald's arm, but Ewald waves him away.

"Don't let the boy see! You'd better give me the matches."

"Of course."

"Say hello to Fru Vik."

"Fru Hall don't you mean?"

"Fru Hall, yes. Say hello from Jesper as well."

Olaf Hall hands the box of matches to Ewald, nods and scoots off along the narrow path that has been cleared. He buys a poinsettia at Radoor Flower Shop in Frognerveien. When he arrives home the hallway is so hot he can scarcely breathe. He removes his shoes. His socks are wet. He pulls them off as well and toddles barefoot into the kitchen where Margrethe is waiting. The fireplace behind her is burning hot. A log falls in a shower of sparks. She doesn't look at him. She is holding her hands in her lap. Will he have to go down on his knees?

"Did you manage that on your own?" he asks.

"Manage what?"

"To light the fire. The draught isn't very good. I can never do it."

Margrethe puts on a smile.

"So there is something I can do."

Olaf disappears again, probably to find his slippers, but returns with the poinsettia he has unpacked.

"Forgive me."

"You should put something on your feet. You—"

"Forgive me," he repeats.

Margrethe looks up and takes the flower. It already needs water. She gets to her feet, runs the tap slowly and sees how the dry, light soil soaks up the water and becomes dark, heavy and alive.

"It's you who should forgive me," she says.

"Nonsense."

"I'll never take coffee down to you again."

Olaf laughs.

"No, we'll drink it in the kitchen. Or the sitting room. Or perhaps in bed?"

Margrethe puts the poinsettia on the windowsill.

"Maybe."

Olaf steps closer.

"Do you like coffee in bed?"

"I might well do. On Sundays maybe."

"Why not other days as well?"

"We don't want to overdo it, do we."

She is standing with her back to him. He has his arms around her. She doesn't know whether she is making him hot or whether he is making her cold. She hears his voice near her ear.

"There's so much I don't know about you. Every day I can ask you something new and get to know you better."

"Me, too."

"Ask me something."

"Do you like red cabbage?"

Olaf Hall laughs.

"Can't you think of something more intimate?"

"Intimate?"

"Personal then."

Margrethe has no idea what questions she should ask. She just chooses the first that comes into her mind.

"What do you dream about?"

"You."

"In which case it'll be a nightmare from now on."

He kisses her neck.

"No. The sweetest dreams ever."

"Don't talk nonsense."

"Shall we have a little lie-down?"

"It's so early . . ."

"I said only for a *little* lie-down."

Margrethe feels him pulling her.

"Here?"

"You like it hot, don't you?"

Olaf takes off his jacket and lays it out on the kitchen floor. They lie down, close to each other. It is painful. Margrethe tries to find a more comfortable position. It is impossible. He takes her hand and draws it down to his belt. She undoes it, closes her eyes and puts her hand inside. She isn't unwilling. Olaf lets out a sigh. That is all. She tries, but it is no good. Olaf holds her again, but she doesn't know what to do in this embrace. She is inadequate. Soon he turns away. She looks at the ceiling, not unhappy, just vacant, but also embarrassed. She sees the heat rising and staying there, under the ceiling.

"Ewald Kristoffersen says hello," Olaf says.

"Where did you meet him?"

"At the cemetery."

Margrethe feels the stabs to her heart, she doesn't want to, but she does anyway and she feels even emptier.

"So that's where you go when you want to cool down."

Olaf Hall is also lying on his back, with his hands behind his head.

"He looked terrible. All skin and bone."

"Is that right?"

"I wondered if I'd have to call an ambulance."

"Was it that bad?"

"Worse. I thought for a moment he was going to expire there and then."

"My God. Then it's been quick."

They lie in silence watching the same heat gliding like a wave of dusty air beneath the ceiling. Margrethe shivers, Olaf takes her hand.

"I really hope he got home safe and sound."

"Do you think . . .?"

"I'm just sorry for the boy who was with him."

"Oh, poor Jesper. Was he there, too?"

Olaf laughs.

"Yes, an inquisitive little fellow. Sorry, it's nothing to laugh about."

"I'll call her. Maj. To find out if everything's alright."

"That's kind of you."

Margrethe gets up, stiff and weary. Olaf stays where he is. He likes lying on hard surfaces. He buttons up his trousers and embraces her again.

"And one more thing. Tell her there's often someone around stealing candles from the graves."

"At Vestre Cemetery?"

"Yes, someone had pinched the candle from Ragnhild's grave and moved it to another one. Can you imagine anything so petty?"

"What did you do?"

"I took it back of course."

"What some people do."

Olaf lets go of her and laughs:

"If it happens again, I'll report the master joiner buried there. Humph, that was mean of me."

Margrethe wipes her hands on her apron, goes into the hall and dials Maj's number. Ewald answers. She wishes it had been Maj. With everyone else, or at least most people, it is the woman of the house who answers, that is just how it is, a kind of arrangement that has developed of its own accord, no deals or planning necessary. Or perhaps it is only because men are less talkative than women? At any rate, one thing is certain: men don't voluntarily chitter-chatter about this and that on the telephone. They get to the point and ring off. Then Margrethe hears something else in the background, the piano.

"Is that Jesper playing?" she asks.

"Yes, he's practising."

"It's so wonderful I thought it was the radio."

"I'll say hello from you and tell him."

"Is it Beethoven?"

"Yes. No sheet music. I suppose you want to speak to Maj?"

"Not really, Ewald. I wanted to make sure you got home alright from the cemetery."

There is a silence up in Kirkeveien 127.

"Yes, I did," he says at length.

"I'm happy to hear that."

"Thank you. You don't need to worry."

"Then we won't."

"Was there anything else?"

"Yes, Olaf says there are apparently some individuals stealing or moving candles from graves. Just so that you know. Are you there?"

Ewald nods, it is a bad habit he has, he nods and gesticulates when talking on the telephone. Then he rings off, stands for a few seconds, bewildered, more doomed than ever. The flat is silent. He suddenly realises he is alone. He almost runs into the sitting room. Maj is standing by Stine's bed. Jesper is sitting at the piano with his hands in his lap, unhappy.

"Fru Vik thought the music she heard was from the radio, Jesper," Ewald says.

Maj turns to him.

"Didn't she want to talk to me?"

"Actually, no."

"What did she want then?"

Ewald has to think.

"She said someone's stealing candles from the graves."

"And she rang to say that?"

"We met the antiquity in the cemetery, you see."

"Olaf Hall?"

"He was tending his ex-wife's grave."

"Why on earth didn't you say?"

Ewald has another think. How long can Stine sleep in here? Soon she will have to have another bed. Soon she will be starting school. Time goes fast. Before you know it. Before you know it, it has gone. Perhaps she can be in the vestibule and Jesper can go in the kitchen? No, then he will be in Maj's way, or vice versa, and neither of the two options can be recommended. What about if he knocks down the wall to the scullery and divides the hall into two? Then probably Fru Vik's empty flat will come crashing down. Ewald curses the architect who wasted so much space on an embellishment instead of making another room.

"I have a lot on my mind," he says.

Maj walks over to her husband and runs her fingers gently through his thin, damp hair.

"Sorry."

Jesper closes the piano and stands up.

"He's the one who steals candles."

Both of them look at him.

"Who is?" Ewald asks.

"The man who took Fru Vik as well."

After Jesper has gone to bed he hears their voices. It's not right that the flat has been left empty. That is Ewald talking. It's not right that it's empty when there's such a shortage of accommodation. Perhaps it's right after all. That is Maj talking. Perhaps it's right that Fru Vik kept it. But mostly Jesper hears the heavy globule of water in his head, the sombre sound which still reverberates. He closes his eyes and is sure he will be at half past two for the rest of his life.

ANNUAL REPORT FOR 1950, FAGERBORG DEPARTMENT
The board consists of: Fru Nordklev (chairman), Fru Lund (deputy chairman), Fru Kristoffersen (treasurer), Fru Larsen (secretary), Fru Arnesen and Frøken Aasland (reserve).

There were five board meetings in 1950.

The board members and voluntary helpers assisted with the X-ray procedures and provided food for fifty German Jewish children on their way through Oslo for the Norwegian Mission of Israel.

The department gave 360 kroner to the crèche teacher at the Rikshospital. 24 elderly people were on the joint trip to the Museum of Cultural History. The Bakkebø Institute for the mentally handicapped in Egersund, the former Slettebø internment camp which was taken over by the Directorate for Property in Enemy Hands, was granted 400 kroner, plus ten pairs of shoes, while the Norwegian Red Cross contributed no less than 250,000 kroner through the Nitedal Charity Matchstick Foundation.

The department's participation in the bazaar and stamp sales produced a good result and no slip-ups. For the Studenterlunden market the department provided eight helpers per day for fifteen days.

Ten baby parcels were given to Oslo Red Cross's Child Aid. One thousand kroner was put aside in the 1951 budget for prizes.

We gave food, shoes, knitted items and other clothing to the needy in our district, 90 parcels in all. In some cases we offered financial assistance. Five older Red Cross members knitted wonderful children's socks and mittens all year.

Oslo, 2/1, signed by Berit Nordklev, chairman.

BUCKRIDE

Herr Lykke is not at school. There are a lot of rumours circulating. In the end it all comes out. In the meantime they have a temporary teacher. He is a young man with round glasses and thin arms. He sits behind the desk with these arms crossed and asks them to read aloud. After a week they start playing him up. After two weeks they begin to miss Lykke. When the month of January is over, he finally returns. By then he is neither the happy Lykke of his nickname nor Løkke. He returns as Uløkke. This is his new name. Unhappy Løkke. Not to his face though. He walks so slowly. He has hardly reached his desk before the bell for the end of the lesson rings. His face is pinched and pale. The chalk turns to dust in his hands. He is no more than a ghost leaning against the blackboard. Jesper follows closely. Jesper watches his every move. Jesper puts everything in context. Uløkke mourns sorrow before it happens. That is exactly what Jesper is doing. He is mourning the death of Ewald, even though Ewald isn't dead yet. It is strange. Jesper feels very close to Uløkke in these days. He wishes he could mourn sorrow before it happens to get it over and done with. No-one in the class dares to play any pranks during this time. Uløkke is off-limits. They can see the pain he is carrying, recognise it and are obedient to the tips of their fingers. But one morning the sorrow, whatever its origin, has lasted too long. His amnesty has run out. Uløkke is overdoing it. The sorrow that the day before had evoked respect has become ridiculous in the course of the night. Jesper senses it at once. He bows his head and can't bear to watch. It is repugnant. It is a disgrace. Sorrow is a lop-sided top hat. The suffering is hanging in strips. The class notices it, too. The beasts of prey can smell rotten flesh, but they are making a mistake, a big mistake, they actually think Uløkke has become harmless as well. Jesper knows they are wrong. He wants to stop what is in the offing. He doesn't know how. He is already flinching. This week's monitor, Ivar from Smestad, puts up his hand. He is given permission to speak.

"How in fact did you become unhappy, Herr Løkke?" Ivar asks.

Everyone in the class, except Jesper, is spread across their desks trying to stifle their laughter. Suppressed hiccups, truncated howls, can be heard nonetheless. Løkke stands behind his desk with his arms behind his back. He stands like that for a long time. How long can he stay there? Only Løkke knows. Eventually the class becomes silent. No-one dares to laugh. A different kind of silence ensues. Jesper analyses it. He has never heard anything like it. It is an intense lull containing everything. Absolutely silent it is not. The sombre globule of water is still in Jesper's head. Ivar from Smestad can't stand it and puts up his hand again.

"Did I say something wrong, Herr Lykke?"

Then what the class has not expected, not even Jesper, happens. Løkke slowly raises his arm and at that moment the bell rings. Is it the end of the lesson? Is it all the church bells ringing at once, in Fagerborg, Vestre Aker, Sagene, Uranienborg and the Priests' Church? Is it both? Has war broken out again or has peace come once more? Perhaps the City Hall bells have gone wrong, Jesper thinks, or is all this happening only in his head? It is the fire alarm. The class sits waiting, ready to run. No-one dares move. The playground is soon full of pupils. The alarm bell continues ringing. Løkke, arm raised, doesn't move. For a moment he looks like a Nazi.

"Shall we die in the flames?" Løkke asks.

No-one answers.

"Shall we just let ourselves die in the flames?" he says.

The monitor stands up.

"The other classes have already gone outside," he says.

"That's because they don't have any discipline!"

Another boy stands up, in the window row, Robert from Frøen. He shouts:

"There's smoke coming from behind the board! There's smoke behind the board!"

Everyone in the class, apart from Jesper, who can't see any smoke, storms out, tripping over one another, knocking over desks, kicking away chairs, spilling pencil cases and ink wells. Then it is quiet again. Løkke takes Jesper's hand.

"Come on," he says.

Jesper tosses his satchel over his shoulder, as he assumes there won't be any more lessons today. In the corridor coats and packed lunches are scattered everywhere. By the steps Løkke lets go of Jesper's hand and begins to walk up the flights of stairs.

"Don't do it," Jesper says.

But Løkke doesn't hear him or he doesn't want to hear. He continues up the steps until he disappears around the landing where the staircase turns. Only his hand is visible on the brown banister. Jesper makes a dash for the last door. In the playground teachers search for their classes and pupils also hurtle around unable to find their usual positions. Everyone seems lost and unhappy. Jesper stands by the wall. It is only now he notices: his head is empty. He is sound-free. The sombre, heavy globule of water has finally freed itself and trickles out. Jesper cries with his ears. Then everyone freezes, in a sudden, random pattern, and looks upwards.

Løkke appears on the roof, between the chimneys. He can just keep his balance. He has to stretch out his arms. He has to crouch down. A sigh runs through the assembled crowd. Some scream and instantly put their hands over their mouths. Don't frighten him. For God's sake. The teaching staff collects by the fountain. Should we call the police? Ambulance? The caretaker suggests he and the gym teacher, Åhlen, simply go up and bring down Løkke, who is now sitting astride the ridge. He is a rider. He is riding Majorstua School into the sunset, which is soon behind the city and turning the mountaintops blue and making Holmenkoll Hill look like a nail scraping the last light from the sky. Løkke is riding. The Deputy Head wants to make him listen to reason.

"Pull yourself together!" he yells.

He shouldn't have said that. Løkke lifts one leg, slides on his bottom down the slippery tiles and stops by the roof gutter where he sits dangling his legs over the edge. More screams. Two girls in the third class faint and are taken care of by the singing teacher, Hultgren. Someone bursts into tears. A boy in the seventh class says: "Do you think we'll get the day off if he falls?" But Løkke doesn't fall. He just funnels his hands around his mouth so that everyone can hear:

"This is just a fire practice!"

Jesper turns and leaves. He walks with his eyes shut and counts the paces inside his head. He reaches eighteen. Then a lorry hoots, Jesper opens his eyes, it is the sewage truck driving past, straight in front of him, and he stands for a moment in the stench, the stench of shit, the stench of all the shit that those with an outside toilet in the yard have managed to shit since the previous time, while the night-soil man standing on the step at the back with a muckrake turns and waves. A fire engine races up at full speed from Briskeby. They are going to extinguish Løkke. An ambulance sets off down Kirkeveien at the same speed from Ullevål Hospital. Jesper throws up outside the Salvation Army Hall. Then he goes inside the butcher's shop and asks Fru Melsom for a glass of water. Of course. Is Jesper unwell? He seems a little pale around the gills. He shakes his head and drinks. Herr Melsom makes an appearance as well and gives Jesper a packet; the paper is already red and soaked.

"For your father," he says.

Jesper doesn't ask any questions, puts the packet in the pocket of his windcheater and goes out. There he meets Jostein, who takes him aside.

"Have you heard what happened to Løkke?"

"You don't have to shout."

"Have you heard what happened to Løkke?"

"What?"

Jostein looks to the left and right and leans closer.

"He was tricked."

"Tricked?"

"He was tricked out of all his money by a woman."

"What money?"

"What?"

"Did Løkke have any money?"

"He took out his savings and lent everything to her."

"How do you know?"

Jostein looks around again.

"Heard it."

"Heard?"

"Yes. And?"

"Well, nothing."

Jostein turns to Jesper and puts his hands behind both ears; he almost takes off and flies over Fagerborg.

"I'm not bloody deaf. I'm just a little hard of hearing."

Jesper walks home thinking: Jostein hears for me. He hears rumours. He sits down at the piano, but doesn't play. When he has looked at the notes for long enough they begin to dance in front of his eyes. Some fall, others rise. Where Zanetti has written *fortissimo* with a shaking pencil the notes burn a hole in the paper. Where he has written *lento* they almost disappear between the lines. Jesper gets up, uneasy, even though his head is empty. Ants crawl up from his toes to his forehead. His mother shouts it is time to eat. He goes into the kitchen. Stine is allowed to sit at the table, in her own chair. His mother feeds her a grey, grainy mush. Ewald attaches the serviette to the top button of his shirt, which is much too big for him around the collar, as all his clothes are. There is some light stew and flatbread on the table. Ewald helps himself. Jesper watches him. There is something. His father has changed. Jesper thinks: he is already dead. Then Jesper sees what it is. It is only his hair. The thin hair that is still in place is plastered across his skull and dyed darker. He has smartened himself up. He has smartened himself up for them, for Maj, Jesper and Stine. Jesper wishes he hadn't bothered. Ewald hasn't smartened himself up. He has just put on an act. He looks like an ad for shoe polish or roofing felt. Jesper can't look anymore and casts his eyes down. Suddenly there is stew on his plate. His mother says nothing. She is busy with Stine, who tries to knock the spoon away. In surprise, Ewald looks around.

"Haven't you heard?" he says.

Maj glances at him.

"Heard what?"

"What happened to Løkke. Don't you know even, Jesper? You—"

Maj interrupts him:

"You don't have to tittle-tattle at the table, Ewald."

"Do you know?"

"Fru Melsom told me. And you don't have to tell Jesper—"

Jesper interrupts her.

"I know, too," he says.

Ewald leans across the table.

"What do you know, Jesper?"

"A woman stole his money."

"Is that right?"

Ewald turns to Maj, who lowers her voice.

"Oh dear, yes. Apparently he met some woman at Regnbuen who pulled the wool over his eyes. And now let

414

that be an end to it. Was that what you were going to say?"

"No, actually it wasn't."

"What were you going to say, Ewald?"

Ewald is silent and gently shakes his head so as not to upset his hairstyle.

"Now I understand better," he says.

Maj lifts Stine up from the chair and puts her on her lap.

"What do you mean? You're talking in riddles, Ewald."

"I've just been to Julius, the hairdresser. As you might be able to see. And he said that—"

Maj is quick:

"Your hair looks really good. I didn't have a chance to say when you came in."

Jesper looks down at his plate. The stew looks like vomit. She is lying. Ewald can hear she is lying, too. She can hear it, too. He sighs:

"Soon there'll only be a few tufts of grass left on the piste. I asked Julius to do the best he could with what there was."

"He's done a great job," Maj says.

Jesper can't stand it anymore.

"What did he tell you?"

Ewald looks up and sighs again.

"Løkke jumped off the school roof today."

Jesper closes his eyes. Maj takes a deep breath and almost drops Stine.

"What was he doing on the roof?"

"Well, you'd better take that up with Løkke. But I assume he was searching for his savings."

"So he survived?"

"Did he bite the dust do you mean?"

"Talk properly! Show a bit of respect at least."

Ewald is rapt in thought, then answers:

"The fire service very kindly caught him. He didn't get so much as a scratch. But apparently he did get a chill on his travels."

"Thank God."

Ewald stares at Jesper, who opens his eyes.

"Wouldn't that have been good," Ewald says.

"Wouldn't what have been good?"

"Landing in the fire brigade's safety net."

For the rest of the evening Jesper pretends to be doing his homework. He just sits at the little desk in the vestibule waiting for the ants to find somewhere they can relax. No-one notices anything because everything is different this evening anyway. After he goes to bed he lies awake. Later, but earlier than usual, his mother comes by, in her nightie. She blows him a kiss and leaves the bedroom door open. Ewald is singing in the bathroom. Everyone wants to be happy. Then he comes by too, in the striped pyjamas he has to wear with a belt. He raises a hand, a casual wave in passing, or perhaps he was just running his fingers through his hair, which is still as sleek. Jesper thinks: everything has already happened. It is terrible. This is the last time he will see his father walk past him, from the scullery to the bedroom. But as Ewald is about to close the door, he hesitates. Is the boy crying? No, it is only a shadow moving across his face. That is how the night touches us. He stands there for a moment. Where does the shadow belong in the darkness? He also leaves the door ajar so that they can hear if anyone is crying. All the doors in the world are ajar. Then Ewald goes to bed. Maj sleeps beside him. Her breathing is calm and regular. It is good to hear. It is good to sleep to. She is his. He is hers. Now he can make the promise. Now he can keep what he promised: to love her until death do them part. He will do that even if she finds someone else. Ewald wakes to fear and desire. A flame burns between his eyes. He can see in the darkness. The pillow is clammy and nearly black. His hair is stuck to it. He pulls himself free. Maj is still asleep. He lies on top of her, as gently as he can. He has to be gentle. He is so thin that she could cut herself on him. He doesn't want to hurt her. He wants to make love to her. He wants to make love more intensely than ever before. She is soft and willing. He wants to penetrate her. She yields to him at first. She yields to him for a while. Then she begins to fight. She doesn't want him. But Ewald doesn't stop. He can't stop. Maj tries to say something. She squirms from side to side. She kicks, punches and groans. She wakes with a scream and pushes him away, but her arms reach out into thin air. She gasps for breath. The duvet is on the floor where a column of light has fallen. Beside her, the bed is empty. Maj sits up.

"Ewald?"

She says it again, his name, it is like a shout this time.

"Ewald?"

She throws her dressing gown over her shoulders and goes into the vestibule. Jesper is sitting up in bed. He sees her approach. Suddenly he has a bad conscience. It is so bad he has to hide his face in his hands. He knows what it is from: Jesper knows before his mother. Jesper is the first to know. She asks tentatively although there are not many places to look:

"Where's Pappa, Jesper?"

"He's bitten the dust."

"Pardon."

"Bitten the dust!"

Maj takes Jesper by the shoulders and shakes him. It doesn't help. She can shake as much as she likes. Then she sees that the dining-room door is closed. Maj lets him go. She lets go of everything she has, wants to break down the door, but comes to her senses and opens it as quietly as she can, so as not to wake anyone. She doesn't wake anyone. Stine is asleep. Ewald is sitting on the floor, leaning against the piano. The dye in his hair has run down his face.

———

The first board meeting of 1951 is held at Frøken Vanda Aasland's on 2nd February. Those present were: Fru Nordklev, Fru Lund, Fru Foss and Frøken Aasland.

Fru Nordklev read the minutes from the last board meeting and the last working committee meeting. She also read out thank-you letters from recipients of food parcels etc for Christmas and other correspondence.

It was decided to drop Fru Wådeland as an auditor. The general assembly was arranged for 7th February.

The following budget proposal was set up by our treasurer, Fru Kristoffersen, who was unable to attend herself as she had just lost her husband and had her hands full for that reason:

Creche fund	2,000 kroner
Holiday camp	400 kroner
Trip for the elderly	400 kroner
Christmas food parcels	400 kroner

| Patient Friends | 500 kroner |
| Grime Farm for children | 1,000 kroner |

(provided that the crèche teacher at the Rikshospital
is paid 720 kroner by other departments)

The board decided to send a wreath to Ewald Kristoffersen's
funeral.

THE SEQUENCE

The worst of it is that she thinks about the bill. How much will this cost? And they won't exactly have a lot to play with in the time to come. Maj folds her hands and looks down. Were two candelabra necessary? And live music? Couldn't she have made do with the organ? Isn't the organ that is already in the gallery live enough? She could have asked Enzo Zanetti to play or why not Jesper? And the coffin? They had cheaper models at the undertaker's. Maj chose the most expensive one nonetheless, a white carved oak coffin. The others seemed so niggardly, or was it the undertaker who said they appeared so *impoverished*? But they all have to go into the same flames whatever. She must have been delirious. At least she doesn't have to bother about another gravestone. Ewald can rest beneath the old one, with his mother, where they will all come to rest one fine day. But an inscription costs as well. She is glad she dropped the commemoration afterwards. She starts crying. Ewald had deserved better. The trio has finished playing *Spring* by Christian Sinding. The priest opens his book to send him on his way with some final words. Jesper doesn't fold his hands. He clenches his fists instead. He has made up his mind: he will never play at funerals. His grandpa, Alfred

Kristoffersen, smells bad. Either he hasn't washed recently or he has bad breath, probably both. They are sitting next to each other in the front row. There is plenty of room, yet it is cramped. Jesper can't move any closer to his mother or he will end up in her lap and she has enough to deal with. His collar is tight and is cutting into him. Soon he won't be able to breathe. Surely this has to finish at some point? Alfred Kristoffersen lays a hand on Jesper's shoulder. Can't the boy sit still for a moment? No, obviously he can't. Alfred can't, either. He interrupts the priest, walks up to the coffin and stands there, with his back to it. He sees farewells from the Fagerbord department of the Oslo District of the Norwegian Red Cross. He sees farewells from colleagues at Dek-Rek. *So you passed the final tape.* What sort of place is that to work? An advertising agency? Fancypants, the lot of them. That isn't work. Alfred Kristoffersen could think of a few things to say about them. But he has other matters on his mind. He wants to say this isn't right. It isn't right that a son should die before his father. Fathers should die first. There is a sequence which you mustn't break. This is what he wants to say something about. Ewald has done his duty, to die before Jesper, despite leaving them prematurely. He could have waited a few years. But Alfred Kristoffersen hasn't done his duty. He has lived too long. He doesn't mind dying, but it hasn't turned out like that. He wants to ask everyone for their forgiveness for being so negligent. He turns to the mourners. The mourners? They look indifferent. Isn't one of them sitting there knitting in the darkness? He is standing face to face with indifference. The chapel is too big. There are too many empty seats. When it is his turn, and may that happen quickly, preferably this evening, he wants the smallest chapel there is. And the funeral will take place in silence. That is the best. His death notice, which will not mention Ewald, his son, should say that "the funeral will take place in silence, in accordance with the wishes of the deceased". They have a little chapel in the basement of Tåsen old people's home. That will do. He can lie there in peace. Alfred Kristoffersen opens his mouth. But his original words get stuck in his mind, get stuck in his throat, and instead he says:

"I never told my own wife, and I doubt Ewald said it so often either, if I know him at all. But dear Maj, you've been a good wife to my frivolous son for all these years, although they were far too few."

Alfred goes back to his place in the front row. There is silence for a few minutes, then the priest enacts throwing three spadefuls of soil for Ewald Kristoffersen's body and soul. Thereafter the coffin sinks through the floor to Sibelius' "Finlandia". Jesper watches the coffin. Where is it going? Will they re-use the coffin? The coffin is a ship. Maj takes his hand as they walk down the central aisle and stop outside on the steps. It is cold, the sun is low between the graves, the snow sparkles. Soon the others follow them out. The solemnities are rounded off by the grave. It was in the death notice. This is the grave. Maj feels guilty. She is ashamed. Couldn't she have given her husband anything better? The man who enjoyed a party so much. She hardly knows what to do with herself, but she has no choice. She has to stand there. She is the widow. The chairman of the Fagerborg department, Fru Nordklev, says:

"Take some time off now, Maj."

422

"It's better to have something to do."

Fru Hall, formerly Fru Vik, gives Maj a hug.

"It's so sad," she whispers.

Maj whispers back:

"I forgot to say we found your ring."

"What?"

"We found your ring in your bedroom."

Maj knows she owes Margrethe an explanation, but Olaf Hall interrupts them, taking off his right glove.

"My condolences."

"I'm sorry there's nothing afterwards," Maj says.

"It was nice here. Don't give it another thought."

Dr Lund says hello to Jesper first:

"Shall we go for a run when the snow's gone?"

Jesper nods. He has no desire to run with Dr Lund, who straightens up. He has no desire to run with anyone.

"If you need anything, just call me, or pop round."

"Thank you."

Fru Lund is of the same mind:

"You look after yourself now."

Maj can barely distinguish between the Dek-Rek colleagues. She shakes their hands one after the other. They seem embarrassed and uncomfortable. The one called Ravn, without really having to, says:

"Now we're going to the Bristol to remember Ewald."

Maj smiles:

"You do that. It's what Ewald would've done."

Ravn brightens up.

"Yes, wouldn't he just!"

And it strikes Maj that life goes on. After the second glass they don't talk about Ewald anymore and by the third they have already forgotten him. Water meets an obstacle and runs round or over it. It is both sad and true, but also liberating. She feels guilty again. Rudjord places his hand on her arm.

"They behave like children when the seriousness of life hits home," he says.

"It doesn't matter."

"But they're good at heart."

Rudjord lets through Frøken Bryn, the secretary, who wants to give Maj a rectangular envelope.

"The boys have had a whip-round," she says.

Maj doesn't understand.

"A whip-round?"

"It isn't much. But maybe enough to get you over the first hump."

Maj still doesn't understand:

"Hump? What hump?"

Frøken Bryn becomes impatient and is offended.

"Well, it can't be easy. Please take the money."

Maj is suddenly cold and happy:

"Thank you all the same. I don't need any support. Give it to the Red Cross Patient Friends."

Fortunately the next is Julius, the hairdresser from the Grand Hotel. He is a short, well-groomed man with a stomach starting at his neck. He doesn't take off his thick gloves.

"Did he really die the day I cut his hair?"

Maj nods.

"I'm afraid he did. So at least his hair was nice for the end."

The hairdresser isn't listening; he is lost in his own thoughts.

"Makes you think," he says.

Melsom, the butcher, pushes him gently on and raises his strong, bluish hand. Maj's fingers disappear inside it and she is frightened she will never get them back.

"A great loss for Fagerborg," he says.

"Thank you for saying that."

Fru Melsom agrees:

"It won't be the same without Ewald."

Maj only sees her now:

"You haven't closed the shop for us, have you?"

The butcher shakes his head.

"When great men pass on there are restricted opening times."

Jesper looks up and thinks: I've closed too. When someone dies you take time off. Then he spots Enzo Zanetti coming over, wearing baggy black trousers over a pair of worn snow boots and a light camelhair coat with loose threads hanging off. Maj retreats a step at first, then she stumbles into him and says, before the Italian lounge pianist, who looks no sadder than on any other day, has a chance to speak:

"Jesper isn't going to stop playing."

Maj reddens as Enzo Zanetti smiles and turns to Jesper.

"I'm glad to hear that. And you, what do you say?"

"Yes, that's right."

"Let's say next Tuesday at half past five then."

"Can I bring someone?"

"Not too many now."

"Just one person."

Enzo Zanetti looks at Maj again.

"You mustn't stand here getting cold."

"Thank you. It'll soon be over now."

Alfred Kristoffersen is the last person to emerge on the steps, bowed and slow, but still determined. Maj hugs him.

"Thank you for your words. They were heart-warming."

The old man is shy.

"It was nothing. Just something I said."

"Are you coming home with us?"

"I don't know."

"You haven't seen Stine, have you."

"I don't know," Alfred Kristoffersen repeats.

"And then you can say hello to my mother, too."

Alfred Kristoffersen scans the cemetery. The trees seem very black against the luminous snow. You can hear the sound of dripping.

"Another time maybe," he says. "Another time."

Then Alfred Kristoffersen walks down the steps and along the path between the headstones, his hands behind his back, so slowly that his shadow clings to the steep banks of snow that are sinking equally slowly under the February sun.

Maj thanks the priest for his trouble.

When they arrive home, Jesper charges up the stairs. However, he stops at the top step and waits for his mother there. It isn't right to hurry on a day like this. He really ought to walk like Grandpa, with dignity, with his hands behind his back and his head bowed. But there is a smell of chocolate cake, heavy, dark and sweet. He wants some. He would most like to resist, but he wants some. He wants to fill his mouth with it. Jesper feels even guiltier. Imagine thinking like that on a day like this. Besides he has resolved not to get fat. He would rather be ill. He would rather die. His mother catches up with him.

"Where do you think that smell comes from?" she asks.

Grandma opens the door, she has heard them long before, and the same aroma draws Jesper into the kitchen. The chocolate cake is on the table, which is set for three. He doesn't dare touch it. He just stares. There are no candles on the cake. No-one has a birthday. There are zero candles. This is year zero. Eventually his mother and grandmother come in. Stine is asleep. She has slept almost all her life. She doesn't know what she is missing. Jesper wants to sit down, but has to wash his hands first. He goes into the bathroom and splashes lukewarm water over them. He looks at the mirror and sucks in his cheeks. Now he is as thin as his father was. Today he can put on some weight anyway. He can't stop himself running back. Grandma is cutting a slice and puts it on Maj's plate.

"I don't understand how you could let them burn him."

"Mamma please! Not here!"

Jesper pulls up in the middle of the floor.

"Burn who?"

"No-one, Jesper. Come on and eat now."

Maj gets up and passes him her piece of cake. Jesper puts his hands behind his back.

"Burn who?" he repeats.

"Who are you taking to your piano lesson? Me?"

"Burn Pappa?"

Maj sits down and glares at her mother, who has nearly finished her piece of cake.

"Was it good?"

Grandma doesn't look up.

"I baked it."

"And now you can see what you've stirred up. Burning, really!"

Grandma wipes her mouth with her serviette and turns to Jesper.

"It's called cremation. All your body goes up in flames and the rest melts in a big oven."

"Teeth, too?"

"Teeth, too. And nails. There's nothing left. Aren't you going to try the cake?"

Jesper shakes his head. He will never chop wood again. Grandma cuts him a piece anyway.

"But *we* don't do that kind of thing. *We* bury everything. Lock, stock and barrel."

Maj is about to bang the table, but gives up.

"That's because there's more room in the country," she says.

"And why should everyone live in a town and be cremated? Can't you move out to us?"

Maj sighs.

"Has Pappa rung?"

"I told him only to ring if there was something wrong. Besides he doesn't like asking the grocer."

"Isn't it time you got a telephone?"

Grandma snorts:

"If you lived closer we wouldn't need one."

"And if there was something, I'm not sure Pappa could make it to the shop, as you know."

"He hasn't rung anyway."

Jesper stands at the window and lets them talk. He will let them finish talking, even if they never get that far. Down in the yard someone has made another snowman, this time his nose is a carrot, or some sort of stick, and his eyes are two milk tops. Jesper doesn't know why, but it upsets him. It isn't right. There shouldn't be any more snowmen there. There shouldn't be any snowmen anywhere. Later in the evening, when Jesper is in bed, hungry and suddenly unhappy, the telephone rings anyway. Maj answers it. She thinks there is something wrong. Something *is* wrong, but not what she thinks. It is the night nurse at Tåsen old people's home. Is Alfred Kristoffersen with them? He hasn't returned back after the funeral he went to earlier in the day. She uses the words *returned back*. They find him later in Vestre Cemetery. He is sitting in the snow not far from the grave where what is left of him, a handful of dust and a wedding ring, will soon be with his wife, son and all the others who will follow.

———

The general assembly was held at Gabelsgate 43 on 7th Feb at 8.00 p.m. (advertised in *Aftenposten* on 31st Jan with the usual week's notice). No-one apart from the board attended.

The annual report and the accounts were read out. The accounts had been audited and passed. No-one had any objections to make. On the contrary, everyone praised the treasurer, Maj Kristoffersen, who despite a difficult time still discharged her duties with flying colours. May she be a model for voluntary work in Norway.

Afterwards there was discussion of new appointments for the board, which according to the rules should be for two years max. It was time for Fru Lutken and Fru Nordklev to step down. Neither wished to be re-appointed. The rest of the board, including the co-opted members (Fru Lessund, Fru Foss, Fru Kristoffersen, Fru Larsen, Frøken Aasland, Fru Lund and Fru Arnesen) chose two members: Fru Dagny Hoffmann and Fru Miranda Dunker.

FINANCES

Jostein is lying on the floor with his eyes closed. He looks like an angel from the way he is lying, with his arms and legs out to the side. He can hear the music in his back, the oscillations that come from the piano and grow in ever greater circles as they become softer and softer and finally disappear in the continuous noise of the world. No-one knows better than Jostein that there is no silence. There is movement everywhere and he feels even the slightest. Jostein almost bursts out laughing. Beethoven tickles. He hears the Italian cough, then the click of a lighter and the flame igniting on the little wick. Soon afterwards there is a drag on a cigarette and his eyes smart, in spite of the fact that they are closed. Jostein opens them. When he can see, his hearing is even worse. He was right. The Italian is standing next to Jesper and smoking. The lighter is on the shelf. Jesper starts from scratch again. He will never be finished with Beethoven. Jostein gets to his feet and goes out. He needs the toilet. Enzo Zanetti watches him until he has gone.

"That boy cannot be here."

Jesper stops playing.

"Why not?"

"He makes me nervous."

"Why?"

"Why, why, why. Why you always ask why?"

"I asked you if I could bring someone."

Enzo Zanetti is grumpy and fills a glass to the brim. He waits before he drinks and looks past Jesper. He is holding the glass with both hands. His Norwegian is more broken than ever. The repairs are obviously not working. He will have to do more.

"I thought you meant your mother. She can be here. But not friend."

"She told me to say hello," Jesper says.

Enzo Zanetti drains his glass and stands at the window with his back to Jesper. The evenings are lighter. It has snowed. Jostein comes back. Enzo Zanetti turns to him.

"What can you hear?"

"What?"

"You heard what I said."

Jostein thinks.

"You're a drunk."

It is Enzo Zanetti's turn to think. In the meantime he recharges his glass and drinks that, too.

"Who says I am a drunk? Apart from you?"

Jostein shrugs. Enzo Zanetti takes a step closer.

"Who says?" he repeats.

Jostein looks down and is no longer cocky.

"Just something I've heard."

Enzo Zanetti laughs out loud and raises his glass.

"In Italy I am teetotaller and here in Norway I am drunk."

The lesson is over before the hour is up.

On his way home Jesper asks first:

"Why did you say that?"

Jostein stops, too. They are outside Berle School. The roof gutters are dripping. Occasionally a chunk of ice loosens and falls to the ground.

"Because it's true," he says.

"It isn't true."

"He said so himself. He was a drunk in Norway."

"You just pretend you can't hear."

"What?"

They continue down Professor Dahls gate, past Vestkanttorget where the skating rink in the square is a pool. A tramp with a rucksack and an umbrella is standing in the middle of it. Soon it looks as if he is walking on water. It still isn't dark.

"You just pretend," Jesper repeats.

Jostein stops again.

"Do you know why we call matchsticks matchsticks?"

Jesper shakes his head.

"No."

"Because the sticks match."

Jostein laughs, he laughs even more differently than before, it sounds like air being slowly released from a lilo.

"That's not true," Jesper says.

"Let's think up something to do."

"What then?"

"That's what we have to think up, isn't it?"

Jostein takes out a lighter and looks around. Jesper grips his briefcase tighter and takes a step back.

"Don't do it," he says.

"Don't do what?"

Jesper steps closer, pointing:

"It's not yours."

"Didn't hear you."

"The lighter. It's Zanetti's, isn't it."

Jostein laughs with a similar release of air, flicks the shiny hammer with his thumb and a flame shoots obliquely from his hand.

"Is it?"

"You pinched it."

"Do you think he'll notice?"

"You have to return it."

"Do I?"

The flame sinks and it is suddenly dark. This is dangerous. Danger lurks in every direction and exists nowhere. Danger is quiet. Jesper takes a deep breath.

"I can take it back for you."

The flame becomes visible again and lights up Jostein's face, which seems dry and alien.

"Why?"

"So that he doesn't notice."

"Take it then."

Jesper hesitates, steps closer, hesitates again, stops.

"Just give it to me," he says.

"Take it then."

"Didn't you like what I played for you?"

Jostein throws the lighter; it burns for a second, then goes out and lands on the melted skating rink. Jesper runs after it. He can hear it hissing somewhere, but can't see it. Then the sound is gone too, but is soon replaced by another. Jesper looks around. By the kindergarten the tramp is fiddling with something shiny in his hands. Jesper ambles over to him. His boots squelch with every step. He isn't Jesus. Jesus walked barefoot or in sandals. No-one is Jesus this evening. His heart is beating. His heart is beating alone. His heart trembles when it beats. Jesper stops in front of the tramp, who lifts the lighter to his mouth and drinks from it, he drains the lighter of fire, then reaches out a hand. The hand is wrapped in a filthy bandage. Only the fingertips are visible, black nails, Jesper counts them and gets no further than four, one finger is missing. Jesper can hear the tramp's heart too, a heavy, irregular heartbeat behind the long, dark-green coat, and a smell of petrol issues from his mouth. Everyone is afraid this evening. Then Jesper takes the lighter and runs back. Jostein is waiting for him. They walk together to Valkyrie Plass without saying a word. They part company at the end. Jostein walks along Kirkeveien while Jesper chooses Jacob Aalls gate. That is the way it is. Jesper thinks: this is the first time I have fallen out with someone. Fallen out? He has to sit down on the steps outside Jessenløkken Greengrocer's. He mustn't cry. He wraps his arms around the briefcase containing his music. If he looks up he can see the moon hanging beneath a lamp post over by Marienlyst. His snow boots are soaked and weigh three hundred kilos each. The lighter is beginning to corrode. Jesper drags himself home. All the rooms are dark except for the dining room, where Maj is sitting over the month's accounts. She glances up. She is about to ask why he is so late, but doesn't. She leaves him in peace. He hangs up his outdoor clothes, switches on the hall light, takes his music from the briefcase, goes to the piano and puts it on the rack.

"Did Jostein enjoy going along?" Maj asks.

Jesper shrugs and lingers.

"The telephone directory has arrived," he says.

"What?"

"Are you hard of hearing, too?"

"Jesper, please."

"It's on the doormat."

"Why didn't you bring it with you?"

Jesper shrugs again.

"Are you playing patience?" he asks.

"Patience?"

Jesper seems unwell, almost offhand in all his embarrassment.

"What are you counting then?"

"Nothing."

"Just nothing?"

"Everything has a cost."

Stine wakes up for a moment. Both of them listen. She lets slip a little whimper and goes even quieter. Sleep makes her sound-less. She has only surfaced from the deep for a gasp of air. Then Maj goes out to fetch the telephone directory. Jesper sits at the table. He sees the piece of paper his mother was working on. It is a bill from Oslo churches: Cremation fee 60 kroner, music 90 kroner, urn 12 kroner, organ 40 kroner, decoration 150 kroner, VAT on the urn 2.40 kroner. It is a fortune. By the decoration expense Maj has put a question mark. Something is written on the back too: *In Norwegian law ashes may not be kept in private possession.* Jesper doesn't hear her come back until she is in the doorway with the telephone directory in her hand. He lets go of the piece of paper and asks:

"Is Grandpa just as expensive?"

Maj laughs.

"Yes, we're not saving on anything."

Jesper gets up and runs his fingers through his hair.

"Well, we're not cheapskates, I suppose."

"What?"

"We're not tightwads, either."

Maj stares at him in surprise until she comprehends what she has heard and takes a step towards him.

"Don't you start talking like your father, Jesper! Promise me that."

Jesper ducks his head, ashamed and furious, and wants to push past her. She holds him back.

"Sorry, Jesper. I didn't mean it like that. Please."

Jesper hasn't got the strength to pull himself free. He rests his forehead against her apron. Later they eat supper in the kitchen. Then he washes his face, cleans his teeth, puts on pyjamas, packs his satchel, hides the lighter under the home economy book and goes to bed. When everyone is asleep, apart from Jesper, and only the apartment block's very own language can be heard, he creeps into the sitting room, switches on the smallest lamp, sits down on the sofa, lays the telephone directory across his lap and slowly skims through. The writing is so small and there are so many names. And after every name there are numbers you have to dial to get through. If everyone rings at the same time what will happen then? Jesper's mind whirrs and he has to start again. It is easier to read music. Then at last he finds his father, among all the people whose names start with K, *Kristoffersen, Ewald*. And he can't help but wonder: how many of these people are dead? How many numbers don't work anymore? Jesper dials anyway. He puts his forefinger in the first hole on the dial, pushes it round as

437

far as it will reach and lets go. He does this six times: 551430. Then he puts the receiver to his ear, but he gets a different tone, an impatient warning, *engaged*. The number he has dialled is engaged. And that fills him with a sorrow so unlike anything he has felt before that he almost stops breathing and has to throw up. Because this sorrow is mixed with envy, with jealousy. Jesper is hurt. His father hasn't got any time for him. Then Jesper realises of course how it all interconnects. It is Jesper who is *engaged* and his father is envious of the living. Jesper rings off.

———

The working committee of the Norwegian Red Cross held its meeting in the nurses' home on 13.3.1951 with Fru Esther Andersen in the chair. First of all Frøken Birgit Henriksen read the minutes of the previous meeting. Then Fru Andersen read the annual report and the accounts. The working committee had agreed to the following expenditure:

Convalescents	7,500 kroner
Patient Friends	2,500 kroner
Retired nurses	2,000 kroner
Hospital volunteers	1,000 kroner
Dishwasher	5,000 Kroner

The working committee had received an application for financial help for crèche teachers at the Rikshospital. This work is expanding and a further teacher has been employed. It was suggested that all departments should contribute 500 kroner per annum, or 50 kroner per month, but they shouldn't commit to more than one year at a time. Tøyen, Grønland and Vaterland had agreed to the 500 kroner already. The suggestion was made that the infant group, which has a surplus, should contribute.

To help finance the Norwegian National Women's Council a flower (a pink carnation) will be sold on the Crown Princess's birthday and the day after. Assistance with sales is required from departments.

Fru Dybvig talked about help packing parcels of clothes for Korea. She also brought up the issue of joint trips for the elderly and asked departments to inform Frøken Henriksen whether they were interested.

Actual expenses will form the basis of the calculation of deductions for a percentage of the bazaar income. Departments who have not previously had a whole table at the bazaar can inform Frøken Henriksen in case they are interested in a whole table. The price is twice a half table. The bazaar this year will be held from Saturday 8/9 until Monday 17/9. April 13th is the fashion show for Oslo District, April 12th a soirée costing 15 kroner for admission. Departments are asked for help with selling the tickets. A deadline will be set for the return of unsold tickets.

Participants at the meeting were invited to tea and sandwiches and were afterwards shown around the nurses' home.

13/3/1951 Else Larsen, Berit Nordklev

FRIENDSHIP

Olaf Hall is leafing through *The Chinese Flute*, which he has tried to restore to the best of his ability. However, it will never be as good as new. Nor is that the intention. An antiquarian book should show its true age, otherwise it is unlikely to be genuine, but it should also be intact at all times. *The Chinese Flute*, however, is not. It has deteriorated. He will have to withdraw it. He mustn't be seen to be selling it. It could damage his name and reputation. And a reputation is even harder to restore. He might be able to sell it to a social climber, one of these nouveaux riche types who have amassed a fortune during the war or come into easy money in shipping and now have to fill their libraries in houses along Madserud allé and Kristinelundveien. They might just as well buy wallpaper. No, Olaf Hall will look after *The Chinese Flute* himself. It could give him a certain pleasure. It could also remind Margrethe of her faux pas. He listens for a moment. She is making different sounds in the house from the ones he is used to. Then he hears the postman. Olaf Hall knows exactly what the time is, 10.40, it is the first delivery. He waits a little before he goes out to collect the post. The air is mild. The gentle wind is drawing the last snow from the shadows. Among all the catalogues is a letter. It isn't addressed to him. It is for Margrethe, Margrethe Hall. Her name is typewritten. The postage stamp is Danish. There is no sender's name on the envelope. Olaf Hall looks up to the kitchen window. Margrethe waves to him. He raises a hand and blows her a kiss. She shakes her head and laughs, but does the same, blows him a kiss, then he goes back to the shop with the post. Margrethe puts on some coffee and sets the table for them. The bread is dry. She cuts thin slices. She wants to ask Olaf whether they can buy a toaster. It would be nice to have toast, at least on Sunday morning. Unless her memory is playing tricks on her, there are still jars of blackcurrant jam in the cellar in Kirkeveien. For a moment she is gripped by panic. There is no order in anything. The panic passes. The coffee is ready. It will soon be half past eleven. Olaf is late today. She is hungry, but refrains from eating while she is waiting. Then she can hear him on the steps. First he goes into the sitting room. Soon he comes into the kitchen and sits down. Margrethe pours coffee into his cup.

"You mustn't catch a cold," she says.

"No. Why?"

"April. It's bitter even if the sun's shining. You just don't notice."

Olaf laughs and pulls her to him.

"It's not so far to the post box."

"You can never know."

He lets go and tastes the coffee, sits and thinks, then asks:

"What do you think we should do at Easter?"

"I don't know. What do you feel like?"

"I'm asking you."

"Perhaps we could go to Nesodden."

"We never open the country house before Whitsun."

"Ah."

"What about Copenhagen?"

Margrethe sits down and butters a slice of bread thinly.

"At Easter?"

"Why not?"

"I could do with a bit of colour."

"You don't need it. You're lovely as you are. Besides you can sunbathe in Copenhagen, too. In Langelinie."

"Maybe."

"And I can visit second-hand bookshops while you visit friends."

Margrethe glances at him.

"Friends?"

"Don't you have any friends there?"

"In Copenhagen? No, not as far as I know."

Olaf gives her the letter. She stares at her name, Margrethe Hall, and tries once and for all to get used to it. The stamp is Danish, the postmark Copenhagen four days ago. She has no idea who it could be from. She slits open the envelope with a knife and takes out the letter. It is also typewritten, just a few lines. She sees everything there at once and her first thought is to show it to Olaf. It is from Bjørn. Just as quickly, she changes her mind. She daren't. She wants to spare him. But she can't carry this alone, either. Bjørn writes:

> Dear Margrethe,
> At some point everyone has taken a bite of an apple and then
> left it. Then, after quite a short time, you see that the flesh

goes brown. The fresh, tasty apple decomposes and goes rotten. If the apple is left for long enough it will decay. It is the cells dying. They oxidise. It is the same with Olaf Hall. He takes a bite of someone and drops them. This is all I want to say. You are a good person. You deserved better.

Regards,

Bjørn Stranger

P.S. I would have made this little speech on your wedding day, but my courage deserted me.

Margrethe puts the sheet of paper back into the envelope. She does it slowly to gain time. After all, she has everything to lose. She is not used to lying. She can't remember the last time she lied, it must have been to herself, if so, and that is quite different, that is a white lie. Lying to the man you live with, to his face, is quite a different matter. She hardens in these few seconds. Olaf Hall asks:

"Who's it from?"

Margrethe hides the letter in her lap.

"From one of Halfdan's old colleagues."

"That's nice. On what occasion?"

"Occasion?"

"Yes, why has he written?"

"Just to congratulate me on the wedding. He didn't find out until recently. That I'd remarried."

"What did you say his name was?"

"I didn't. Wilhelm Juul. They studied together at Ås Agricultural College. Halfdan and him."

"But is he in Copenhagen now?"

"Yes, as a guest lecturer at the university."

"Guest lecturer. That's nice."

"Yes, Halfdan was also offered it in his day. But he didn't want it. He . . ."

Margrethe puts the letter in her apron pocket and gets up. She is drained. She doesn't need to say any more. She has to stand by the sink with her back to Olaf. She can't look him in the eye. He gets up too, thanks her, although he hasn't eaten anything, he has only drunk a cup of coffee. He places a hand on her shoulder. It strikes Margrethe at once that he has read the letter, he has already read it, he knows how to open envelopes and close them again.

"I'm just going for a walk," he says.

"Do you want me to go with you?"

"You don't need to."

"Are you going to the cemetery?"

"Damm's. They have a new catalogue."

When Olaf has gone and Margrethe hears him closing the gate behind him, she bursts into tears. She doesn't know how long she stands like that. She turns on the tap and rinses her face in cold water. Then she goes back to her routine. Her routine will pull her together. She tidies the kitchen and washes up. It is important to keep calm. Lies require calm. With every movement she finds some common sense she needs to rely on. It doesn't help. She has to get rid of the letter. She could burn it in the fire. What good will that do if he has read it? She can go to the hairdresser's and have a perm. It has been quite a time since she had one anyway. She feels unkempt. She can ring for an appointment today. So she looks good for when Olaf returns. She hangs her apron on the hook in the pantry, puts the jug of cream in the refrigerator and stops, her hand on the smooth, cold door. What good is having nice hair if this is true? It can't be true. Margrethe suddenly feels guilty. She is ashamed. How could she believe such a thing? How could she even believe something like that about Olaf? Instead she feels an immense affection for him. She is sorry for Olaf. She mustn't believe the cowardly, vengeful mother's boy of a stepson, who runs off with his tail between his legs. Margrethe closes the refrigerator door, puts her apron back on and goes into the sitting room. There is enough to do: the dusting, watering the flowers, beating the carpets. She will find ways of passing the time. She knuckles down to the work with a joy that is stronger than ever because the joy comes from a place so deep in her it needs extra strength to raise it. It feels like exoneration, a relief, with all the lightness that brings. Then Margrethe sees the book lying on the coffee table. It is *The Chinese Flute*. The cover is stained. The spine has stains on. Her mood sinks again. She slides back down to the depths whence her joy arose, now it lies in ruins. Did Olaf leave it there to remind her of the damage, to remind her that it was her fault? Margrethe sits down on the sofa. She is a stranger here. She will never get used to these ways, this language, this past. Perhaps Bjørn is right: Olaf has taken a bite out of her and thrown the rest aside. Now she is decomposing. Now she is in decay. She wants to put *The Chinese Flute*, this worthless copy, somewhere else, get it out of her sight. She doesn't. She daren't. She is on the verge of tears. She doesn't cry. It is a choice. Once again she prevails. She doesn't know what she has prevailed over, but she has. She walks over to the window. The gate is closed. Along the fence there is still snow, dirty patches. It is all dirty. She can't see Olaf. She

445

rushes into the hallway, dials Maj's number and soon Maj is on the line.

"This is Maj Kristoffersen, hello."

Margrethe smiles.

"How are you?"

"Is that you, Margrethe?"

"Yes, sorry, I'm not disturbing, am I?"

"No, no. Stine's asleep and—"

"I just wanted to hear how you were."

"I'm taking one day at a time."

"And Jesper? How's he taking it?"

"He doesn't say much."

"I suppose he never has."

"And he's fallen out with Jostein. The butcher's son."

"It'll pass. They'll be friends again, you see."

"I don't know. I'm worried. It's almost too much of a good thing sometimes. No, dear me, what did I say?"

"But he's still playing the piano?" Margrethe asks.

Maj laughs.

"Apparently he's finished with Beethoven and he's into someone called Atie."

"Satie."

"Satie, that's right. You should come and listen to him. Can you come?"

"Yes, I'd like to."

There is a short silence, wasting valuable time, but they themselves would perhaps claim the contrary, it is a comfort just knowing the other person is there. In the end Maj says:

"And you? How—?"

Margrethe interrupts her:

"You found my ring, did you?"

"Yes, it was—"

This time Maj interrupts herself:

"Do you know what we two should do today?"

"No. What do you think?"

"We should go to a fashion show!"

"Fashion? No, honestly, I couldn't."

"Of course you can. The Red Cross is arranging it. At one o'clock. And I'll bring the ring with me."

"I look so awful, Maj. My hair and—"

"I'm sure you don't."

"You haven't seen me."

"There are two of us anyway. I look like a hag."

They agree to meet at the National Theatre in an hour. Margrethe gets herself ready, as well as she can. She has a bad feeling, which she can't shake off. She is not sure what the cause is, what direction it is taking. It is too early to wear a spring coat and too late for a winter coat. She puts on a jacket. Luckily it is fur-lined. She puts Bjørn's letter in her bag and writes a note for Olaf. She bumps into him on the way out.

"Are you going to the hairdresser's?" he asks.

Margrethe looks down.

"The hairdresser's? No, I was just going to do a bit of shopping. And to meet Maj."

"Maj Kristoffersen?"

"Yes, she's had so much to deal with. First Ewald, then her father-in-law."

"You think of everyone, Margrethe."

"We were neighbours, you know."

Olaf puts two fingers under her chin and raises it so that he can look into her eyes.

"But you have to think of yourself, too," he says.

Then he drops his hand, goes in, stops and pats his bag.

"I can cook. I've bought some whale steaks."

Margrethe catches the tram in Frognerveien and feels like getting off at every stop. Think of herself? Is her hair really that awful? She should have worn a scarf. But the conductor doesn't give her a strange look; on the contrary, he smiles and gives her the change, 25 øre, with a little bow. She picks up again when they reach the long, gentle descent, Glitnebakken, which leads to the centre itself, the theatres, the cinemas, the hotels and restaurants. How many times can she pick herself up? Margrethe gets off at the National Theatre, where Maj is already waiting. She has Stine with her. Margrethe leans over the pram and the sight of the little person, who opens her eyes at once and smiles in her own way, makes her forget everything else, apart from the time that has passed since their last meeting. Is it Ewald she looks like? Then she gives Maj a hug, they hold each other and for some moments it is impossible to say who is consoling who. Passers-by on this rather chilly but clear morning in the middle of April, office workers, housewives, newspaper boys, actors and students will only see a mutual embrace and they will probably be warmed by that. Afterwards they walk the short distance along Karl Johans gate to the Grand, where the show is due to take place in the Mirror Room itself. But there they discover from the doorman that the show has been moved to Hotel Bristol, to the Mauriske Hall. Maj regrets coming, she doesn't want to go there, but can't say no now. They dash around the corner, up Rosenkrantz' gate, Maj hoping they don't meet anyone from Dek-Rek, she doesn't know why, she just doesn't want to see them. They slip into the dark foyer of the Bristol, where the perfumes of all the ladies in front of them still cannot repulse the smell of tobacco, alcohol and fatigued shirts. It smells of Ewald on a bad day. Maj shudders and turns away. No less than four members of the working committee, dressed to the nines, as well as the vice-president of the Norwegian Red Cross, Jens Meinich, receive them. Maj and Margrethe both feel so insignificant in this company that they have to smile, as there are two of them. The cloakroom lady is happy to look after Stine in the meantime. Then Margrethe has to go down and powder her nose. Fru Nordklev comes from the opposite direction and looks towards the stairs.

"Was that Fru Vik?" she asks in a low voice.

"That was Fru Hall."

"Then Fru Vik really has lost weight."

And there is someone from Dek-Rek after all. A man gets up from behind the grand piano. It is Rudjord. He waves to Maj, who goes to meet him. Actually she is glad to be able to slip away. Rudjord shakes her hand.

"How are you doing?"

"Oh, so-so."

"You look good anyway, if I might say so."

Maj blushes and shakes her head.

"Now don't you do an ad job on me, Herr Rudjord."

He laughs and lights a cigarette.

"I should've rung you ages ago, but I've waited. It's about Ewald's severance pay and pension. Perhaps the time's right now?"

"Is there something wrong?"

"No, no. Not at all. Could you pop by the office one day?"

Maj nods and scurries back to Margrethe, who is waiting in the Mauriske Hall. They find two free seats at a table between some pillars. The place is full of ladies, ladies of all ages, except under thirty. There is a buzz. It is reminiscent of a swarm of bees surging to and fro. Then there is a sudden silence and the ladies stand up, Maj and Margrethe too. *Not at all*, Maj echoes. What has Ewald been up to now, now he is dead? Margrethe grabs Maj's arm, almost sending her flying. Princess Astrid enters the room. She is accompanied by the vice-president and two aide de camps from the Royal Palace and they sit down at the table nearest the stage. It can start. The Fred Thunes Orkester plays a potpourri. Afterwards the M.C. takes the micro-phone. His voice is familiar from the radio, but the rest of him is not so familiar. He greets the royalty and the volunteers and emphasises that the income from this matinee is going to a holiday camp for orphans. This triggers a round of applause. The vice-chairman of the Norwegian Red Cross also has to say something, and talks about the organisation's work, far too much, in the opinion of most people there, he makes a point about the international side of the operation, of the *operation*, and in this context mentions Korea. In the same way that we received help after the war, it is our duty to help others: *We are also part of the world*. Then it is finally the models' turn. They are equally pretty, all three of them, but one is last year's Miss Oslo, Bente Sørum from Slemdal, and she takes the prize. First of all they show off a simple evening outfit. Skirts are still calf-length, but a chequered pattern on the cardigan is in now. Moreover they are so tight around the waist that the models look like hour-glasses on heels. How can they breathe? Incidentally, none of the outfits can compare with the blue dress Maj tried on at Steen & Strøm. She feels a deep sigh inside herself. Everything inside her is from *before*. Then there is more music from the Thunes Orkester, "*Ha min sympati*", and the drummer, the vocalist on this occasion, sings:

> *Take my affections*
> *It's all in my affections*
> *Or what I want to give.*
> *We, like everyone else,*
> *Must have faith in each other*

Afterwards the models come back, now sporting light leisure-wear and each of them their own original English beret, in black, navy blue and bottle green. These elicit a particularly enthusiastic response. Margrethe leans over to Maj.

"Did you remember my ring?"

Finally the radio voice, with a certain ardour this time, can introduce this year's bathing fashion, such as might be enjoyed on Huk and Ingierstrand beaches this summer. The beachwear is all in two parts, bold but not vulgar, even though it reveals more than it hides. Again this sigh inside Maj, maybe a sigh that runs through all the ladies present, as none of them is under thirty, as mentioned: she could never in this world wear anything like that. Her figure isn't as trim as it used to be. Not that she is fat now, but her body is no longer co-operative, it bristles, it is resistant and quarrelsome. It obeys only one word: *widow*. Sorrow is also a roll of fat. That is how she sees it. The Thunes Orkester plays the national anthem and everyone stands up. Maj collects Stine from the cloakroom lady and Margrethe is allowed to push the pram to the National Theatre. Before they part company, Maj gives her the ring, which she puts into a little envelope left over after Ewald's funeral. Margrethe quickly drops it into her bag. Maj has more to say. She is dreading this:

"Now you mustn't get angry, Margrethe."

"Angry? Why—?"

"He isn't tricking you, is he? I mean Olaf."

"How can you say such a thing? Tricking me?"

"You're angry."

"I'm not angry. I just—"

Maj gets to the point:

"I'm thinking about your empty flat. And—"

"It's only temporary. Olaf says it isn't wise to sell now."

"Alright. Sorry."

"You don't have to be. I understand very well why you're asking."

Maj watches Margrethe striding out along Glitnebakken, beneath the luminous advertising sign at the top of the corner building, towards Drammensveien: TIDEN GÅR, GJENSIDIGE BESTÅR. Time passes, but Gjensidige Mutual Insurance Company remains. Soon Maj hears the chimes from the City Hall towers. It is three o'clock. She thinks of Ewald every hour and every half-hour and sometimes every quarter of an hour. She will have to move to another town to stop thinking about him, and it is not even certain then she will be able to. Nor is it certain that she wants to. Ewald should see her now, she thinks. What would he think? That he will never get to see her wearing a two-piece swimsuit? Maj goes back to Rosenkrantz' gate, to Dek-Rek, she might as well get it over and done with. She leaves the pram downstairs and takes the lift with Stine in her arms to the offices on the sixth floor. The men in the design room stop work for a moment and say hello, still shy. These fashionable young men, who are normally big talkers and sweet-talk women into submission in the moonlight, are suddenly compassionate and confused. Maj understands. It is not her charisma and curves that have an impact, far from it. Those days, as mentioned, are gone.

"Thank you for the present," she says.

The boys nod, and breathe out: Oh, it was nothing. They just had a whip-round for a bit of dosh. It was our pleasure. How many times did Ewald Kristoffersen buy a round for them? Then they have to take a peek at Stine, the spitting image of her father, they say, mother too, they no longer know what they are saying, how difficult can it be? The secretary, Frøken Bryn, accompanies Maj to Rudjord's office and is more than happy to take care of the tiny tot in the meantime. Maj sits down in the little lounge Rudjord has created in the corner, it is less formal there.

"Can I offer you anything?" he asks.

Maj shakes her head.

"No, thank you. I've just come to say I accept the gift after all."

"The gift?"

"Which Ewald's colleagues collected."

"Ah, yes, of course! I'm happy to hear that."

Rudjord fetches the envelope and passes it to Maj.

"That'll help with Jesper's music lessons," she says.

"Excellent."

"He plays the piano."

"You must be very proud of him."

"And one more thing."

"Yes, of course?"

"Can we be informal with each other, the way we were before I became a widow?"

Rudjord sits down again and lights a cigarette.

"Fine. I apologise. And Fru, I mean Maj, you're always welcome here."

He places some other papers on the table and shuffles through them.

"As I said, Ewald was a visionary man."

"Yes, he knew he was going to die."

"You call a spade a spade. I like that. But he wasn't a visionary in only that way. He had ideas, well, visions."

"That's nice of you to say so."

"It's true. And he increased the premium of his life policy in the last year. Yes, I assume you know we have a lawyer who takes care of this."

"Where did he get the money from for this?"

"Where? He had it deducted straight from his wage."

Maj has to look away for a moment, her head is hurting, it hurts to remember all the times she told Ewald off for frittering away money. But it won't hurt now. It will lighten the load. She collects herself and looks at Rudjord again.

"Does that mean—?"

She isn't allowed to finish her question.

"I'm afraid this case has taken a turn. The insurance company didn't approve the upgrade as Ewald knew he was going to die."

"Surely he didn't know for certain?"

"The insurance company deems he did. And they're supported by the hospital."

"But he hasn't lost his money, has he?"

"No, no. Ewald, I mean you, will be paid according to the original policy and what Ewald paid in extra."

They sit in silence, then Maj puts the envelope in her bag, gets up and says:

"At least it shows his goodwill."

Rudjord accompanies her to the door and stops.

"I liked the way you spoke," he says.

"The way I spoke?"

"'Now don't you do an ad-job on me.' But does it mean you don't trust me or us? Or the industry, for that matter?"

Maj holds her bag with both hands.

"You exaggerate a little. Sometimes."

"How so?"

"For example, it's absolutely impossible to get your sheets as white as in the advertising pictures.

"But you *dream* of getting them that white?"

"Yes, perhaps."

"And that's what we sell. Not lies. But dreams."

"I think there have to be limits."

Rudjord laughs and opens the door.

"Frøken Bryn will order a taxi for you. We'll pay."

"That isn't necessary."

"Maybe not. But we'll do it anyway."

Maj takes the lift down again, puts Stine, who has been asleep the whole time, in the pram, and waits outside. The wind is colder now; there is a sudden draught on her back and neck whichever way she turns. Fortunately the taxi arrives promptly, a black Mercedes, around the corner from Bonde-heim Hotel, and pulls up in front of her. The driver alights onto the pavement, pushes his cap back and looks at his passengers. This is what they call a big move. Has the whole of the pram got to come? But when they fold it up there is enough room in the boot. The driver would prefer to put the child there too because he has new leather covers and doesn't want them messed up, whether it is vomit or the other end. Maj is able to reassure him. The child is house-trained. No cause for concern. And should anything happen she will certainly make sure it happens on her coat. At length she gets into the back with Stine on her lap. She has never been in a taxi, or a car, without Ewald. She thinks about everything she has to do for the first time again. The blocks of flats and the wall along the Rikshospital in Pilestredet glide past in a grey mist. Maj has the feeling she is at the very bottom of the town, so low are the seats. They pass Frydelund Brewery and Bislett Baths, the smells of malt and chlorine mix inside the car. Dreams? It is men who dream. They dream at women's cost. That is how it is. In Norabakken there is a horse with its muzzle in a burlap sack. On the cart are leaves, gravel and twigs, the last load of winter. Maj wants to pay anyway, to be sure, but the driver is able to assure her that Dek-Rek has already coughed up and if he takes the money he will have to offer to drive her again. She hasn't got time for that. Maj asks the driver to hoot his horn so that Jesper, if he is at home, can run to the window and see his mother and little sister in a taxi. But she can't see him. So the driver helps her to get the pram into the house. When she opens the door to the hallway she sees a satchel and a pair of brown shoes thrown on the floor. In the dining room Jesper is sitting on the piano stool. Jostein is standing next to him, leaning against his shoulder. They are obviously friends again. They don't notice her. They are in their own world. She leaves them there. It is their world. She just stands watching the two boys. They are still children, but the war, of which they remember barely anything and yet cannot forget, has cast a shadow over them that causes their childhood age to lose its meaning. They are already carrying the darkness of adulthood. They are children in camouflage. Stine, on the other hand, has no burden to carry, except that she has to grow up without a father, of whom she is hardly likely to have any memories, only of his absence, quite different from the loss that Jesper and Jostein share. Memory is sorrow. History is reconciliation.

———

On April 17th the board meeting was held at Fru Dunker's. Apart from Fru Else Larsen the whole board was present, including Fru Nordklev and Fru Lutken.

Treasurer, Fru Kristoffersen, informed us that the working committee has refunded 186.31 kroner, which constitutes the ten per cent charge to hire a stand at last autumn's bazaar. We have also received an application from a lady for some clothes. After making enquiries it was decided not to offer any help.

The matter of the new chairman was discussed, without finding a solution as none of the present board members was able to take over the post.

An application had been received from Fru Krogh, who

lives in Egne Hjem in Adamstuen, for a good, thick carpet, but the board was unwilling to accept such a request.

With reference to the September bazaar it was discussed which items should be raffled. The board was unanimous that we should concentrate on three big prizes this time instead of a large selection of smaller items, as we have done previously.

Our contribution to the sale of the "Crown Princess Flower' was a great success, as 14,000 pink carnations were sold in the Fagerborg District. The department will receive no income from this.

LARS SAABYE CHRISTENSEN is the author of novels, poetry and short-story collections. His international break-through came with *Beatles* (1984), since translated into many languages, and for *The Half Brother* he was the winner of the Nordic Council Literature Prize in 2001. *Echoes of the City* is the first in a planned trilogy.

DON BARTLETT is the acclaimed translator of books by Karl Ove Knausgård, Jo Nesbø and Per Petterson. His translation of Roy Jacobsen's *The Unseen* was shortlisted for the Man Booker International Prize in 2017.